AL 639:	*Halifax, we have a flameout on our Number Three engine. Do you copy? We now have no, repeat, no engines!*
HALIFAX:	*Understood. All engines flamed out.*
AL 639:	*Affirmative.*
HALIFAX:	*Do you have hydraulics?*
AL 639:	*Affirmative, but we're descending rapidly. We're declaring an emergency, Halifax. We're goin' down!*
HALIFAX:	*Okay, 639, we are alerting all shipping and other aircraft in the area. Just keep us advised.*
AL 639:	*Halifax, this weather's bad news. It's goin' to be hairy. Any, ah, thing about sea conditions you can give us?*
HALIFAX:	*Not a lot. Reports coming in of moderate to heavy seas in your vicinity with swell. That could mean six-to-eight foot wave troughs.*
AL 639:	*Sweet Jesus! You guys had just better be praying for us, that's all.*
HALIFAX:	*We're with you, 639. We have you on the screen, but we're getting, er, some breakup now on the R/T. Are you below three thousand?*
AL 639:	*Affirmative. We're at two...not good... in ther... flamin...*
HALIFAX:	*639, d...*

D0921450

STALKING HORSE

MICHAEL DELAHAYE

Tudor Publishing Company
New York and Los Angeles

Tudor Publishing Company

ISBN: 0-944276-50-4

reprinted by arrangement with Charles Scribner's Sons

Printed in the United States of America

First Tudor printing—June 1989

*This one for
my mother and father,
with love.*

Author's Note

THIS BOOK is self-evidently a work of fiction. Airlantic Airlines and the SP-3 aircraft are imaginary. However, whenever I or my characters refer to specific incidents or accidents involving real aircraft and/or real airlines, the reader may assume that they have actually happened and that the details have been drawn from official reports. This applies notably to the "Miami Incident" of May 5, 1983, involving a Lockheed TriStar powered by Rolls-Royce engines.

For the record, Rolls-Royce was approached at the research stage of the book but its aircraft engine division at Derby, U.K., declined to help on the grounds that "the specter of mishaps, however unlikely, does not encourage people to fly." An offer by the company to have its chief legal officer check the manuscript before publication was in turn declined by the author. Without my knowledge or permission, Rolls then passed on details of the book to the U.S. National Transportation Safety Board in Washington, the world's foremost civil air-crash investigation body, who, true to their reputation for openness, promptly gave me all the access and information Rolls had refused.

A particular debt of gratitude, therefore, to Dave Thomas, formerly of the N.T.S.B. and now of the U.S. Federal Aviation Administration; to Dennis Grossi of the N.T.S.B.'s Bureau of Technology; to Paul Turner, senior cockpit voice recorder specialist in the Bureau's Engineering Services Division; and, not least, to Brad Dunbar, one of the N.T.S.B.'s public affairs officers. Any similarity between any of my characters and any real N.T.S.B. employee, past or present, is unintentional and entirely coincidental.

Finally, my thanks to Dr. Jamie Shea at NATO headquarters, Brussels, for his time; to my former BBC colleague Sue Crowther for her help and hospitality in Washington; to the people of Chatham, Cape Cod, Massachusetts—particularly Bill Crockett and Dan Wolf—for their extraordinary kindness to an off-Cape limey; to those in Bulgaria who helped me but cannot be named; to my editor, Dominick Anfuso; and, as always, to my wife, Anni, for reasons that by themselves would fill a book.

—M.D.
Oxford
1987

STALKING HORSE

MICHAEL DELAHAYE

Prologue

Time present and time past
Are both perhaps present in time future,
And time future contained in time past.

—T.S. ELIOT, "Burnt Norton"

THE HEADQUARTERS of the North Atlantic Treaty Organization is a low, sprawling building to the northeast of Brussels. When it was erected in the mid-1960s, it was actually intended as a barracks for the Belgian army. According to those who work there, the best thing about it is that it's on the road to the airport.

Yet it is here that the fate of Europe, maybe the world, could one day be decided. During the opening stages of the next world war, it is here that the representatives of NATO's sixteen member states will meet in emergency session around an elongated horseshoe table to give their agreement to any request by the military command for "nuclear release."

Such an eventuality is of course unthinkable—except for those believers in prophetic symbolism who note that just ten miles down the road is a small town whose name has entered the English language as a synonym for defeat, disaster, and destiny.

Waterloo.

Adrian Medcalf arrived at his office in NATO's Department of Political Coordination just before 8:00 A.M., sublimely unaware of the extent to which his carefully ordered existence was about to be disrupted.

A confirmed bachelor, most of whose forty-three years had been dedicated to achieving a state of emotional self-sufficiency, Medcalf had never felt closer to celibate Nir-

3

vana. A morning hadn't gone by during recent weeks when, inspecting his uncannily youthful face in the mirror, he hadn't congratulated himself on having escaped the demanding spouses, rebellious offspring, school fees, and crippling mortgages—not to mention ulcers and coronaries—with which most of his contemporaries had burdened themselves. From where he now sat at his desk there stretched before him another two decades of steady promotion and rising salary. The prospect of being looked after from cradle to gravy train had never seemed more assured.

Glancing through the batch of letters already opened by his secretary, he left the still-sealed buff envelope till last in the belief that it would contain an internal memo of no importance. Even after reading its contents, he found it hard to believe there hadn't been a mix-up.

But it was no mistake, and as Adrian Medcalf read the words ". . . immediate and indefinite attachment to the Central Monitoring Division," the effect was as if he had been told he was to be ". . . taken from here to a place of execution."

An attachment to another department within NATO headquarters meant only one of two things: impending promotion or a sideways shunt off the main track into a siding— and CENMON was the ultimate siding. It was a standing joke among the British, delighting as ever in the sort of childish wordplay which excludes foreigners, that the Central Monitoring Division contained more old buffers than Paddington Station.

Still clutching the memo, Medcalf looked up to see his secretary standing before him.

"It's Herman Van Kleef on the line," she said quizzically, hand over the telephone mouthpiece. "He says he'll show you round whenever you're ready."

*   *   *

In common with most others in the building, Medcalf had long ago learned to avoid engaging the deputy head of CENMON in even polite conversation for fear of being trapped for half an hour. The man was certifiably hyperactive, with a face as red and round as one of the Edam cheeses from his native Holland. Only someone with Van Kleef's manic interest in everything and anything could be genuinely enthusiastic about CENMON.

"Tremendous to be having you with us, really very good," said Van Kleef, going on to explain at length what every new recruit to NATO HQ knew within a week of joining—that the Central Monitoring Division's job was to trawl the airwaves, to listen in to all the broadcasting from Eastern bloc countries, internal and external, news and propaganda, truth and falsehood; to transcribe and translate, record, and analyze; to drive all who worked in the department slowly round the bloody twist.

The place spawned metaphors of an agricultural nature—wheat and chaff, needles in haystacks, straws in the wind. With his evident interest in idiomatic English, Van Kleef seemed to know them all and a few more besides. CENMON's daily output, he told Medcalf, was "a mountain of paper topped by an avalanche of tape," 99.999 percent of which was sheer dross but which, "like the ton of rock and shale," had nonetheless to be scrupulously sifted for "the milligram of gold" which could signal a change of policy, a change of leadership, or a subtle but crucial shift in emphasis on any matter from the deployment of nuclear missiles to the display of religious paraphernalia in public places.

With a growing sense of despondency, Medcalf followed the Dutchman through room after room of whirring tapes and chattering keyboards. The words ". . . immediate and indefinite attachment" seemed now more like a term of life imprisonment than a death sentence.

*   *   *

His first inkling that there might be more to CENMON than had hitherto met his jaundiced eye came when Van Kleef unexpectedly funneled off down a corridor and, standing before a closed door, tapped a number into its coded security lock. This, the Dutchman announced casually, was "Intelligence Liaison," the unit for which he was personally responsible.

Medcalf was surprised. He had never heard of any such department, nor had he ever seen a mention of an intelligence body in any internal directory. On the contrary, it was common knowledge that, as a mere umbrella organization for the defense of its sixteen member states, NATO had no intelligence arm of its own. The secretary-general had even been publicly quoted as complaining that the only behind-the-scenes information he was ever able to glean was from the NATO ambassadors at their regular Tuesday lunches in his private dining room.

Yet once through the security barrier, Medcalf found himself in a large open-plan office which, with its glass divisions and potted plants, could have been easily mistaken for the general office of any large European banking or insurance company. The only outwardly remarkable feature was the BURN bin beside each desk, which he had only ever seen in one other place—the CIA headquarters in Langley, Virginia. He was impressed; since the rest of the building relied upon shredders for the disposal of confidential material, Intelligence Liaison had to be special.

No sooner had his interest been aroused, however, than Van Kleef was beckoning him like Lewis Carroll's White Rabbit down another tunnel.

It led to a windowless room with several dozen plush cinema seats bolted to a floor that raked down to a large, slightly concave screen. Stale cigarette smoke hung in the airless atmosphere, taking Medcalf back to the misspent Saturday afternoons of his youth in the local Gaumont. Van Kleef shut the door and turned.

"Sit down, Medcalf, and let me tell you about Intelligence Liaison. First of all, a question for you: Where's the best place to hide a diamond?"

Nothing that came from Van Kleef, however non the sequitur, was capable of surprising Medcalf. He shook his head.

"But in a glass of water, of course!" responded the Dutchman. "Which is why Intelligence Liaison is here in CENMON. The Central Monitoring Division is so transparently boring that nobody would ever think of looking for anything secretive or sensitive inside it." He smiled. "And I wouldn't blame you for thinking that, in the same way, nobody would ever think of somebody as transparently boring as myself being put in charge of such an operation!" As he spoke, the Dutchman moved to the front of the room and pushed a button. "Now let me show to you something you will most likely have already seen. Only this time I want you to look at it with a particular care."

From a box attached to the ceiling high up behind Medcalf's head three shafts of colored light—blue, green, red—penetrated the smokey haze and, the palette becoming the picture, merged on the screen into a troupe of young gymnasts marching in formation and waving. A second later, a sound track blasted in with upbeat martial music. The gymnasts were followed by a more ragged group of adults holding bunches of flowers above their heads. The actuality sound dipped and gave way to the voice of a Bulgarian television commentator.

There were banners—red banners—with words on them written in Cyrillic script. Medcalf was unable to determine what they said, but the scene was instantly familiar: the chanting crowds, the large square with its distinctive yellow cobbles; the lineup on the mausoleum in self-conscious imitation of another lineup on another, larger mausoleum more than a thousand miles away; the party hierarchy waving from the elbow in that peculiarly economical way of East

European leaders which made them look even more like cardboard cutouts; and the president himself center-stage. Most of the television-viewing population of the world had seen it.

The picture froze.

"You recognize it, yes?" said Van Kleef. "How could you not, eh?"

"Sofia . . . the attempted assassination of the Bulgarian president," replied Medcalf. "A couple of weeks ago."

"Correct. November seventh, to be perfectly accurate—the anniversary of the Bolshevik Revolution. But this is the bit I wish you to take a particularly close look at . . ."

The picture moved again. The camera was now close in on the central group standing on the balcony of the mausoleum of Georgi Dimitrov, founder of the modern socialist republic, great leader of the Bulgarian people. Momentarily it cut to the cheering parade, and then back again to the celebrity lineup. Knowing what was coming, Medcalf instinctively held his breath.

The scene had subtly changed, although only one man on the mausoleum seemed aware of it—the man to the president's immediate right, Stanish Lubinov, the minister for foreign affairs. Lubinov's hand, which a moment before had been waving to the crowd, was now clutching his right temple. For a full three seconds the figure was immobile; then, like a mannequin in a shop window, it tumbled forward, hand still to head, onto the parapet. Only then did those around the foreign minister seem to appreciate what had happened amid the cacophony of music, singing, and shouting.

The over-modded music continued to blare, but the crowd was now scattering like storm-lashed corn, while the camera, uncertain where to point itself, was panning wildly around the square—from the mausoleum to the former royal palace opposite, to the tall buildings on either side, and finally back to the mausoleum where the Politburo's place had now been taken by armed militia crouching behind the parapet.

There was a cut, followed by a close-up of a large sign reading GRAND HOTEL BULGARIA on a rooftop. But only when the camera slowly pulled back from the sign did one see it in relation to the mausoleum and the square, and realize that a period of some hours had elapsed. The area was now cordoned off with red tape and, except for a few soldiers, was deserted.

There followed handheld shots of a bathroom, the camera panning from shower to washbasin to lavatory tank. On cue, a hand lifted the lid of the tank to reveal and then remove a dismantled rifle and telescopic sight.

Van Kleef pushed the button on the video projector and the screen went blank. His face was even more flushed than usual.

"Now, remembering that you have seen that film before, what did you notice about it this time."

Medcalf squinted at the screen.

"Principally what I noticed about it the first time— the fact that it was allowed to be seen at all. It struck me then as remarkable that the Bulgarian authorities should have allowed their own people to see it; more remarkable still that they should have invited the world to join in. Yet they must know the West picks up all their television transmissions."

"As you say, remarkable. Anything else—about the events themselves?"

"Only the obvious—that the assassin, whoever he was, got the wrong man. Assuming he was aiming for the president."

Van Kleef rubbed his hands together.

"Exactly. But why?"

"I don't understand."

"Why did he hit the wrong man?"

"Because, well, because he missed the right one!"

Van Kleef smiled. There was a hint of his former manic self.

"Think about it, think about it . . . As you yourself have said just now, that is to assume that the gunman was aiming for the president. But let me show you another thing." He picked up a large manila envelope without making any immediate move to open it. "Now, the commentator on the film was telling us what we have all come to accept as the official Bulgarian government version of the events—that the assassin was staying as a guest in the hotel, that just before or during the march-past he got up onto the roof, fired his rifle from behind the large illuminated sign; then he ran back to his room, dismembered the rifle, and hid it in the lavatory tank—before walking out the front door and escaping."

Medcalf slowly nodded, attempting to recall the newspaper accounts that he had taken only passing interest in at the time.

"So far so well," continued Van Kleef, sliding a couple of large ten-by-twelve color prints from the manila envelope. "Let us then look at these photographs that have been taken from the film. First, this is a computer-enhanced copy of the end shot of that pull-back from the hotel sign to the mausoleum . . ." He handed it to Medcalf. It had an unreal look about it, as though an artist had touched up the fuzzier lines with a pencil. "If you remember," Van Kleef said, "there were soldiers both on the roof and at ground level and that has given our experts in photogrammetry a very convenient clue to the scale of the picture. From it they have been able to calculate the height of the building and deduce two things—that the gunman fired from no more than 130 meters away, and that, assuming he hid himself behind the sign, he would have been firing down at an angle of about thirty-five degrees . . . a perfect angle in fact and with no sky behind the target to distort his perceptions."

Van Kleef focused on Medcalf's face, like a schoolmaster checking that one of his duller pupils had fully understood.

He continued, "And if we now look at the second photograph, we find it is the close-up picture—again enhanced—of the dismembered rifle which we saw being removed from the lavatory tank. You recognize what sort it is, perhaps?"

If this was an intelligence test, thought Medcalf, he was going to fail. Nothing interested him less than the technicalities of armaments. Rather than admit his ignorance, though, he remained silent.

"Then I will tell you. It is an Austrian Mannlicher—one of the finest hunting rifles available. And it is fitted with a telescopic sight made by—a name you will know—the West German company Zeiss. Again, one of the finest money can buy." He shuffled the prints back into the envelope. "So now what do you say?"

Medcalf sought refuge in facetiousness.

"That the man must have been drunk at the time."

To his surprise, Van Kleef nodded vigorously; then added, "Or, if he wasn't drunk, he must have been aiming for Foreign Minister Lubinov after all—and not, as everybody has assumed, at the president. Because, my friend, there is no way he could have missed his target with that equipment and from that vantage point. My ninety-seven-year-old grandmother has never as much as fired a catapult but even she could not have missed under such conditions! So our question now is a very different one, is it not? If we dismiss the likelihood that the man was drunk, we have only two possible theories—either the intention was to remove Foreign Minister Lubinov from the political scene, in which case a seeming assassination attempt on the president made the perfect cover—or the whole thing was a propaganda exercise to persuade the world that the security and stability of the state had been gravely threatened, in which case the foreign minister was just an unfortunate stand-in for the president. Well, do you not agree?"

Medcalf had survived fifteen years at NATO headquarters as a political analyst by avoiding such questions. First law of survival: Never respond to any question of a hypothetical nature that has YES or NO as its only possible answer.

"I can see there are persuasive elements in what you say," he fenced. "An elaborately staged assassination attempt would certainly be a good excuse for the imposition of tighter government controls—martial law, the purging of dissidents, that sort of thing. It's hardly a new trick, though—not when one thinks back to the burning of the Reichstag. All totalitarian regimes, left and right, use the same political manual when it comes to means and ends."

The Edam face cracked into a broad, beaming smile.

"I'm relieved to see, Medcalf, that the secretary-general's assessment of your talents was entirely correct."

Medcalf felt suddenly better about the attachment. As one who had consciously maintained a professional profile barely above baseboard level, he was frankly surprised to have made such an impression.

"But we must not delay," added Van Kleef, reaching for a telephone. "The secretary-general said he wished to see us in his office before you . . . before we tied matters up. I will tell him we are on our way."

The secretary-general was in an expansive mood, displaying that capacity for levity in high office which members of the British aristocracy seem uniquely adept at carrying off without any loss of esteem—coupled in his case with an ability to appear inordinately busy while having all the time in the world for whomever he was with. "Charm" seemed a singularly inadequate word to describe such an amalgam of qualities, and yet it was the one most often used by those who frequented His Lordship's large upper-floor office.

"You'll have a drink, won't you?" he asked, already setting up the glasses.

Gazing at the collection of English watercolors around the walls, Medcalf was drawn to the only vaguely martial item in the room—a glass case containing two perfectly modeled toy soldiers, circa early eighteen hundreds. They were a gift from the president of West Germany and the story about them, their symbolic importance, was well known in the building. One was an infantryman of the First Prussian Guards Regiment; the other his counterpart in the English First Regiment of Foot Guards. As the plate pointed out, the German and the Englishman had once fought alongside each other—before the Foot Guards had become the Grenadiers, the regiment in which the secretary-general himself had served with distinction in the fight against Hitler's Germany.

"So, this Bulgarian business . . . I gather you go along with Herman's theory," said the secretary-general.

Medcalf wasn't aware of having gone along with any theory—still less Herman's.

"Well, I—"

"Which certainly would fit the pattern that seems to have been emerging from Bulgaria over the last few days—the widening of the yellow security zones along the frontiers, the tightening up on visas, the stridently nationalistic editorials in *Rabotnichesko Delo*." He glanced at Van Kleef and back again to Medcalf. "Don't speak Bulgarian, do you?"

"No, sir."

"Ever been there?"

"No, sir, can't say I have."

"Not to worry. The real question is what it all adds up to. How much do you know about the place?"

Medcalf quickly switched his gaze to one of the English landscapes. The truth was that he probably knew more about macramé and basket-weaving. The Department of Political Coordination from which he had been plucked only an hour earlier was concerned solely with monitoring the internal politics of the NATO member states. Accordingly, most of his time and energy over the last decade and a half had been spent not divining the aggressive intentions of the Communist states on the other side of the Iron Curtain but, more mundanely, assessing the chances of countries like Italy and Holland staying within NATO after their next general elections—or, to put it more bluntly, predicting the chances of the Alliance surviving the very democracy which it had been set up to protect.

With some difficulty Medcalf now racked his brain for memories of all those briefing documents that had passed across his desk during the days since the assassination attempt.

"Well, you will appreciate, sir, that it's not my speciality, but naturally I am aware of the Bulgarians' special relationship with the Russians, going back—if I remember correctly—over a century to the time Tsar Alexander II freed them from the Turks. Offhand, I can't think of any other Eastern bloc country that regards the Soviet Union as its liberator rather than its conqueror."

There was an impish smile on the secretary-general's face. Medcalf's hasty rummage through "A Hundred and One Handy Facts About Bulgaria" had amused and, in a small way, impressed him; if nothing else, it demonstrated the man's ability to think on his feet. It reminded him of the old trick employed by MI6 recruiting officers: ask each candidate to recall the registration number of the bus or taxi that had brought him to the interview. Nine out of ten would admit they hadn't a clue, but the bright one, knowing that nobody would ever be able to check, would simply make it up.

"Good," he said, and turning to Van Kleef, was about to say more but was interrupted by his chef de cabinet poking his head around the door.

"The French ambassador is here, sir. Shall I ask him to wait?"

The secretary-general gave a theatrical shrug as though to indicate that he was, as ever, a victim of the schedules of others. He was confident, however, that Medcalf's attachment to CENMON would be a great success.

"Oh, and good luck!"

Saturday evening with the boys in Old Town Alexandria, outside Washington. It was a ritual that had outlived even its symbolic importance, except insofar as it had come to epitomize Matthew Di Coiano's sham fatherhood.

Like all rituals it seldom deviated from its prescribed path: a stroll around the shops and sights, up and down King Street, a bite at Bilbo Baggins, a couple of scoops of Häagen-Dazs, and a self-conscious avoidance of any talk of how things had been when they had all been together as a family. There were the occasional indiscretions—as when one of the boys would let slip something "really great" they had done with Mom and John, or Joe, or Mark—and they would know from their father's forced smile that the mention had caused him pain.

There was a limit to how far a father could blind himself to reality and, as Di Coiano watched his two sons run ahead of him, he knew that he was their father in a biological sense only. It hurt him but, given his separation from Margaret two years earlier and her custody of the boys, it could hardly be otherwise. He was a "guest father"—wheeled out for the occasional special appearance but no longer a regular member of the cast.

"Hey, Dad, can we go in the Torpedo Factory, Dad?" demanded Bobby, at twelve the elder by two years.

"Sure, but not for long if you want to eat."

They rushed ahead into the arts and crafts shopping mall

which had originally been what it was still called, although with its exposed pipes and walkways it more resembled the inside of a ship.

"Back here in ten minutes! Got it?" he shouted, unsure how much had registered with the disappearing backs.

Following them inside, he wandered through a small art gallery and a couple of pottery shops, declining offers of assistance with a slow shake of the head. It was out of season and the well-heeled locals in this chic residential area of the capital on the far shore of the Potomac were singularly resistant to the charms of impressionist pottery, idealized views of the old port, and all such folksy knickknackery. The stoical expressions of those behind the desks were almost enough to make Di Coiano grateful for a regular income, even if it wasn't the job he most wanted.

As so often, some sixth sense told him the beeper was about to go off a split second before it did. He unclipped the Bellboy from his waistband and checked the number to call on the liquid crystal display.

It was as he feared.

There was a telephone on the desk just ten feet from him. He caught the eye of the graying Bohemian woman whom he had repulsed a few seconds earlier with a curt, "Just lookin', thanks."

"Mind if I use your phone?"

When she hesitated, he added, "It could be an emergency" and, displaying his N.T.S.B. identity card, said, "I'm a crash investigator with the National Transportation Safety Board . . ."

She turned the phone toward him.

It picked up on the second ring.

"Jean? This is DC."

"DC, hold on just a second, will you."

He held, listening to the babble of voices in the background. There was now no doubt in his mind and, as he stared at a colony of pottery toadstools, he knew the next call would have to be to Margaret to tell her that she would have to pick up the boys in Bilbo Baggins. Just like old times. Almost.

"DC, you still there?"

"Still here. Go ahead, tell me how you're going to ruin my weekend."

"It's a big one. A fully loaded Airlantic SP-3 out of New York bound for Rome ... disappeared from the screens after the reported flameout of all engines over the sea."

Cradling the receiver beneath his chin, Di Coiano pulled the current GO sheet from his back pocket and flattened it on the desk. He scanned the list of names and phone numbers and grunted to himself when he saw who had been designated IIC—investigator-in-charge—for that week's emergencies.

"How many of the team've you managed to contact?"

"Nearly half. The initial assembly point will be in the conference room here on the eighth floor. Just as soon as you can make it."

He laid the phone back gently on its cradle and recalled how, crossing over Key Bridge on their way here, the boys had pointed out the great clunking slabs of ice that choked the Potomac from shore to shore. They'd figured it would have been possible to walk right across to the Jefferson Memorial. It needed no feats of imagination now to reckon how long two-hundred-plus passengers ditched in the North Atlantic would survive at this time of year.

He was at the federal aviation building on Independence Avenue within the hour, bag packed and ready to go he knew not where or for how long. On the way in he had scanned the radio bands, but there had been no word of any crash. As always, it was a painful privilege to be among the first to know; aware of those destined still to hear the news—wives, husbands, lovers, parents, who within the hour would be checking frantically and fearfully the flight numbers on those slips of paper left on bedside tables and kitchen bulletin boards.

The security guard nodded him through the white marble entrance hall to the western elevator to take him up to the National Transportation Safety Board. The elevator stopped briefly on the second floor to let in diners from the canteen, the smell of grilled meat and French fries reminding him he was missing his own dinner.

He got out on the eighth and crisscrossed through the maze of glass-partitioned offices to the small, windowless conference room on the north side of the building. A quick head count told him that the GO team was near complete.

Doug Murphy, the investigator-in-charge, snapped a single sheet of paper beneath his nose. It was an FAA Special Alert. Di Coiano started to read the details but got no further than the opening paragraph when Murphy called for attention.

"I don't think there's any doubt that we'll be pulling staff off other investigations to help out on this one, gentlemen. Worse still"—he turned to a map draped over the blackboard—"it looks like we're dealing with a ditching a couple of hundred miles off the coast in water that could be two, maybe three, miles deep." He pointed to a spot far out to sea, just off the Continental Shelf to the south of Nova Scotia. "The weather prospects aren't good. The last report was of six-foot waves with a nor'easter winding its way up from South Carolina and expected to hit the area within forty-eight hours."

He didn't need to expand. A crash on land was bad enough but at least there was wreckage to examine; no matter how twisted by heat and impact, it was seldom that it didn't give up its secrets in time.

By comparison, investigating a crash at sea was an exercise in frustration. Salvage operations were lengthy, expensive, and rarely succeeded in recovering anything more than fragments. Although both the flight data recorder and the cockpit voice recorder—the so-called black boxes—were built to survive depths down to nearly four miles and carried locating radio beacons which would emit a sonar signal for thirty days, they still had to be brought to the surface. In the meantime, investigators were totally dependent upon the ATC tape, the crew's last recorded exchange with the Air Traffic Control staff back on land.

"What I suggest, gentlemen," Murphy concluded, "is that we all stay in the building, get something to eat, and wait for more information to come in from the airline, the Coast Guard, and the search and rescue services. By then we might be in a better position to decide where to set up the command post."

Murphy was in his element—once again on the flight deck, briefing his crew before takeoff. Di Coiano felt a mixture of sympathy and contempt for the man. A heart condition had cost Murphy his pilot's license eight years earlier and it was generally known that he had suffered a minor stroke in the last year, although at the time his confinement had been officially put down to exhaustion. Now nearing sixty, he should have left the industry long ago but had doggedly, pathetically, clung on. If need be, he would have swept the hangar floors to remain a part of it. True, the man had a reputation for running a tight ship, but, if he was seldom challenged, it was because no one wanted to be responsible for his death in harness.

Yet disputes and disagreements were an essential part of any investigation—part of the dialectic process by which the truth was arrived at—and the prospect of working on a major accident under Murphy genuinely worried Di Coiano, particularly since the nature of this crash made it inevitable that there would be a host of conflicting theories.

Apart from pleading incapacity through sickness or bereavement, there was only one way out. At the first opportunity he took Murphy to one side.

"Doug, I think I, well, I might have a problem with this one."

Murphy looked more hurt than surprised.

"I can't imagine what. Our names have all been on the GO sheet since Thursday."

"It's nothing to do with the makeup of the team. It's— it's the airline. Airlantic is my old company. If it'd been just an incident or a minor accident, then I could've stretched a point, but on a big crash like this I would . . . well, I guess I'd feel kinda compromised by old loyalties."

"I wasn't aware there was that much love lost between you and Airlantic," Murphy snapped. "Not after the way they fired you."

DC felt the slash of claws across his face but curbed his response.

"All the more reason why I shouldn't be involved."

"Well, I'm sorry, DC, but this isn't a decision I can make." Murphy rubbed the back of his neck. "I only know what's on the sheet. You're down there in black and white as heading the Human Performance working team, and as far as I'm concerned, what's on the sheet is what's on the team. If you want to press it, you'll have to go to the chairman. Sorry, but that's the way it is."

With a flick of the hand, Howard R. Shepherd—"your esteemed chairman," as he was fond of terming himself—indicated one of the low armchairs that put the sitter at the immediate disadvantage of having to peer over the desk. Di Coiano repeated his reasons for being pulled off the investigation but this time took care to avoid the word "loyalty" and talked instead of a possible "conflict of interest."

Shepherd didn't reply immediately. He stood up and took two steps to the north-facing window which gave onto the Mall. Every building of any prominence was illuminated by floodlights. As he stared in the direction of the Washington Monument off to the left, a DC-9 taking off from the National Airport on the other side of the Potomac passed within several hundred feet of the top of the obelisk. For a moment it was caught in one of the beams of light, then instantly disappeared into the darkness. He spoke without turning.

"D'you know, this building, this office, is exactly midway between the Monument and the Capitol? I noticed it the first time I stood at this window and then, when I checked the map, I found it was really so. There has to be some sort of significance in that, don't you think, DC?"

Di Coiano was silent. He hadn't come to discuss matters of local geography—still less to get involved in verbal sparring with a man who prided himself on cutting through the sensitivities of his staff with the discriminating delicacy of an oxyacetylene torch.

"Well, what do you think it could be, this significance?" Shepherd repeated. "A kind of symbol for the N.T.S.B.'s traditional compromise between integrity and pragmatism? You've got to admit it's a pretty damned paradoxical sort of organization—a uniquely independent body, removed from the Department of Transportation by congressional amendment to keep it above politics, and yet run by political appointees; a place staffed by dedicated professionals like yourself but headed by a presidential arse-licker like me!"

He turned to see Di Coiano's reaction. But Di Coiano wasn't playing the game and, like a playground bully suddenly tired of taunting a weaker child, Shepherd returned to his chair.

"I can see the difficulty," he said to Di Coiano's surprise, "but there's no way I can spare you. Christ, we've got three GO teams in the field already. This'll be the fourth." He paused as though suddenly struck by an idea. "Tell you what I'll do, though. I'll put Scott Collins on Human Performance with you. That way, any areas of potentially conflicting interest with Airlantic and you can get Scott to handle them. He could do with breaking in on a big one like this."

Di Coiano couldn't bring himself to look at the man. Shepherd had dug a pit for him and he had walked right into it, eyes open.

"Why don't I give Scott a buzz now and get him to rendezvous with you in the canteen?" said Shepherd, lifting the phone.

Unconsciously adopting an old Mafia trick, Di Coiano had chosen a seat in a far corner of the canteen in order to be able to see "Shepherd's Boy" Collins before he saw him. He didn't have to wait long. Collins advanced toward him, looking as keen as a hound for the hunt. He lowered his tray onto the table.

"This is great news, Matt."

"You mean that two hundred and however many people are probably dead?"

Instantly he regretted the remark. It was cheap. Even so, it served to point up the difference between their two temperaments—the Latin and the Anglo-Saxon.

"Hell no, 'course not. I meant it was, well, great for me to find myself working with you on a big investigation like this. That's all, I swear, Matt."

Di Coiano laid down his fork.

"Look, Collins, we'd—"

"Please—Scott."

"Look, Scott then, we'd better get a couple of things straight right off. First, if you're going to call me anything, I'd rather you call me what everyone else calls me around here—DC. I know it's corny and I've heard all the jokes about my grandfather being DC-1 and my father DC-2, but I've gotten used to it over the years. Second, I normally work on my own in the GO team. This dynamic duo idea of you and me on Human Performance has been dreamed up by our esteemed chairman. It was not my idea and, you might as well know now, I don't like it."

"I understand that, DC."

"Good. The other thing is that you and I are different kinds of animals. We come from different backgrounds—I'm talking about flying experience now. Your background's military, mine's civilian. It's the difference between F-16s and 747s—and that's one helluva difference in anyone's book."

"Sure," came back Collins, "but that's what GO teams are all about, isn't it? Bringing together different experts with different disciplines, different backgrounds, but with a common motivation."

DC didn't reply. The thought went through his head that the kid had an answer for everything. Except that, for all his boyish enthusiasm, this was no kid. Collins was no less experienced a pilot in his field that DC was in his. And combat trained with it. On reflection, DC suspected he had made a fool of himself.

"What I mean, Scott, is that, well, it can take time in this business to get to know people you haven't worked with before."

Collins gave a dismissive flick of the hand.

"Hey, don't worry. I can imagine how you feel. You just want to get on with your job and here's this hot-dog rookie shoved at you. I understand."

DC got up to fetch himself a cup of water. When he returned, Collins was reading the FAA Special Alert.

"It talks here about the crew reporting a triple flameout, but it beats me how all three engines could have failed on this bird. I thought the engines were all independent of one another—deliberately so."

"Don't read too much into first reports," said DC, conscious of again adopting an avuncular tone. "Things are rarely what they seem in this business. That report may talk about flameouts but it's just as likely that a mechanic left his screwdriver behind a panel and short-circuited the instruments."

"You really think it could be that wide of the mark?"

DC didn't reply. It wasn't the job of a Human Performance specialist to know about the hardware—at least not in any detail. But as a former pilot with type rating on SP-3s, he could think offhand of only two probable reasons for the flameout of all three engines: volcanic dust or ingestion of wildlife—and neither of them was even remotely likely thirty thousand feet above the Atlantic south of Nova Scotia.

PART ONE

◈ 1 ◈

"CHATHAM . . . right here on the southern tip of Cape Cod."

Doug Murphy kept his finger on the spot on the wall map of the U.S. eastern seaboard, while the rest of the GO team craned forward, first to fix the spot and then to mark it on their own maps resting on the small tables bolted to the chair arms.

"As a command post, Chatham should serve us pretty good," continued Murphy. "It's got its own municipal airport, which'll enable us to fly in and out direct, and there's a fair-sized fishing port; so, if the boats pick up anything, they can bring it right in there. And of course there's a Coast Guard station."

"Accommodation?" asked a voice from the back.

"The usual arrangement. A modern motel a couple of miles out of town. Conference rooms permanently at our disposal, direct-dial phones, telex, typewriters—stenographers if we need 'em." He indicated a pile of paper on the table before him. "The details are all here. The plan is to fly up there at first light."

DC looked at his watch. It was already past midnight. Nobody was going to get much sleep tonight. He looked around for Ben Lieberman, the head of the audio lab, but failed to find him. It was unlike the conscientious Lieberman not to be present at a briefing, even though the job of lab members during an investigation was to stay behind in Washington and back up those in the field.

DC was suddenly impatient; thinking over what Collins and he had discussed in the canteen—the improbability of a triple flameout with three independent engines—he knew he had to have a word with Lieberman before the team took off for Chatham.

"Any spottings, any wreckage yet, Doug?" asked one of the structural specialists next to DC.

"I admire your optimism," replied Murphy, "but nothing. Come daylight, we might have some reports. Meantime . . ."

DC switched off. The meeting looked like it would drag on another hour through its own sheer momentum. He walked up to Murphy's desk, picked up one of the sheets still warm from the Xerox shop with a muttered "Things to do," and slipped out of the room. Murphy, he guessed, would interpret his action as discourtesy or pique, but he really didn't care.

A minute later, on the other side of the building, he was rapping gently on the door of Room 825-A, the laboratory complex of the N.T.S.B.'s Department of Technology. He peered through the small wire-reinforced peephole.

Total darkness.

He tried the knob but its five-digit combination lock had been set. More in frustration than in hope, he knocked again, harder. He cursed and was about to give up when a wafer of light cracked the darkness. A silhouette . . . and a tumble of the lock.

"Didn't you know Mr. Bell has invented a marvelous device for talking over distances?"

If it had come from anyone other than Ben Lieberman, DC might have taken offense in his present frame of mind. But Lieberman had license to abuse. The man was a genius, able to get more out of an inch of tape than most investigators could extract from a ton of wreckage. Genius had to be indulged.

"We were too poor to have such things where I come

from," DC deadpanned. But as usual Lieberman was his match.

"Hey, look, if you came here to give me a rendition of 'O Sole Mio' to the tune of 'Mulberry Street Blues,' you can turn right around and go back the way you came. Unless you want me to join you in a chorus of 'My Yiddishe Momme.' There's serious work going on here."

DC spun him around and pushed him back along the corridor toward the audio lab.

"That's just what I need to talk to you about. One way or another, I need to hear the Air Traffic Control tape of this SP-3 before we fly off for the Cape tomorrow morning. Correction—today. Now, I know it's asking a lot at this time of night, but if both the cockpit voice recorder and the flight data recorder are a couple of miles beneath the waves it could be our only clue, Ben."

Lieberman gave a derisive snort.

"So what the hell do you think I've been doing here for the last two hours—making bagels?"

"You mean you've already got it?"

Lieberman nodded in the direction of the room next door.

"It's on the machine now in the listening room if you want to take a seat. I'm still working on the timings."

DC shook his head. "Beniamino, you're a regular, fucking miracle."

"Yeah, that's what the midwife said."

DC sat in one of the half-dozen plush chairs arranged around the T-shaped wooden table. Copies of the U.S. government "Standard Instrument Departures (Civil)" were strewn across it together with scratch pads and pencils. On the corner next to the tape decks was a still-hot cup of black coffee where Lieberman had left it. DC pulled it toward him.

Like most investigators, DC's feelings about the listening room were ambivalent. He had attended too many "seances" here ever to feel comfortable. For it is in this room, barely twenty feet by ten, that the tapes from the cockpit voice recorders and Air Traffic Control logs are replayed—tapes which, on all too many occasions, represent the last words of a doomed crew. Because the playback equipment is the finest—the deck is a Swiss-made Nagra—the voices heard within the acoustic-tiled room have a quality that is eerily lifelike.

DC watched Lieberman put on headphones, spool through the quarter inch, cue it up, and take his seat next to the machine.

At least there was one thing to be grateful for: They were alone. Normally on such occasions friends and colleagues of the crew members—sometimes even family—were required to be present to identify and separate voices. Identifying a charred or mangled corpse in a morgue might be more grisly, but hearing the spools spin out their acoustic ectoplasm here in the listening room could be a hundred times more traumatic for those who had known and loved that corpse as a human being.

"Okay," said Lieberman, "we're picking up the Halifax ATC about forty-eight minutes into the flight. You ready?"

DC took a mouthful of the coffee and nodded, aware of the anticipatory tensing of his stomach muscles as the tiny room was suddenly filled with the hum of an ATC tower.

TRANSCRIPT EXCERPT: HALIFAX ATC—AIRLANTIC SP-3 AL 639

HALIFAX: Airlantic 639, proceed on zero four two heading.
  AL 639: Ah, Halifax, we've, ah, had a flameout on our Number Two engine.
HALIFAX: Okay, you need any special handling?
  AL 639: Negative, sir. We think we, ah, have an isolated technical problem here.

HALIFAX: 639, you want to put in somewhere quick?

AL 639: Negative, sir, but if you can give us a vector back to New York we'd appreciate it.

HALIFAX: Okay. Why don't you turn right heading two two zero and when you get a moment you can give us your ETA for New York.

AL 639: Two two zero, turning ... Ah, Halifax, we have like, ah, something crazy here ... looks like our Number One engine is now flaming out. Do you copy? We're losing our Number One engine.

HALIFAX: Understand, 639, losing Number One engine. You got two [Number Two engine?] turning?

AL 639: Negative [apparent misunderstanding]. We've only one now and, ah, we're gonna try to restart our Number Two engine.

HALIFAX: Okay, we copy you. You've lost both your Number Two and Number One engines. You want to put in somewhere instead of returning to New York?

AL 639: Affirmative. Guess we need to get this mother back on the deck.

HALIFAX: Okay, we're looking at the possibilities right now. At the present time, continue on that New York heading. You are cleared to descend to any altitude you require. We just need to know how many people you got on board and amount of fuel. Have you restarted Number Two or Number One engine?

AL 639: Not yet, sir. We're still trying. We'll keep you updated on that situation ... Ah, we have two five four on board, including six laps and twelve crew. And fuel, about a hundred and forty—one four zero—thousand [pounds].

HALIFAX: Okay, 639, we got it. It's, er, looking kind of difficult to get you in someplace near. Halifax and Gander are both below freezing with driving snow and, er, visibility right down to zero. Suggest you maintain your present heading and we will advise.

AL 639: We read—maintain present heading. There sure is something weird here that we can't figure. We need to get down, ah [as?] soon as possible.

HALIFAX: Okay, 639, we're working on it. It might have to be Boston.

AL 639: Ah, sure hope we can last that long. The weather's turning real sour.

HALIFAX: Okay, we appreciate your situation.

AL 639: Halifax, we have a flameout now on our Number Three engine. Do you copy? We now have no, repeat, *no* engines!

HALIFAX: Understood. All engines flamed out.

AL 639: Affirmative.

HALIFAX: Do you have hydraulics?

Al 639: Affirmative, but we're descending rapidly. We're declaring an emergency, Halifax. We're goin' down!

HALIFAX: Okay, 639, we are alerting all shipping and other aircraft in the area. Just keep us advised. We should be able to hear you down to twenty-five hundred feet. Right now your squawk shows you at two hundred miles south of us.

AL 639: Halifax, we're now at, ah, five thousand feet and experiencing some turbulence. Our indicated airspeed is two five zero. This weather's bad news. It's goin' to be hairy. Figure we could have problems lining up on our approach to the water. Any, ah, thing about sea conditions you can give us?

HALIFAX: Not a lot. Reports coming in of moderate to heavy seas in your vicinity with swell. That could mean six-to-eight-foot wave troughs.

Al 639: Sweet Jesus! You guys had just better be praying for us, that's all.

HALIFAX: We're with you, 639. We have you on the screen, but we're getting, er, some breakup now on the R/T. Are you below three thousand?

Al 639: Affirmative. We're at two [unintelligible] . . . not good . . . in there . . . [unintelligible] . . . I don't know . . . Number One flaming out . . .

HALIFAX: 639, do you read . . . do you read, 639?

◆ 2 ◆

"Now, I am going to take you somewhere of great interest to students of history, and to Englishmen in particular." Van Kleef's tone was that of a parent who had planned a surprise family outing. "And you would be better to bring your coat. You will have good need of it."

Medcalf followed the Dutchman down to the parking lot in front of the building. There they climbed into Van Kleef's aged Mercedes and, skirting the circle of national flags, swung right onto the three-lane highway. Flecks of sleet spattered the windshield and melted on impact.

Just before the airport, they joined the Ring Road and followed the Route de Mont St. Jean southward through the Forêt de Soignes. Medcalf had a fair idea where they were heading, although why on a day like this, he was at a loss to explain. As for asking, he knew there was no point.

"Does nuclear war worry you?" asked Van Kleef without apparent reason. When Medcalf didn't immediately reply, he added, "I'm just curious, you understand. We all work in this place and in theory we all live and breathe the prospect of nuclear extermination. Yet you will never guess it if you sit in the canteen for only five minutes. Most of our colleagues seem to worry more about their pensions. Ironic, is it not?"

At the back of Medcalf's mind lingered the suspicion that the question was less innocent than it seemed. Van Kleef was incapable of saying "Good morning" without implying an interrogative.

"No more than death itself worries me," he answered guardedly.

Van Kleef seemed satisfied. He pointed to some frozen cattle draped in comical tarpaulin jackets; then picked up. "Personally, I feel the same way. The only death that is truly relevant is one's own—in the final analysis, so to say. Whether others die their deaths at the same time is as irrelevant as if ... as if a planet exploded on the other side of the universe." He slapped the wheel. "*Phutt!* It's like when people talk about the world's worst air crash. There is only one worst air crash and it is different for different people because it is the crash in which you personally are involved."

The sentiment was so close to Medcalf's own feelings and, in the nonchalance of its delivery, so far from what he suspected to be Van Kleef's that he felt sure the Dutchman was again trying to draw him out—to set him up for a verbal ambush. He was beginning to resent being obliquely interviewed for an unspecified job he had neither sought nor wanted. Yet he knew that not to respond would itself be a response.

"Or the crash in which someone you love is involved," he said rather belatedly. The words sounded as hollow as they were.

Van Kleef nodded vigorously but said nothing.

Ten minutes later, they parked at the foot of a huge and perfectly conical man-made mound dwarfing the scattering of hotels and restaurants below. The cast iron lion at its summit was barely visible in the driving sleet.

Medcalf had visited the battlefield perhaps half a dozen times—it was an obligatory sight for the occasional English house guest—but never at this time of year. In summer there would have been coaches and tourists tramping the fields for miles around to the justified annoyance of the local farmers, but today it was deserted.

Like an energetic schoolmaster, Van Kleef led the way up the mound two steps at a time with a reckless disregard for his excess weight and high blood pressure. At the top he grasped the railing that ran around the base of the lion's plinth and with his free hand indicated landmarks in the flat snow-covered patchwork of fields below. His voice came in gasps.

"Straight ahead, you can make out La Haye Sainte ... and over there to the right of it, La Belle Alliance, where Wellington and Blücher finally joined up after the rout of the Imperial Guard ... You know, do you, that Blücher wished it to be called the Battle of La Belle Alliance? ... What could have been more appropriate? The British and the Prussians combining forces to defeat the French. But Wellington vetoed it in favor of Waterloo because it sounded more English and would be easier for his countrymen to pronounce!"

He gave a hearty laugh that turned into a cough. Medcalf waited for him to recover and, seizing the opportunity to score at least one point, remarked:

"I thought most historians now accepted that it was simply Wellington's practice to name battles after his head-quarters of the previous night."

"Oh, that too, that too," agreed Van Kleef. "But it's not so good a story!"

The sleet had turned to a freezing rain, which now trickled down inside the collars of their raincoats. Van Kleef fell silent, scanning the fields with the concentration of a lookout in the crow's nest, his ungloved hands glowing like embers. Medcalf, too, was suddenly subdued. He recalled Victor Hugo's description of the visionary mist that was meant to haunt the battlefield at night—"the hallucination of disaster ... the whirlwinds of specters exterminating each other"—and shivered. In the reflecting ripples of the snow-crusted furrows it required little imagination to people the plain with infantry and cavalry, with glinting sabers and flashing cuirasses; to hear in the wind the cries of dying men and horses.

When Van Kleef spoke again, his voice had lost its levity.

"You know, Medcalf, it is good to come up here. It gives one historical perspective and in our jobs it is very important to retain that. It makes one realize that we are only the latest page in the latest chapter of the latest book; and, more than that, that whole volumes have gone before us."

"And you need to come literally to a high place to get that perspective?" Medcalf's skepticism was edged with irritation.

"It helps, it helps—particularly here. Look around you and remind yourself that sixty thousand men died in these fields, many of them buried where they fell. Killed not by mortar, bomb, gassing, or even a neat burst of machine-gun fire, but by being hacked and stabbed, by a scything saber slash across the neck or a bayonet in the groin from a man who looked you in the eyes as he delivered it." He turned and added, "We were talking in the car about personal deaths. That is a personal death—for both the man who inflicts and the man who receives. Imagine it—sixty thousand individual acts of murder committed in just sixty hours."

Again there was the note of challenge in the Dutchman's voice—a challenge which again, and for all that he found it tiresome, Medcalf couldn't refuse.

"Double that number died at Hiroshima—in circumstances no less ghastly," he said.

"True but different. Hiroshima was not a hundred and twenty thousand acts of murder but a single act of murder with a hundred and twenty thousand victims."

"I doubt that those who died appreciated the distinction."

"Of course not, but *we* should. Do you think the crew of that American bomber over Hiroshima would have been prepared to kill a hundred and twenty thousand Japanese individually—even after you had persuaded them that not to do so would have prolonged the war and entailed the deaths of many times that number of their own compatriots? The most insidious aspect of modern warfare, Medcalf, is that it has depersonalized death; it has eroded our inhibitions about killing our fellow human beings. That is the true abomination of the nuclear age we live in."

"So what lessons do you draw from all this?" asked Medcalf. "That war was better in those days, more responsible somehow, because men were required to think about each death they inflicted? It doesn't seem to have stopped them from doing it."

He was surprised at his own acerbity, which he suspected owed more to his present physical discomfort than to any intellectual conviction.

But Van Kleef smiled, apparently satisfied at having again goaded him into such an uncharacteristic display of emotion.

"Oh, I draw no lessons. I leave such things to the political analysts like yourself. I merely observe—and it is not very profound—that this little piece of ground has seen everything. It is what you call a microcosm of European history. In 1815 it was the Germans and British slaughtering the French. Remember those toy soldiers in the secretary-general's office—the Prussian and the Englishman, standing side by side? A hundred years later it would be the British and French against the Germans. Then, next time around, the British, French, and Russians against the Germans. And now, with our NATO headquarters only a little up the road, all of us against the Russians. The only lesson I draw is that history is a game of consequences: the result of one confrontation will determine the configuration of the next—who will be with whom, who against whom."

Medcalf turned. "And Bulgaria, where does Bulgaria fit into this game of consequences?"

"That is for you to find out. Your flight leaves tomorrow—from London Heathrow."

It took Medcalf a couple of seconds to react.

"Flight? What flight?"

"Your flight to Sofia, of course. We've even managed to book you into the Grand Hotel Bulgaria itself which should—"

"But I'm an analyst—a deskman, for God's sake!"

"Which is precisely why you were picked—for your analytical talents. That and the fact that whoever we sent would have to assume the identity of an Oxford historian by the name of Dr. Stephen Chanter. The real Dr. Chanter was one of the last to get a visa in his passport before the latest clamp-down. He was going to Sofia to research a book about the Balkan Wars but, in the interests of more immediate history, kindly agreed to postpone his trip and allow us to borrow his passport. Of the ten short-listed candidates for the job, you were one of the closest in background, age, and physical appearance. Not *the* closest, I have to admit. The final choice was between you and two others—but they had families and dependents, you understand."

He looked at Medcalf meaningfully, soliciting sympathy for the other short-listed candidates. When none was forthcoming, he cleared his throat and continued: "Times have changed, Medcalf. We no longer need spies in the old sense. Technology has taken over from technique—or, to use the spookspeak of our Transatlantic cousins, HUMINT has given way to SIGINT and COMINT. When one side can intercept the airwaves of the other and photograph the insignia on a man's epaulet from a hundred miles up, who needs a vulnerable biped in a shabby raincoat with imperfect hearing, impaired sight, and a mental processing system which, seven times out of ten, will misinterpret the data anyway? The only times humans are required these days is to act as messsenger boys—and that's what you are to be."

"To take or receive?"

"To receive. In that strangely animal-fixated argot of which your English secret service seems so fond—perhaps it is the early influence of nannies and nurseries—you are to be a 'retriever.' Not a mole or a carrier pigeon, but a good, dependable retriever. Not very glamorous, I know, but in this case, I assure you, vitally important. We must know the truth behind that assassination attempt, Medcalf.

A professional assassin using professional equipment doesn't miss at that range—and a Communist government with a reputation for Byzantine secrecy assuredly doesn't then go and broadcast such an incident to the world. Not without a reason. And if there's a reason, there must be a plan—and if a plan, a time scale. We have only one informant within Bulgaria who is in a position to know the answers and you are our only possible means of communication with that informant."

"And how, in God's name, am I to identify him? Does he have a code name or is there some absurd conversational exchange we have to go through?" Medcalf caught a sudden glimpse of himself sitting on a park bench, a trench-coated character beside him muttering, "Tonight, comrade, the red kipper swims upstream."

"No, no," said Van Kleef, his laugh again breaking into a cough. "But yes, our friend does have a name—a code name, if you like. It is 'Bogart.' "

"As in Humphrey?"

"Precisely. I assume our friend is something of a film enthusiast. But you must not worry. All you have to do is act normally—at least what might be considered normal for an Oxford academic researching a book on prerevolutionary Bulgaria."

◆ 3 ◆

CAPE COD is the cartological equivalent of a Rorschach test; everyone sees in its outline something different, something personal. Few, though, have bettered Thoreau's description of it as "the bared and bended arm of Massachusetts." The ten-mile-wide biceps jut thirty-five miles out into the Atlantic before flexing abruptly north and narrowing into a forearm, which at its extremity flips back landward in a clenched fist that is credited by local trawling skippers with hanging on to the fog a day or two after it has cleared the mainland. Hence, the Cape's nickname: "the pesky peninsula."

In the late fall of 1620 the inner grip of this fist—now Provincetown harbor—was the first mooring place of the *Mayflower* after its departure from Europe several months earlier. As every Cape Codder will tell you, it was here and not at Plymouth that the Pilgrim Fathers set foot on the shore of their New World; here, too, that they signed the Mayflower Compact, the first known charter of a government of the people, by the people, for the people.

After barely four hours' sleep and close on two hours in the air, the dozen passengers aboard the twin-engined Beechcraft Super King Air were mostly unappreciative of the history beneath them as they made their final approach into Chatham Municipal Airport on the southern tip of the Cape—the elbow of Thoreau's arm.

Sitting in a window seat, DC sensed the engines change tune, shook himself out of a doze, and took in the grim monochrome landscape below: the occasional clusters of white clapboard houses amid dark expanses of Scotch pine.

At some point during the flight the pilot had mentioned that the outside temperature was below freezing. DC didn't doubt it, seeing the banks of snow piled up on either side of the runway. With the weather eye of a former pilot, he also noted the direction of the windsock veering ominously between southeast and east.

The air-taxi pilot too should have noted it but, unnerved by the accumulated flying hours sitting behind him in the cabin, he misjudged the crosswinds and dropped the Beechcraft hard onto the deck with a squeal of protesting rubber. Sardonic smiles were exchanged among the GO team; one crash investigation at a time was quite enough.

Half an hour later, DC was unpacking his bag in the motel. As Doug Murphy had predicted, it was the usual cheerless, characterless accommodation, designed less to appeal to all than to offend none. Its only redeeming feature was that it blended so unassumingly with the landscape that, but for the sign on the highway, hordes of potential guests might have driven past without noticing it. Judging by the keys in the racks, the GO team were just about the only guests in the place.

In the bar and restaurant a brave attempt had been made at "local atmosphere" by the addition of captain's chairs, oars, and harpoons—yet in such profusion that the overall impression was of a marine lumber room. Old black-and-white photographs of the countless wrecks grounded on the back side of the Cape were dotted around the walls, while above the fireplace a pair of swordfish engaged in what would have been mortal combat had they not been screwed to the brickwork.

DC looked at his watch. It was still only half past eight. If he phoned now, he might be able to have a word with the boys and apologize for dumping them the previous evening. He knew from his own childhood that they were at the age of garnering memories, good and bad, that would stay with them for the rest of their lives. Like most estranged fathers, he guessed, he wanted those memories to be good in respect to himself and marginally less so in relation to their mother. He was aware that there was something unpleasantly calculated about his building up emotional credit in the minds of his children, but equally aware that the previous night's experience was likely to go down on the debit side as "the night Dad abandoned us and Mom had to come and pick us up."

Margaret answered, her vocal cords pinched with resentment. The boys had already left for school, been collected by a neighbor five minutes earlier. She had explained to them as best she could that what had happened hadn't been their father's fault but, yes, obviously they had been upset. Implied by her tone if not actually stated was the addendum that it was no longer her job to make his excuses for him. She would tell them he had called.

He laid down the receiver and, although he tried to put the call out of his mind, he knew it would rankle for days to come.

At least he had managed to uncouple himself from Scott Collins before leaving Washington. He had sent "Shepherd's Boy" off to interview the families of the crew to check on their physical and psychological condition—ailments, worries, intake of alcohol and medication, etc.—during the twenty-four hours prior to the flight. It was a purely routine chore but a necessary one and, since all three crew members had lived in New Jersey, it could safely be assumed that Collins would be out of his hair for the next thirty-six hours at least.

The bedside phone rang. For a moment DC thought it might be Margaret calling back to smooth things over. But it was the front desk, relaying a message from Murphy to all members of the team to meet in the conference room. He sighed. It was time for Captain Murphy's preflight checklist.

Murphy was feeding sheets of paper through a photocopier in the corner of the room, while a girl presumably recruited from the local employment agency sat pecking at an electric typewriter. Everybody else was sitting around the long oblong table, sipping black coffee and massaging tired eyes. Already the ashtrays were filling up. The scene resembled more the end of an all-night poker session than the start of a major air-crash investigation. As DC took one of the remaining seats, Murphy came to the head of the table but remained standing.

"Okay, team, the situation is like this. Still no reports of any sightings. At this moment a fifty-mile radius from the aircraft's last reported location is being searched by military spotter planes because it's beyond the range of the Coast Guard. I repeat, we have no report yet of any survivors or wreckage but"—he glanced at the clock on the wall opposite—"they've only been up there since first light. Meanwhile, a couple of trawlers from Provincetown are in the area joining in the search. How long they can stay there is anyone's guess. The weather's closing in and the meteorologists—am I right, Bert?—are now forecasting the imminent arrival of that nor'easter I mentioned back in Washington."

Bert Turner, the weather expert, nodded and, at Murphy's prompting, stood up to add:

"The wind's already swinging around from southeast to east and in these parts that's regarded as the danger signal. You may have seen as we flew in that the local Coast Guard station was flying the gale warnings. Another twenty-degree swing north and within twenty-four hours we could have eighty-mile-an-hour winds—that's hurricane force—gusting to over a hundred. The only good thing to be said about it is that whatever's floating out there will be blown toward the coast."

Turner sat down again and Murphy, brandishing a copy of the Air Traffic Control transcript prepared back in Washington by Ben Lieberman, continued: "Most of you'll already have seen this, and you'll know that it doesn't, well, it doesn't make good reading. On the face of it, it looks to me like a case for the power-plant boys. Agreed, Jo?"

Jo Kaplan, the team's engine specialist, twirled a pencil between his teeth and rocked back on his chair. Now in his late fifties, Kaplan took pride in being a former engineer instead of a former aviator like most of those around the table—happily describing himself as "just a grease monkey among the coconut heads."

"That's certainly the way I read the transcript. The flame-out on all three engines could indicate one of two things—a loss of fuel or a loss of oil, assuming we discount birds and volcanoes. Personally, I'm inclined to go for the fuel. We're checking the fueling records at JFK right now, but it's my hunch that we're looking at a case of bad fuel management by the air crew . . . Now, I'm not discounting oil altogether; there're plenty of cases of oil seals failing and leaking the entire contents of an engine, and we most of us here have come across them in the course of our work. But there's no case I know of where it's happened to all three engines on the same aircraft virtually simultaneously." He paused and cast his gaze slowly around the table; nobody challenged. "I try to keep an open mind on these occasions, like we all do, but frankly I find it impossible to imagine three separate oil seals failing on three separate engines, all within minutes of one another."

There was a rustle of paper from the other side of the table as Gordon Stafford, the systems expert, held up his copy of the transcript to attract Kaplan's attention.

"Hold it there a second, Jo. I'm not sure we can dismiss an oil loss that easily. I have to say I find it equally hard to accept that an experienced flight engineer could have accidentally starved all three engines so early in the flight." He referred to the transcript. "Right here on the second page we have the crew talking about having—here it is—a hundred and forty thousand pounds of fuel still on board. So you're asking us to believe that somehow the flight engineer screwed up on his cross-feeding and was then so dumb that he didn't realize what he'd done even when engines were flaming out all around him. Hell, Jo, I—"

Kaplan cut through the unfinished sentence with a slash of his pencil.

"Gordon, I think you're forgetting how quickly events move up there in that sort of situation. Chances are the guy was too preoccupied with shutting down engines, going through the checklists, and preparing for fuel dumping and ditching. The crew were probably already too far behind events to ever have any chance of catching up with them, still less getting back in front." He tilted back his chair, addressing now the whole team. " C'mon, you guys are the ex-aviators here. Imagine yourself at thirty thousand feet with engines flaming out all around you." He referred to some figures he had scribbled on his scratch pad. "You know how much time they'd have had? I'll tell you. By my calculation they'd have been dropping at a rate in excess of fifteen hundred feet a minute. That gave them no more than fifteen minutes in which to try to restart engines and, when that failed, get everything ready for ditching: dump fuel, prepare passengers, check weather reports, run through checklists, and line up the aircraft for the final approach." He spread his hands wide, appealing now directly to Stafford. "Put yourself on that flight deck, Gordon, and tell me you honestly think the flight engineer would've been reading his manuals and checking his circuit breakers. But . . ." He tilted forward again, hands coming together. "I'm not saying my theory is necessarily the way it *did* happen; only the way that, with the information available, seems to make the most sense. And, well, you guys know me well enough; I'm kind of old-fashioned where these matters are concerned . . ."

There was no immediate response, from Stafford or anyone else. With a career spanning thirty-five years, Kaplan had many times expounded his belief that the present generation of pilots and flight engineers were taught to put too much faith in their instruments and too little in the seat of their pants. His view ran counter to popular opinion in the modern civil aviation industry, but within the N.T.S.B. it had been too often proved right to be ignored.

Stafford stared grimly at those around the table and then back at Kaplan. He was on tricky ground.

"So you're saying the crew panicked," he said curtly.

"You're twisting my words, Gordon," Kaplan countered. "I'm saying the crew might've been less alert than they should've been and paid the price. When fire's raging through your house, you tend to forget that it's just as important to turn off the gas as turn on the hose."

Sitting on the opposite end of the table, DC was struck as always by the generation gap which seemed to characterize the makeup of every GO team he had ever worked on—the neat divide between the fifty–sixty-year-olds whose training, either as pilots or engineers, dated back in some cases to the Second World War, and the thirty–forty-year-olds like himself who had started their careers about the same time as the first 747s were being introduced in the early seventies. Jo Kaplan was indisputably a fine engineer but an engineer who had learned his trade in the days when a pilot exerted his personal muscle power on an aircraft by pulling on levers connected by rods and wires directly to the flying surfaces. Philosophically, he had never really come to terms with the new "theology" of hydraulics and electronics; for him it was as hard to accept that a pilot in the cockpit could move the rudder two hundred feet away by operating a valve to redirect fluid under high pressure as that he should move the cup of coffee in front of him six inches to the left by the mere application of his brain power. He accepted that it happened because the causal link was undeniable, but he had little faith in the principle that made it happen. But, whereas a lesser man might have hidden his skepticism behind a mask of arrogance, Jo was always the first to deprecate his own unease with modern technology—to declare, only half-jokingly, his conviction that the hydraulic pipes merely concealed the old wires.

It was impossible not to like such a man but, as one who had sat in the left seat and was only too aware how hard it was for a dead crew to argue its case, DC now felt angry at the way Jo was already forming his own judgments—and thereby influencing those of the rest of the team—without a shred of supporting evidence. He knew he was in danger of opening up that other divide which afflicted most GO teams—that between the aviators and the engineers—but it had to be done before Jo's speculative judgment contaminated the team's collective subconscious and became the accepted wisdom.

"Jo, I'm sorry, but I can't let your hypothesis stand without some objection. I know we're all committed to an open exchange of ideas here but, well, I'm sorry, but I regard it as"—he searched for a word that would be diplomatic but failed to find one—"irresponsible to make that sort of snap judgment on what little we know so far. Hell, we haven't yet seen the aircraft's history or maintenance records and we're still waiting for—"

He never finished. Murphy's authority as investigator-in-charge fell upon his words with full flattening force.

"Now, just cool it, will you, DC! It was me who asked Jo for his opinion and, as the one in charge of this investigation, I'm making it clear that I'll not tolerate any rank-pulling by aviators over engineers. Aboard this ship, every man is entitled to his own opinion."

Murphy's complexion had darkened by several shades and it was noticeable that he was holding the back of his chair for support. Kaplan cast a glance at DC and with a discreet scything motion of his hand indicated that, while he personally had taken no offense at DC's remarks, it was in the interests of everybody to let the matter drop.

Reluctantly DC complied, choking down his anger in a sullen, resentful silence that was to last for the remaining fifty-five minutes of the meeting. Too late he found the word he had been searching for: not "irresponsible," but "inappropriate."

◆ 4 ◆

THE MORE Medcalf learned of the ways of Intelligence Liaison, the more he wondered. Returning home to his flat in the early hours of the morning, he was amazed to find a man—well-dressed, thirtyish, middle-management type—sitting in his living room reading a copy of *Newsweek*. More surprising still was that the man himself showed no signs of alarm, but casually laid aside the magazine and stood up.

"Just put your bags together for you," he said with an English accent that was a shade too impeccable. "Oh, and whilst I remember, your tickets."

"You in the habit of doing this?" asked Medcalf, ignoring the ticket held out at arm's length.

The intruder smiled knowingly. It was not the first time he had been so challenged. He laid it on the coffee table.

"It's what I'm paid to do."

"In which case you must be on overtime by now."

The man's expression changed. He had been happy to indulge Medcalf's sarcasm so far, but the play-acting was over. His tone was suddenly clipped and business-like.

"You will find in your bedroom one of your suitcases already packed with enough clothes to last up to a week. You will also find in the case a couple of academic books and papers and a wallet containing traveler's checks in the name of Dr. Stephen Chanter and a couple of photographs of your 'wife,' Katherine, and two 'children,' Sarah and Paul. Please be certain to take everything with you—including, of course, this . . ."

The outstretched hand held a British passport. This time, Medcalf complied.

"Dr. Chanter's passport, complete with Bulgarian visa. The photograph has of course been replaced by your NATO mug shot. The physical details—age, height, hair—should be close enough not to attract attention. We must just hope that the Bulgarians didn't copy Chanter's photograph when they entered the visa in London—or at least that, if they did, they won't compare it with yours when you enter the country. It goes without saying that you must leave behind anything—clothing, possessions, documents—which might indicate your true identity. I've been through your clothes and checked them—laundry marks, embroidered initials, that sort of thing. And of course your luggage labels have been changed. Now, if you don't mind, your hands."

He didn't wait. Grasping Medcalf's hands, he splayed the fingers and felt up the cuffs. It had all the no-nonsense professionalism of a hangman preparing his victim for the drop.

"Good—no rings, no identity bracelets. Anything round the neck?"

Medcalf mouthed a "no."

"Fine—then we're all done. Only one thing left and that's the most important." He dropped an envelope on the coffee table. "A little bedtime reading for you. Your new identity—

everything you and perhaps others will ever want to know about Dr. Stephen Chanter. Remember to destroy it before you leave in the morning. Oh, and one other thing—the DS."

"The what?"

"The Durzhavna Sigurnost."

It took a second or two for the words to register; at past midnight after a tiring and disorienting day, Medcalf's mind was putting up the shutters of its own accord. Yes, he had heard of the DS—the Bulgarian secret service. He knew that they were organized along the lines of the Russian KGB, whose dirty work they were often reputedly called upon to perform abroad. He knew that in 1978 the DS had been credited with the murder in London of Georgi Markov, the Bulgarian emigrant writer and broadcaster for Radio Free Europe. Markov had been hit in the thigh by an unidentified assailant carrying an umbrella as he walked across Waterloo Bridge. An autopsy had revealed the presence of a minute metal pellet containing the poison ricin. He also knew that the DS had been implicated in the attempted assassination of the pope three years later, although the extent of their involvement had never been clarified.

"What *about* the DS?" he asked petulantly.

"Just be careful. All the usual precautions plus a few more. Don't under any circumstances be tempted into changing money on the black market." Medcalf's eyes narrowed into an expression of world-weariness. Even the secretaries in the typing pool knew that Communist governments used unofficial moneychangers as agents provocateurs to trap foreigners. "And, surveillance," continued the other. "Assume it at all times even if there is no apparent evidence for it." He grinned in anticipation of a good line. "Just remember that the only time a Bulgarian waiter empties an ashtray is to change the batteries."

Medcalf didn't attempt to conceal his contempt for this jumped-up security guard who seemingly spent his life rummaging through other people's underwear. What he hadn't suspected was that the man would have also had access to his personal file.

"I was going to add," concluded the intruder, "a warning about honey traps but I gather sex isn't really in your line, so I needn't bother. Each one to his own, eh?" He smirked, gave the room a cursory once-over, and, before Medcalf had a chance to react, was gone.

Two miles away, despite the lateness of the hour, the light was still on in one of the upper-floor offices of the NATO building. But the mood of the figure who sat behind the desk was very different now from that which Medcalf had briefly witnessed earlier in the day. The jaunty British air, the blend of military and aristocracy, had evaporated. Instead, the secretary-general was staring grimly through his squared-off glasses in the direction of the deputy head of CENMON seated in the leather armchair opposite.

"So on balance, and despite your earlier reservations about his psychological makeup, you are telling me, Herman, that you now believe Medcalf is capable of doing the job."

Van Kleef shifted noisily in his chair. He was aware that both his personal judgment and his professional reputation were on the line.

"On balance, sir, yes. He is as complacent and egocentric as his file suggests, emotionally entirely self-absorbed, but beneath that I detect a lively, if lazy, analytical capability and even a moral conscience that will respond to a little goading. Obviously we could have wished for better, but at least he will know the right questions to ask and can be counted on to bring back accurate answers. In this respect, his ignorance of the Bulgarian scene will be an advantage; he goes with few preconceptions."

The secretary-general removed his glasses and wiped them on a handkerchief pulled from his breast pocket.

"And his ability to survive?" he asked.

"Minimal."

"So how long do you give him—three days, four?"

"Less than that. I'd be surprised if he goes beyond two."

The secretary-general reached across his desk to call the car that would take him back to his residence.

"Good," he said. "Better than I had hoped."

♦ **5** ♦

EVENING. It had been a long, frustrating day, and, coming on top of his altercations with Doug Murphy at the morning conference, it almost made Di Coiano wish he had joined Collins interviewing the relatives of the crew members in New Jersey.

There was a feeling of impotence among the team. The ATC transcript had been raked over a hundred times but, without so much as a square inch of wreckage, speculation had merely spawned further speculation to the point where it was impossible to start any sentence with the words "assuming" or "if we assume" without producing jaded grins all round.

Representatives of the airline, the air-frame manufacturer, the engine manufacturer, and the pilots' association had arrived throughout the day, bringing with them boxes of records and passenger lists. On the roof a short-wave radio antenna had been rigged up to beam in instant information on the progress of the search out at sea.

But no wreckage had been sighted, no life rafts, nothing. Not even an oil slick. The local radio stations talked of "hopes fading." They were wrong: Any hope had long since disappeared.

Late in the afternoon, Murphy had convened a second meeting to establish the working groups within the enlarged investigation team, augmented as it now was by interested parties. As head of the Human Performance group, DC had finished the meeting with a team of three beneath him: Apart from Collins, he now had the airline pilots' representatives and a member of the Airlantic personnel department. The only thing either could contribute were the crew records, which indicated a degree of experience well above the average. A little to his surprise, DC found he had known none of them personally during his own time with the airline.

In the cheerless conference room men were now standing about in huddles of twos and threes, poring over charts and documents and periodically stretching, coughing, and belching.

The investigation was entering that depressing stage all too familiar to DC—when walls as well as tables disappeared beneath paperwork, and smokers, abandoning hope of locating ashtrays, started flicking their ash directly into the air in the belief that they were thereby fulfilling some fundamental imperative uniquely sanctioned by both ecology and religion. Ashes to ashes, dust to dust.

Thinking back to Jo Kaplan's theories about crew negligence, DC studied the results of the flight engineer's last three simulator tests with particular care, looking for the slightest sign of instrument neglect, indecision, or sluggish reaction. There was none; the results were as good as any he had seen. He tossed them onto the table and looked at the clock. It was nearly eight.

The bar was deserted except for the barmaid and a young woman at one of the corner tables, her head turned away toward the window. DC perched himself at the bar and ordered a large "rye and dry."

He felt like a guilty schoolboy. Murphy, a strict teeto-taler, always let it be known that he regarded an investiga-tion base as an extension of the flight deck: clear chain of command; scrupulous discipline; and at all times dry. But whatever powers he may have had to enforce the first two, there was nothing he could do about the third. Even so and although DC told himself he didn't care what Murphy thought about alcohol, it was apparent that most other members of the team did and, if only for the sake of a quiet life, were prepared to abide by their chief's unofficial strictures. One thing was for sure; if the motel had entertained any hopes of making a killing on its bar takings, it was going to be disappointed.

The barmaid was talking about her dogs. DC was uncer-tain how the subject had arisen but listened politely.

She was on the wrong side of forty-five, he guessed. There was something desperate about her, about the way she spoke and moved. The up-tilted eyes and permanent smile were a public declaration to an indifferent world that she intended to win through against the odds. "Life is for living" was the message they tried so hard to convey, but the truth was that mere survival had become an end in itself. Fifteen, twenty years earlier she might have been judged attractive, but the cruel overhead lighting revealed gray roots at the parting of her blond hair and a skin that had grown slack with age. The smell of cheap scent, which on a younger woman might have been a turn-on, wafted intrusively across the bar every time she reached up to place one of the glasses in the overhead rack. Her dogs, DC suspected, were most likely her only faithful companions. He felt at once depressed by her and sorry for her and, despite his own preoccupations, listened to her prattlings with a show of attentiveness.

Looking in the mirror, he was aware, just to the right of her head, of a figure advancing toward the bar, empty glass in hand. It was the young woman who had been sitting in the corner.

The juxtaposition of images was startling—of youth and age caught momentarily in the same frame, as though the barmaid's younger self were hovering behind her in a past that had suddenly been made spatial.

The illusion passed but not its impact. As the younger woman came closer, DC kept his eye on her advancing image while the mirror permitted a scrutiny that in other circumstances would have been impertinent. No longer listening to the barmaid's chatter, he studied the image as one would study the picture of a pretty girl in a magazine—appreciatively and without embarrassment.

The image smiled, catching him off balance. He swung around.

"I'm sorry, I didn't mean to stare." His eyes dropped to her glass. "Please . . . what'll it be?"

She regarded his confusion with detached amusement.

"Really, you don't have to. I'm very emancipated. In fact, let me prove it by getting you one."

"Tell you what, I'll get this round. You get the next if we're still drinking."

It was a clumsy remark; the sort a man might make to another man, a drinking buddy. Where, he wondered, was all this Italian blood sloshing around in his body? Whatever had happened to the subtle seduction technique of "the Latin lover"?

She sensed his embarrassment and gave a light laugh.

"My name is Terry Morrow and my drink is a white wine and soda. And thank you."

"And I'm Matt Di Coiano, but everybody calls me DC."

There was hurt in the barmaid's eyes as she took the order. DC sensed that the present scenario was painfully familiar to her and wanted somehow to cushion the blow. But again his handling was inept.

"We were talking about dogs, weren't we, er . . ." He realized he had made no effort to find out the barmaid's name. "You, you got any, Terry?"

Not now, she said, but plenty when she'd been a kid. She went on to swap comments with the barmaid about various breeds, effectively excluding DC from the conversation. He didn't mind; it gave him a chance to observe her.

Early thirties, he judged, and with expensive tastes. Every accessory—the simple gold chain around her neck, the Cartier watch, the plain twisted braid gold bracelet—had a discreet aura of quality about it. The soft brown hair that fell in curls just skimming the shoulders looked entirely natural but, even to DC's untutored eye, had been expertly cut and styled, and contrasted cruelly with the barmaid's split ends. She had the one commodity DC prized most highly in a woman: She had class. Beneath the gaze of her dark brown eyes he felt like a gas station attendant in his crumpled jacket and scuffed shoes.

Somebody else entered the bar—not a member of the investigation team—and attracted the barmaid's attention. As soon as she was gone, Terry leaned across and whispered.

"Her name is Cathy."

It was a rebuke, but done in a gentle, good-humored way that was calculated not to humiliate. DC smiled sheepishly.

"Thanks. I'm not very good at that sort of thing."

"Men seldom are, but I get the impression you're more sensitive than most." She sipped her drink. "Anyway, what are you doing in this storm-lashed, godforsaken, frozen wilderness in the middle of winter?"

"Oh, there's a group of us here to investigate that crashed airliner that went down in the Atlantic yesterday evening. I work for the National Transportation Safety Board in Washington."

"You mean you're a real-life air-crash investigator?"

"You make it sound like a private eye or something. It's not as glamorous as people think."

"So tell me about it."

A warning bell sounded in DC's head. The press. She didn't look like a reporter but the best reporters never did. The same was true of every profession. The best doctors didn't walk the wards with stethoscopes around their necks, just as the best pilots didn't strut around hotels in their uniforms. Only those who aspired to the top of their professions but still had a long way to go modeled themselves on the stereotype images.

He had been caught out by reporters before and lulled into indiscreet remarks. Maybe that had made him paranoid, but it wasn't beyond the wit of an enterprising newspaper editor to find out where the investigation team was based and dispatch a reporter under cover. And what better cover than a pretty face and engaging manner?

"First, how about you telling me what *you* are doing here?" he answered, deflecting the question.

"Oh, I'm a writer. I'm just doing an article for a magazine. The changing face of Cape Code in winter; the Cape the visitor never sees—you know the sort of thing. Long on words, short on facts. It's what in the trade they call 'a color piece.' "

The answer did nothing to dispel DC's suspicions. There was a certain double-bluff subtlety in the reporter masquerading as the folksy magazine contributor.

"Which magazine you work for?"

"Whichever will take my work and pay for it. I'm your ultimate freelance—or mercenary, depending on which way you look at it."

Still he wasn't convinced.

"Would I have read any of your articles?"

"Depends how long you normally have to wait to see your dentist."

He tried several more questions but short of asking outright for a sample of her work, there was no way of checking her story.

Suddenly there was a hint of irritability in her voice.

"Look, what is all this third-degree business? Are you on the payroll of the writers' union or something? Have they asked you to check me out to see whether I'm undercutting minimum rates? Is that it? When you said you were an investigator, I thought you were talking about air crashes."

He gave a nervous laugh.

"I'm sorry. I just . . . well, I just wanted to be sure you weren't a member of the press sent up here to do a little eavesdropping on the investigation. It wouldn't be the first time."

She shook her head in disbelief and some of the brown curls fell across her face.

"Now I've heard everything! Just hold it there and don't go away."

With a flick of the head she slipped off the barstool and disappeared through the door. Two minutes later she was back, clutching a photocopy of a magazine article. She offered it to him for his scrutiny.

It was from *Cape Cod Life*—an article on the history of patchwork quilt making. The byline, TERRY MORROW, appeared prominently beneath the awful punning headline, DO YOU HAVE A QUILT COMPLEX?

"It's something I did quite a while back," she said. "Just read it through and, when you've finished, tell me whether you really think the author is likely to be an undercover reporter for *The Washington Post* or *New York Times*."

The headline and byline were enough to convince him. He handed the copy back without reading further.

She pointed to his glass.

"My turn, I think."

DC was seized by a boldness which, if he had had time to think about it, would probably have deserted him. But there wasn't likely to be another chance, and there was always the possibility of Murphy or somebody else appearing on the scene. He placed his hand over the glass.

"I've a better idea. I don't know about you but I've got to get out of this place, even if it means getting soaked. After twelve hours, I feel like I've been vaulted in a tomb. What d'you say to our finding someplace a little more . . . congenial?"

She seemed surprised but not displeased.

"I thought you were working on this big investigation."

"Which is why I need to get away for an hour or two. Clear the mind."

She smiled and glanced at the rain-lashed window.

"I'll go and slip into my wetsuit."

"While you're doing that, I'll call a cab."

"No need. My car's out back. And unless there's a place you have in mind, I'm told there's a good restaurant about five miles west along Route 28. I was going to check it out for the article anyway."

◆ 6 ◆

THERE IS something uniquely unnerving about assuming another man's identity. If sleep, to borrow the poet's metaphor, is a little death, then impersonation is a little murder. It is the ultimate invasion of privacy. Actors are seldom aware of it because they generally impersonate the deceased or the imaginary, but not so Adrian Medcalf, as he checked in at London Heathrow's Terminal Two for the Balkanair flight to Sofia.

He had flown from Brussels to Heathrow as Adrian Timothy Medcalf, NATO political analyst. Then, somewhere between Terminals One and Two—perhaps as he stood

motionless on the moving walkway—he had assumed the
identity of a man he had never even met. As though it had
been sprayed on. By the time he had popped his Medcalf
passport in the Terminal Two postbox, as per instructions,
the transformation was complete. He was a different man.

He passed most of the flight making up for lost sleep—
when not being pressed by the stewardess to try a shiny red
Bulgarian apple. The fact that she clearly believed it to be
some sort of treat, a national delicacy even, only heightened
his growing feeling of disorientation.

He seemed to have been living through a kaleidoscope
of experience in which events made patterns but little sense.
It was hard to credit that this was really how NATO
operated—tossing their senior deskmen behind enemy lines
with paper-thin disguises mugged up from a couple of sheets
of biography. If it was, it showed a callous disregard for the
safety of their own people. Where had been all the training,
the painstaking preparation? Unless one counted an hour
with a mad Dutchman viewing videos, visiting historic bat-
tlefields, and discussing "personal death"—followed by an
encounter in one's own flat with a licensed intruder. Not
forgetting of course the slap on the back and cheery "Good
luck!" from the secretary-general. It was like being pushed
out of a plane with a folded parachute and an instruction
manual to read on the way down.

And yet, on reflection, the whole process did seem to
have been informed by a curious logic. Although rushed, it
had never given the impression of being improvised. It was
even possible that all the training and knowledge he needed
to survive was there, but in such a concentrated form that it
would require days to dissolve into his consciousness.

"Ladies and gentlemen, welcome to Sofia. You are kindly
requested to remain in your seats until the aircraft has come
to a complete rest. For your information, the temperature
outside is two degrees below the zero. Thank you and
good-bye."

Again time, space, and experience all seemed to have been telescoped. In one respect it worked to Medcalf's advantage. He went through Passport Control in such a daze that he quite forgot to worry about whether his own photograph would be checked against Chanter's original.

Outside ten minutes later, he stood on the steps of the airport building looking for a taxi to take him to the Grand Hotel Bulgaria, Ruski Boulevard—and to his surprise realized that Dr. Stephen Chanter of Oxford University had arrived safely in Sofia.

♦ **7** ♦

THE RESTAURANT was everything the motel was not. In a word, authentic. There was the same whaling paraphernalia but, whereas in the motel, it had been self-conciously displayed like something off the set of *Moby Dick*, here it was just part of the ambience of the place.

The air was heavy with the smell of cooked fish. Huge steaming bowls of quahog clam chowder passed by at nose level on their way to tables so close together that to reach the farthest corners they had to be passed from one customer to the next. The place had a life that mercifully predated sterilization, pasteurization, and all the other barren "izations" of the late twentieth century. Potential health hazards abounded—chipped crockery, fingered cutlery, rough wooden tabletops—all no doubt teeming with invisible bacterial life that, back in the culinary clinics that passed for restaurants in Washington, would have slain half the clientele.

Like a landed fish thrown back into the water, DC felt suddenly revitalized. A waitress appeared, quoted from memory the blackboard menu at the far end of the room, and, having committed their order to paper, crab-stepped away between the tables.

Terry waited for her to be out of earshot.

"Have you noticed how the letter *r* doesn't exist on the Cape?—chowdah, lobstah, even crackah! I warn you, it can be very infectious. You've only to listen to the wash-ashores."

"The what?"

"The wash-ashores. They're the year-round residents who pretend they were born here—and, if there's one thing the locals can't stand, it's a phoney. Even among themselves they insist you're not a true Codder till you're third-generation."

Sitting by her side on the bench seat, DC had to turn to face her. As he did so, he was aware of the sensuality of their proximity, of a sexual static that crackled between them, bridging the thickness of cloth between their bodies. He was sure she felt it, too. Yet she made no effort to move away. The enjoyment seemed mutual.

"This all for the article? Or did you know it before?" he asked.

She laughed, flipping back her hair to reveal a small gold ear stud.

"When I was a girl, the family had—rented, rather—a summer house at Eastham. My mother died when we were young. My father was the worst sort of tourist you can imagine—always trying to be more Catholic than the pope. He'd insist on holding authentic clambakes down on the beach, while all the true Codders were doing it in the convenience of their own backyards. He used to organize my brothers and me like we were his private army, giving us all names that defined our duties—stone-finder, fire-tender, rockweed-gatherer, clam-digger—and try to persuade us that, before the Pilgrims arrived, this was how the Wampanoag Indians did it! Can you imagine?"

"And which were you?"

"Usually Little Squaw Rockweed-gatherer. The boys could never be trusted to get the right sort of weed, the kind with the oval airsacs. My father always figured girls were naturally more conscientious than boys." She returned his gaze. "And you, where did the young Di Coiano spend *his* summer vacations."

A sad smile came to DC's lips.

"Oh, nothing so grand as clambakes on the beach. I'm not sure I even knew what a vacation was. I was a street kid—a child of Little Italy. New York, you know?"

"Mulberry Street?"

"Close enough. But this was before the classy restaurants moved in, before the Chinese starting moving north of Canal. My grandparents emigrated from Italy in the 1920s—I'll spare you tears by skipping the chapter on Ellis Island—and started up a delicatessen on the corner of Mott and Grand. Ricotta, mozzarella, latticini freschi! ... It's still there, still thriving: DI COIANO'S DIARY STORES—my grandfather had trouble with the language; so, as a kind of tribute to him, it's always been left as DIARY on the sign." He shrugged. "And that's about it. We all lived above the shop. My father finally took over the business in the early fifties, grandfather joined his cronies playing bocce on Houston Street, and we kids got most of our amusement chasing each other up and down the fire escapes. They talk these days about kids being streetwise; well, I guess you could say we were tenement-trained. I tell you, the way we moved up and down the outside of that block made Spiderman look like some kinda geriatric cripple."

"Happy memories?"

"I guess so. But it's always the small things you remember. Like you and your father's clambake. I still have the smell of the parmigiano and prosciutto in my nostrils. I remember standing behind the counter—I had to get up on tiptoe to see over it—and my mother making up customers' orders and slipping us kids slivers of salami from the slicer. Like it was some kind of Host—the wafer to keep us good Catholics, the salami to keep us good Italians."

"And did it work? I mean did it keep you good Italians?"

DC could see what made Terry a good writer. She had the knack of every time picking up on scraps of conversation, of grabbing hold of the end of the rope before it slipped away, and then deftly lashing it to a new length so that it never seemed like a fresh topic was being broached. He was aware that more was being drawn from him than he would normally have volunteered at this stage in a friendship but, equally, he knew a flip answer wouldn't satisfy.

"Depends what you mean by 'a good Italian.' A good Italian would have stayed with his family and today would be running the family business alongside his brothers. But I had ambitions. Even as a five-year-old, I knew what I wanted to be." He paused, wondering about the wisdom of sharing a family intimacy with a stranger, but carried on. "I tell you, the only way my mother could ever get me to eat all my tagliatelli as a kid was to tell me that nobody ever became a pilot unless he logged his daily input of pasta." A look of mock incredulity crossed Terry's face, encouraging him to continue. "Gospel truth, I promise you . . . She totally convinced me that there'd come a day when the head of TWA would ring up and say, 'Mrs. Di Coiano? We've got your boy Matteo here; says he wants to be a pilot. We'd sure like to have him on board but, well, the records suggest there was some problem with his dinner on March twenty-third, 1952. Would you confirm, please, that he did finish his pasta that day?' "

They both laughed and then fell suddenly silent. It was the mention of flying—that and the fact that here they were warm and happy, and alive. In DC's case it was compounded by a feeling of guilt. He was conscious of Murphy's ghost sitting Banquo-like at the end of the table to remind him that socializing on the job was "unprofessional."

"I get the impression you don't think there's much hope," she said quietly, reading his thoughts.

The waitress returned with their order. It was over a minute before DC replied.

"It would require nothing short of a miracle. People tend to think of ditching in the sea as almost routine because of all that life-vest spiel the stewardess goes through before the flight. In fact, it's extremely rare, but when it does happen, the impact and damage, far from being less, can be even greater than a crash into the ground."

"I didn't realize. I always imagined that it would be, well, I guess a bit like coming down in one of those old-fashioned seaplanes."

"That's what most people think, and for obvious reasons the airlines do nothing to persuade them otherwise. It's an unwritten law in the industry that you never talk about safety in front of the public. It's like sex in front of children. Ask a manufacturer if his aircraft is strong enough to survive a ditching, and he'll tell you it has a high structural integrity and a demanding fatigue spectrum! Cut through the gobbledygook and you'll find the truth is more simple ... For a start, most modern wide-bodied jets—the SP-3 included—have engines slung beneath the wings, which in most cases will be ripped clean off as they plough into the water. If they stay on, they'll as likely as not drag the wings off the fuselage—and with the wings go your buoyancy bags, the empty fuel tanks. That's assuming, of course, that the crew has had time to complete the fuel dump before impact."

"Are you saying it's safer to crash on land then?"

"Depends ... but at least on land there's always a chance of the aircraft bouncing or sliding to a stop. On water the stop can be virtually instantaneous—within one second—and with horrendous G forces that'll rip seats from their anchorages and concertina the fuselage. Then you have to start worrying about the problems of evacuation ..."

"And?"

"Let's put it this way: The manufacturers will tell you their aircraft are capable of staying afloat twenty-five minutes—and more. But that's on the basis of dunking models in test tanks. In reality, most of today's designs have never been tried out in a real sea with real waves. Almost everything about the ditching capabilities of a modern wide-bodied jet is theoretical." There was a sadness in his eyes. "Don't kid yourself, Terry, the only hope in this case is that we'll find some scrap of the aircraft that'll tell us why it went down in the first place."

They drove back across country through a landscape whipped by hurricane-force winds. The nor'easter had arrived. Blue and white mailboxes advertising the *Cape Cod Times* quivered on their stalks by the roadside. At the occasional intersections, the overhead traffic lights swung wildly like Chinese lanterns in a drunken procession.

Neither of them spoke, awed by the elements and half-fearful that the car itself might be picked up by a freak gust and hurled deep into the pines. The low, strung-out exterior of the motel was almost welcome when it finally came in sight.

The clock in the lobby said it was a quarter to midnight. During the drive back, DC had thought of inviting Terry to take a nightcap in his room, but the antiseptic ambience of the motel with all its associations of work and duty now drove any further thoughts of romance from his mind. With an absurd chasteness—not even a peck on the cheek—he wished her a good night's sleep and headed for the conference room. He had a pretty good idea what he would find.

Murphy sat alone at the head of the table, paperwork spread out before him. His expression was unmistakable—that of the parent who had waited up for the stay-out child and was going to take time and pleasure in delivering a well-rehearsed lecture.

"Sure is wild out there," DC said casually, pouring himself a coffee from the machine.

But Murphy was not to be deflected.

"DC, there are certain things you've clearly not understood about the way a GO team works."

DC felt his anger rise. Murphy could say his piece but he, DC, was not prepared to trade personal insults. He laid the coffee on the table and bore down on Murphy from the other end, his voice firm but controlled.

"Before we go any further, Doug, are you talking about GO teams generally or GO teams headed by yourself?"

"I should hope there was no difference when it came to matters of discipline and procedure."

DC sensed he had the advantage. There was a defensive tone in Murphy's voice. He pressed on.

"Me, too, Doug—and, if you're talking about tonight and the fact that I chose to leave this place for a couple of hours, then you'd better know the procedures I observed before leaving. First, the desk clerk knew which restaurant I had gone to; second, the beeper was in my pocket at all times; third, there was nothing to be done by the Human Performance group that had not already been done—and fourth, there's nothing in any rule book I've ever read which says I have to ask your permission every time I want to leave the room or, if it comes to that, the building."

He picked up his coffee and drank. It was a gesture of defiance and contempt. Murphy wasn't even worth staring down any longer.

"It depends on who you leave with," said Murphy.

The girl on the front desk had obviously been interrogated. It wasn't beyond Murphy to ask to see the guest register.

"And what does that mean—since we've established that I've breached none of your precious procedures?"

"D'you know who that young woman is—the one you left with earlier?"

"Yes, but I don't have to answer to you about her. And neither does she. She's a guest in this hotel, as you damn well know."

"She's also a journalist." There was triumph in Murphy's voice.

DC's grip loosened on the paper cup. So this was what it was all leading up to.

"No, Doug, she's a writer. She works for a magazine. She specializes in heavy, in-depth articles on New England patchwork quilting and regional cookery. She didn't even know what we were all doing here."

"Until you told her."

DC felt suddenly tired.

"Doug, I'm not going to argue with you. It's midnight and—"

"And I'm not going to argue with you, DC. For your own sake, though, you'd better take this on board. However you choose to define her—and I don't care if she's the emeritus editor of *Embroidery and Crochet Monthly*—that young woman is a member of the press corps. Now, you know the rules and, in case you've forgotten them, I'm reminding you of them now: All contacts with the press are handled through the board's public affairs officers. We have one on the team with us here and there is another back in Washington. For the moment, all inquiries are being handled by Washington. Anything you divulge to that young woman about this investigation—and I mean anything—is unauthorized and will make you liable to disciplinary procedures. Do you—"

DC crumpled the cup and threw it into the bin just inches from Murphy. It was as calculated as spitting on his shoes.

"Sleep well, Doug," he said, making for the door.

To his surprise, Murphy was on his feet. For a moment DC thought the man was going to hit him. Then he saw the sheet of paper in his hand.

"What's this?"

"Take it and you might find out. Since you seem to have stopped listening when people talk to you."

DC took the sheet but waited till he was in the corridor before reading it.

It was a telex from Collins in New Jersey. It seemed that the initial information about the crew on board the doomed SP-3 had been wrong. There had been a last-minute replacement of the rostered flight engineer.

The name of the man who had stepped in was Gerald C. Aldridge.

DC stopped, let his head fall forward, and took a deep, slow breath. If it was Fate that had decided he should be on this particular investigation, Fate had a strangely twisted sense of humor.

♦ 8 ♦

MEDCALF knew there was something wrong the moment he woke up. He opened his eyes and, shifting his buttocks to another declivity in the corrugated mattress, surveyed the hotel bedroom by the crack of early morning light squeezing around the edge of the internal shutters.

Most of the details were familiar from the previous night. The room was high and narrow with two single beds in opposite corners. There was a writing table by the window, much of its surface taken up by a large Russian-made radio, the size of the old-fashioned tube radios he recalled from his childhood. The carpet was stained and worn, a great and growing crescent of moisture being accounted for by the water that leaked perpetually from the lavatory tank in the bathroom before flowing over the threshold into the bedroom. The reading light on the wall above him hung limply on its wires, apparently wrenched off by a previous occupant, while on the bedside table to his left sat a blue plastic telephone of a cheapness and nastiness that would have disgraced even a child's toy box in any Western country. Given the technological progress represented by these various objects, it was hard to believe that the Eastern bloc nations were really the masters of electronic eavesdropping they were famed to be.

He knew then what was wrong: It was the quiet. He had never stayed in any hotel in the center of a capital city and known such silence. No cars, no motorbikes, no horns. He got up, pulled back the shutters, and pushed open the window.

There appeared a frosted glass plate. Upon it were etched skeletal trees in a neat park with wooden benches and elegant nineteenth-century buildings in the Viennese Baroque style, the entire scene rendered two-dimensional by freezing fog and the absence of moving, human forms.

It was not the Sofia he had expected. Back in Brussels, he had imagined a cityscape of functional gray buildings inhabited by functional gray people—a down-trodden population in a run-down country. This was not it.

As his eyes became accustomed to the scene, muted colors appeared like the emerging tints of a Polaroid print. The buildings grew yellow, cream, and beige—the benches in the park pale green. He leaned out. Ruski Boulevard sixty feet below seemed paved with blocks of yellow chocolate. They led, he knew but could not see, to the Ninth of September Square, the scene of the assassination attempt.

Slowly, the picture gained depth and perspective. A gilded onion dome topped by a two-barred cross appeared above a rooftop to the right, while in ironic but appropriate opposition to the left the symbol of the new order, a huge five-pointed red star, teetered on a green stalk above "Party House," the headquarters of the all-powerful, all-pervasive Bulgarian Communist Party.

He retreated to the bathroom and, grateful for a trickle of tepid water, showered and shaved, thinking again of the totally unrealistic nature of his assignment. By pretending to research a book on Bulgaria's prerevolutionary period, he was somehow to establish contact with a local informant who would—somehow, again—make himself known despite the perpetual official surveillance.

He got dressed and, removing from his case the guidebook to Sofia so thoughtfully provided by his late-night visitor, took it with him down to the restaurant.

Breakfast was a serve-yourself affair of cold salami, cheese, and bread, washed down with a choice of tea or something which its Cyrillic label proclaimed to be "WBenc" but which turned out to be one of the Western world's great gifts to the East, the ubiquitous "Shveps."

Two maroon-jacketed waiters circled the central table in a desultory fashion, replenishing items as they ran out. This at least was what Medcalf imagined their function to be. Closer observation, however, afforded him his first insight into one of the fundamental principles of Bulgarian socialism: that the greatest reward of a "service" job—be it in a hotel, restaurant, shop, or government office—was the opportunity it continually afforded to demonstrate one's equality with one's fellow men by a display of stony indifference to their every request and requirement. If, as in this case, one also had a monopoly on the bottle openers, one was then in the truly enviable position of being able in addition to exert a measure of real power.

Pushing all thought of croissants and coffee in La Grand'

Place out of his mind, Medcalf pressed open his guidebook—purchased, he noticed, from Collet's Bookshop, Charing Cross Road—and, while his stomach protested at the unaccustomed ingestion at this hour of cheese and salami, started work on the itinerary for the morning's academic peregrination.

That the memory of Charing Cross Road should prompt a genuine sense of loss was just the first revelation in a day that was to be full of them.

◆ **9** ◆

DICK SEEWARD, one of the structural specialists, was the first to greet DC at breakfast.

"I guess you've heard the news."

"What's that?"

"They've found some wreckage."

"You're putting me on. When?"

"Twenty-four hours ago, it seems, but we've only just heard. A trawler from Provincetown came across a section of the tail yesterday morning. When the storm warnings went out, the skipper decided to stay where he was to the north of the worst of the weather and ride it out, figuring he could always make a run into Halifax if he had to."

DC helped himself to a large orange juice from the serving table.

"So why the delay? Why the hell didn't he radio in and tell us?"

"Trouble with the radio. At least that's his story." Seeward winked. "More likely he was fishing somewhere he shouldn't. They all do it up here. As with the fish, the skill's in not getting caught. Anyway, he's due in to P-town about ten o'clock—with his catch."

DC was still puzzled. "Why doesn't Murphy get him to bring it into Chatham and save us all some time? I thought that was the reason we were based here—because of the airport and the harbor."

"Yeah, well . . ." Seeward smiled. "Seems there's a bit of ill feeling between the P-town fishermen and the Chatham fishermen we didn't know about. There's a local agreement that the P-town skippers keep three miles off the coast—outside the Chatham men's 'territorial waters'—but there're a few mavericks up there who've a habit of sneaking in under the fog and trawling the local lobster pots every once in a while. That sort of thing doesn't do a lot for neighborly relations."

"So how does Murphy plan to get the wreckage down here?"

"Just load it on a flat truck and drive it down to the hangar at the airport. He's briefed the P-town harbor master pretty thoroughly about handling it—although I doubt that it'll've been kindly treated by our trawling friends—and of course we'll have to send somebody up there to keep an eye on things. The whole operation shouldn't take longer than a couple of hours." A glint of excitement came into his eye. "Then at last we might be able to get this so-called investigation under way. Don't know about you, but just sitting on my butt sifting through manifests and maintenance documents was really getting to me."

DC sympathized and then out of the corner of his eye noticed Terry enter the room. She looked stunning in well-cut dark slacks and a loose-fitting cream silk shirt. Heads turned. There was the same freshness and natural elegance about her that had so struck him in the bar the previous evening. He felt proud and possessive—laughably so. Like a love-struck adolescent, he wanted everybody to know that he'd already struck up a friendship. She was his—so lay off, fellows.

She gave a fleeting smile of recognition in his direction as she helped herself to the buffet, but then headed for a single table on the other side of the room. Several more times he attempted to catch her eye but failed. It was her instinctive sense of tact, he told himself.

"See you in the hangar later then, I guess," said Seeward, pushing back his chair and adding, "unless of course you'd like to do my job for me and go up to P-town to see this tail section off the boat."

But DC's attention was elsewhere. Still he stared across the room, but still Terry acted as though unaware of his attention. Finally, her breakfast finished, she got up to leave. He watched her back disappear through the front door and followed, catching up with her as she stood at the front desk. The lobby area had diplomatic immunity, he figured.

"Not leaving already?" he said.

"Not yet. Just checking how long it takes to get to Provincetown these days. They've built a new road since I was last here."

The words were out before he could stop himself:

"You mean you're going to P-town this morning?"

"That was the idea. Why, am I going your way?"

Too late, DC remembered his run-in with Murphy the night before and the warning about fraternizing with members of the press. He hesitated.

"Depends what you'll be doing there?"

"Oh, I just want to take a look—see how the town has changed. My article, remember?"

DC reasoned with himself. To tell Seeward that he would happily volunteer to go up to P-town to supervise the unloading of the tail section would put him ahead of the game, which could in itself be useful in dealing with Murphy if there were any more snide suggestions about his neglecting his duties. Murphy could hardly object if he was doing not only his own job but somebody else's too. He might object if he found out that he was hitching a ride with Terry but, hell, she wasn't going to be interested in tagging right along to the dockside to view a piece of twisted metal; she had other things to do. Anyway, since when was he so worried about what Murphy thought, for Christ's sake?

They had been on Route 6 for about an hour when an incongruous Italianate bell tower rising three or more hundred feet above sea level pierced the horizon.

"Make you feel kind of homesick?" Terry asked.

"Uh?" responded DC in the passenger seat.

"The *Cam-pan-ee-lay.*" She pronounced the word with an exaggerated Italian accent. "The Pilgrim Monument. It's a copy of the Torre del Mangia in Siena. At least that's what the guidebook says. I'd have thought it would've held some magic for a second-generation pasta-pusher like yourself— the spot where the Pilgrim Fathers landed, commemorated by an authentic bit of old Europe."

DC looked hard at the gray granite monstrosity dwarfing the town that was now coming into view beneath it. It looked as out of place as a crucifix in a bordello.

"Look, I've never been to Italy, but I can tell you—and every drop of *vin santo* in my veins confirms it—that that pile of stone bears as much relation to the Torre del Mangia as a Saturn Five sitting on its pad at Cape Kennedy. My grandfather would have called it '*uno scherzo*'!"

They pulled up in the harbor parking lot. The wind had dropped since the previous night but it was still strong enough to bounce the car on its springs. And it was raining. Terry pulled a scarf from the glove compartment and wrapped it around her head. It gave her face an appropriately Puritan look, he thought.

He checked the time. Throughout the journey he had been deliberately cryptic about his reasons for coming to Provincetown.

"You going to tell me what it's all about or do I have to guess?" she said at last. "Or do you still think I'm working undercover for *The New York Times*?"

"If I told you I came just for your company you wouldn't believe me."

"I might."

The words took him by surprise. There was a seductive softness in them that invited a response in kind. She tucked the loose strands of hair inside the scarf, inclining her face slightly toward him. He was aware that once again the line between business and pleasure was being subtly eroded and had to remind himself that he was an integral part of a major air-crash investigation—a crash in which 254 people had lost their lives. He owed it to them—at least to their relatives—if not the Murphys of this world, to play his full professional part in the investigation. He responded brusquely:

"One of the trawlers picked up part of the missing aircraft's tail. That's all. It's due into harbor in about half an hour."

As he had feared, she felt repulsed. An invitation to greater intimacy had been declined. Torn up and scattered to the wind.

"Then I'd better not delay you any longer," she said. "I guess you'll know where to find the car when you want to be driven back."

He felt both better and worse for being alone again. Terry seemed to have a unique capacity for screwing up his emotions that was both pleasurable and disquieting. And on both counts dangerous.

He found the harbor master without difficulty—a large barrel of a man with a baseball hat and parka—and introduced himself. It was obvious the man thought he hadn't been trusted to freight the wreckage back to Chatham without supervision—and resented DC's presence. Bit by bit, though, he thawed, as DC persuaded him that he had no desire to muscle in on his show. It was just "regulations," he said, that a member of the N.T.S.B. be present on such occasions—a bore but, well, that was in the nature of regulations, wasn't it?

The gulls appeared on the horizon before the boat—an avian escort hovering above the mast in expectation of a good feed on the dockside.

As the blue-and-white seventy-footer came closer, DC noticed that the rails and even the wires around the bows were lagged in thick ice. He pointed it out to the harbor master.

"Sure, that's quite common this time of year. They'll've been fishing for halibut off the Continental Shelf. The spray coming over the bow freezes on contact with the metal and starts to build up. Can be real dangerous if it's not hacked off. There've been cases of boats becoming so top heavy they've turned turtle."

There was no sign of the tail section on the deck as the trawler tied up—just a jumble of nets, floats, plastic baskets, and winding gear. DC turned again to the harbor master.

"You sure this is the right one?"

But the harbor master was already pointing to a long length of tarpaulin covering an object wedged between the wheelhouse and the gunwale.

"I think you'll find that's your tail section there."

He was right, and ten minutes later, as the tarpaulin was rolled back, the SP-3's port horizontal stabilizer emerged, battered and buckled but seemingly complete with its elevator.

DC collared the trawler skipper and took him back to his wheelhouse to get out of the drizzle. He explained that, as the one who had found the wreckage, the skipper would be required to make a sworn deposition before a court reporter and that in his statement he would be required to outline the exact circumstances surrounding its retrieval—time of day, compass bearings, condition of sea.

The skipper tugged off his woolen hat and grinned like a mischievous schoolboy.

"Could be kinda difficult, that sort of thing," he said.

Seeward had guessed correctly; they'd been fishing in somebody else's part of the pond, and there was now every likelihood that the skipper would lie to cover his wake. Yet it was vital he be persuaded to tell the truth. DC tried the standard lecture on the basics of air-crash investigation—the paramount importance of precisely locating wreckage, whether on land or at sea, to determine whether a part had fallen off in flight or on impact. The lives of every air passenger could depend on it, he stressed. But the skipper merely nodded, occasionally rubbing the three-day stubble on his chin and grimacing.

DC realized that more devious measures would be required:

"You were riding out the storm well to the north of its vortex, right?" he said, staring through the window of the wheelhouse. "I think the satellite pictures I saw last night showed you not far off Halifax . . ."

It was a bluff but, from the flash of concern on the man's face, it had had the desired effect. DC continued:

"All we need to know is at what point you came across the wreckage and at what time. No need to give us your course from beginning to end; we can work that out from the satellite material—if we need to. Anyway, I guess that in that storm you'd've been more concerned with staying afloat than doing any fishing."

"Right . . . right," the skipper agreed. The grin had gone.

Off-loading the tail section proved trickier than expected. Eventually it had to be trussed in a rope cradle and, using the trawler's own inboard hoist, gently dislodged from its resting place between the super-structure and gunwale. Then, with the trawler bucking in the harbor swell, it was precariously swung out over the sea, through 180 degrees across the stern section, and onto the back of the low-loading truck on the dock.

As the underside passed within a few feet of DC, his eye was caught by a dark, fanned-out stain—as though applied with a spray gun—on the tip of the stabilizer, extending a couple of feet back from the leading edge.

He watched the thirty-foot section being secured and cushioned between two sets of vertical wooden supports, and then pulled himself up on to the trailer to examine the stain more closely. He ran his finger along it and sniffed.

He couldn't be sure but it smelt like burned engine oil. A detailed examination and analysis would have to be carried out back at Chatham but, at first sight, it looked as if the slipstream had carried burning oil from the port engine over the tail as the aircraft had dropped toward the sea. Although the wreckage would have been buffeted by the waves and manhandled by the trawler crew, the freezing air and water had bonded the already tacky substance to the metal like a glaze.

The implications of the stain were obvious. If it *was* engine oil, it would strongly suggest that at least one of the flameouts had had nothing to do with loss of fuel. Kaplan would have to eat his words.

"Interesting?" asked a female voice.

He recognized the kerchief before taking in the face, and was glad.

"Could be. Looks like the port engine was spewing oil before the crash." He again examined his fingertip. "This would've been some of the last of it. See, it's burned. The engine would've been running so hot by that time that the friction would've ignited what little was left."

He yelled to one of the two men lashing the ropes.

"Hey! Put a piece of tarpaulin or something over the tip here, will you? Just to protect it."

The man was a dour type to whom a lump of metal was a lump of metal, whether it had fallen off the back of a truck or the back of an aircraft. He nodded in the direction of the Pilgrim Monument.

"Sure you wouldn't like us to gift-wrap the tower while we're about it?"

DC was going to make a smart reply but noticed Terry wrapping her arms around her body in a theatrical shiver.

"I guess it's best," she shouted through the rain, "if I meet you back at the car when you're through."

They were back on Route 6 and heading south again when Terry said:

"I can see what makes you a good investigator."

"What's that?"

"You have a deductive mind."

DC grunted. "Sometimes. My problem's always been that I'm more interested in the practical than the paperwork. Trouble is that when you're on what they call the Human Performance side like I am, it's more a question of psychology than engineering—nuts of a different kind. Pilots, it's believed, only understand other pilots, not the machines they fly; that's strictly for the engineers."

"And that leads to tensions within the team?"

"Human nature is human nature. It's natural for an engineer to resent it if an ex-pilot on the team like myself uncovers a major mechanical fault that he's missed, just as I'd feel sore if he discovered the pilot was an alcoholic and I hadn't. Like our fishermen friends, we each have our territorial waters, and we guard them jealously."

There was silence between them for a long time. DC suspected what the next question would be; in any conversation it generally came up around this stage and was invariably preceded by a lengthy pause.

"Why did you stop flying, DC?" she asked.

He pushed himself back in the passenger seat and sighed.

"Terry, it's a long and complicated story. It also has a lot to do with this particular investigation. D'you mind if I tell you some other time, preferably when this is all over? I'd like to think that we'll still know each other then."

She smiled. "Sorry, it's obviously the latent *New York Times* interrogator coming out in me again. 'The Great Quilt Cover-up: We name the Guilty Men!' But just tell me this: How do you become an investigator? D'you have to take a test, or what?"

"That's an easier one. Sure, there's a test of sorts but not the kind you'd expect. What they need to know is not how good a pilot or engineer you are—that's taken for granted—but how observant you are. It's not enough just to look; you've got to be able to see."

"Meaning?"

"Well, there's a standard trick they play on most applicants. They give you two photos of a light aircraft that's crashed—nose in the ground, tail in the air, crumpled wings, usual sort of thing—and ask you to compare them and say which way the aircraft was spinning prior to impact. Clockwise or counterclockwise?"

"And which is it?"

"Neither—that's the point. The photographs are of two different planes but of the same type. It's not one crash, but two. That's what is meant by seeing as well as looking."

◆ 10 ◆

FOR the first few minutes of his walk east along Ruski Boulevard, Medcalf conducted himself with the self-consciousness of a man who believed his every step was being monitored by closed-circuit cameras.

Only after a hundred yards did he start to relax sufficiently to take in his surroundings.

Again his preconceptions of Bulgaria had been wide of the mark. Judged by appearances, the people of Sofia were prosperous, even fashion-conscious. The women in their furs and fine leather boots were a far remove from the archetypal daughters of toil with headscarves knotted beneath their multiple chins; some would not have looked out of place on the Champs-Élysées. Of the men, a high proportion were in uniform. They walked as though to the beat of hidden metronomes, keeping their arms rigidly by their sides lest swinging them spoil the lines of their exquisitely tailored greatcoats.

Referring only to the mental map he had memorized over breakfast, Medcalf kept deliberately to the "monumental" side of the city, as he felt might befit an academic engaged in researching a book on the prerevolutionary period.

As soon as he saw the equestrian statue of Tsar Alexander, "The Liberator," he knew he was in Narodno Sobranie Square. It must, he thought, be the Romanovs' only surviving memorial anywhere in the world. He stopped and looked about him, unaware of the figure who had marked him out several seconds earlier and was now advancing from behind.

82

"You have dollars, pounds you are wishing to change? I give you good rate."

He sprang from the man as from the carrier of a contagious disease. Just when he was beginning to think that he had successfully merged into the local scene, here was proof that he was as conspicuous as an Eskimo on the Equator. And in all probability about to be compromised.

"*Né, né,*" he stammered, recalling one of the half-dozen words of Bulgarian he had picked up from the girl at the hotel reception desk, and launched himself across Ruski Boulevard in the direction of the most prominent landmark that presented itself—the huge Neo-Byzantine pile of the Alexander Nevski Church a hundred yards up the hill to his left.

A couple of minutes later, the freezing air catching in his throat, he parted the heavy green curtains across the church entrance and entered a sanctuary of incense and candle wax.

Belatedly he realized his stupidity. How did he know that his importuner had not in fact been Bogart, that the man's offer to change currency had not been an opening gambit?

He swore silently to himself. There was nothing he could do now, except trust that, if he was and it was, he would try again.

He felt suddenly angry with Van Kleef and the whole infantile game that he was being obliged to play. If Bogart had made known to Van Kleef his desire to pass on information, why could he not at the same time have arranged a rendezvous? If not a precise time, at least a place. The present arrangement seemed decidedly hit or miss, absurdly amateurish, and therefore the more dangerous for both parties.

He sat down against a wall on a wooden bench and, his eyes adjusting to the gloom, focused on the huge central candelabra. Their polished brasswork glowed dully in the morning twilight struggling through the segments of dirty yellow glass. From walls of glaucous gold, traumatized saints, apostles, prophets, and patriarchs stared down upon him in neurasthenic stupor—according well with his own feelings of impotence.

To his discriminating eye, the place had all the appearance of a Christmas grotto decked out by Liberty's window dresser. There was not an inch of floor, wall, arch, niche, or cupola that was not covered in mosaic or inlaid in marble, onyx, or alabaster. It represented the worst form of *fin de siècle* excess—Gustave Moreau after one absinthe too many. The Art Nouveau style he could cope with in moderation, but it was like Chinese ware: A single item displayed in a neutral setting could be stunning; put them together and the effect was of a bazaar. As now.

"You like?"

He had not noticed the figure that had quietly slipped onto the bench beside him, but this time he managed to control his instincts and with the manners of the well-bred Englishman was even prepared to lie in the interests of courtesy.

"Very impressive."

He didn't turn to look at the questioner, reasoning that if this wasn't Bogart it was most likely a DS man whose job was to keep an eye on him and check out the story in his—or rather Stephen Chanter's—visa application. A modest display of erudition, however, would not go amiss.

"Built around the turn of the century, I imagine."

"You are very correct," replied the other. "It was built to memorialize the two hundred thousand Russian soldiers who have given their lives to liberate our country from the hated Turkish occupiers in 1878. It immortalizes the fraternal love and gratitude that we Bulgarians will always feel toward the great Russian people. In 1878, you will know, they have given us our freedom, and then in 1945 our socialism."

Medcalf was glad he had not turned to look at the man. His averted face could betray nothing. He nodded in apparent agreement.

"You are English?" asked the Bulgarian.

"Yes, English."

"You are on holiday here?"

Medcalf didn't answer immediately. If this was a genuinely innocent encounter with a native who merely wished to practice his English under the guise of a little patriotic propaganda, fair enough; but, if so, he didn't want to get drawn into a protracted explanation of his reasons for being in Sofia. On the other hand, if his interrogator was really a secret service man, it would be necessary to maintain and actually promote his assumed identity of Dr. Stephen Chanter of Oxford University, here in Sofia to research a book.

"No, I am not on holiday," he replied at last. "I am doing some study." Before the man had time to pursue the line, he turned and asked:

"And you, what do *you* do?"

"Me? I am a student here at the university," replied the Bulgarian, delighted that his conversational gauntlet had at last been picked up.

Medcalf scrutinized the face. It was hard to tell in the half-light but the man looked too old to be a student. The high Slavic cheekbones accentuated the sunken eyes and the hollowness of the unshaven cheeks. He would have guessed him to be in his late twenties; even early thirties. As though sensing his suspicions, the man added:

"We go to university older in Bulgaria. First, we must make our military service."

There was silence between them. Medcalf watched as a verger figure in black made his rounds of the offertory candles. Plucking them from their holders, he tutted over each like a gardener uprooting weeds, and then with a notable lack of reverence tossed them into water-filled tins to fizz and die. The man's personal timetable apparently allowed no discrimination: All lighted candles, irrespective of length, were treated with the same ruthlessness.

"How long you are staying in our country?" asked the Bulgarian.

"About a week."

"That is not long. You have need of a guide—someone to show you around. Sofia is small in geography but she is big in history."

Medcalf had no ready response. He suspected he had only to hint at compliance and the man would attach himself to his side limpet-like for the rest of the week. This did not suggest itself as the likely action of a Bogart. Surely, he reasoned with one of the painted prophets opposite, an informant would wish to pass on his information as quickly and discreetly as possible, not be seen as the constant companion of a foreigner in the streets of the capital. Contact with foreigners was specifically discouraged by the Bulgarian government—even the most casual encounters were meant to be reported.

He stared hard at the painted prophet and made up his mind: The man had to be a DS agent, an official government minder. It followed that he had to do everything in his power to throw him off—without arousing his suspicions.

"I prefer to see things alone," he said firmly but he hoped not impolitely. "It is the way I normally work. I find it difficult to think with other people around."

The Bulgarian chuckled in the gloom.

"I know the expression. 'I vant to be alone,' yes?" He drew out the word "vant" in perfect Garboesque fashion. "It is okay. I understand. But please, you see the underneath here; there is a very fine display of icons. Many people miss them because they do not know."

Medcalf gave a civil smile, grateful that the man seemed at last to have taken the hint.

"And do not forget," added the Bulgarian, now standing, "to buy a record of Boris Christoff and the Alexander

Nevski Choir. It has been recorded here in this church and is very fine. It is up for sale in the church shop at the entrance, but I think I see only one. And now I go and leave you at peace."

An outstretched hand materialized in the half-light.

"My name please is Sergei."

Medcalf shook the hand and watched Sergei head for the entrance. Instinctively, he wiped his palm on his trousers. He remembered the story of Georgi Markov on Waterloo Bridge, of the poisoned pellet in the thigh, and wondered, not altogether frivolously, whether he had now been impregnated with some diabolical "death dust." In his own mind, in its present heightened state, nothing was too fanciful.

♦ **11** ♦

DC stood talking to the airport manager in the small downstairs reception area. It had a casual, homey feel to it. A jar of love hearts sat on the counter for anyone to dip into and a machine in the corner dispensed soda while an old-fashioned kerosene heater warmed the atmosphere to a level of fragrant coziness. A large map dominated one wall but was almost totally obscured by the collection of signed shirttails of those who had made their first solo flights from the airport.

"They're all in there if you wanna go through," said the manager, indicating the direction of the hangar next door. "We had the wreckage off the truck over an hour ago."

DC gave his hands a final toasting over the stove.

* * *

Despite the cold, the hangar doors had been rolled back to provide the maximum light. About a dozen assorted Pipers and Cessnas had been pushed to one end to make room for the section of the SP-3 tail.

It looked like the full team had been got together for the inspection, some standing, others on their haunches, and one even lying flat on the cold concrete to examine it. The tail could barely be seen amid the press of bodies. DC wondered what they had made of the oil stain and whether it tallied with his own assessment. He walked up behind Dick Seeward, who was one of those down on his haunches.

"So what d'you think?" he asked in a confidential whisper.

Seeward half turned.

"Hi!—and thanks for doing the supervisory bit. What do I think? Well, it certainly didn't drop off in flight. I can tell you that for nothing. You can see from the damage to the root that it was ripped off by the impact—together, I'd guess, with the wing engines and the flaps. In that weather, with those seas and without the benefit of engine power, I'd say the pilot had an impossible job on his hands."

"What does it tell you then?"

"Oh, he seems to have been doing all the right things, if that's what you mean. From the position the jackscrew is jammed in, I'd say his pitch attitude was somewhere between eleven and fourteen degrees, which is what the manual advises for a ditching. With landing gear up and flaps at landing setting, that've brought him in at about one-tenth above stall speed. His real problem, though, would've been in judging the final approach. The book says to observe the crests of the waves and come in at an angle to them—which is fine in theory but not a lot of help at night in the middle of a storm. Like asking an automobile driver heading for a wall at eighty to check which way the bricks are running." He moved one of the team members to one side to show DC the severe crimping along the leading edge. "I'd say they hit the waves head-on. Never had a chance, poor bastards."

DC was about to press Seeward on the stain when the group gathered around the tip of the tail parted. He stared in disbelief.

It had to be a trick of the light.

He circled round to take a closer look. On the way, Collins greeted him like a long-lost buddy and asked whether he had got the telex about the stand-in flight engineer. DC pushed past him without answering.

It was no illusion: The oil stain had gone—been removed. He started to doubt the veracity of his own senses and memory. But no, there *had* been a stain, and not only had he seen it, he had also pointed it out to Terry. He had even asked one of the loaders especially to cover it up for the journey to Chatham.

He looked around, wondering who to tell about it— Seeward, Kaplan, Murphy? But the more he thought about it, the more absurd he realized it would sound. Who in God's name would deliberately wipe away evidence like that? And why? What was he suggesting?

It might always have happened accidentally, of course; some well-meaning individual thinking the corpse should be hosed down before being presented to the pathologist. In which case it would be argued that there had been a failure of communication and command on the part of whoever had been responsible for overseeing the move from Provincetown to Chatham. All Murphy's doubts about his suitability as an investigator would be vindicated. He could imagine the line of questioning: Had he personally escorted the truck all the way back from P-town or simply waved it off and made his own way back? And if the latter, how and with whom? Then there would be the innuendo: that his mind might have been more on his job if it had been less on his chauffeur.

He wasn't going to give Murphy that satisfaction. But he was going to find out what had happened, if only to confirm his own sanity.

He returned to the airport reception to find the manager. There was nobody there, but a staircase led upstairs to a staff lunchroom and, as he suspected, the manager's office. Going up, he realized that he hadn't even taken the truck driver's name. Perhaps Murphy would have a point about his mind being elsewhere.

"Look," he said to the manager, "you don't happen to know where I can find the truck driver who brought that tail back here? I figure I might've left a notebook in his cab."

"Billy Conway? Sure thing. You know he's not from around here?"

It had been a bad morning, and looked like being a worse afternoon.

"So where'll I find him?" DC asked, fearing the worst.

"A few miles north off Route 28."

"But I thought you said he wasn't from around here."

"That's right, he's a Virginian. Moved to the Cape ten years ago. Quite a character, Billy. Has been just about everything in his time. He used to be a fisherman; had his own fifty-footer. Seen that gash down his face? Got it out on Georges Bank fishing for halibut. They were pulling in the line too fast, when one of the hooks flew up, caught him just below the eye, and ploughed a furrow down his cheek. Anyway, that kinda put Billy off fishing. Makes his money now playing poker and doing a little truckin' on the side."

Billy Conway stood in a corner of his yard, levering a tire off a wheel. Seeing the taxi draw up, he laid down the lever and wiped his hands on a dirty piece of toweling.

"I sure appreciate folk who come and settle their accounts in person," he said, as DC got out of the taxi.

DC remembered him now from the dockside. It was Conway who had suggested gift-wrapping the Pilgrim Monument. Again, he let the remark pass.

"There's something I want to check with you about this morning," he said.

Conway cocked his head to favor his unscarred cheek—a gesture DC also recalled from earlier. He suspected it was why he hadn't noticed the scar before.

"Just wanted to check whether you had any problems this morning—between P-town and Chatham."

"And what sort of problems might you have in mind?"

There was no point in tiptoeing around the subject.

"Well, did you have to leave the truck at any time? Stop for a bite to eat or anything like that?"

Conway looked resentful.

"I did just as you said and took the load direct to the airport—no lunch, no coffee, not even a piss."

"So you never left the wreckage on its own—not even for a minute."

"That's what I just said, wasn't it?"

DC looked down at the ground. There was no reason to think the man was lying.

"Mind if I take a look at the truck?" he asked.

Conway shrugged, holding out a still-dirty hand in the exaggerated gesture of a waiter showing a customer to his table. The truck was in a far corner beneath an open barnlike structure.

"Nothing but trouble, this load," Conway remarked as they crossed the yard. "You can tell your friend at the airport that next time he wants something like this moved he can call in a specialist from Boston or New Bedford. Nothing but trouble, that's what it's been."

The repetition of the phrase prompted DC to probe further.

"How do you mean, trouble?"

"Well, the supports that had to be rigged up on the truck, the time spend loading it, and, as though enough time hadn't been wasted already, the police then checkin' everything over."

"Police?"

"Sure, they pulled me off the highway at Eastham. There's a Visitors Center there with a large parking area. Closed this time of year."

"But you said just now you hadn't stopped"

"I didn't. It was them that stopped me."

There was nothing to be gained from disputing the point.

"Why did they stop you?"

"Figured I was carrying an 'abnormal load' or some such fancy phrase; said I should've checked with 'em before setting off. Any load over twenty-five feet long requires notification—Massachusetts law or some damned fool thing. First time I'd heard about it—and I've been running thirty-foot loads up and down Route Six for five years now an' never been stopped. Told 'em that but it didn't make no difference."

DC impulsively caught Conway by the arm and swung him round.

"Listen, this could be important. Tell me exactly what they did and what they said. First of all, which police were they?"

"Massachusetts State."

"You recognized them?"

"Not the men, but you can't mistake the cars."

"But wouldn't you normally expect to know the local officers? It's a small community, the Cape, surely—the sort where everybody knows everybody else, particularly the local cops."

A sheepish grin crept across Conway's lips.

"Depends on your business. I've a deal with the cops:

They don't bother me and I don't bother them. Leastways I thought that was the understanding."

"So what did they do?"

"Like I told you, pulled me off the highway. Got me out of the cab; walked around the truck, pulled on ropes, checked knots. Questions: Where'd I come from? Where was I heading—that sort of thing."

"And then?"

"Then they took me to the car and went through my papers."

"Both of them?"

"No, just the one."

"So where was the other all this time? With the truck?"

"Could've been. I couldn't say for sure. The car was parked around the side of the Visitors Center."

"You mean, out of sight of the truck."

"Guess so. The truck was on one side of the building; the car on the other."

DC pulled a notebook from his pocket and bent it open. He handed it to Conway together with a ballpoint and got him to draw a rough diagram of the highway, the building, and the two vehicles in their respective positions. Studying the crude, grease-stained drawing, he felt a strange and disturbing sense of exhilaration. There was one more question:

"Conway, this could be important—vitally important. How long were you in the car alone with the one officer and out of sight of the truck? Don't answer immediately. Think about it."

Conway ran his finger slowly down his scarred cheek.

"Must've been twen'y minutes. This cop in the car insisted on running my driver's license and trucking registration through the state computer—over the two-way. Then asked me a lot of damned fool questions about where I was based and how far I carried. Reckon they were strangers to the Cape—didn't seem to know the area."

"You didn't get a number—car, badge?"

Conway shook his head.

"I just wanted to get back on the road."

DC was sure there were other questions he should ask but his mind was racing with what he already knew. He turned to the truck and for the second time that day clambered up on the tailgate. The ropes and coverings had been removed but the pair of large wooden vertical supports were still bolted in place. If somebody had cleaned off the oil stain between P-town and Chatham—whoever—they would have had to use a good quantity of solvent to cover the area. Chances were that some of that solvent would have splashed around and ended up on the truck itself.

It was an impossible task to sort out one stain from another. The wooden floor of the truck was already black with a thousand different marks, none of them looking any fresher than the rest.

But the vertical supports were more promising. They had been cut from fresh, damp timber and retained the soft nap left by the path of the saw. DC summoned up in his mind the picture of the tail as it had been loaded onto the truck and recalled that the oil stain would have been less than a foot from the rear support. He then examined the support with microscopic intensity.

There were differences of tone in the surface of the wood, but nothing one could call stains or marks.

Conway had been watching the performance with growing amusement.

"When you goin' to bring in the sniffer dogs then?" he asked.

Quite inadvertently the remark reminded DC of something he had forgotten—the importance of using *all* one's senses when carrying out an investigation. Not just sight, sound, and touch.

He put his nose to the top of the support and sniffed. The smell was unmistakable: gasoline. With the scent now in his nostrils he got down on all fours and sniffed the trailer floor. Again it was unmistakable.

"Don't look as though you'll be needin' them dogs after all," remarked Conway with a grin.

DC pulled himself up again.

"What do you normally carry on this truck?"

"Timber, building materials, that sort of thing. Mostly lengths of clapboard."

Again, DC's training as an investigator came back to him: Avoid the leading question, the sort that might suggest a particular answer. He had to ask about the gasoline without asking about it.

"What about machinery—pumps, chain saws?"

"Sometimes."

"Recently?"

Conway looked skyward.

"Nope, can't say recently."

DC put out a hand and pulled him up onto the trailer.

"Smell that," he said, indicating the rear support, "and then tell me what you think it is."

Conway did as he was told. His answer was immediate.

"It's gas." For the first time he looked genuinely surprised.

"So where's it come from?" DC asked.

Conway couldn't rightly say but the tarpaulin, when he located it at the back of the shed, also smelled of gasoline.

◆ 12 ◆

MEDCALF neither went below to see the display of icons nor did he buy the only remaining record of Boris Christoff and the Alexander Nevski Choir. Instead, he left the church as soon as he reckoned Sergei was out of the way and set off straight ahead down a wide boulevard.

Again he was reminded of Paris. Every street in this part of the city seemed to have been built to a Napoleonic edict that no thoroughfare should be less than sixty feet wide. He crossed over a major intersection and, following a left-hand curve, eventually came into the Ninth of September Square— face-to-face with the scene he had viewed two days earlier on Van Kleef's video projector.

He stood across the road from the Mausoleum of Georgi Dimitrov, Father of the Bulgarian Nation, Son of the Bulgarian People, and now, Holy Relic. He felt no desire to go inside; he would leave that to the ghouls and the party faithful. In fact, the whole business struck him as very odd—that the highest honor any Communist state could award its leaders was to be stiff, stuffed, and stared at.

By chance he had arrived a couple of minutes before the hour, just as the ceremonial guard was about to change.

He watched as the new guard, immaculately tailored in gray topcoats, white accessories, and calf-length black boots, emerged from the ground floor of the National Bank a hundred yards away and marched toward the great block-house of white Vratsa stone, rifles raised, bayonets fixed.

Coming level with it, they broke into a funereal goosestep, swinging and slapping the right hand across the chest and, with each delayed footfall, sending a small shockwave up the body to escape through the long eagle's feather on the front of each man's astrakhan shako.

It was a bizarre anachronism—as though the old Tsar's bodyguard, locked away like Pharaonic retainers in the bank vault for the last hundred years, had been let out to scandalize the modern Communist state.

It was then that he caught sight of Sergei—standing no more than fifty yards away, half-hidden behind the mausoleum. There was no mistaking him, but barely had his mind registered the fact than the Bulgarian ducked again out of sight. He was to catch similar glimpses another three times during the morning: at the bottom of a stairwell in the National Art Gallery, at a brass tap in front of the National Mineral Baths, and then in the underpass that links the Ninth of September Square with the Largo, the capital's administrative center. Strangely, the Bulgarian always seemed to be waiting, never following; always half-hidden, never completely. It was as though he *wanted* to be seen.

Back in the square, Medcalf sat on a bench in the park behind the mausoleum to rest beneath the bare chestnuts and silver birches. The city's ornamental pools had all been drained to protect them from the sub-zero temperatures, and for several minutes he looked on as small children played football in the large pool in front of the Ivan Vazov Theatre, squealing in delight each time the ball ricocheted unpredictably off its scalloped corners.

He felt uneasy. He was, he concluded, the victim of a less than subtle form of intimidatory surveillance. Even at this moment and even though he couldn't see him, he had no doubt that Sergei was sitting, standing, or leaning no more than a hundred yards away. He could feel the man's presence as though the two of them were caught in the same force field.

What should he do? Presumably "Bogart," if he were trying to make contact, would be as aware of the situation as he was and would simply bide his time until an opportunity presented itself. But it was hard to see how such an opportunity could ever present itself unless he, Medcalf, made a positive move. The problem was that, in throwing off Sergei, he might also lose Bogart.

A twinge in the stomach reminded him that it was time to find some lunch. He left the square and, for the first time, ventured "downtown"—away from the yellow-cobbled boulevards with their oppressive blend of Habsburg and Romanov architecture, away from the swish of the official Chaika and Mercedes cars—and into narrow metaled streets choked with fuming Ladas, Skodas, and Moskviches, where yellow trams sparked and crackled against overhead wires, lacing the atmosphere with the busy smell of electrical discharge.

It was another city. Here there were signs of an almost-Western consumer society: shops and crowds, flower stalls selling bunches of hothouse chrysanthemums; outdoor cafés with young girls sitting in fur-collared coats sipping cups of steaming liquid; even that ultimate symbol of urban capitalism, the parking meter. There were signs too of something else—a cause more for civic disgrace than pride—in the number of parked cars whose owners had carefully removed the windshield wipers lest somebody else do the job for them.

Then, with the relief of one who finds that at least one of his preconceptions is correct, he came across his first line.

He guessed it to be for meat or bread but, following it to its head, he found instead crates of bananas. They were evidently a seasonal delicacy—and a ludicrously expensive one, judging by the size of the banknotes that were changing hands. Even for card-carrying Communists, it seemed, there was a certain cachet in being seen consuming this exotic fruit in public, and for streets around he was to come across members of the new banana-bearing bourgeoisie holding perfectly peeled specimens at arm's-length with all the self-consciousness of a Westerner flashing his gold Rolex.

Fifteen minutes later he was sitting in a self-service cafeteria, shunting cold French fries, white beans, and shashlik around his plate. His earlier anxiety had now given way to impatience. He just wanted to get the whole stupid business over and done with and be back in Brussels—behind his own desk, in his own bed, and at his own table in his own favorite restaurant.

He no longer even cared about standing out as a foreigner. He pushed the plate to one side and placed the guidebook open on the table for all to see.

In was a ten-minute walk via the underpass to TSUM, the government-owned department store, the Bulgarian equivalent of Moscow's GUM. He entered through the main door and found to his amazement that the place had been decked out for Christmas. Silver tinsel was draped over the counters; large star-spangled plastic globes dangled down the central stairwell; while on the ground floor a small crowd had gathered around a platform supporting a figure who, in red coat and flowing white beard, had to be Father Christmas.

Except that he was actually "Father New Year." Similarly, although he was surrounded by figures that resembled angels, they had all been shorn of their wings. The whole thing was a sham. Con-mas.

It struck Medcalf as both sad and comic. Communism allowed no Christmas but the old celebrations still continued in a modified, government-approved form. Like the imperial guard outside the mausoleum, the institution was too deeply ingrained in the national consciousness to be discarded in its entirety. Just as the early Church fathers had been obliged to fix the date of Christ's birth to coincide with the old pagan Saturnalia, so the fathers of the modern Communist state had been forced to compromise in the face of an equally irresistible emotional reality.

Without looking around, he assumed Sergei had followed him in. He could only hope that Bogart was even closer by. The trick now, he reminded himself, was to lose the one long enough to enable the other to make an approach in relative security. He headed for the elevators.

The double doors scraped back and disgorged their human cargo. As one of the first in, he was able to survey his fellow travelers without difficulty. At least a dozen others had piled in after him, forcing him onto tiptoe. He winced as the woman next to him jammed a sharp-edged shopping basket against his leg.

The buttons indicated seven floors and a basement.

Comforted to see no sign of Sergei in the lift, he scrutinized the profiles for a likely Bogart and picked out two possible candidates. One was smoking in a nervous, almost desperate fashion and occasionally even glanced over his shoulder in his direction. The short-list was reduced to one.

They reached the fourth floor. Still the smoker was there. Then the fifth.

By the sixth Medcalf knew he would have to take the lead. He was already feeling hot and slightly queasy. The doors opened and he elbowed his way through the pack. As he came alongside the smoker, he too started moving forward—as though on cue.

The stage was set.

Most of the sixth floor was taken up by electrical and plumbing spare parts. Allowing the smoker to lead the way, Medcalf watched as he made for a section displaying large electric motors. He trailed behind and finished up about twenty feet away at a counter given over to variously shaped heating elements for kettles, washing machines, and hot-water tanks. There was still no sign of Sergei but, if only in his mind, Medcalf could hear him running up the stairs; could imagine him frantically checking out each floor in turn.

The smoker moved on in the direction of the plumbing section, which was dominated by hundreds of blue plastic hip baths, stacked up one inside the other. He started to scrutinize one of the baths, flicking ash on the floor behind him as he leaned forward.

Suddenly Medcalf understood: Arranged as they were, the baths provided a perfect screen against prying eyes. This time he made no pretense of keeping his distance but came to within a few feet of the smoker, even mimicking the way he ran his finger along a rough edge of the plastic where the mold had failed to close.

The man looked up sharply. They were the only two in that part of the section. His eye went to Medcalf's finger as it ran along the ragged edge. He spoke—in Bulgarian.

Medcalf nodded foolishly. Again the smoker spoke, again in Bulgarian, but this time pointing to the ragged plastic. Medcalf gave a helpless smile.

"Sorry, I do not speak Bulgarian."

The smoker's eyes darted to left and right. He had the look of a startled stoat.

"American?" His voice was a strange, shrill whisper.

Medcalf shook his head.

"British."

A sort of panic began to set in. Abandoning all interest in blue plastic hip baths, the man spun on his heels and set off back toward the electrical section. The last Medcalf saw of him, he was talking animatedly to one of the store assistants.

◆ 13 ◆

DC returned to the motel unde-
cided on his course of action. There was a message waiting
for him from Collins to say that Murphy had brought the
evening conference forward an hour to seven o'clock and
expected everybody to be present. As the desk clerk handed
him his key, he glanced up at the bank of pigeonholes
behind her. Terry's room number, he recalled, was 128. The
key was in the slot; she was out.

He gave the matter of the disappearing oil stain more
thought in the shower. He needed to confide in somebody;
to bounce his hunches and theories off someone who had
the technical expertise he lacked; to persuade himself that he
wasn't building an elaborate structure on a foundation of
thin air. In the end, Murphy would probably have to be
told, but not yet. There was nothing Murphy relished more
than shooting holes in a half-baked, ill-thought-out theory.
He considered having a word with Jo Kaplan. After all,
Kaplan was the engines expert on the team—but the man
had too much of a nuts-and-bolts mentality to apply his
mind to a case involving the possibly deliberate destruction
of evidence.

That left only Dick Seeward. He and DC had been on
the same course at the Board's training center in Oklahoma
City. They had always gotten along well, had been in the
habit of drinking together. More than anyone else on the
team, Seeward had that rare capacity for being able to
handle a vast amount of information and still come up with

the most pertinent questions. When he was sober. DC decided he would tackle him after the conference.

The conference room was deeper still in paperwork. Another couple of crates had come in during the day with the arrival of more people from Airlantic. He picked up a bundle at random.

It was Flight 639's passenger list. He flicked through pages dense with print—Baker, Benenson, Bracciolini—and wondered why putting the names in alphabetical order should have the effect of robbing them still further of their individuality. Perhaps because it was another act of arbitrariness—that same arbitrariness that had determined they should be on a doomed aircraft in the first place. Of course there was a purely practical reason for it. Yet no one would ever lay out a cemetery in alphabetical order for the convenience of the bereaved.

Beside most of the names there was a small red tick, signifying that next of kin had been informed. He tossed the list back on its pile and took a seat at the back of the room. It was five to seven.

By Murphy's standards, it was a short meeting. Apart from the discovery of the tail—and DC had already heard Seeward's views on that—there was little to report.

The media, said Murphy, looking meaningfully in DC's direction, were making a lot about the fact that among the passengers had been a party of Italian parliamentarians returning from an official visit to Washington at the invitation of Congress. The aviation correspondents, meanwhile, were speculating that fuel contamination was the most likely cause of the triple flameout—despite the N.T.S.B.'s assurances that the fueling procedures at JFK had been checked and declared faultless.

More constructively, continued Murphy, attempts were still being made to locate the rest of the wreckage by zeroing in on the acoustic beacons attached to the aircraft's flight data recorder and cockpit voice recorder. The problem was that if, as seemed likely, the wreckage was at least three miles below the Atlantic, the beacons' range at the surface and the strength of their signals would both be greatly reduced—and getting a fix on them that much more difficult.

He flipped over a blue and beige map showing in graphic relief the submarine peaks, crevices, and canyons of the ocean floor. To many in the room, DC included, it came as a surprise to realize that plains and mountain ranges existed below the waves on a comparable scale to those on land. Murphy pointed to an area two hundred miles southwest of Halifax, Nova Scotia.

"The spot where the tail was picked up, taking into account the drift factor, indicates the area of ditching was about here," he said, "at a point fifty miles beyond the edge of the Continental Shelf where it slopes down to the Sohm Abyssal Plain. The depth of the plain is seventeen thousand, four hundred feet—three and a third miles. A naval seabed recovery vessel is at this moment trailing a hydrophone along a course roughly parallel to the shelf but it's looking increasingly like the wreckage has rolled all the way down into the abyss." He removed his glasses and pinched his nose. "In short, gentlemen, we're talking about a considerable feat of maritime engineering. Perhaps an impossible one. Frankly, the people I've talked to—both on the salvage and the electronics side—think the chances of even locating the wreckage are, well, pretty remote. I guess I don't have to remind you gentlemen that it took seventy-three years to find the *Titanic*—over here off Newfoundland—and that was in water not three and a third miles deep, but two and a third." He looked around the room at the double row of downcast faces. "I know, we're not used to working this way—with only a section of tail and an Air Traffic Control recording to go on—and, believe me, I share your sense of frustration. It's hardly the most appropriate image, I know, but let me remind you that murders have been solved without a body before, and with the assembled talent and experience I see before me, I'm confident it can be done again."

DC stifled a groan. Lieutenant Murphy of Homicide addresses his men! The man had become a parody of himself.

The meeting broke up and, seeing Dick Seeward talking to his own three-man team, DC went over and put a hand on his shoulder.

"Dick, can I have a word with you—in private?"

Seeward turned.

"Sure, why don't you come along to my room in five minutes? I've got a bottle of lubricating spirit there that might compensate for our current lack of hardware."

Seeward handed him the glass of bourbon and plopped in a couple of ice cubes from the bedroom refrigerator.

"Okay, shoot."

DC sat in the armchair by the window, cradling the glass in his hands, and recounted the story from start to finish. It was not a polished performance and, as he had expected, Seeward homed in on the most pertinent question:

"Why didn't you take a photograph of this oil stain when the tail was right there on the wharf?"

DC stared at the ice clinking in his glass.

"It was raining, I was cold and wet, and the camera was in the car. And yes, that's no excuse."

Seeward closed the fridge door and perched on the side of the bed.

"I see. Well, it's an intriguing tale, I grant you, but, let's face it, totally circumstantial. First, you're suggesting that somebody—for reasons unknown—destroyed a piece of potentially relevant evidence because it was there wh' truck left P-town and gone when the truck arrive' ham. Second, you're pointing a finger at a co' because as far as you know they were the only ones to have access to the wreckage during the journey. And third, you're suggesting that they used gasoline to wipe away the stain because there was evidence of it on the trailer. Am I right so far?"

DC gave a hesitant nod. "Right."

"Okay," resumed Seeward, still perched on the bed but now leaning forward, a cross between The Thinker and The Drinker. "A number of questions seem to me to follow logically from that ... One, who apart from an aviation expert would know that that oil stain was relevant to the crash investigation? Two, assuming the police were genuine, who would've had the authority to order them to do a clean-up job? And three, how can you be sure the gasoline didn't get there by some perfectly innocent means?" He straightened himself. "Let's face it, DC, to say you've been sniffing trucks and detected traces of gasoline is, well, it's not exactly the most persuasive evidence for the sort of conspiracy you seem to be suggesting."

DC hung his head. He'd asked for the opinion of a man he respected and he'd got it. Seeward poured himself another generous bourbon and proffered the bottle. DC declined.

"So you think I'm making something out of nothing. That it?"

"I didn't say that. A mystery remains—how to explain that the oil stain was there when the truck left P-town and gone by the time it arrived at Chatham. What you haven't convinced me of is that there was any sinister intent in its removal."

"So what would convince you?"

Seeward thought a moment.

"I suppose if you were to turn up a rag stained with aviation engine oil and gasoline at that Visitors Center at Eastham. That would be a start."

"And in the meantime?"

"Up to you. Personally, I'd be more sure of my facts before I floated this one before the likes of Murphy and Kaplan." He swung his feet up on the bed and stretched out, staring upward, eyes defocused. "Perhaps you should also consider how relevant that stain was in the first place. Again you could be leaping to conclusions that are, well, less than justified. You say the oil was definitely burned—sticky like varnish, you said—which means that, if we assume it came from the port engine, that engine must've been on fire. Yes? Yet there's no suggestion of any engine fire on that ATC tape. On every occasion the word the first officer uses when talking about the engines is 'flameout,' which I've always understood to mean the opposite of a fire—that the engine's normal combustion flame has gone out, *not* that the engine itself is on fire. I don't know of any other interpretation."

DC was aware of now fighting a rear-guard action. The drink was starting to have its effect on Seeward and, although the mind was still lucid, his speech was beginning to slur. Soon there would be no point in pursuing the argument.

"Dick, the tape breaks up at two and a half thousand feet. The fire could've started after that," he said half-heartedly.

Seeward raised himself on one elbow and waggled a reproving finger.

"Could've, sure. But a lot else *could've* happened too. Once you get into that game, there's no end to it. That oil that you saw on the tail plane *could've* been picked up in the sea not in the air, just as it *could've* come from the trawler and not from the aircraft. Speculation is cheap, DC, but in the end we have to come back to what we have in our hands. The tape may be incomplete but at the moment it and the tail are the only goddamn evidence we've got."

"So you figure Kaplan's right—it was all a screwup by the flight engineer. It's going to be another case of, 'If the crash doesn't kill the crew, the inquiry will'!"

Seeward got up from the bed and topped up his glass again before answering.

"I accept Kaplan's theory as one possibility—and, yeah, at the moment it's looking like the most likely, now that we've been able to rule out fuel contamination and miscalculation on the ground. Now I know it's not what you want to hear but I have to say that, like Jo, I find it hard to swallow the triple-oil-leak hypothesis. The chances of three seals failing on three engines on the same aircraft at the same point in the same flight must be—I don't know—a million to one? Two million? Three million?"

He waved his hand dismissively and then propped himself up on the pillow, spilling some of the drink on the turned-back sheet.

"Look at it this way, DC ... You have three cars traveling abreast along the highway, all in perfect mechanical condition, regularly serviced, checked over before every trip—only, instead of their normal fuel tanks, they're all hooked up to the same gasoline tanker rolling along behind. Then, at a certain point along the highway, three-quarters of an hour into the journey, they all come to a stop—one after the other." He slapped the bedside table. "One! Two! Three! Now, I ask you, are you seriously telling me that, if the choice is between them running out of oil and running out of gas, you'd say they'd all run out of oil? Well, are you?"

DC didn't respond. He drank down the contents of his glass and got up to leave.

Seeward stood up and blocked his way. It was the act of one called upon to tell a colleague a painful home truth.

"DC, will you take a word of advice given in that spirit of the cockpit confessional in which we were both trained?"

DC sighed. "Go ahead."

"Remember when we were both being put through our paces in Oklahoma? Remember what that instructor guy told us about the technique of investigating—about how there were only two things you needed to know? One was that Sherlock Holmes quote—you remember it?—'My dear Watson, when you have eliminated the impossible, whatever remains, however improbable, must be the truth.' The other—and right now just as relevant—was never to let skepticism become cynicism or tenacity obsession."

"And you think I'm in danger of going that way?"

Seeward raised his glass.

"I'm just saying this: Never forget that most air accidents are still caused by human error—and don't dismiss everything Murphy and Kaplan say just because you don't get on with the guys. Sure, they can both be pains in the ass, but they've been doing this job longer than both of us put together and, if only for that, we owe them some respect."

DC unhooked Seeward's hand from his shoulder. Before leaving, he paused in the doorway and said evenly:

"You don't think maybe we owe something to the crew of that flight as well, Dick?"

♦ **14** ♦

BACK AT HIS HOTEL, Medcalf was feeling tired and foolish. The emotional tension and sheer physical effort of foot-slogging around Sofia had caught up with him.

He opened the door to his room to find the tide still coming in; the soggy crescent on the carpet had now swelled to within inches of his bed. In any Western hotel he would have picked up the phone and complained to room service. Now, so strong was his desire to avoid further contact with the natives, so overwhelming his feeling of helplessness, that he ignored it.

He opened the window a fraction to counteract the effect of the central heating; threw off his coat, scarf, and jacket; and lay down, oblivious even of the corrugations in the mattress.

Whether due to tiredness or paranoia, the room actually seemed taller and narrower than before. The feeling that had been creeping up on him all day suddenly declared itself head-on: He was a laboratory rat in a man-made labyrinth.

Yet even a rat might have fared better. Not only had he been made a fool of, he had made a fool of himself—from his initial contact with Sergei in the church to his farcical pursuit of the smoker in the department store. The catalogue of errors was too painful to review. Instead, he allowed his mind to float like a rogue planet drifting through space, mercifully unconstrained by the orbit of consciousness.

But the pull of the present was too strong for him to escape it entirely and, despite himself, his thoughts kept returning to the identity of Bogart.

Within thirty seconds the truth had grown from a pin-prick possibility to a blinding certainty. Bogart was Sergei; Sergei was Bogart. Had to be! He raised himself on one arm.

The signs had been there all along but, like a man touring a town with the wrong map, he had blithely dismissed every landmark as an obstacle. The only thing he knew about Bogart—Van Kleef had told him—was that he had chosen the name because he was something of a film buff. And what had Sergei said when he, Medcalf, had tried to throw him off in the church? . . . "I know, you vant to be alone." Yes, he had definitely said "vant." The cinematographic allusion was undeniable. Now equally undeniable in Medcalf's mind was that only one in a thousand Bulgarians of Sergei's generation would ever have heard of Greta Garbo, let alone be able to quote her most famous line. And that one in a thousand would have to be a film buff.

In an instant all was clear. The meeting in the church had been intended as a subtle introduction. Under cover of the interior gloom, Sergei had been trying to make himself known—but Medcalf, all of a jitter after his encounter with the moneychanger minutes earlier, had not merely misread the sign; he had failed even to recognize it *as* a sign.

He could have laughed out loud at his own idiocy. He had spent—wasted!—an entire day sedulously avoiding the individual he should have been pursuing.

The only consolation lay in the thought that on Sergei's past form he would now have no difficulty making contact with him. It was four o'clock. He would have a couple of hours' rest in his room, eat in the hotel, and then take a long, circuitous walk around the city center with frequent stops along the way.

The first snow of winter—a month late according to the receptionist—was falling as Medcalf emerged from the hotel at eight-thirty. Along the cobbled length of Ruski Boulevard the five-globed lamp posts glowed a pale green without casting any discernible light.

He turned left into the Ninth of September Square, past the darkened window of Aeroflot on the corner, and across the parade ground between the old royal palace and Georgi Dimitrov's mausoleum. He shivered. The hidden arc lights behind the mausoleum's columns shimmered an eerie turquoise. He thought of the enbalmed body within and, quickening his pace, headed downtown for the area around Vitosha Street, where even at this distance he could see the comforting sparks of the trams lighting up the snow-pocked sky.

Three hours later, at close on midnight, Medcalf was retracing his steps across the deserted parade ground, padding slowly through snow that was now several inches thick. The slightest sounds carried clearly in the acoustically deadened air and, as he passed the mausoleum, he could hear the guards twenty yards away whispering like naughty children after lights out. It was a reassuring reminder of humanity in an alien city—for despite countless stops along the way he had made no contact with either Sergei or anyone else. Again, he had failed.

◆ 15 ◆

DC picked up the bedside telephone.

"Front desk," came the cheery response.

"Can you tell me please if Miss Morrow—Room 128—is in the motel?" DC asked.

There was a pause. Then:

"Miss Morrow's key is not in its slot, sir."

"Will you put me through to her room then, please."

"Sure thing."

Terry's voice sounded unusually tight—almost jumpy. Perhaps it was the lateness of the hour; it was past ten o'clock. As soon as she recognized him she seemed to relax a little, but it sounded like an effort.

"I was kind of wondering," said DC, doodling nervously on the small message pad by the phone, "and this may sound like an absurd suggestion to make to anyone at this hour of night, but I was wondering if you'd like to take a walk."

"A walk?"

"Well, a walk across the parking lot and then a short drive actually. And you'd be doing the driving—again."

"Where did you have in mind? No, don't tell me; keep it as a surprise. I'll see you in the lobby in five minutes."

DC put down the receiver. He was surprised by his own boldness and by the positive effect it had had. The easy camaraderie of his relationship with Terry had triumphed over his more usual ineptness in such situations. For no reason that he could articulate he slapped the side of the bed; the mere prospect of being with her again had lifted the depression that had weighed upon him since his talk with Seeward two hours earlier.

"I suppose it figures," she said as they walked across the tarmac. "Most of the great explorers had Italian origins—Amerigo Vespucci, Cristoforo Colombo. And now, the latest in that great line: Matteo Di Coiano!" She trumpeted a mock fanfare. "So what new worlds are we off to plunder? What native hordes to subjugate?"

DC climbed into the passenger seat and plucked the tattered AAA map from the glove compartment.

"Don't like to disappoint you but its one of those Visitors Centers up the coast. The one at Eastham, off Route 6. We must've passed it on the way back this morning." He pointed it out on the map.

"No trouble," she said. "It's on the turning that leads down to the Coast Guard beach. I don't have to tell you, I guess, that it might just be closed right now." She turned a mischievous smile on him "You try this trick on many girls?"

The parking area around the large rustic building was deserted. DC directed Terry to pull up some distance away from it. He snapped on the interior light and studied the rough sketch which Billy Conway had done, showing where his truck and the police car had been parked. Terry said nothing. Then, taking a flashlight, he opened the door.

"I shouldn't be gone more than five minutes," he said, indicating as subtly as he knew how that whatever he was going to do he preferred to do alone.

Any hopes he had harbored of still finding the tire tracks were soon dashed. The drizzle of earlier in the day had turned what little snow was left to a Jell-O slush. Still, if Billy's sketch was even only approximately correct, the police car and the truck had been so positioned as to make it impossible for the occupants of the one to see what was going on in the other.

He swept the area with the flashlight and picked out two large yellow litter bins. He examined first the bin farther from where the truck would have been parked.

It was empty except for a couple of scraps of candy paper still stuck to the bottom of the inside container.

He zigzagged through the puddles across to the other bin, telling himself that nobody involved in such a clean-up operation would have been so stupid or careless as to leave the incriminating evidence in a trash can anyway.

And he was right.

He spent another couple of minutes searching the area for clues before giving up and returning to the car with only the negative consolation of knowing that, if the police had been responsible for the clean-up but with quite innocent intentions, they had acted most curiously in not throwing the dirty rags or paper in the most obvious receptacle. As "evidence," though, it wasn't even circumstantial. Dick Seeward's warning ran through his mind; he was becoming obsessive.

Having dragged Terry from the warmth of the motel and again taken advantage of her driving ability, he felt he owed her at least a partial explanation for his garbage-hunting activities.

"You remember that oil stain I showed you on the tail?"

"Sure."

"Well, some interfering SOB wiped it off before the tail reached Chatham. I thought there was a chance of still finding an oily rag or something."

"Why here?"

"Because this was the only place the truck driver remembers stopping." He decided not to mention the police. "I'm sorry, I've dragged you out here for nothing."

She didn't respond. Instead, she flicked the ignition key, and instead of heading back onto the main highway swung to the right past a large board announcing they were now entering the Cape Cod National Seashore.

"My turn to take you exploring," she remarked with a cryptic smile. "I'm going to take you somewhere no desk-bound executive from Washington, let alone a vacation-deprived kid from Little Italy, has ever gone before—boldly or otherwise."

They traveled about a mile along a winding road carved between densely packed pines. It led to an old clapboard Coast Guard house a hundred yards back from the shore, long disused, its white paint curled like bark.

"This is what they call the back side of the Cape," she said, bringing the car to a halt alongside the house, ". . . the thirty-mile strip of coastline that faces onto the Atlantic. And I warn you now: It's wild. Enough ships have been wrecked here to form a continuous wooden wall all along the coast if they were put stem to stern—five thousand, according to the last reckoning." Like a parent playing with the fears of a child, she eyed him for some reaction before continuing. "When there's a nor'easter like the other night, the sea will gobble up ten feet of cliff in a single bite. Snap! One storm, back in seventy-eight, they had winds here gusting up to 140 miles an hour. An entire length of the coast disappeared overnight—houses and everything."

She opened the car door.

"Come on, I'll show you."

"You're not serious," DC protested.

"Oh, it'll be all right. The waves are satiated. They'll have gorged themselves on the cliff faces last night. Bring the flashlight."

DC couldn't remember ever having walked on a beach at night before. There was a sensuous quality to it—of experience at one step removed, of risk and unreality, as his feet sank into the sand and his head was buffeted by the salty sea spray.

On both sides they were dwarfed by nature. To the left were sixty-foot cliffs—curtains of striated sand and earth, their gathered tops defined by the snow still caught in the tufts of sparrow grass. To the right were great curling combers that reared and plunged with the regular pounding of a steam hammer—tons of water raised up at a scoop, suspended in air, then dumped and left sizzling on the shore. Nature was showing off, demonstrating its power in an impressive but pointless display of physical prowess—a muscle-bound macho doing push-ups on the beach.

He felt a strong impulse to hold her close to him—a gesture less of sexual desire than of human companionship in the face of the daunting elemental might all around them. Yet he held back for fear of rejection and let her walk ahead of him.

He pulled the flashlight from his pocket and, directing its beam onto the sand, stumbled forward as the imprints of seagulls' feet, dead crabs, and razor-clam shells moved across the bright oval like specimens beneath a biologist's microscope.

"You never told me you were a mooncusser," Terry said over her shoulder, her hair wound across her face by the inshore breeze.

"A what?"

"You've never heard of mooncussers? Back in the old days, they used to come along here with lanterns to give the impression of vessels at anchor in the hope of luring boats out at sea onto the shoals. Then they'd plunder the wrecks. The trick didn't work if the moon came out."

"Which is why they were called mooncussers?"

"Right. When Congress voted funds to build lighthouses along this coast during the last century, the locals complained that it would ruin the economy. Like modern-day muggers complaining of street lighting!" The wind carried her laugh back to him above the sound of surf. "Rumor has it that most of them became lawyers, real estate brokers, and motel operators!" As though it were all part of the same sentence, she added, "Take my hand."

At first he doubted he had heard correctly; then he saw her hand held back toward him and grasped it.

He felt a surge of excitement of a kind he hadn't known since his first date—a feeling that anything was possible, that he had only to reach up to pluck a handful of grass from the clifftop.

They half-walked, half-ran in silence for a hundred yards or so. He felt no tiredness. Her grip tightened in response to his and seemed to transmit its power through his body and back again, the blood in their veins pulsing to the same ebb and flow. After the days of pent-up anger and frustration, he wanted to throw back his head and shout, to howl against the crashing of the waves. All thought of the investigation, of Doug Murphy, Jo Kaplan, Dick Seeward, of oily rags in garbage bins was pummeled into a billion sparkling globules and drained back into the deep.

He stopped and, instead of shouting, laughed out loud. For no reason and yet every reason. He could feel his hair plastered down on his forehead, and as he now looked at hers he saw that it, too, was soaked by the spray.

She stood before him in the weak moonlight. There was nothing submissive in her expression, nothing demure; but the hint of a smile that challenged him to take the next step. The smile of an enchantress.

Delicately, as though handling precious porcelain, he rested his hands on her shoulders and said:

"Will you come to New Jersey with me tomorrow? There's someone I have to see, to interview. It's not going to be easy and, well, I could do with your support."

The smile spread.

"So long as it's strictly on business."

He kissed her lightly but lingered on her lips, framing her damp cheeks between his hands, and released her.

"Strictly business. I promise."

He wondered what she now expected of him. That he would follow the example of the sea and the cliffs? Throw her down on the beach and ravish her? Even given the impracticality of the thought he was as tempted as any man would have been. But another, stronger emotion asserted itself—a desire to hold back, to hold on a little longer to the exquisite sense of expectation. There was no rush. She had agreed to come with him to New Jersey, and for the moment that was more than enough. It would be a long journey—a long day and, necessarily, a long night. Best of all, they would be far removed from the hotel and all its inhibiting associations. He would wait and, waiting, savor the anticipated pleasures.

He took her hand again. Silently, like a couple of courting kids, they walked back along the beach.

Returning to the motel, he found Murphy still sitting where he had last seen him—at the top of the table in the conference room. He looked beat. The air was heavy with stale nicotine and human sweat.

"Doug, I think I should go to New Jersey tomorrow to interview the flight engineer's widow," DC began. "The usual thing. Collins thought it better left to me when he realized there'd been a last-minute crew change. He's already seen the wives of the captain and first officer."

"Did you know him?" asked Murphy, looking up.

"Aldridge? Only casually." He feared his voice was betraying him, as he realized that, given an evasive answer, Murphy was quite likely to check up. "We flew together a couple of times."

"You won't feel . . . compromised?" Murphy gave each syllable of the word its full weight. The wound DC had inflicted back in Washington when he had tried to get off the investigation had not been forgotten.

"I think I can handle it," DC replied.

Murphy stood up and walked over to the coffee machine. He returned with two cups and held out one to DC. It was a peace offering.

"DC, I don't like strains—you know, personal tensions—on any team. What I'm saying is, well, it's good to have you back in the loop. Dick was telling me you went up to P-town for him and I know he appreciated that. I repeat what I said at the conference yesterday: With all of us pulling together, we can crack this thing. I know it."

"And you still lean toward Jo's theory," DC said, trying hard to maintain as neutral a tone as possible.

"It's the only one that makes the least sense at the moment. You know the old saying: 'When you've eliminated the impossible, whatever remains, however improbable, must be the truth.' "

DC did a double take. It was the second time in a matter of hours that he had been fed the line about the impossible and the improbable. First Dick Seeward; now Murphy. And yet he was sure Seeward would not have broken the confidence of their earlier talk. It was chillingly insidious—the Goebbels principle at work: REPETITION MAKES TRUTH.

At the risk of opening up old wounds he felt bound to respond, but from experience he knew that to attack Murphy head-on would only lead to another flare-up. The best way to argue with the man was to demonstrate to him, coolly and convincingly, that fuel starvation was just as "impossible," by his own definition of the word, as simultaneous oil loss on three engines. But it was going to need careful handling.

"Doug, you know I'm not a power-plant specialist but, looked at from the standpoint of crew behavior, I have to say that I find it equally inconceivable that any crew could have been led into such a crucial error over fuel. It's not as if fuel management is in the hands of the flight engineer alone; any action on the flight deck relating to fuel or altitude has to be monitored by a second crew member. That's what the loop is all about."

Murphy showed no signs of violent reaction. Encouraged, DC continued.

"Even if we assume that the flight engineer hadn't been watching his gauges, the SP-3 has a whole row of fuel low-pressure lights that would have warned him long before any flameout. To me the idea of his being trapped into a fuel error—and so early on in the flight when he'd have been fresh and alert—is, well, I have to repeat, inconceivable."

"Impossible?" asked Murphy. There was a knowing tone in his voice that put DC immediately on guard.

"Impossible in these circumstances is what I'm saying, Doug."

Murphy moved across to one of the gray filing cabinets in the corner of the room and pulled open the second drawer down. He ran a finger from the back to the front and plucked out a couple of sheets of paper with the self-conscious posturing of an amateur actor exaggerating his actions for the benefit of those at the back of the auditorium.

"What d'you think of Republic?" he asked, returning to the table, the drawer of the filing cabinet trundling home behind him.

"The airline?"

"Right—Republic Airlines. What do you think of them?"

DC sensed a setup but was baffled by the sudden switch of subject.

"Damned fine operators; one of the best."

"Maintenance of aircraft? Caliber of crews?"

"Again, the best."

"So you'd happily fly with them?"

"Sure, without hesitation—passenger *or* pilot."

Murphy weighed the sheets of paper in his hand. The milieu had changed from the theatre to the courtroom. No longer an amateur actor, he was now attorney for the prosecution, about to spring a trap on the expert witness. He launched the papers in DC's direction, observing their glidepath down the table with professional interest.

"I agree with you all the way, DC. Now, remembering that, take these away and refresh your memory . . . N.T.S.B. incident briefs, file numbers 5004 and 5024 respectively. They might change your mind about the impossibility of a fuel error. And one other thing: What you were saying about the loop—never forget that the same bonding which makes a crew work as a team can occasionally result in misguided acts of group loyalty. It's not beyond possibility that those fuel warning lights *did* come on, that the crew were alerted to their error but hoped they could unscramble the situation before it had to be formally notified."

DC couldn't conceal his surprise. "You're seriously suggesting that they play-acted their bafflement—all that talk on the tape about 'there sure is something kinda weird here that we can't figure'—just to protect their own backsides?"

"Seriously suggesting, no. I'm just saying it must still be regarded as within the realm of probability and therefore shouldn't be ruled out just because you and I have both been up there and still feel a strong natural affinity to the guy in the sky. That's all." He glanced quickly away to the clock and reached for the telephone. "What d'you want to do about tomorrow? Fly or drive?"

"Er, drive," said DC, still stunned by Murphy's suggestion.

"I'll book you a car and tell 'em to have it here by seven. And don't forget to read those incident briefs like I told you."

PART TWO

◆ 16 ◆

IT WAS day two in the Bulgarian capital for Adrian Medcalf, alias Dr. Stephen Chanter, and a night's fitful sleep had done nothing to refresh either of them.

Standing now before the bathroom basin, razor in hand, Medcalf stared at the tepid trickle that emerged from the "hot" tap and at the hole where a plug might have gone, had there been a plug. With a capacity for self-mockery he didn't know he possessed, he reflected that, although it was a filthy Western habit to shave in one's own dirty water, such habits had as surely contributed to Britain's greatness as the playing fields of Eton. Here, in short, was yet more evidence of a Communist conspiracy—a conspiracy that meant he wouldn't be able even to rinse his dirty capitalist socks when the clean ones ran out.

The desperation of the previous evening had now been replaced by a brand of fatalism bordering on indifference—a condition to which he had attached the fittingly medical label Bugger Bogart Syndrome. B.B.S., for short.

It was in this mood that he had already decided upon the morning's singularly unadventurous program. Since everything else had failed, he would repeat his original itinerary and go again to the scene of his first encounter with Sergei, the Memorial Church of Alexander Nevski.

Besides, it was Sunday.

*   *   *

A single bell was summoning the faithful to prayer as he kicked the snow off his shoes and parted the heavy green curtains. Inside, an Eastern Orthodox priest with full gray beard and black stovepipe hat was walking in front of the altar. Before him in the body of the church a clutch of short, hip-heavy old women in headscarves rolled around the marble floor like a collection of babushka dolls.

Medcalf walked again to the wooden bench along the back wall but this time, instead of sitting, he remained standing. He allowed several seconds for his eyes to adjust but, even so, could see no sign of Sergei. Suddenly, the toll of the single bell gave way to a rapid, more tinny tinkling of smaller bells.

He looked back to the altar. The priest now had a golden crown on his head. A pair of young acolytes in gold vestments were bowing deeply before him and kissing his hands. He took a bunch of lighted candles in each hand and in an elaborate gesture, the significance of which eluded Medcalf, first held them apart and then crossed them over, repeating the movement several times. From somewhere high up a choir started to sing.

The voices swelled beneath the great dome and reminded Medcalf of something that up till now he had quite forgotten.

During their earlier encounter, Sergei had made two specific suggestions, both of which at the time he had summarily dismissed: to buy a copy—the last copy—of the record of Boris Christoff and the Alexander Nevski Choir, and to visit the exhibition of icons in the crypt.

After so many disappointments and embarrassments, he was now wary of his capacity for fanciful deduction. Even so, there had to be some significance in the fact that Sergei had specified that the record was the only one left. Was it really too far-fetched to speculate that it might even contain a message?

He walked out of the body of the church and into the entrance area where the souvenir shop was situated. He looked among the records on display but could see no trace of the name "Boris Christoff." Not trusting his rudimentary knowledge of Cyrillic script, he finally asked the old woman behind the counter. She spoke only bad French but her words left no room for doubt: The last copy of the record had been sold the day before.

He turned away, despondent. Then back again.

How did he get to the crypt?

She directed him out of the church, to the right through a pair of ornately carved doors, and down a wide marble staircase.

It could not have been more different—a crypt of cool white walls that sprang without a break into vaulting arches that met overhead. Against the walls, at eye level and spaced a couple of feet apart, were brilliantly colored medieval icons, predominantly red and gold, each illuminated by a single light.

He could feel the painted eyes following him as he walked around—eyes that blazed with an extraordinary intensity, totally unlike their catatonic cousins in the church above. With heavy-handed propaganda, the multilingual notices pointed out what was obvious—that these were one of the few vehicles by which an oppressed people, living under a Turkish occupation five centuries long, could express their sense of national identity and patriotic pride.

"So you come after all."

The voice was instantly familiar.

"You did say it was worth a visit, I recall," Medcalf responded, concealing his relief beneath a cloak of nonchalance.

It was up to Sergei to make the next move. For all Medcalf knew, the place could be swarming with DS men who had bugged every light fitting, but he had to assume that Sergei—or "Bogart," as he now thought of him—knew what he was doing.

"You are having a successful visit, I think," said Sergei. "You have been seeing a lot of our fine capital . . ." He paused as though his next sentence was intended to carry a particular significance. "But I think you have still not found what you are coming here to find."

There was something infuriatingly oblique about the man. Medcalf could feel an attack of B.B.S. coming on. Staring straight ahead, he said briskly:

"Then perhaps you had better provide it while you still have the opportunity."

Sergei gave a little laugh and moved off to the left, toward the corner of the crypt farthest from the entrance. Medcalf waited a second and followed.

"And what, my friend, do you wish to know?" Sergei asked when they'd come to a stop.

"Whatever you wish to tell."

"Ah, there are many things. You will have to be more particular."

With the greatest difficulty, Medcalf controlled himself.

"Then let us start with the assassination attempt on your president."

Sergei looked at him and smiled. He whispered a "Shhh!" and gripped Medcalf lightly by the elbow. "Here, I think," he said, "is not a good place to speak. We go upstairs and find another place—a better place. There we will be able to speak about all these things."

◆ 17 ◆

ON REFLECTION, it had been a mistake to drive from the Cape to New Jersey; it was already late afternoon by the time they crossed the Tappan Zee Bridge, the skyscrapers of Manhattan fifteen miles downriver standing out like a geological formation in the dying rays of the winter sun.

They turned south off the interstate onto the Garden State Parkway and within half an hour were in the heart of New Jersey "prosp-urbia," the manicured greens of its myriad golf courses hidden beneath a foot of snow.

"I forgot to tell you," DC said as they neared the Aldridge house, "you'll be needing your shorthand. I'm assuming you have it."

"Check. Ready for takeoff when you are, Captain," Terry replied in an attempt to lighten his mood.

He took a wrong turn, cursed, found the right one and, five minutes later, drew up outside a two-story house clad in cedar shakes with an incongruous white neoclassical front porch. It was the only house on the road where the snow hadn't been cleared from the driveway.

He got out, opened the door on Terry's side, and forced a smile. It was a long time since he had felt so tense about an interview.

"Look, I'll tell you now before we go in," he said. "This is the part of the job I hate. I'm going to need all the support you can give me."

129

She gave his hand a reassuring squeeze and nodded in the direction of the house.

"She expecting us?"

"I phoned ahead this morning before we left. Aldridge's brother and his wife are staying with her. Ready?"

It was the brother who met them at the door. He introduced himself with a curtness that left no doubt he regarded the visit as an unwarranted intrusion into their private grief, then led the way into the living room where Mary Aldridge was seated on the sofa beside her sister-in-law, hands clasped in a pose worthy of a Victorian painting.

There was an unmistakable aura of hostility about the two women—a tight-lipped, narrow-eyed resentment that went beyond mere annoyance at the intrusion. It was just as DC had feared. He wondered whether he should, after all, have had Collins do the interview.

He introduced Terry with a deliberately casual reference to its being her job to make notes of what was said, and took an armchair opposite the sisters-in-law. Aldridge's brother, he noticed, had meanwhile perched on one of the upright chairs in the dining area, removing himself from the arena of interrogation but clearly signaling his intention, like an overprotective lawyer, to maintain a watching brief. Terry drew out a notebook and pencil.

DC had never been to the house before, but he had met Mary Aldridge on maybe a dozen occasions at social functions organized by Airlantic when he had still worked for them. The impression he had gained then was reinforced now: of a self-contained individual, sure of her own beliefs and opinions; a standard-bearer for the Moral Majority, whose lack of sympathy for the spiritual weakness of others tended to manifest itself as indifference and arrogance. In that respect she and Aldridge had been well-matched and part of her anger now, DC suspected, was that her grief had made her vulnerable, exposing her with her defenses down. Head high, hair scraped back, she stared at him with a determination not to afford him the supposed satisfaction of seeing her break.

Normally he would have offered his condolences, but on this occasion he was aware that the sincerity of any such words would have been immediately questioned, no matter how genuine in reality. He made do with an apology.

"I'm sorry to have to put you through this, Mrs. Aldridge."

She sensed the opportunity given her and seized it.

"You don't have to apologize, Mr. Di Coiano. Gerald would have understood the necessity perfectly. He respected procedures and knew their importance—as you know." She added the last words in a tone of perfect neutrality that seemed calculated to leave him wondering how far they were intended to wound. "I shall answer your questions to the best of my ability and recollection, Mr. Di Coiano."

The lines had been drawn: Mrs. Aldridge, Mr. Di Coiano.

He started on the routine questions and soon realized that her answers had been not just rehearsed, but actually committed to a mental clipboard:

NO, Gerald had not been receiving any medication—neither tranquilizers nor antihistamines . . .

NO, of course Gerald had not taken any alcohol within the eight hours before the flight . . .

YES, to the best of her knowledge, Gerald had managed to get in at least six hours' sleep before the flight . . .

YES, Gerald had seemed absolutely normal. If he had sensed he was in any way unfit, he would have been first to admit it.

DC listened, observing the tight knot of fingers and their effort to retain a grip on composure. Only once did the voice falter—when she recalled her first realization that something serious had happened.

As a crew member's wife, she said, she had often had calls from the airline about delays and technical problems, but always accompanied by the assurance that there was nothing to worry about. This time the call had been different: Instead of the normal assurance, the airline's director of flight operations had pointedly asked whether she was alone. When she had said she was, he had advised her to call someone in—just to keep her company.

"It was then, Mr. Di Coiano, that I knew."

There was a note of pride in her voice—pride that even when the airline had attempted to deceive her for the best of motives, she had neither been duped nor had duped herself, but had insisted on staring reality in the face.

The pride spread by association to the other two members of the family, as they sensed the interview was over. It had been an immaculate performance; the ordeal had been survived with dignity. The brother stood up and made a play of pushing in his chair beneath the table.

DC didn't move.

If ever an interview had to be conducted with thoroughness, even ruthlessness, it was this one. And he knew he wasn't going to get a second chance.

He had no reason to believe the woman had lied in her answers, but the extent to which she had so obviously rehearsed them bothered him. Above all, he needed to be sure—as much now for his own satisfaction as for the Board's—that nothing was being held back, whether deliberately or through a subconscious desire to expunge the memory. The family had evidently read the initial newspaper speculation about the triple engine failure being due to fuel contamination and had concluded that any blame was therefore well removed from the cockpit. Neither they nor the press would have had the slightest notion of the way the investigation was turning.

"Mrs. Aldridge," DC said, noting the outrage on the sister-in-law's face that he should pursue the interrogation further, "I'm sorry to press the point, but are you sure your husband didn't have anything on his mind the day of the flight—something that he might have confided to you or even something you didn't know about but may somehow have suspected?" He hesitated. "Financial worries perhaps? A domestic row before he left?"

The brother was in before she could answer.

"Mr. Di Coiano, such questioning is irrelevant and . . . and gratuitously cruel in view of my sister-in-law's emotional state. It's unforgivable!"

DC's eyes didn't move from the widow. Still holding her gaze, he said evenly: "Mrs. Aldridge, will you kindly ask your brother-in-law to remain quiet or to leave the room."

She looked across pleadingly to her brother-in-law, but he chose to misread her plea as one for assistance. He walked across and stood between them.

"Mr. Di Coiano, I think you and your colleague have outstayed your welcome in this house. We are not unaware of your personal involvement in this case, and in view of that I would say it was singularly ill-advised of you to decide to conduct this interview yourself. Indeed, it seems to have affected your professional objectivity."

The man was standing so close that it was impossible for DC to stand up without toppling over backward. Yet he was not going to put himself at the psychological disadvantage of having to look up to him as he spoke—which seemed to be what was intended. Having no other option, and with a sense of the ridiculous, he addressed the man's groin.

"I'll ignore what you've just said and ask you only this: *My* professionalism aside, are you aware of the extent to which your brother's professional reputation is at stake in this investigation?"

There was no response, although it occurred to DC that a knee in the face was not out of the question, given the man's volatility and self-appointment as Guardian of the Aldridge Family Honor.

The legs stepped to one side, however, revealing Mary Aldridge's shocked features. A voice came down: "I think you had better explain that remark, Di Coiano."

"Sit down and I will," responded DC bluntly, sensing he had regained the advantage. Fleetingly he caught Terry's eye and as quickly looked away. The brother took an armchair adjacent to the sofa on which the two women sat. For the first time DC noticed that, although there was no facial similarity, he sat in the same way as Gerald Aldridge himself had sat at his panel in the cockpit—body erect but head jutting forward, the unnaturally long neck giving the impression of a turtle trying to balance on its hind legs. There was a probing rectitude about the pose which for DC was uncomfortably reminiscent and which at this moment he could have done without.

He knew he should not divulge details of a current investigation prior to the official findings. On the other hand, the Board's own policy, proudly and publicly declared, was that it related factual information about an accident to anybody at any time, and it was a fact—in the strictest sense of the word—that there was a divergence of opinion within the investigation team.

More to the point, there was no other way he could see to persuade Aldridge's widow to give the answers that were required. As for Terry's presence, it was too late now to worry about the ethics of her being made privy to such information; it was no longer a question of whether she should or should not be trusted. She had to be.

Keeping the language simple but not avoiding the necessary technicalities, DC ran through the options that faced the investigation team and explained the current debate over oil loss and fuel loss.

As he had suspected, it was the first inkling the family had had that Flight 639's crew might be held to blame, and they knew enough about the workings of an air crew to realize that fuel management was primarily the responsibility of the flight engineer. Aldridge's brother was quick to demonstrate he knew more.

"Di Coiano, such a suggestion only confirms my earlier judgment about your unsuitability for this investigation. You had good reason to dislike my brother, we all know that, but I never imagined any human being would stoop so low as to carry out a vendetta against a dead man, to ... desecrate his grave for reasons of personal retribution. I shall be writing a report of this meeting to the chairman of the National Transportation Safety Board and you may be assured that I will spare no details."

DC stared across the room. The determination to spare no details was mutual.

"Do that and you will most likely achieve your purpose, if that purpose is to lose me my job," he said quietly. He switched his gaze back to Aldridge's widow, although the words were still addressed to the brother. "You'll also help ensure that your brother is blamed for the loss of 254 lives—since at this moment I'm probably the only member of the investigation team who is convinced that the fault, whatever it was, was not his."

The brother was again on his feet.

"Do you take us for fools, Di Coiano?" he sputtered. "Do you expect us to believe that your colleagues are also fools? From my talks with Gerald over the years, I know enough about modern aircraft and the way they're operated to know that only an incompetent idiot could have been misled into the sort of fuel miscalculation you're suggesting, and I trust you'll grant that, whatever your personal feelings about my brother, he was neither incompetent nor an idiot. Men with his experience and unblemished record do not run out of gas at thirty thousand feet!"

But the brother was wrong—as the incident briefs which Murphy had given DC the previous evening proved.

"Before you write that letter to my chairman you'd better hear me out," said DC. "The fact is that even the most experienced crews have their occasional lapses." He put his hands together. "I guess you've heard of Republic Airlines . . ."

"Of course."

"Well, in 1983, they had not one, but *two* low-fuel emergencies in as many months—both involving DC-9's, both due to crew error. In the first, the captain was distracted when the autopilot knob came off in his hand shortly after takeoff, with the result that the crew forgot to switch on the center fuel tank boost pumps. Both engines cut out and the aircraft dropped nearly 23,000 feet before they were able to get the situation back under control. Then, just two months later, the crew of another Republic DC-9 suddenly discovered in mid-flight that tanks which they thought had plenty of fuel in them were nearly empty. When the low fuel warning lights came on, they found that a circuit breaker had been tripped—pulled out—and this had disabled the fuel gauges in such a way that, instead of returning to zero, they'd 'frozen' at the reading they were giving when the power had been cut off." DC straightened himself. "I need hardly add that in both cases the crew members were supposedly monitoring one another."

"What are you saying, Di Coiano?" asked the brother, his tone only marginally less combative than before.

"I'm saying that human beings are just that—human. No investigator likes to blame the crew, but at the back of every investigator's mind is the fact that eight out of ten of all air accidents involve some measure of human error."

"Yet you said just now that you were probably the only member of the investigation team who was convinced Gerald was *not* at fault. I ask you again: *What are you saying?*"

DC's head dropped forward, then jerked up.

"Look, I guess it's well known that I didn't like your brother, and I think the feeling was pretty mutual. You'll have to forgive me, but I found him humorless, pompous, and unbearably self-righteous—in short, a pain in the ass."

Terry looked up from her pad in astonishment, but DC quickly continued. "He was also the best damned flight engineer I ever flew with ... and I worked with enough of them in my time to be able to judge. What I am saying is this—that, in the eyes of my colleagues on the investigation, your brother's length of service is not the proof of his infallibility that you think it is. In a perverse way, it may even count against him. Any pilot will tell you that the most dangerous flight engineer to fly with is not the rookie going through his checklist like a multiplication table, but the overconfident guy with ten, fifteen thousand hours under his belt who's done it all and seen it all—because he's the one who'll know all about fancy balancing acts with the fuel tanks, he's the one who'll try to trim the aircraft by crossfeeding all the engines off one tank instead of running each engine off its own ... and he's the one who'll then be momentarily distracted by a gauge mal-function or a pretty stewardess when the time comes to switch tanks."

"And you're saying this is what your colleagues on the investigation believe Gerald could have been guilty of?" asked Aldridge's widow, her voice trembling.

"Something along those lines, yes."

"But *you* don't believe it."

DC was aware that the tables had been turned. She was now the one asking the questions.

"Let's say I'm ninety-nine percent certain. I repeat, I can't think of any other flight engineer whose competence I could be so sure of."

"So what is that one percent of doubt?"

"The reason I'm here this afternoon; the reason I asked you those questions which your brother-in-law found so offensive. You see, if your husband *did* suffer a mental aberration of some sort, it could only be explained by a circumstance wholly outside the normal run of things. Hence my question about possible financial worries or domestic rows. The answers, Mrs. Aldridge, are important—important to me, important to you."

There was a sudden softening of her features as she looked to her brother- and sister-in-law.

"Robert, Patricia, will you be good enough to leave me alone with Mr. Di Coiano. Just for a minute—please." She released her hold on her sister-in-law's hand. The brother looked surprised but this time her expression left no room for ambiguity.

"If that's what you want, Mary," he said, a suggestion of the spurned protector in his voice.

Terry looked to DC to determine whether she, too, should leave, but the widow raised a hand and said, "You will be needed to record what I have to say, Miss . . . Morrow, isn't it?"

DC felt suddenly sick. There *was* something after all. His judgment about Aldridge had been wrong. Murphy, Kaplan, Seeward—all were about to be vindicated. In all the talk about fools and idiots, there had been only one—himself.

"Mr. Di Coiano," Mary Aldridge began when the door had closed behind the other two, "I want you to know that Gerald was in as good a spirit as I had ever seen him when he left here for that flight the other afternoon." She paused, fighting to retain composure. "My husband and I were very close. We none of us in this life truly know each other, but I knew Gerald better, I believe, than anyone, his own mother—God rest her soul—included, and I give you my assurance that he had not a care in the world—not over money, health, or me. As for a domestic row . . . when you have been married for thirty years, Mr. Di Coiano, you come to realize that such things are not worth the energy expended on them. Gerald's last words to me were to be ready and packed for a weekend away as soon as he got back." She looked up from her hands and fixed DC with her pale eyes. "Mr. Di Coiano, you knew Gerald professionally; I knew him personally. We cannot both be wrong."

DC rubbed his face in disbelief. He could have hugged her.

"But why ... why did you send your brother- and sister-in-law out of the room?"

"So you could be assured that I was telling the truth," she replied simply. "Had they remained here, you would have had no way of knowing whether or not I was inhibited by their presence and perhaps reluctant to reveal an unpalatable truth. Without them here, there is no reason for me to keep up any pretense. They will, of course, be thinking the worst, and I will have to explain to them as best I can ... But you have been honest with us—painfully, even brutally so—and I think we owe you as much in return. I'm sure that's how Gerald would see it."

"So now you know."

They were several miles from the Aldridge house. DC spoke the words staring straight ahead at the road.

Terry turned to him, puzzled.

"Know what? That Gerald Aldridge wasn't to blame for the crash?"

"I was thinking more of the question you asked me on our way back from P-town. Remember? Why I stopped flying."

"Sure—but I don't feel any wiser because of what I've heard this afternoon."

"You mean you can't guess?" He pulled off the road into the parking lot of a plush, three-story establishment which announced itself not as a hotel or motel but, for no apparent reason, as a LODGE. The words BAR and RESTAURANT were displayed below, accompanied by a pair of discreet rosettes testifying to the establishment's excellence—or exorbitance. It was not till five minutes later in the bar that DC finally gave Terry an answer:

"I stopped flying because I was fired. Somebody blew the whistle on me. That somebody was Gerald Aldridge."

He delivered the words in the staccato rhythm of a newspaper headline, waiting to see whether she was sufficiently intrigued to want to read on.

"Well, at least I understand now why you disliked the man," she responded.

"Oh, I disliked him long before that. The man was a self-righteous, self-satisfied jerk. Nothing gave him greater pleasure than catching out a colleague, even if it was only to tell him his zipper was undone. Professionally, though, he was the tops. It hurts me to have to say it."

DC studied his glass for a few seconds.

"Ever heard of 'the loop?' " he asked.

"Sounds like a contraceptive device."

"Could be—except that it's meant to save lives rather than prevent them. It's a training system for flight-deck crews. Most of the world's big airlines now use it. The idea is that, instead of each crew having his own duties and minding his own business, you monitor one another's and if you detect what you think is a mistake, particularly a departure from standard procedures, you challenge and say so. And if you don't get a response, you holler until you do."

"Even at the captain?"

"Even at the captain. He's still in charge of the aircraft but, since he's also within the loop, his actions are no more sacrosanct than anybody else's. I won't say we all liked it—and for the Old Guard it came particularly hard—but most of us had to admit that it made for much greater safety. Too many accidents in the past were caused by crew members not questioning the decisions of their superiors even when they knew they were wrong. There were occasions when captains were totally immobilized by heart attacks but the cockpit voice recorders revealed that the other crew members sat there dumb while the aircraft dived into the ground at several hundred miles an hour."

He ordered more drinks and looked around. It was Happy Hour and the bar was filling up.

"So, are you going to tell me how Aldridge lost you your job, or not?" she asked with characteristic bluntness. "I assume the loop is relevant to the story."

He looked away, belatedly aware of how far he had committed himself. It was like being in the confessional again, or at least what he could remember of it from his childhood. The difference was that this time there was no hope of absolution. The chairman of Airlantic wasn't going to materialize in shining raiment amid the brass and burgundy leather and give him his old job back in return for a dozen Hail Marys. Still less for a dozen Bloody Marys. But if one was going to confess, it was hard to imagine a more attractive confessor as he looked at her now in the soft lighting of their corner niche. He would happily have gone down on his knees before her. Instead, he picked up a matchbook and tapped it nervously against the table.

"We were coming into Fort Worth after a particularly grueling transatlantic flight. It was a real shitty night and we were making an instrument approach. Weather conditions were what they call 'marginal'—another way of saying 'foul' —and we all knew there was the possibility of having to divert to another airport. Aldridge had been bugging me most of the flight, even more than usual. All I wanted was to get off that aircraft, get to the hotel, and hit the sack . . . Well, we made two approaches and each time overshot. It's a harum-scarum business, overshooting; you've got between two and three hundred ton of aircraft behind you, the ground coming up at 250 feet a minute, and a maximum of five seconds to make the decision before you're committed. And at the back of your mind is the knowledge that, if you get it wrong, there's going to be blood on the end of the runway."

He looked up and laughed. "I mean, if you think about it, the whole business is crazy. What other industry can you think of that requires decisions involving millions of dollars of equipment and the lives of hundreds of people to be taken in five seconds? And the trouble is that, no matter how hard you fight it, each time you make an overshoot you get more tense. By the time you come in on your third attempt your nerves are strung like piano wires." He paused to take a drink. "See"—he indicated the glass—"I'm getting tense just talking about it!

"Anyway, we were on the third approach and Aldridge, as flight engineer, was reading out the altitude figures down to decision height. That's the height at which, if you can't see the runway, you have to abandon the attempt and overshoot. At least, that's what the rule book says . . . Well, he got to the decision height and there was still no sign of any runway; so I did what most pilots do—I sneaked down just another few feet to be absolutely certain. It was then that Aldridge broke in: 'You're below decision height, Di Coiano. I advise you to overshoot." I bristled. I knew I was breaking the rules, but it was the way he'd said it, his choice of words—like a school monitor who's caught a younger boy stealing chalk. If he'd said something like, 'Don't you think we ought to consider the diversion?' then okay, I could've taken the hint. But no, that wasn't his style; he had to personalize it: 'I advise *you* to overshoot.' And not 'Captain' but 'Di Coiano'—just like that pompous brother of his this afternoon. It really got to me; it was so damned typical of the man."

"So what did you do?"

"At first I just ignored the remark, made out I hadn't heard it. There was still no sign of the runway and I'd decided to overshoot anyway. But of course he repeated it—which is what the book says you do: Keep hollering until you get a response. Well, he got his response all right. With all the Anglo-Saxon at my command, I told him to shut his f-ing mouth. I knew the moment I said it that he'd do his damnedest to have me crucified, but I thought I'd be able to handle it, particularly since the first officer had remained quiet all this time."

"And he reported you?"

DC nodded.

"That was only the half of it. That's what I expected him to do and I was prepared for that, even if it went to official inquiry level. Knowing the first officer disliked him as much as I did, I figured it would be a case of two against one as to what I'd actually said. I had no worries about the cockpit voice recorder because it wipes itself automatically every half hour and I knew it had been well beyond that by the time we'd diverted and landed at Houston. What I hadn't reckoned with was the extent of the guy's deviousness. Without telling anyone, the sneaky son of a bitch had pulled the circuit breaker on the CVR immediately after our third overshoot, which meant that my every word, expletive not deleted, was on the tape. He'd screwed me well and good."

"But, whatever the niceties of the loop, wouldn't the recording show that you'd been provoked?"

"Perhaps, perhaps not. Certainly, I don't think there was any way I could've avoided several months' suspension. But that was ruled out by what happened next . . . I was back at the hotel when the first officer told me about the tape and, for the first time in my life, I just lost all control of myself. I found Aldridge eating down in the restaurant, pulled him out of his chair, and slugged him there and then in front of fifty witnesses. I even managed to fracture his jaw. And of course that was it. All things considered, Airlantic was very understanding. Obviously I had to leave, but the reasons for my departure were suitably sanitized by the airline's medical department. The chairman even got Aldridge to agree to a deal—that he wouldn't press for an inquiry if I not only left the company but also turned in my pilot's license. In terms of retribution, he'd gotten more than he wanted—the satisfaction of knowing he'd deprived me forever of the opportunity to do the one thing in life that meant most to me. With my license gone, I couldn't even fly a single-engined trainer, let alone another airliner. As for my public display of the martial arts, I had had the sense—luck actually—not to be in uniform at the time."

"And that's it?"

"That's it—end of story . . . except that I was fortunate in having friends who thought it was an awful waste that a good pilot should spend the rest of his life selling insurance and put in a good word for me with the National Transportation Safety Board. Airlantic's medical officer had done such a convincing job—gave me something called Ménière's disease—that everybody really did believe that I was just one more talented pilot deprived of his living by Fate. To this day none of my colleagues at the Board, not even the chairman, knows the real reason for my leaving Airlantic. The story that circulated—and I've been happy to go along with it—is that I was pushed out after failing my six-month medical, and without even the offer of a desk job."

They both fell silent—he still tapping the book of matches; she studying him as though looking at a picture in a new light and finding in it features which she had previously been unaware of.

"You really are an extraordinary guy," she said at last.

"You mean you never thought I'd hit a man ten years older than myself as he was eating his dinner?"

"More extraordinary than that. I never thought you'd be defending his memory after the way he'd bitched up your career. From what you say, there were few people you disliked more before the incident and certainly nobody you had better reason to dislike after it. Yet here you are, trying to salvage his reputation—and the man's dead, for Christ's sake! I don't understand it."

DC gave a pained grin.

"I'm not sure I do. I certainly don't feel any different about the guy just because he's dead. But look at it this way: Who else had better reason to be sure Aldridge was psychologically incapable of making the sort of elementary fuel error he's accused of? And after what his wife said this afternoon there can be no doubt."

"But it doesn't follow that you have to start a personal crusade to prove the guy's innocence."

"You mean I should do nothing—take a perverse satisfaction in allowing a corpse to be dragged through the mud? Maybe I'm just a better investigator than I thought. Maybe that's the ultimate irony—that Aldridge should have to depend for the restoration of his reputation on the efforts of someone who wouldn't be an investigator in the first place if it wasn't for his action!"

"So you're going to pursue it."

He looked at her, almost pleading.

"Hell, Terry, how can I *not* pursue it? It's my job!"

She suddenly got up, saying she had to go to the ladies' room. The subject of Aldridge seemed to have strangely rattled her. He knew he should have kept it to himself and determined, as soon as she returned, to talk of other, more pleasant matters. Like how they were going to spend the rest of the evening . . .

It had been no accident that he had chosen this place for a drink, and he was sure she was astute enough to have spotted that, apart from the bar, it offered both a fancy restaurant and accommodation. Nothing had been said, but he had noticed the bathroom bag inside her executive case when she had taken out her shorthand notebook. Options had clearly been kept open. Thinking about it, he felt again the pleasure of anticipation steal over him, now sped through his body by tiredness and alcohol. And, this time, without any feelings of guilt. By any standards, he'd put in a hard day's work.

But the woman who'd gone into the ladies' room wasn't the same one who emerged three minutes later.

"I figure you'll need to do some thinking, so I'm going to leave you alone to get on with it," she announced, sitting down but with her eyes on the door over his shoulder. "I'm going to spend the night with a girlfriend in Manhattan."

For a second or two he stared, uncomprehending—like a man who'd stepped into an elevator only to find it was a revolving door. It was the first he had heard of any such plan and there had been plenty of time for her to mention it on the journey from the Cape.

"She . . . I mean, is she expecting you?" he asked.

"I've just phoned. I told her I'd be there in an hour."

"You haven't got time for a meal first?"

"No. I'm sorry, but she's arranged something." She smoothed her dress as though about to get up again, but he put a hand out to stop her. He still didn't understand.

"Look, is it—I don't know—is it something I said? You think I shouldn't have told Aldridge's widow her husband was a pain in the ass, is that it? For Christ's sake tell me—at least let me know where I went wrong!"

Her reaction was the same as he had witnessed once before, during their first meeting in the motel bar when he had pressed her to find out if she had been sent by a newspaper on a snooping expedition. It was the reaction of the cornered tigress.

"DC, just give up on this, will you! It was you who said this was a business trip, and the way I see it that business is now done." She dug into her executive case and slapped her notebook on the table. "There's your interview with Mrs. Aldridge. There's no charge. It's been a pleasure to do business with you. Now please, I must go."

He shook his head in bewilderment.

"Look, at least let me drive you wherever you're going."

"That won't be necessary. I can get a cab. I'd rather."

She stood up, catching the table with her case and spilling his drink.

"I'll . . . I'll see you back at the motel," she added half over her shoulder. "Tomorrow night, maybe."

He rose and caught her hand just as it was about to slip beyond reach.

"Terry, for Christ's sake, will you just listen to me—please!" He was shouting. He didn't care.

She stared around the room, her face now flushed with anger.

"People are looking, DC. You're making a scene. Let *go*, will you!"

But still he held. Forcibly, he swung her toward him.

"Terry, I'm not going to let you leave like this. Not without an explanation. I thought we had something."

"You cannot 'have something' with someone you don't know," she retorted, mocking his inept phraseology.

All around, conversation had stopped. The barman was looking across with a knowing grin. Without another word, she wrenched her hand free and, head down, rushed for the lobby.

He watched as she spoke to a brown-liveried doorman who then stepped outside and beckoned into the darkness. A second later, a taxi drew up and took her off into the night. Without even a backward glance.

He sat, dumbfounded—not even aware of the looks he was now attracting. In the space of five minutes he had gone from being "an extraordinary guy" to an uncouth farmhand trying to pick up a princess. The only possible explanation was that he had said something to spark off the reaction, and yet for the life of him he couldn't think what. A trickle of his spilled drink ran off the table onto his trousers. He blocked it with the paper coaster, pocketed the notebook and, indifferent to the eyes that followed him, went up to the doorman in the lobby.

"The lady, she got her cab to Manhattan okay?" he asked.

"Manhattan?" The doorman looked puzzled. "If you mean that lady just now, she was going to La Guardia Airport."

His jaw dropped. How many more lies was he about to discover?

"Tell me," he asked, "is there a telephone in the ladies' room?"

The doorman answered with the patience of one convinced he was dealing with a lunatic.

"No sir, the only public telephone on this floor is right here in the lobby." He pointed a white-gloved finger at a booth twenty feet away.

"The only one?"

"The only public one, yes sir."

For nearly an hour DC sat in the car in the lodge parking lot. It had dropped below freezing again and periodically he had to run the engine to keep warm. On the other side of the road a pizza parlor was doing a roaring trade, its customers barely visible behind windows streaming with condensation.

To acknowledge that the evening had not turned out as planned rated as the understatement of the year.

He thought back to the exhilaration of the previous evening when he and Terry had walked along the shore hand in hand. He hadn't imagined it; there *had* been the feeling of something special. For both of them it had been the declaration of a shared emotion, the more sincere for being unstated. Or so he had thought—for whatever he had found on the beach he seemed to have lost in the bar.

He blamed himself. He had forced the pace and overdone it. The invitation to come with him to New Jersey had carried blatant overtones of seduction which, if they hadn't been clear at the time, had become clear from the length of the journey.

Yet she had agreed to come. And what about the bathroom bag in her executive case? Besides, she had also shown herself quite capable of handling tricky situations with skill and tact and, if this one had not been to her liking, she would surely have found a more subtle way to deflect him. As it was, her precipitate walkout had left him feeling shabby—like a teenager on the dance floor whose erection becomes an object of girlish giggles.

But it went deeper than embarrassment.

He thought back to the scene in the bar, this time seeing himself as he must have appeared to her and everybody else. A shiver ran through him. By this all-too-public display of emotion he had forfeited not just his pride, but his dignity—a thing of inestimable value and, once lost, as irretrievable for a man as virginity for a woman. At least that was how his mother would have seen it. With her innate good sense—her Italian instincts tempered by American experience—she had never had any time for Honor, which she said led only to absurdity or death; or for Pride, which was concerned only with cutting *"una bella figura."*

But Dignity . . . Dignity, in his mother's words, was "the common man's Nobility." It was something a man carried within him which, irrespective of rank or social standing, assured him of the correct conduct at all times, in any company, in happiness and in adversity. It reflected a man's proper estimation of his own worth and, because it glowed within him like an inner light, it determined other men's estimation of him. For "without dignity, Matteo, no man can call himself a man."

And in the bar with Terry he had lost it.

Like a fallen angel, he felt a sudden craving for the company of those similarly cast down—for the comfort and protection, the locker room intimacy, of male company in its rawest form. On its simplest psychological level, he needed to hide his blushes behind a little braggadocio and a smutty joke or two. Within half an hour, he told himself, he could be in Manhattan, find a bar, and drown his discomfort in liquor.

Yet he hesitated. There remained within him a vestige of that former self-respect. Alcoholic oblivion was not the answer.

There was an alternative—to immerse himself again in the investigation; to drive all thought of Terry to the back of his mind by concentrating on his other preoccupation of the moment.

What had Dick Seeward said? "We have to go on what we have, even if it's only a scrap of wreckage and an ATC tape." Something like that.

He reached for his briefcase on the passenger seat, pulled out the transcript of the tape, and forced himself to read by the inadequate glow of the interior light.

All the old frustrations nagged at him. Reading any transcript of the tape of a fatal crash—whether the Air Traffic Control exchanges or the cockpit voice recording—was like watching a murder being committed behind a shower screen. There was also an uneasy sense of privilege—the privilege of both "being" on the flight deck and knowing that one would be leaving it safe and whole at the point of impact. More honestly, it was a form of voyeurism.

Even though he had lost count of the number of times he had read the present transcript, it still evoked the same uncomfortable emotional response in him. Even in print, the co-pilot's voice carried a doomed resonance, and he found he had consciously to slow himself down as the drama of the triple engine flameout unfolded with the grim inevitability of a three-act Greek tragedy. He reached the last page and the crew's final garbled communication before atmospherics and the curvature of the earth silenced them.

He looked up from the page and frowned.

Something didn't add up.

He read again from the top of the page.

Again something in that last communication didn't tally. At least not as it was transcribed.

Yet why had he not noticed the incongruity when he and Lieberman had listened to the tape in the audio lab back in Washington? Had the immediacy of the actual voices dulled his comprehension of what they were saying, or did the transcript differ from the tape?

And if it did and he was right on this point, then he might be right on a whole lot else—on the cause of the oil stain on the tail, on the reason for its removal, and on his faith in Gerald Aldridge's competence as a flight engineer.

He had to hear the tape again, even if it meant driving through the night to Washington and dragging Ben Lieberman out of bed.

◆ **18** ◆

AT THE INTERSECTION of General Gurko Street and 6th September Street in the seedier part of downtown Sofia stands a large five-story building of smooth sandstone ashlars, dwarfing all adjacent buildings like a fifteen-year-old in a class of tens. The initial impression of slab-sidedness is mitigated by a deeply undercut ground floor rimmed by thick square pillars and, at roof level, a broad eave supported by exposed concrete joists in imitation of the old Bulgarian architectural style.

Closer inspection reveals that all ground-floor windows are heavily barred; closed-circuit cameras scan every exposed flank; and for no apparent functional reason the north elevation facing onto General Gurko Street bows slightly outward like the side of a ship, producing a nautical effect that is echoed by the rigging of antennae on the roof.

But the most surprising feature is the one that is missing.

For, while every other governmental building in the Bulgarian capital proclaims its identity from a block away in bronze lettering or incised chisel strokes, the only mark of identification anywhere along the 120-yard frontage of this building is a single blue-and-white enamel plaque measuring three inches square and bearing the number 30.

But then the occupants of Number 30, General Gurko Street, are not in the business of publicizing themselves, for this is the Ministry of the Interior—the headquarters of the Durzhavna Sigurnost, the Bulgarian State Security Service.

It was from here in 1978 that the order went out to murder Georgi Markov, the Bulgarian émigré in London. According to some, it was also here that DS officers, acting on orders from Moscow, planned the assassination of Pope John Paul II three years later—although others who know the workings of the DS better find it hard to accept that the Bulgarians would ever have mounted such a crude and clumsy plot relying, as it did, upon the services of a deranged Turk. According to this latter school of thought, the assassination attempt was more likely the work of the security agencies of *the West* who, directing Mehemet Ali Agca and his colleagues through third parties, deliberately involved Bulgaria's resident DS officers in Rome so that both they and their masters, the KGB, would be publicly discredited by the guilt of association. If true, it was probably the first time that the DS had been ensnared by its own devious methods.

Colonel Vassili Arenkov arrived at the Gurko Street headquarters in a spotless white shirt, a black leather jacket, and an exceeding ill-humor. He had received the call about the British suspect just as he had been etting off with his family for lunch at a fashionable restaurant on the slopes of Mount Vitosha. He would be furious, he told himself as he followed the Ring Road, if Sergei had got it wrong, even though that fury might be abated by his delight at for once catching out the cocky, rat-featured little bastard. The man was a creep—which, Arenkov had to admit, was what made him good at his job.

"I assume this is more than just your intuition," Arenkov grunted as Sergei slipped him the two-page typed report.

That was the other trouble with Sergei: He committed everything to paper in the knowledge that this was the surest way of keeping his name before his superiors. There was hardly a file in the building that did not contain something from him. Put it all together and you could fill an entire floor! He was a strange type, reflected Arenkov. He had no family and was said to have no private life. Apart from his work, the only thing that seemed to interest him was Western cinema—an obsession sadly unshared by any of his colleagues, who found his habit of dropping one-line quotes into normal conversation odd and tedious. The typists on the third floor had grown so used to being told in fractured English, "Frankly, my dear, I don't give a damn" that they no longer registered the slightest surprise.

Arenkov read through the report twice, feeling Sergei's watery eyes searching his face for signs of reaction. At the end he had to concede that Sergei had probably not gotten it wrong. It was all too familiar: a Western academic or businessman traveling on some flimsy pretext and always just after something big had happened politically—the invasion of Afghanistan, another change of leadership in Moscow, or, as now, something directly related to Bulgaria itself. The West really must think they were all idiots in Sofia not to see through such patent "fishing expeditions." And the caliber of the people they sent! Rank amateurs. His eight-year-old son could do better. Well, there was one thing: The Warsaw Pact countries need never fear defeat or disadvantage on the espionage front so long as the other side sent across people like this.

Sergei was still looking, spaniel-like, for approval.

"How long has this character been in?" Arenkov asked with a callous determination not to gratify his junior colleague.

"Nearly two hours," replied Sergei. "Colonel Krusteva is already in the building. She's been in over the weekend on another matter."

Trust Sergei to know that.

"Then you had better tell her I will be requiring her services in the interrogation room."

Sergei smiled. "I took the liberty of alerting her to that possibility, Colonel."

Arenkov was not disappointed by what he saw on entering the interrogation room. The specimen—Dr. Stephen Chanter of Oxford University—fitted his preconceptions perfectly.

He was glad he was out of uniform. A uniform might be impressive but it was his experience that casual wear was often just what was needed to suggest to an easily intimidated suspect a similarly casual attitude to rules, regulations, and the treatment of detainees. With luck and Colonel Krusteva's help he might yet make lunch on Mount Vitosha.

Colonel Krusteva—Anelia—followed him in, taking her usual seat at the end of the table, equidistant between the two men facing each other across it. She was wearing a uniform—tight-fitting, well-cut, and, as ever, provocative.

Her childhood training as a gymnast had given Anelia not just an enviable figure but the professional poise to display it to advantage. More than that, she had that certain bloom which Arenkov had often noted in women in their late thirties—particularly brunettes like Anelia. It was hard to define, but it was a self-confident awareness that, although youth had passed, the structure of their faces and figures had held up and, having survived thus far, would serve them with only minor deterioration for at least another twenty years. "Good bone structure" was the usual explanation, but in Arenkov's opinion it had as much to do with an attitude of mind.

He pulled his chair into the table and threw a fleeting, conspiratorial smile in Anelia's direction in recognition of the fact that this was familiar ground for them both.

Together, they had perfected the interrogation procedure over nearly three years. It hadn't started out as a conscious double act; just a convenient coupling of colleagues of equal rank—he, a specialist in Western penetration techniques and she, the most proficient linguist in the building, versed in English, German, French, and Italian.

At first she had been content to work just as an interpreter but it had soon become clear to them both that there were the makings here of what was known as the Hard Man/Soft Man Act—or in this case, Soft Woman. As an interrogation technique it was as old as the hills, but, because human nature was similarly unchanging, it was eternally effective.

For Arenkov, it also offered the joy of partnership with Anelia. Like actors who played the same scene on stage every night, there was an intimacy in knowing each other's part, reading reactions, feeding cues—an officially sanctioned intimacy which had become for him a sublimation of the sexual relationship which he craved but which was denied him not just by his own marital status but, more effectively, by the fact that Anelia herself was married to a senior DS officer in the same building.

With an upward tilt of the chin, he signaled to her that it was time to begin.

"The colonel here, he is wishing to demand you some questions," she said, addressing the suspect.

Reluctantly, Arenkov switched his gaze. Chanter's face, he again noted, was weak and decadent. No, it wouldn't take long.

*   *   *

As usual, the first questions were all predictable—Chanter's reasons for being in Sofia, his knowledge of Bulgaria prior to his visit, the intended length of his stay. As usual, Arenkov's eyes flitted mothlike around the room as he formed the question, but each time realighted on the suspect's face for the translation.

The Englishman did rather better than he had expected. Perhaps he even knew a thing or two about interrogation. He had, for example, stood up respectfully when, he, Arenkov, had entered the room but had displayed his independence of spirit by sitting down again without being told. He also clearly understood the importance of maintaining a level and consistent gaze with his inquisitor, aware that not to do so might imply evasiveness. The chances of lunch on Mount Vitosha were diminishing.

But as the questions became more detailed and probing, Arenkov was gratified to see that the old lie-detector format was as effective as ever. It was noticeable how often Chanter's eyes were now wandering toward his interpreter in a search for understanding, sympathy, and protection. It really was extraordinary how well the setup worked. It was as if the suspect's eyeballs were attached to polygraph pens—eyes straight ahead: truth; a flick to the right: untruth.

The interview moved quickly into its next phase—and Anelia's turn to take the initiative.

At first she had delivered her translations of Chanter's answers in a tone that was straight and sensitive, betokening a sympathetic ear and a willing tongue. Chanter had looked reassured. But now her tone was changing and, listening to her translations, Chanter was displaying the first signs of real unease. No longer straight translations of his answers, her words now seemed—just from her tone of voice—more like ironic commentaries on them. It was as though she had started off believing his story but, after hearing it thus far, had come to the conclusion that it was not worthy of her professional services.

They had arrived at the moment which Arenkov enjoyed most. Retaking the initiative, he started to fire rapid questions not at Chanter but at Anelia, his voice increasingly edged with impatience. As she tried to interpret them, he interrupted and piled on still more questions, each one louder than the last, each one less coherent, until eventually Chanter was cut out of the interview altogether.

Already demoralized and now seemingly powerless to influence his own fate, Medcalf watched the extraordinary play between interrogator and interpreter with growing alarm, as the interrogator grew even redder and the interpreter, judged by her jabbing hand thrust in his direction, seemed to protest that she was doing the best with the material available but it wasn't her fault if that material was third-rate! And all in a language of which he understood not half a dozen words.

For the first time, he felt naked fear. The man before him was out of control, capable of anything—the silence all the more threatening for being implied through a third party who, once an ally, now seemed concerned only to protect her own reputation.

Suddenly, the interrogator was on his feet, the veins in his neck standing proud like hawsers. Instinctively Medcalf drew back. He knew just how the victims of the Inquisition must have felt as the brands were removed from the brazier. Would it, he wondered, be a personal dusting up by the interrogator himself, or a meticulous working over down in the cells by a couple of his trained thugs? In the end, would it matter anyway?

First signs suggested the later. Brushing past him with a parting obscenity, the interrogator stalked from the room, slamming the door behind him.

The interpreter sighed. "The colonel says it is not for him to decide what will happen to you. He must to go to talk with a superior. In the meanwhile you will wait here please."

It was a strange way of putting it; as though he had some choice in the matter. Then with perfect poise and quite unruffled by the previous exchanges, she removed a cigarette from the packet left on the table by her colleague and, lighting it, added: "I think you are in some very great danger. The colonel, I think he is not believing your story."

✦ 19 ✦

IN THE EVENT, DC had neither to drive through the night nor drag Ben Lieberman from his bed; dumping the rented car at the airport, he took the New York–Washington shuttle and arranged with Lieberman over the telephone to meet him in the audio lab "around midnight."

Lieberman's large round face filled the rectangular peephole of the lab door like a badly framed painting. A second later the door opened with an immediate protest.

"You realize this could break up my marriage. It's the third night in a row I've had to work late."

"Don't worry about it," DC consoled. "Blame it all on me."

"That's fine, but you're not going to have to face my wife first thing in the morning."

DC knew Miriam Lieberman well—a small, fiery woman; a zealot in every way.

"Yeah, well, I can see your difficulty," he said with the trace of a smile. "Just send her my warmest regards. Shalom!"

Lieberman led the way into the listening room, remarking over his shoulder, "It'd have been easier if I could've told her what it was all about."

"I'm not entirely sure I know myself," DC responded. "You said on the phone that you'd done some filtering work on the tape."

Cueing the tape on the Nagra, Lieberman kept one of the speakers of his headphones cocked behind his ear so he could carry on the conversation at the same time.

"Well, it's not a great improvement, but I've managed to clean up the cockpit end a little, take out some of the atmos rumble. Nothing I can do about the static. D'you want to go from the top of the transcript?"

DC nodded. "From the top—but Ben, I want you to come and sit here at the table and follow through the transcript with me. There's a reason which I'll explain afterward."

Lieberman looked puzzled. Since when did anyone ask the chauffeur to sit in the back? He ran the tape, but instead of taking up his normal position next to the deck monitoring the levels, he pulled out one of the half-dozen red chairs at the T-shaped table and, sitting down, adjusted his glasses over the typed transcript that DC had placed before him.

As the recording neared its end, DC snatched surreptitious glances at him both to check that he really was following the transcript line for line, and when it came, to see his reaction to the last exchange between the ATC and the SP-3's crew—the half-dozen lines which in the transcript read:

HALIFAX: We're with you, 639. We have you on the screen, but we're getting, er, some breakup now on the R/T. Are you below three thousand?

AL 639: Affirmative. We're at two [unintelligible] . . . not good . . . in there . . . [unintelligible] . . . I don't know . . . Number One flaming out . . .

HALIFAX: 639, do you read . . . do you read, 639?

Without taking his eyes off the transcript, Lieberman leaned back and stopped the tape. His expression had remained unchanged from beginning to end—a model of impassive concentration. Not so much as a flicker of reaction.

"Well, doesn't anything strike you?" DC asked.

Lieberman laid out the four sheets side by side, scanned them again from left to right as though the texture of the paper might hold a hidden clue. He looked up.

"Sorry, DC. It's late. My mind isn't functioning too well."

"Nothing in that last exchange between the crew and the ATC?"

Lieberman's eyes dropped to the last page, rested on it five seconds, and again floated up.

"Well, it's the only bit that's given us any trouble—technical trouble—and that's because of the breakup. As we've indicated on the manuscript, parts of it are unintelligible."

"But let's assume that the words of the transcript, such as we have them, are correct. Is there nothing *then* that strikes you as strange—I mean in relation to what has gone before?"

Lieberman rolled his large head from side to side.

"You're going to have to spell it out, DC. I tell you, I'm better at party games before midnight."

DC moved around the table and, standing over Lieberman in the coaxing but vaguely threatening manner of a schoolteacher with a slow child, took him through the transcript again from the beginning.

"Look, Ben, we have a clear sequence of events." He reached across the table to retrieve the red felt-tip with which he had been marking his own transcript. "First, we have a flameout of the Number Two tail engine." He made a red dart in the margin at the appropriate reference. "We then have a flameout of the Number One, the port engine"—another dart—"followed a little later by a flameout of the Number Three starboard. Agreed so far?" There was a

movement of Lieberman's hair which DC took to be a nod.
"So—Two, One, Three—all out. In between these successive
engine losses, we also have references to attempts to restart
the engines. Both Halifax ATC and the first officer on the
flight deck are quite specific. Here, for example . . ."—he
stabbed the second page—"Halifax asks: 'Have you restarted Number Two or Number One engines?' and the
first officer replies: 'Not yet, sir, we're still trying.' And he
carries on: 'We'll keep you updated on that situation.' But
then the last engine, the Number Three, flames out on them
and they decide to call an emergency and make preparations
for a ditching. But even then, technically, there would have
been no reason for them not to continue trying to restart
those engines. If they'd been following the manual, they'd
have kept back at least ten tons of fuel, more than an hour's
worth, after dumping the rest. Just in case."

DC pulled out the chair next to Lieberman's and, instead
of standing over him, now sat down beside him, the better
to gauge his expression.

"Now, Benjamin, let me ask you this: Is it your impression from what you hear on the tape and from this transcript that the crew managed to get any of those engines
restarted?"

"No, the impression I get—"

DC cut him off with a raised hand.

"Do you think that if they *had* managed to get any one of
those engines restarted, they'd have told Halifax ATC—in
other words, that we would have a record of it on the tape
and transcript?"

"Sure. As you pointed out, the first officer says he will
keep them updated."

"So there's no way that he would have failed to mention
a restart?"

"No way I can see. Even on a single engine they'd have
had enough power to limp back to New York; it could've
been a lifesaver."

There was perspiration on DC's upper lip as he continued, jabbing the pen into the margin of the last page: "So what do you make of this last exchange, this reference to 'Number One flaming out'?" He circled the words with a flourish of red felt-tip.

Lieberman stared at the page but didn't respond.

"What I am asking, Ben, is why the crew feel it necessary to mention that their Number One is flaming out when we already know it is out—they told us back here on the first page. See? 'Looks like our Number One engine is now flaming out. Do you copy? We're losing our Number One engine.' And the ATC confirms it: 'Okay, we copy you. You've lost both your Number Two and Number One engines.' Couldn't be clearer. And yet here they are on the last page in this last exchange—on their final glide path for a ditching—repeating it! *Why?* By that time you'd expect them to have a dozen other things on their minds."

Still Lieberman was silent. DC stood back, arms flailing in exasperation.

"Well, there're only two possible explanations, aren't there? Either they *had* managed to restart that Number One and didn't tell us—and you agree that it so unlikely as to be ruled out—or the transcript has got it wrong and there is something else on that tape."

"Like what?" asked Lieberman, hurt by the implied accusation that he personally might have made a mistake in the transcription.

"Like: 'Number One, flames *coming* out!' "

"You mean they're reporting a fire?"

DC leaned forward, hands splayed on the table, his face inches from Lieberman's.

"That's exactly what I mean, Benjamin. That's the only thing that makes any sense. The flame is not out, it is *coming* out. Number One engine is on fire!"

Lieberman stood up and, returning to the tape deck, wound the quarter-inch back a couple of feet. He switched the Nagra to Play and listened again to the last exchange, first with headphones, then without. He then repeated the operation but this time slowed the tape down to a deep rumble on playback, removing his glasses to aid his concentration. DC waited; he needed no second or third hearing to be convinced.

Finally Lieberman put his glasses back on.

"You could argue it either way, DC, but I can see what you're getting at. There's about a third of a second gap between the syllables 'flam' and 'ing' which is covered by static breakup and could accommodate the extra syllable to give you 'flames coming out.' Perhaps, strictly speaking, we should've transcribed that section as 'Number One flam . . . [unintelligible] . . . ing out.' I'll make sure it's amended. On the other hand, I have to say you're reading into it more than is justified. There's no evidence to suggest that that extra syllable—assuming it's not just a natural pause anyway—is the one you're claiming. Frankly, on the evidence of what has gone before, it could just as likely be an 'er,' 'um,' or 'ah' . . ."

"In the middle of a word, for Christ's sake?"

"Sure, in the middle of a word. Look again at the transcript and you'll see that the first officer has done exactly that a couple of lines earlier." He scooped up the pages from the table. "Here we are. The bit where he's talking about ditching. He asks, 'Any, ah, thing about sea conditions you can give us?' "

DC sensed he was losing the battle of words.

"But what about the *logic* of his statement, Ben? Explain to me why he should repeat that the Number One is flaming out when we already know it is out and are sure that it hasn't been restarted?"

Lieberman busied himself with spooling back the tape, talking over his shoulder.

"DC, one thing you learn very quickly in this job is not to question the logic of what people say; that way you end up hearing only what you want to hear. It's one of our endearing conceits as human beings that we all think we speak logically. But I swear to you, you analyze any snatch of conversation—in a bar, on the street, over the telephone—and you'll find it's riddled with repetition, inconsistency, and non sequiturs."

DC sat watching Lieberman's back as he removed the spool, slid it into its neatly labeled box, and returned it to its neatly labeled shelf. The man was right—and wrong. Surrounded by the tools of his profession and handling the raw material of his trade, he was acting and thinking according to a mental rule book—correct, disciplined, and totally unimaginative. It was a standing joke that the worst qualification for a pilot was imagination, but Lieberman clearly believed the same applied to audio technicians. The only hope was to get the man out of his environment; take him somewhere totally alien.

But at one-fifteen in the morning?

A few seconds' thought suggested just the place. DC stood up and placed a comradely hand on Lieberman's shoulder.

"Ben, I appreciate your help—coming in like this. Now, you must let me repay you. You got your car outside?"

"DC, you don't have to repay me for anything. There's no—"

"No, no, I insist. There's a place just ten minutes from here. We can sit down, have a couple of drinks."

"DC, it's past one o'clock in the morning."

"No trouble. This place stays open till three, sometimes later."

"I mean my wife will be waiting, and anyway I need the sleep."

But DC was already holding up his coat.

"Benjamin, I tell you, it's on your way home—lower part of Wisconsin. A small nightcap will help you sleep all the better."

*   *   *

Lieberman surveyed the place with undisguised amazement.

"This joint run by the Mob or something?" he asked, taking in the gold-striped wallpaper, crystal chandeliers, red velvet upholstery and, in the middle of it all, a three-foot gilded cherub on a plinth, its vitals tickled by jets of water arcing up from the basin below.

DC knew he had chosen well. No question, it was Lieberman's first encounter with twentieth-century Italian baroque.

"Does every Italian bar have one of these cherub things?" Lieberman asked.

"It's not a cherub, it's a putto," said DC, handing him a cognac that came nearly halfway up the balloon glass. "Cherubs are Christian; putti are pagan. Apart from that, cherubs have smaller balls—if they're allowed any at all."

Lieberman looked at his glass and resigned himself to a lengthy session.

"Now let me explain to you why that transcript could be the key to a whole lot else," said DC, leading the way to a far corner.

"Don't you see," he concluded, after telling Lieberman the story of the disappearing oil stain, "the reference to a fire in the Number One engine explains it all—and particularly why it should have been burned oil."

"I'm not sure I see the connection," said Lieberman wearily. "Where's the link between the loss of oil and a fire?"

"Fifth-grade physics, Benjamin . . . When an engine loses oil, it first heats up and eventually seizes up and, if there isn't a fire already, repeated attempts at a restart—which we know were made here—will soon start one. The bearings actually fuse together. Whatever residue of oil is left by that time will first be caramelized and then ignited. I tell you, it all adds up."

Lieberman screwed up his face, stifling a yawn.

"You could be right, DC, but you're talking to the wrong guy. It's not my specialty, this sort of thing." Longingly he eyed the clock over the bar. It was now well past two. "I just . . . just don't see what you're looking for from me."

DC felt a sudden sympathy for the drooping bundle of human frailty opposite. The spirit was willing but . . .

"Ben, I'm sorry. It's just that, well, I suppose I need someone to tell me I'm not going mad. Everybody I've talked to so far—Murphy, Kaplan, Seeward—they've all lectured me on the need to stick to what is known for sure. But what they really mean is that, in the absence of *anything* being known for sure, the most obvious textbook explanation—human error—will have to be deemed the probable cause. It's like saying that, because you can't find the body, a murder *must* have been committed. In fact, Murphy is now talking in those very terms. And I just can't accept that."

"As an investigator or as a former pilot?" asked Lieberman.

"Both. In this instance, the two are inseparable," DC replied, going on to tell Lieberman about his interview with Gerald Aldridge's widow and how it had reinforced his earlier conviction.

"And yet every time I suggest oil loss as a possible alternative to fuel loss, I get the same response: 'Three engines with independent oil systems don't lose their contents at the same time. Therefore the cause of their failure must be loss of fuel . . .' Q.E.F.-ing.D.! It's become like a goddamn tape itself!"

Lieberman studied his cognac.

"Well, I can't help you on that one. You need an engines expert—someone who knows about these things."

"Right, Ben, but who? Our resident expert Kaplan has already made up his mind; he's got the rest of the team supporting him, and I can't approach anybody else for fear that news will get back to the Board that I'm working outside my specialty without authorization. And you can imagine the pleasure Murphy would get writing a report to the chairman about that!"

For more than a minute neither spoke. At the end of the room, the barman was telling a risqué joke to the small cluster of male customers seated on high stools around the bar. They suddenly erupted into a wail of forced laughter—the laughter of men anxious to persuade themselves they were having a good time. It struck DC as sad and hollow. Yet this, he reminded himself, was the sort of company which he had so craved just a few hours earlier. He knocked back his drink and turned in the expectation of finding Lieberman already asleep over the table. But to his surprise he was erect and alert.

"There is one man you could talk to," Lieberman said cryptically, "and there's no reason why anybody at the Board should ever know about it."

"So tell me, for Christ's sake!"

"His name is Schofield—George Schofield. He used to work with Rolls-Royce—often acted as the company representative on investigations involving Rolls engines. Before your time with the Board, this would've been. He was the finest engineer I ever came across—the sort who could tell what had happened to an engine just by listening to the cockpit tape. You know, I don't think there was a thing that guy didn't know about aircraft engines . . . Trouble is, he could be dead by now."

DC winced. "Thanks, Ben," he drawled sarcastically. "He sounds like just the man I need."

But Lieberman hadn't finished.

"It'd be easy to find out, though. When he retired—must've been five years ago—he sent me a card with his home phone number on it. He and his wife were buying a small retirement cottage in the country and he was keen I should visit them if ever I got the chance. I've still got the number on file back in the office. If you rang him now at least you'd know whether he was still alive."

"Now?" DC exclaimed. The brandy had clearly gone to Lieberman's head.

"Why not? It's seven in the morning there."

"Where, for Christ's sake?"

"Britain, of course. I just told you: He worked for Rolls-Royce. He was at their aircraft engine division in Derby, England. That's why I say you can be sure the Board won't find out. If you took Concorde out of Dulles, you could be there and back in twenty-four hours."

DC sat back and studied Lieberman's expression. He detected a hint of mischief about the lips. His bluff was being called. Was this burning desire of his to determine the truth a pose, or was he really prepared to go to the ends of the earth? At least, to the other side of the Atlantic.

"You'll go back to the lab and dig out that phone number?" DC asked.

Lieberman leaned forward. "Look, if it'll guarantee I get to bed before dawn, I'll ring the guy myself to tell him you're on your way! Meantime, I can cover for you with Murphy by telling him you and I are getting the FBI to help us clean up that tape some more."

DC stared at the clock, then back to Lieberman. He drew a deep breath and drained his glass.

"It's a deal."

♦ 20 ♦

"YOU HAVE NOT DONE very well, Dr. Chanter."

There was an air of patronizing playfulness in the voice that caused Medcalf to avoid the gaze and stare fixedly at the pack of menthol cigarettes on the table. He wasn't going to set himself up a second time for her judgment.

"I mean," she continued, drawing on the cigarette, "most of your colleagues durate three, often four days before they are being caught."

Medcalf looked up, prompted by the laughable quaintness of her English. She was smiling but, to his surprise, without the sneer her words had conveyed.

"But I expect that in this case Mr. Van Kleef knew the need for quickness," she added.

He could almost feel his pupils dilate. Had he heard correctly? Had she really said "Van Kleef"? Whatever, he recognized the ploy for what it was: an elaborate trick to draw him out, along the lines of "We know everything already, so you might as well try to save your own skin." He remained silent but aware that his features might already have betrayed him. Considering the derisory training he had been given for the journey and the fact, as it now seemed, that he was not the first to be sent to Sofia, he could well believe that the DS knew all about CENMON, Intelligence Liaison, and Van Kleef. Even so, her next utterance came as a shock.

"Bogart."

She let the word drop between them like a primed grenade.

"You are coming here to meet with this Bogart, yes?" She laughed. "And now you are meeting with him, but you are not understanding because him is a her."

"You mean *you* are Bogart?" The words were out before he could check himself.

Again, she seemed amused by his stupefaction.

"Of course. You, like those who have come before you, have assumed Bogart has to be Sergei because Sergei likes to impress foreigners with his knowledge of Western cinema. That is why I have chosen the name and that is why you all come to this place at the end. It makes it more easy for me. I know I will meet you finally and also in a little privacy. We have a saying in Bulgaria: If you are being chased by a wild boar, the most safe place is on his back."

Medcalf glanced over her shoulder toward the door, but she gave a dismissive flick of her cigarette.

"Colonel Arenkov? Oh, you do not worry about him." She indicated a concealed button beneath the table. "He will not return until I will signal to him that you are ready to confess. You see, he believes I am using my feminine charms upon you. It can take a long time. At least half an hour . . . But first, my name it is Anelia. Your name I am not wishing to know, but I am sure it is not Dr. Stephen Chanter. And yes, there are things that I must tell to you and that you must listen and remember."

Although Medcalf's mind had been thrown into confusion by the interpreter's—Anelia's—revelation, he was to have no difficulty with his memory, such was the already heightened state of his perceptions after Arenkov's performance. For the next twenty minutes he was to listen and remember as Anelia's words poured forth, her pace speeding up or slowing down according to what she gauged to be a Westerner's capacity to understand material which was at times more historical then political. She began with the historical.

"You have heard of Macedonia, yes?"

He had—just. It was filed away in the same compartment of his memory that housed all those other geographi-
cal anachronisms that made up the Balkan ragbag of the
last century—Herzegovina, Moldavia, Montenegro, Rumelia,
Transylvania—and which for Westerners of Medcalf's generation were only marginally more real than Ruritania. As to
Macedonia's location on a modern-day map, he would have
placed it—correctly—to the southwest of Bulgaria, now split
between Yugoslavia and Greece.

"For we Bulgarians," she continued, "Macedonia is very
dear because it is truly a part of our country. In the time of
the great Bulgarian Empire of the Middle Ages, the shores of
the Macedonian lakes of Ohrid and Prespa have been the
seat of our tsars. Its people are our people, but always
obligated to lie under foreign rulers. This is why in the years
since our liberation from the Turks we are always trying to
make Macedonia again a part of the Fatherland. But every
time we are being impeded . . . For a few months after our
liberation in 1878 the Russians have given it back to us, but
then your Mr. Disraeli has forced the Russians to take it
from us again and has given it instead to the hated Turks,
the same people who had oppressed us for five hundred
years! Since then we are trying many times to have it back.
The reason why we have joined with the Germans in the
two world wars is because they have promised to give us
Macedonia if they will win, and for a short time during the
Second World War we have occupied it . . ." She drew
deeply on her cigarette, the exhalation of smoke mingling
with a sigh. "But of course the Germans did not win and so
after the war the land—our land—was taken away from us
again."

She paused to check that he had understood. Satisfied,
she continued.

"So you can see that we have a very great love for this
piece of earth called Macedonia and will never relinquish

our aspirations for it. That is why—and this is what you must tell to Mr. Van Kleef—our government is now planning a new invasion. The assassination attempt upon our president is a part of it, for it was really the work of one of my colleagues in this building. He was ordered to shoot the Foreign Minister who stands next to the president so that it will seem like the president has been the target. I know all this from my husband because he is an important man here. He says to me that sometime very soon a man will be arrested for the assassination and he will be a Yugoslav. He will be innocent, of course, but the government will say he has confessed to be part of a Yugoslav plot to make fall the Bulgarian government. This will happen very soon—perhaps even tomorrow or the day after, I do not know. But soon. At the same time there will be explosions in the other towns of Bulgaria. One is already being planned by our officers at Plovdiv. Again our government will say that these things are a part of a Yugoslav plot and they will say that it is therefore necessary for Bulgaria to widen her border with Yugoslavia for her own security. Then they will use this imagined threat as a reason for our soldiers to cross the border and to occupy Macedonia."

Medcalf listened, stunned. Despite his anger at the way Van Kleef had set him up, he recognized that the information was political dynamite and, viewed in the cynically dispassionate terms in which these things often had to be measured, worth sacrificing the lives of perhaps a dozen agents to secure. Not that he, in his own NATO career as an "in-house" analyst concerned solely with monitoring the cohesion of the Alliance's member states, had ever had any direct experience of such issues. Faced now with Anelia's revelations about Macedonia, he could say only:

"So you will at last have the land you love."

The remark caught her off-balance. She had expected something rather more astute, but responded:

"Yes—and no, because this is a bigger story than you are thinking. For sure our government wants Macedonia—all Bulgarians want Macedonia—but this invasion is not all the plan of our government. It is, first, the plan of the Soviet leaders in Moscow who have a lot bigger ideas. I think you can guess what these are."

"To invade Yugoslavia and bring it under Soviet domination?"

"Of course, and it is a very clever, a very beautiful plan for them. They are using Bulgaria as—how you say?—their 'stalking-horse.' It will seem like only a small dispute between two East European countries. There will be no Warsaw Pact soldiers—not at first—but only Bulgarian soldiers. Bulgaria, it is true, is a member of the Warsaw Pact but these will be Bulgarian soldiers acting only in the defense of Bulgaria. That is what the government will always say and it will be believed because it is well known that we Bulgarians are so trusted by the Russians that we do not have Russian troops placed on our earth. But then, when our soldiers will be in position, the Russians will follow us into Macedonia with their 'fraternal support' and very soon all of Yugoslavia will fall, because you know it is already very fragmented."

Seeing the skeptical expression on Medcalf's face, she stopped and asked, "You are not believing this?"

"I am not an expert in these matters," he replied. "Yes, I believe everything you say about the Russians' intentions to use Bulgaria as a cover for the invasion of Yugoslavia. I just don't think it will be that easy. The West is not as stupid or impotent as it sometimes seems. You're imagining that the NATO countries will just sit back and let it happen. They won't. At first they may give only diplomatic warnings, but, if necessary, they will respond with force."

"Like they did in Afghanistan, you mean?" Her tone was scathing.

"The circumstances in Afghanistan were very different," Medcalf retorted.

"That is true; they were a lot more clear—and still NATO was unable to do up its mind until it was too late to do anything." She leaned forward across the table, her slate-gray eyes wide with a strange fervor. They reminded him of the icons he had seen in the crypt of the church. "You tell me then what your NATO friends will do if Bulgaria will invade Yugoslavia. Will they send soldiers and arms to help the Yugoslavs in their heroic resistance—like they have sent them to help the Hungarians in 1956, the Czechs in 1968, the Afghans in 1979, the Poles in 1981? Will they?" She threw back her head in derision. "I think they will not, because that will be to risk a nuclear confrontation. No, they will say this is not a NATO country that is being threatened, these are not Warsaw Pact soldiers who are invading, and anyway the Yugoslavs, not like the Afghans, they are already Communist. This is not our battle, they will say."

She paused, triumphant. But only for a moment.

"And I am telling to you this—by the time that it will be obvious that Russia is involved, it will be too late for NATO to do anything. You will still all be sitting on the German plain waiting for the Soviet invasion from the one direction where it will never come. While you will barricade the front door, the Russians will let themselves in at the back."

"You think the invasion of Yugoslavia could be only a first step along the way to taking over the whole of Western Europe?"

"I have not said that, and I do not know that, but if I will be you, I will be worried. History shows us that all empires—the Roman Empire and yours, too, the British Empire—must keep on growing, keep on conquering new lands. Or they die." She threw back her head, aware of having been sidetracked.

"But these are matters for Mr. Van Kleef to decide. What is most important is that you tell to him what I have said. NATO must know that these things—the confession of the Yugoslav, the bombs, the invasion of Macedonia—are not what they will seem, and if NATO will take immediate action, strong action, then perhaps the Russians will not risk more. But if NATO will do nothing, it will be too late to do anything!"

She glanced at her watch and her voice was again calm.

"When Colonel Arenkov will return, you will confess to him that an old friend who works in your Foreign Ministry has discovered that you are coming here to write a book and he has asked you to find out as much as you are able about the assassination attempt upon our president during that you are here. When the colonel will ask you who is this friend, you will give to him the name, Douglas Saunders. You remember that? That will convince him because there is a real Douglas Saunders in your Foreign Office and we are being told by the KGB that he is really a member of your MI6." Reading the apprehension in Medcalf's face, she added, "And do not worry if you will have problems; I will translate only the correct answers."

Medcalf's apprehension remained.

"And what will happen to me then?"

"You will sign a statement which will confess to your small guilt and you will be put on an aircraft to Washington. Sergei has done a very good job of following you and he knows that you have talked to nobody and have learned nothing. I have seen his report. There is no reason to keep you in prison here. Such things cause only diplomatic problems and, at this moment particularly, Bulgaria is not wishing to attract this sort of attention to herself. I promise you this is what will happen."

"But I came from London. Why send me to Washington?"

She smiled.

"It is a way to insult you British. It is a way to show to your MI6 that we know they are acting only on the orders of their American masters. When somebody is throwing his rubbish in your garden at night and you think you know who he is, you return the rubbish to his doorstep to show to him that you know it is him who do these things. Now . . ."

He watched her hand slip beneath the table to press the button that would cue Arenkov's return. Quickly he raised his own hand to stop her. Uncharacteristically, he felt genuinely curious about the woman. Why was she telling him all this? Why should she, a Bulgarian and by every indication a patriot as well, risk her life to help her country's enemies? And not for the first time, it seemed.

"You are playing a dangerous game," he said.

She shrugged. "Perhaps—but do not think that it is for my love of the West or of your capitalism. Do not think that I will ever beg for your political asylum. In your English dictionary I find that 'asylum' also means a house for mad people, and I am not wishing to live in a place like that. I am Bulgarian and I will die here in Bulgaria. All I am wishing is that Bulgaria will be more Bulgarian and less Russian. Just like you British are now the slaves of Washington, so we Bulgarians take our orders too much from Moscow I think." Medcalf shook his head in implied disagreement but she continued. "You smile as if to say I am wrong about you, but I think it is you who is wrong if you think you British are really independent. We at least have no Russian soldiers in our country, but you, you have American soldiers *and* American missiles. But that is another argument. You have read Tolstoy?"

The sudden switch in thought took Medcalf by surprise.

"A long time ago."

"Then perhaps you will remember what Tolstoy says about Christianity . . . 'If I seem to you like a bad Christian,' he says, 'then you must blame me. But blame *me* and not the path I tread. If I know the road home but go along it drunk, staggering from side to side, that does not make the road a wrong one.'" She paused and smiled wisely. "It is the same with Communism. Here in Bulgaria we are trying to become more sober, but Russia I think is becoming drunk and is losing the way ... We are not wishing to be the sixteenth republic of the Soviet Union. For five hundred years the Turks are calling us 'Bulgar-Vilayet,' the Bulgarian Province. Then under the Russian tsars we have become Russia's 'little Slav brother.' That is enough. Now, we are wishing to be only 'drougari'—comrades, equals."

"And that is not what Moscow wants?"

"Moscow wants us to be comrades but not equals. Moscow will help us to have Macedonia. But some of us are looking at history and we are seeing what has happened in the past when we are agreeing to help bigger nations in their plans because we have thought they can help us in *our* plans. Each time, in two world wars, we have lost. Each time in seeking more territory, we are finishing with less."

"And this time?"

There was a hint of humor at the corner of the eyes.

"You have a saying in your country about eating your cake and having it. In Bulgaria we say something similar; we say it is not possible for the wolf to be replete and the lamb to be intact. So I think also it is not possible for us to have Macedonia and for Bulgaria still to be independent from the Soviet Union. That is why I tell you all this."

◆ 21 ◆

"KIRK LANGLEY" announced the black-on-white sign before the cluster of buildings straddling the A-52 road from Derby to Ashbourne. All around, the English countryside lay deep in a powdery snow—as pretty as an adman's dream.

DC expressed surprise that the road had not been cleared. Laconically, the taxi driver explained that the local authority had been caught out by the "exceptional weather"—just as it had been caught out every year for as long as anybody could remember. In Britain, he added, the weather was always "exceptional."

From what DC had seen so far—which admittedly was only the three-mile stretch from the railway station—the county of Derbyshire was infinitely more desirable as a place to live than the town of Derby. He could understand why George Schofield had moved out when he had retired from the aircraft engine works.

The taxi turned right onto a minor road bounded on either side by high snow-capped hedges and then, a mile farther on, turned right again up a lane defined solely by tire tracks. They stopped outside Number 20, a small brick-and-tile–clad cottage with bits tacked on over the course of a couple of centuries. DC handed the driver a five-pound note and told him to keep the change.

"That's very decent of you, sir," said the driver, adding with a hint of irony, "Have a nice day now." It was already dusk.

*   *   *

George Schofield stood in the doorway, beckoning him inside and out of the cold before he introduced himself.

He was smaller and more frail than the mental picture DC had built up, softly spoken, and with a face that seemed fixed in a state of perpetual geniality. If DC hadn't known he was an engineer, he would have guessed him to be a minister of the church.

George led the way through a narrow white-washed corridor into a low-roofed sitting room dominated by a grand piano. A log fire crackled in the grate without generating any appreciable heat. Schofield's wife, Edith, appeared and immediately took over, talking about her husband as though he were a medical specimen in a bottle on the mantelpiece. He had had a stroke barely six months ago, she said; had been temporarily paralyzed down his right side; was no longer a young man when all was said and done, what with the arthritis which had already stopped him from playing the piano, and— she concluded with a look of preemptive menace—was under strict orders from Dr. Morgan not to exert himself.

DC was left in no doubt that, if Edith had had her way, he would not have been invited. Then, as abruptly as she had broached the subject of her husband's health, she announced that she would get them some tea, and left.

George smiled. "You mustn't mind about Edith. She means well. As soon as we've had our medicine, I'll take you across to the pub and we can talk. You'll stay for supper, of course. Good."

Tea was dominated by another monologue from Edith on how George had given his best years to Rolls-Royce and the aircraft industry. More than once George protested, "My dear, I'm sure Mr. Di Coiano hasn't come three thousand miles to hear this!"—but in vain.

For a frustrating half hour, DC sat silently on a sofa covered in floral fabric, sipping from a china cup whose design of red and yellow roses almost matched that of the sofa, which in turn almost matched the curtains. Framed in silver on the piano sat a color photograph of a wedding couple. As Edith chatted, he occupied his mind by trying to determine whether the bride or the groom looked more like a Schofield. He decided the groom was their son.

"I'm taking Mr. Di Coiano across to The Bell," said George at last, anticipating his wife's protests by adding, "He says he's never been in a real British pub, so it'll be a novel experience for him. And don't you fret, we'll be back in good time for supper."

Leaving the house, they set off across what seemed to be a field but which was curiously dotted with little upright wooden shacks like sentry boxes. DC quizzed George about them as they plotted their course in the direction of the illuminated pub sign a hundred yards away.

"Oh, you mean the allotments," said George. "The whole field is divided up into small strips about thirty feet by ten. The strips are then rented out to those who don't have gardens but want to grow their own vegetables—lettuces, sprouts, potatoes, even strawberries. Mostly town dwellers, of course. The sheds are where they keep their tools."

Outside the pub, they knocked the snow off their shoes on the iron by the door before entering a world of warmth, pungent with the smell of exhaled tobacco and human exertion.

The "bar" was nothing more than a serving hatch, flanked on each side by cards carrying small packets of salted peanuts which, as they were sold, revealed more of a scantily clad female figure beneath. The locals, DC guessed, were easily entertained.

George ordered two pints of something DC didn't catch and pointed out a free table next to the open fire. A minute later, he laid the pair of straight-sided glasses on the table and eased himself in behind them.

"Bass," he declared, indicating the glasses. "See what you think of it. Oh, and sorry about that little lie earlier. I'm sure you've been in a British pub countless times before, but it was the only way I could think of to get us out of the house. Now then, Ben told me on the phone you had a problem; said something about it being, well, 'confidential' was the word he used."

DC took a sip of the beer and gave a noncommittal grunt. He pulled his briefcase up onto the bench seat and handed George a couple of cuttings he had torn from the in-flight newspapers on the way over.

"Ah, I thought it might be this one," said George, seeing the headlines. "Strange business. Flameouts like this happen most often with two-man crews, of course—DC-9s, 757s, and the like. Almost always fuel mismanagement; a case of somebody not watching the shop. It's more unusual with a three-man crew, but not unprecedented."

"That right?" DC was surprised Murphy hadn't mentioned such a case.

"Oh, yes, there was an incident not that long ago involving a TriStar owned by some foreign airline. I can't remember all the details—old age, you know—but it was the usual story of troubles never coming singly. The crew made an initial error in converting liters into kilograms and fed the wrong fuel figures into the flight management computer. They were then delayed by a headwind and an occupied runway, and eventually landed with just fifty kilos in the tanks. It was that close . . . Anyway, what can I do for you on this one?"

"Well, I figure it'd be a help if you could just look through the relevant documentation—it'll take quite a few minutes—and then tell me whether in your judgment it still adds up to the sort of thing you've just mentioned."

George peered over his half-frame spectacles.

"Do I gather from that that you have doubts?"

"Let's just say at this stage that I'd value your opinion. I don't want to prejudice your findings in advance." He placed a pile of documents on the table. "You have all the important paperwork here: the aircraft's maintenance sheets and fault reports, a copy of the aircraft's Tech. Log, crew histories and simulator results, the initial report on the wreckage found so far, and the transcript of the ATC tape. You'll also find the airline's mechanical reliability reports and mechanical interruption reports going back six months."

But George wasn't the sort to be rushed. He slipped a hand into his jacket pocket and produced a pipe and pouch.

"Marvelous institutions, pubs," he chuckled. "Wild horses wouldn't drag Edith over here. Comes from being brought up a Methodist, you know." He packed the bowl and lit up, pulling the bundle of papers toward him as he did so.

For nearly three-quarters of an hour DC said nothing, only interrupting George to buy him another drink—"Just a half this time, thanks"—and to help clarify the occasional piece of American officialese.

He felt like a man on trial awaiting the verdict of the jury—or, perhaps more accurately, the judge's summing-up. To take his mind off it, he watched a couple of young men at the next table playing a strange game that involved striking coins with the heels of their hands to make them skid across a board. He was tempted to ask them how the system of scoring operated but, except for alternating outbursts of celebration and obscenity, the game was being played in earnest silence.

Looking back at George, he just hoped Ben had been right about the old man's exceptional powers of intuition but was uncomfortably aware that Ben would have last seen him five years earlier—before his stroke.

Finally, George laid the last sheet facedown on the pile beside him and tapped out his pipe on the coal scuttle.

"That it?" he asked. The tone of voice suggested there had been no surprises.

"Apart from another half dozen crates back in the States," responded DC. "But you've seen all the relevant material."

"And your colleagues have done all the obvious things, like checking the airport fuel records. Nothing out of order there?"

"Nothing. The aircraft definitely took off with seventy tons of fuel on board—the correct fuel—and, as always, it was checked for contamination prior to the flight."

"And no chance that somebody might've interfered with the aircraft on the apron? No opportunity for some joker to have slipped a bag of sugar into one of the tanks or anything like that?"

"Absolutely none. JFK has probably the tightest airport security in the world."

"So any fuel mismanagement, if that's what it was, must have been in the air—by the crew."

"Cor-rect—if that's what it was."

"So—now, don't tell me—the current hypothesis is that the flight engineer had been doing some fancy tricks with the crossfeeds and at a critical moment was distracted. Am I close?"

"Couldn't be closer," responded DC eagerly. For the first time he felt George really might be capable of unlocking the mystery. George sucked on his empty pipe.

"Hmm. Well, the only problem there"—he riffled through the pile of paper and pulled out the crew records—"is that the flight engineer doesn't look the sort to fool around. Fifty-two years old, close on fifteen thousand flying hours—more than half on type. Experience alone can be misleading, of course, but in this case it's backed up by some quite exceptional simulator records. He seems to have had a remarkably unblemished career." He blew on the pipe to clear the drawhole, adding as an afterthought, "I'm assuming your colleagues have ruled out oil loss on the grounds that the idea of three engines losing their oil all at once is inconceivable."

"Right."

"And, of course, the paperwork would seem to support them. There's nothing here about any of the engines having problems with oil leaks prior to the flight. Which would seem to bring us back to where we started—a straightforward case of fuel mismanagement . . . Unless there's something else I should know." The words were delivered with a studied lightness.

DC told him of the oil stain on the tail and his theories about the last exchange on the ATC transcript. Without going into detail, he added his personal testimony to Flight Engineer Aldridge's competence, adding quickly, "Not that all this proves a damned thing of course."

George swiveled the pipe in his hand.

"Hmm. I thought there had to be more to it. People don't normally come three thousand miles just to try the beer. So you believe your colleagues have got it wrong?"

DC spread his hands.

"I don't know what I believe—mainly because I don't have the expertise that you have. But, if it doesn't sound too much like nonsense, I know what I *don't* believe—and I don't believe that that particular flight engineer was capable of that particular error. I just want to know if there is any way—any way at all—that all those engines could have lost their oil at the same time."

"Well, there's always coincidence," said George, "and one should never dismiss it entirely, even though in this case the odds would be quite astronomical . . . The only other possibility, of course, is a maintenance mistake common to all three engines—incorrect replacement of seals or some such thing—but, well, you can see for yourself from the records, the engines had had their last overhaul more than a hundred flying hours earlier and had functioned perfectly for at least a dozen sectors. If the wrong seals had been fitted during an overhaul, the error would have shown itself within a couple of hours of the first flight that followed it."

There was silence. George rattled the pipe stem between his teeth and added speculatively:

"The other point that has to be made, of course, is the old saying that an accident is something that happens after a number of incidents. These things are always signaled well in advance if only somebody is prepared to take note. Remember the DC-10 crash outside Paris in '74 when that cargo door blew off—and how a carbon-copy incident had happened to another DC-10 over Ontario two years earlier? The trouble is that the incidents seem to come to light only *after* the accident. But if you could find a precedent for all engines flaming out in flight—other than because of fuel starvation—then, well, you might have something. Personally, I can only think of two possibilities . . ." DC looked up, hope suddenly rekindled. ". . . birds and volcanoes. But I imagine you'll have already discounted them."

DC lapsed into silence. He was aware of his mood changing, of George's pipe fetish becoming intensely annoying. The ambient charm of the olde English pub with its low beams and colorful locals had turned as sour as its strange-tasting beer.

He took a grip on himself, acknowledging one of the uglier truths of human nature—that we are invariably more kindly disposed toward those we think can help us than toward those we know can't.

It wasn't George's fault that he hadn't come up with the answer. It was his own fault for having invested the whole journey with an almost mystic significance, for seeing genial George as a latter-day seer in a distant land with all the answers if only one made the effort to seek him out and sit at his feet.

In fact, everything George had been able to offer could have been just as easily—certainly more cheaply—communicated by telephone. He should never have listened to Lieberman. Like all ideas hatched in the unreality of the early hours, this one should have been reconsidered by the more reasonable light of day.

On their way back to the house across the frozen field, he told George he would not after all be able to stay to supper. George protested but, pointing to the falling snow, DC argued that if he didn't get a taxi back to the station now it might be impossible later.

Well, why didn't he stay the night and catch the early morning train up? countered George; it would be no trouble, he was sure. But DC was adamant; he was already booked into a hotel near Heathrow and, he half-lied, had promised to be back in Washington by the next afternoon. The truth was that in his present depressed state he didn't think he could take another of Edith's monologues.

It was past one o'clock in the morning when DC finally checked into the Heathrow Post House. His exhaustion was total. He had thrown the dice and lost. It was, he now acknowledged, his lowest point since the investigation had begun.

It was ironic, he thought, that he should have hit the low point in a hotel room. When he had been flying, he had always looked forward to the hotel at the end of the trip as the reward for a job well done; after you had taken care of a planeload of passengers, it was somebody else's turn to take care of you.

In those days there had been a quiet elation in such exhaustion—in the anticipation of a hot tub and fluffy towels, a change of clothes, drinks in the bar, a meal out with the rest of the crew, the joshing and easy camaraderie, the jokes and the stories—and the unstated awareness of all around the table that, sure, it was an artificial life, but a good one, too, and therefore to be enjoyed while you were entitled to it. Depending on the length of the stopover, there might also be a nightcap back in the hotel bar before turning in for the night. Sometimes alone, sometimes not.

There had never been any conscious striving to "score." It was, as one colleague had put it, "easy go, easy come." Flying induced a relaxed attitude to questions of morality, abetted by those twin enemies of marital fidelity, absence and opportunity. When one so regularly crossed time zones and date lines, one tended to regard all barriers with the same nonchalance. He had never told Margaret and she had never asked, but he was sure she had guessed. He had always said that any woman who married an airline pilot had to be a saint or a fool, and she was neither.

And now? There had been only one high point in the last few days, just as there was only one voice that could now lift him from the quicksand of self-pity. He recalled her parting words—that she would see him back at the motel—"tomorrow night, maybe."

Tonight.

He looked at his watch and calculated that it would be just after eight o'clock in the evening in Chatham. He hesitated a second and then picked up the bedside telephone in the full knowledge that he was courting further disappointment.

For several seconds the sound of his own heartbeat was echoed by the distant dialing tone. Christ, how he hated telephones!

"Pilgrims Motel, Chat-ham, can I help you?" said a snappy voice.

"You sure can," he responded in unconscious imitation of the room clerk's upbeat tone. "I'd like to speak to Miss Morrow—Miss Terry Morrow in Room 128, please."

"If you will just hold a moment, sir."

He held. Minutes passed, and the longer he held, the greater, he persuaded himself, were the chances of Terry being found. He imagined her in the bar talking to the barmaid, whose name he still couldn't remember. Or at that

instant walking into the lobby from outside, wet and wind-
blown, unknotting the scarf she had worn at Provincetown
and shaking her head so the curls tumbled around her face.
He even rehearsed an opening line.

"I'm sorry, sir, but Miss Morrow doesn't appear to be in
the motel right now. I've called her room and had her paged
in the restaurant and bar but there's no answer."

"And you're sure she hasn't checked out?"

"I'm sure, sir. Her room is still occupied. Perhaps if you
were to call again later . . ." When DC made no response,
she asked, "Do you want to leave a message?"

He thought, but there was nothing to say, nothing that
wouldn't sound trite.

"No, it's okay. And thanks for trying."

He dropped the phone back in its cradle. His whole
being ached with a craving that bordered on addiction.
Corny as it sounded at his age, he had never known anything or anybody to have this effect on him before.

♦ **22** ♦

IT TOOK Medcalf several seconds
to bring himself mentally up to date and to realize, as he
rubbed the drowsiness from his eyes, that he was sitting in the
rear of a Russian airliner, cruising above the storm clouds of
the Atlantic at 550 miles an hour. Bound for Washington
and—thank God—freedom.

He also thanked God for Anelia. Following her instructions, he had had no difficulty acting out a breakdown
before Arenkov and confessing to having been suborned by

the British Foreign Office into becoming a freelance spy on a one-off mission. Indeed, the colonel had given the impression that he couldn't wait to get the whole business wrapped up and resume his normal weekend activities. So it was that like somebody else's litter—Anelia's analogy had been singularly apt—he had been driven to the airport and bundled onto an Aeroflot Ilyushin airliner flying Moscow-Washington via Sofia. He could still taste the sweet, sickly liquor he had been given in the departure lounge. "A farewell toast," they had said, explaining that since he was the only one going, he was the only one obliged to drink it.

Compared with what he had already been through, the next stage of the journey, he told himself, was going to be relatively straightforward. The aircraft would land at Dulles International Airport; he would "deplane"; wait in line at Immigration; pass through on Dr. Stephen Chanter's British passport; and head straight for the nearest international telephone booth to contact Van Kleef in Brussels. Van Kleef would then either tell him who to get in touch with in Washington or, more likely, would send someone to the airport to pick him up and take him away for debriefing. With luck, he might even suggest he take the next plane back to Brussels.

There was only one problem: There was no U.S. entry visa in Chanter's passport.

For the young black immigration officer it was a first. He had encountered any number of excuses and explanations in the course of his work, but never before had anybody slapped a passport under his nose and declared that it was not his.

The senior plainclothes officer who led Medcalf off to a sideroom was equally perplexed. The man before him with the curly hair and crumpled suit claimed to be British but, although he certainly sounded it, he had not a shred of documentation to prove it. Nor any evidence to corroborate his claim that his name—his *real* name—was Adrian Timothy Medcalf. The only documentation the guy could offer was a passport which passed every test of authenticity, photograph included, but which, perversely, he insisted was somebody else's.

"So what are you doing here, for Chrissake?" the immigration officer finally screeched in exasperation.

That, replied Chanter/Medcalf, was "an intelligence matter," the highly confidential nature of which prevented his going into details—but if he would kindly allow him to make a brief call to Brussels, Belgium, he was sure the present confusion could all be resolved very quickly and to everybody's satisfaction ... The officer protested: Did he think the United States Immigration Department was some kinda free international telephone service for the use of aliens and illegal immigrants?

"How about a local call, then?" Chanter/Medcalf asked. "How about your ringing the British Embassy and getting them to send someone out here? Only, as I say, make sure they understand that it's an intelligence matter."

The immigration officer eyed the Brit carefully. What was to be lost by it? Until the matter was cleared up, neither of them was going anywhere.

Medcalf's first sight of the embassy man who appeared an hour later confirmed his worst fears. He had personally heard the immigration officer specify that it was an intelligence matter, exactly as he had asked. And what had they sent? By the look of him, some gofer from the Protocol Section barely old enough to shave!

"Hello, I'm Porter," the lanky figure announced, flapping a large bony hand in Medcalf's direction. "I gather you've got a spot of trouble with your passport."

Medcalf told him as much as he deemed wise, specifically excluding the details of Anelia's message for Van Kleef.

Porter was impressed. He had clearly never heard of CENMON or Intelligence Liaison and would probably have been hard-pressed even to say where NATO had its headquarters. Every now and again he let out at prolonged, low whistle, followed a second later by a thoughtful "Je-sus" as though what Medcalf had to say was in the nature of a divine revelation.

"Of course," Porter declared, "I'll have to get somebody else from the embassy on this. I must admit this sort of thing's a bit beyond me. I'm actually only the assistant cultural attaché—with additional responsibility for handling British citizens who've lost their passports, which is why they sent me. Actually, this is only my second posting. I was jolly lucky to get Washington."

Medcalf made no attempt to conceal his impatience. Thinking about it, he reckoned he would have fared better if on arrival he had claimed to be a Soviet defector seeking political asylum in the West. At least they'd have sent the right man.

But Porter was eager to please and two hours and three phone calls later, Medcalf found himself sitting in the back of a British Embassy Jaguar, surrounded by mahogany veneer and expensive leather. Beside him on the back seat as they headed along the highway into the capital was a man who had introduced himself as Malcolm Cunningham.

"I'm the MI6 rep here, although nominally I'm just a third secretary. Spend most of my time flitting between Foggy Bottom and Langley—sorry, the State Department and the CIA. Frankly, there are times when I think I have more contact with them than they have with each other!"

It was dark and it was wet and, despite catnaps on the plane, Medcalf could feel the time difference and the delayed shock of his Bulgarian experiences catching up with him. He had also taken an instant dislike to his traveling companion.

"Look, we've booked you into the Hay Adams," said Cunningham as the illuminated obelisk of the Washington Monument made its first fitful appearance between sweeps of the Jaguar's wipers. "I don't know whether you're familiar with it, but it's a super place right opposite the White House in Lafayette Square, full of Old World charm and civility. More than a touch of Fortnum's about it—wing-collared flunkeys and potted bay trees, that sort of thing. We normally put our visiting dignitaries there. Costs a bloody bomb, mind you!"

Medcalf grunted unappreciatively.

"Sounds fine, but we need to talk before I collapse. Either that or I should phone Brussels."

Cunningham was smoothly reassuring.

"Don't you worry. It's all in hand. Better I think that you don't phone Brussels actually. Herman Van Kleef can't debrief you over the phone anyway. The usual form in this sort of situation is for us to do the debriefing here and send the results on to CENMON via an encrypted cable, which will take it straight into Intelligence Liaison."

"But this could be urgent," put in Medcalf, thinking now of Anelia's warning about the imminent announcement of the Yugoslav's confession to the assassination attempt.

Cunningham gave the armrest a pensive stroke.

"In which case, I'd suggest this: that we stop at the Hay Adams, get you booked in, give you time to freshen up a bit—and then we can go on to a grill just round the corner where you can tell me all about it."

"In a *restaurant?!*" Medcalf declared in a tone of disbelief. Was this man who spent so much of his time "flitting between Foggy Bottom and Langley" seriously suggesting he reveal information that could stop or start a world war between mouthfuls of filet mignon and within earshot of waiters and fellow diners?

Cunningham laughed. It was the laugh of an old hand at the game.

"You've been too long in Bulgaria, Medcalf. Quite understandable of course, but I promise you there are no hidden microphones in this place. Besides, in my experience people who've just been through what you've been through usually remember far more on a full stomach in pleasant, relaxed surroundings than they ever would perched on one of those bum-numbing tubular steel monstrosities in some whitewashed broom cupboard of an interrogation room."

Still Medcalf struggled to come to grips with Cunningham's bizarre suggestion.

"Look, I don't want to be difficult or melodramatic, Cunningham, but I honestly think this sort of thing should be done in . . ."—he groped for the word through the gathering fog of his fatigue—". . . well, don't get me wrong, but a more professional manner. My last words with Herman—"

Cunningham's reassuring hand had moved from the armrest to Medcalf's forearm.

"And don't you get me wrong either, Medcalf. Herman Van Kleef is a decent enough chap and no doubt very clever with it, but—strictly between you and me—he takes his job just a wee bit too seriously. Whatever Herman may think, Intelligence Liaison is never going to replace the individual secret services of the various NATO member countries, certainly not while it's having to rely upon— with all due respect—part-time messenger boys like yourself. As a central clearinghouse, it may have its uses, but I have not the slightest doubt that whatever you've brought back from Bulgaria, we already know all about it from our own sources in the field. I'll lay money on it—penny for a pound."

The Jaguar had pulled up beneath the Italianate portico of the Hay Adams Hotel. Across Lafayette Square a floodlit White House stood behind its new antikamikaze ramparts. The rain meanwhile had turned to a freezing sleet. It accorded well with Medcalf's mood; dinner with Cunningham, he feared, was going to tax more resources than he felt able to summon in his present condition.

"So how reliable is this interpreter woman, would you say?"

The sneer in Cunningham's tone matched the expression of professional cynicism that he had worn throughout Medcalf's account of his meeting with Anelia in Sofia. Medcalf pushed to one side his half-eaten steak.

"If you mean by that, is she in a position to have access to such secrets, I should judge the answer is yes. She's married to one of the high-ups in the DS."

"How high up? What's his rank?"

"I don't know but I imagine Van Kleef must know. All I can say is that personally I found her entirely credible. Besides, I can't see why she should put herself at such risk for nothing."

Cunningham's eyebrows shot up like twin drawbridges.

"What did you say your job was at NATO headquarters, Medcalf?"

"Look, do we have to ... You know very well I'm an analyst in the Department of Political Coordination on indefinite attachment to—"

"And you've never heard of disinformation? It seriously hasn't occurred to you that this woman's story may be nothing more than an elaborate ruse? Just think about it for a moment. What if the Warsaw Pact is planning to launch a full-scale invasion of Western Europe across the German plain—now, as we speak? What better diversion than to persuade NATO that the real attack is coming through Yugoslavia, so that we deplete our front-line forces in Germany and send half of them scampering off on a wild-goose chase to the Balkans! A classic rerun, in fact, of the deception we played on Hitler during the Normandy invasion—

although I suppose you're too young to remember that ...
Look, I take no pleasure in saying this, Medcalf, but this
woman seems to have cast some sort of bloody spell over
you."

Medcalf bridled—as much at Cunningham's cheap shot
at establishing seniority as at the implication that Anelia
might have duped him. The man could have been no more
than five years older—forty-eight at most.

Yet, in one respect, he had to admit he was right. Anelia
had indeed cast a spell over him. Perhaps it was the prison-
like surroundings of the DS headquarters and her exceptional courage, but he had come to think of her as a Leonore
figure in his own personal production of *Fidelio*—and could
recall without the slightest difficulty the boyish face, the
widely spaced gray eyes, the short flicked-back hairstyle—
"*Wie ein Engel im rosigen Duft, ein Engel, Leonoren ...*"
Or perhaps he was just a closet romantic who could satisfy
his latent sexual appetite only through the medium of opera.

But no, Anelia had not lied to him—of that he was
certain. Of course she would have passed the information to
whoever Van Kleef had sent, but he fancied she was glad
that it had been he. She hadn't so much given it to him as
entrusted him with it.

None of which was an answer to Cunningham's innuendo.

"Look, I am simply relaying to you the information as I
received it," he said petulantly. "You can believe it or not,
as you choose. But, for what it's worth, *I* believe she was
telling the truth."

Cunningham smirked.

"You mean the truth as *she* believed it. You realize,
don't you, that there's always the possibility she, too, may
have been duped by a higher authority—by this husband of
hers even—and was passing on a lie without realizing it? It's
one of the oldest tricks in the book."

Medcalf finished the Perrier in his glass and looked
around the crowded grill. He was ready to go. If Cunning-

ham wanted to play the endlessly-reflecting-mirrors game, he could find another partner.

"When will you talk to Van Kleef?" he asked bluntly.

Cunningham caught the attention of a waiter and performed an elaborate mime of scribbling in the air.

"When what? . . . Oh, in a couple of hours. There are one or two people in the State Department here I need to have words with first. That way I might be able to give Van Kleef a useful gloss on this woman's story." He read the incipient protest in Medcalf's expression. "Yes, and I know it's urgent. I've told you before—don't worry. We're not novices at this game, you know." Savoring Medcalf's exasperation, he added playfully, "In fact the Bulgarians have already arrested a Yugoslav for the attempted assassination. It came over the wire this afternoon."

◆ 23 ◆

WITH the self-assurance of a former airline captain and the practiced, albeit assumed, panache of a Concorde passenger, DC checked in at Heathrow Airport just half an hour before departure.

To his surprise, there was a message to call a telephone number. He asked the check-in girl if she recognized the area code but she didn't. Having gathered some change from the bookshop on the upper floor, he found a public phone next to it and tapped out the number. George Schofield answered.

"Mr. Di Coiano, I apologize for this but I knew only the

time of your flight and not your hotel. I have something for you. I think it may be what you want."

After so many disappointments, DC would permit himself nothing more than mild curiosity.

"What is that, Mr. Schofield?" he said flatly.

"Something I got out of the company library earlier this morning. Thinking back on what I told you last night, I thought it might be worth a try. I don't know why I didn't think of it before."

"The company?"

The money was running out. He fed in all the remaining coins he had.

"My old company—Rolls-Royce. They have a technical library, which has a section devoted to all the incidents and accidents involving Rolls aircraft engines over the years. I found this report and it *has* happened before—what we were talking about. But you must have a look at it for yourself."

In the background, DC heard his own name being paged. It was a final call—a personal final call. The flight was due to take off in less than fifteen minutes.

His thoughts spun like a Vegas slot machine. Even if George could be relied upon to post the document, whatever it was, it would take days to arrive; even by air mail it could be as long as a week. Perhaps Rolls could be persuaded to telex it, but that would require authorization and, with it, explanation. There was only one other course of action.

"Mr. Schofield—George—tell me frankly whether in your judgment this report is so important that I should miss my flight for it."

There was silence on the end of the line as he watched his remaining money dwindle on the liquid crystal display. Looking over his shoulder, he saw that a long line had now formed at the bookshop checkout; it would take at least five minutes to get more change. And again his name was being called, a degree of urgency now insinuating the well-modulated tones: "Will Mr. Di Coiano, a passenger on Concorde flight BA 189 . . ."

"I think it is," said George at last.

It wasn't said with quite the ringing conviction DC would have liked, but the decision was made. At least his only baggage was hand baggage; there would be no need to retrieve suitcases from the belly of the aircraft. He briefly considered asking George to meet him at the hotel or even the airport, but he was sure that Edith would never permit it.

"George," he shouted as the last tenpence disappeared from the display, "I'll be with you just as soon as I can!"

Four hours later DC was back in The Bell, in the same seat and with George again beside him, although this time with a glass of whisky before him. If the peanut pinup next to the bar had lost more of her modesty bags, it wasn't noticeable.

"May the fifth, 1983," said George, sliding a large buff envelope across the damp tabletop. "An Eastern Airlines TriStar en route to Nassau from Miami."

DC untwisted the string closures and, taking care to avoid the beer slops, slid out a typed report thirty pages thick and bearing a large CONFINED stamp. He looked at the stamp and then at George. Had he stolen it?

"It's all right; they photocopied it for me," said George. He hesitated before adding, "Since I'm now retired, I had to give your name, but as soon as I told them you worked for the N.T.S.B., there was no problem."

An alarm bell rang in the deeper recesses of DC's mind but it was quickly muted by the first paragraph. It was his turn to read and George's to monitor his expression . . .

Eastern Airlines Flight 855, a Lockheed L-1011 powered by three Rolls-Royce RB-211-22B turbofan engines with 172 passengers and crew on board, left Miami International Airport at 08:56 on May 5, 1983, bound for Nassau in the Bahamas. The flight should have been a mere hop taking no more than fifty minutes, but nineteen minutes after takeoff the low oil pressure light on Number Two engine, the one in the tail, came on. The aircraft was at 15,000 feet.

The engine was shut down and the captain, aware of deteriorating weather ahead, requested clearance to return to Miami to land—which was granted.

No sooner, however, had the flight engineer completed the shutdown checklist for the Number Two engine than the low oil pressure lights illuminated for both the wing engines, Numbers One and Three. The oil quantity gauges for all three engines now read zero. The crew notified Miami Air Traffic Control but indicated they believed they had an instrument failure, "since the chance of all three engines having zero oil pressure and zero quantity is almost nil."

Five minutes later, at 09:28, the Number Three engine flamed out and the aircraft, still eighty miles from Miami and over water, began a gradual descent. The flight engineer instructed the senior flight attendant to prepare the passengers for a ditching in the sea.

At 09:33—another five minutes later—the Number One engine flamed out. The aircraft, now with no engines operating, started to fall at a rate of nearly a third of a mile a minute. It was still fifty-five miles from Miami. Warned that a ditching was imminent, passengers adopted the brace position, while Coast Guard aircraft and patrol vessels headed for the scene.

During the descent the captain repeatedly attempted to restart the engines but without success—until 09:38 when the Number 2 tail engine fired at the third attempt. The aircraft was at 4,000 feet, continued dropping to 3,000, but then on the single engine picked up and leveled off at 3,900. Passengers and flight attendants remained in the brace position until just before touchdown back at Miami Airport at 09:46. Fires were noted in both wing engines and were extinguished.

DC looked up at George, his mouth gaping like a goldfish. "That's it," he said, his voice hushed with excitement. "I can hardly believe it. It's an almost exact replay of the Airlantic flight!"

"Preplay rather than replay," put in George. "It's what I

told you: the incident that precedes the accident. But read on. This is the fascinating bit: the cause." He flipped over the page for him.

When the aircraft was examined on the ground, it was found that the master chip detectors on all three engines had been fitted without their oil seals, known as O-rings.

These detectors are two-inch-long plugs—no bigger than an automobile spark plug—which fit into the main oil return pipe. They are tipped with a magnetic probe which draws the metal filings out of the oil as it flows over it. At regular intervals they are changed so that the particles can be examined in the laboratory to give an indication of the extent of wear on the engine's internal parts and thus warn against any potential failure.

There is one master plug per engine and each should have two O-ring seals. Without these, the oil will leak out of the engine during flight under normal operating pressure.

Further inquiries into the Miami incident revealed that the night before the flight, two of Eastern's mechanics had been assigned to change the plugs on the aircraft. Usually, the replacement plugs came with the O-rings already on them. On this occasion they were *not*, but, since the sealed plastic bag in which they were packed had a "serviceable parts" tag on it, both mechanics assumed without checking that the O-rings were on and fitted the plugs accordingly. They were wrong.

DC stopped reading and just stared in front of him.

"Jesus," he exclaimed. "This is just unbelievable—so simple and so stupid. Half a dozen two-bit rubber washers are left off, and two hundred tons of aircraft start falling out of the sky. A procedure that must've been performed thousands of times without mishap fouls up because for once the usual parts aren't together and the guy doing the job doesn't notice the difference. And not just one guy, but *two*, for Christ's sake! That's the incredible part—that neither of them noticed." He whistled through his teeth. "I wouldn't have believed it . . ."

"I'm glad it interests you," said George. "I was rather afraid you might think you'd been dragged back here on a fool's errand."

DC pushed the report to one side and for the second time in twenty-four hours pulled the Airlantic documentation out of his briefcase.

"There's just one problem," he said. "I don't recall any mention of those plugs being changed on the Airlantic aircraft prior to the flight." Snapping the pages, he leafed back through to the section dealing with the aircraft's maintenance history and ran a finger down the page. "No, you see, the only mention is of the 'A' and 'C' checks. The 'A' check was done a week earlier and the last 'C' check was two weeks before that. What does that tell us about the plugs?"

"I'd say they were changed as part of that 'A' check the week before," said George. "There's one way to find out, of course."

"Go and see Airlantic, you mean?"

George snorted a stream of gray smoke.

"It's not for me to tell you your job, but that's what I'd do."

PART
THREE

◈ 24 ◈

MEDCALF awoke the next morning to the sound of *WTOP Newstime* on the radio alarm. He knew it was *WTOP Newstime* because it told him so every ten seconds. It also told him that the Bullets had been trounced the night before by Cleveland; that there was congestion on the beltway; and—scam of the week—that the U.S. Navy had been charged six hundred and forty dollars apiece for their lavatory seats. The usual mix of flash and trash.

He dozed and when next he surfaced it was to hear the chords of an organ and receive, courtesy of the Gospel Spirit of Washington, the comforting message that "old Christians never die; they just sleep away in Thee." This time he rolled over on his back, aware now of the buzz of traffic along Pennsylvania Avenue. There was no longer any possibility of escaping reality. "Oh, Lord," concluded the voice by his pillow, "we pray you this day to walk the corridors of the institutions of suffering. I'm Doctor Robert Baker. Amen."

How long was it since he had been in America? Two years, less even. Yet always there was this early morning culture shock—soon to be followed, he knew, by the aggressively egalitarian familiarity of bellhops, desk clerks, and bartenders all demanding to know "How are *you?*" while still bound by a linguistic puritanism that decreed the correct response to be not "Well," but "Good."

Unable to face a full American breakfast—his confused physiology was still digesting the dinner of the previous evening—he opted for a coffee and Danish in the coffee shop off the main lobby. Taking in the immaculately laid tables, Steinway grand, and potted bay trees sprinkled with tiny white lights, he headed for a window seat that looked onto Lafayette Square and the White House beyond. In the middle of the square a large placard erected by antinuclear protestors exhorted passersby to "Have a nice Doomsday."

A group of a dozen or so sharp-suited Italians were huddled around tables in the corner near the Steinway. Their voices were familiar to Medcalf from the night before when he had heard them outside his room as he had been dropping off to sleep. Dismissing the possibility of a Mafia summit, he asked the waiter if they were attending a business convention.

"No, sir. They're Italian parliamentary representatives on an official visit here as guests of Congress." The waiter nodded in the direction of the White House through the window. "They're due over the road in half an hour, an'll be checking out of here after that. Back to Rome, I guess."

He saw Cunningham before Cunningham saw him. Her Britannic Majesty's Resident Spook was paying off a taxi directly beneath the window and looking distinctly less composed in the morning light than he had in the gas glow of the grill the night before.

DC got up to intercept him in the lobby.

"Ah, Medcalf, thank God you're here!" Cunningham gasped. "I had an awful feeling you might have wandered off to do some sightseeing or something." Smoothing down his hair, he nervously scanned the tapestries and wood paneling. His hand remained fixed to his head as though with so much else on his mind he had forgotten to remove it. "Look, we've got to talk, but not here."

"How about the coffee shop?" suggested Medcalf, pointing in the direction of his half-consumed coffee and Danish.

The idea was vigorously brushed aside.

"Heavens, no! Best thing, I think, is if we go for a walk. Got your coat?"

A minute later Medcalf reemerged from the elevator threading an arm through his coat and still mystified by the abrupt change in Cunningham's demeanor. Why was the man suddenly so concerned about surroundings, when only twelve hours earlier he had poohpoohed the possible dangers of talking in a crowded grill?

They set off at a brisk pace, skirting the east flank of the White House and heading south down Fifteenth Street. By keeping a step ahead and refusing to look over his shoulder, Cunningham contrived to prevent any conversation—until they reached Constitution Avenue where he had to wait for the lights to change. Medcalf, coming alongside and increasingly irritated by the air of mystery, broke the silence.

"Do I assume you've talked to Van Kleef?" he demanded.

Still Cunningham refused to respond—until they had crossed over Constitution and were out in the open, in the middle of the Mall and heading up the grassy slope toward the towering Monument. Even then the response hardly rated as an answer:

"From talks I had last night and this morning at the State Department, this whole business is rather more complicated than either of us could have guessed when we last met, Medcalf. It seems—" he broke off abruptly as a jogger in mittens and earmuffs padded past. "It seems that what your Bulgarian interpreter friend told you is the truth—but only a part of it. The question is whether she chose not to tell you all or simply didn't know all."

An icy wind was whipping down from the Capitol, funneled between the great blocks of public buildings on either side of the Mall. Every one of the flags ringing the base of the Monument was rigidly extended, pointing like signposts in the direction of the Lincoln Memorial. As he turned up his collar, cursing his failure to bring a scarf, Medcalf was reminded of his trip with Van Kleef to Waterloo just days earlier, when again he had come close to catching pneumonia. What was it about him, he wondered, that made people drag him off to exposed, windy places whenever they wanted to discuss anything?

"Cunningham, I haven't a clue to what you're talking about," he said peevishly. "Will you kindly explain before we go any further."

Cunningham stopped, glanced around, and stamped the ground.

"It's not that simple. Technically you don't have the necessary security clearance for me to tell you everything. On the other hand, if we accept the American principle of the need to know, I suppose you'll need to know most of it if we are to have a hope of salvaging the situation." He shot a sideways glance, eyebrow cocked. "I tell you, Medcalf, this little jaunt of yours to Sofia has set more feathers aflutter in the intelligence dovecote than you can possibly imagine. And they're going to take some smoothing. Over the next few hours you and I are going to have to concoct a pretty plausible tale for your friend Herman Van Kleef or we're done for!"

Medcalf was puzzled. Why should he "concoct" *anything* for Van Kleef?

"Hold on," he said. "Herman Van Kleef is my boss."

"Wrong—or, rather, no longer. Van Kleef, NATO, CENMON, Intelligence Liaison—you can forget the whole bloody lot of them. As of now, Medcalf, you're under the direction of MI6 which, in practical terms and so long as you're here in Washington, means you answer to me . . ." Another sideways glance—this time to indicate that the seniority he had affected in the grill the night before was now for real. Following the direction of the flags, he struck out toward the Reflecting Pool and the Lincoln Memorial beyond. "First of all, tell me this: Are we right in thinking that Brussels has every reason to believe you're still in Sofia?"

"If you haven't been in touch with Van Kleef to tell him I'm here, then yes."

"But Van Kleef will be expecting you to be picked up by the Bulgarian authorities any time now, I imagine. So one way or the other he'll be expecting to hear from you pretty soon."

"Or you. Look, I thought you said last night that the usual form on these occasions was for you to do the debriefing here and then pass it back to Brussels ... I have to repeat, Cunningham, I have not a clue to what all this is about."

Cunningham didn't respond. Propelled now by a following wind, he was again in fast-forward mode. Finally, when they reached the foot of the Reflecting Pool, he stopped and, staring straight ahead, said:

"I'll tell you then—but before you hear it, you must understand that if you ever repeat a syllable to anyone else you'll be a dead man. It's that sensitive."

Medcalf was inclined to laugh out loud. It was like a line from a bad spy movie. Cunningham had been too long in Washington. In New York a man was judged by the amount of money he earned; here apparently he was judged by the number of secrets he knew or the number of cover-ups he was involved in.

Cunningham took a deep, melodramatic breath and, in a conscious effort to capture the spirit of Gettysburg, held the sad, stony gaze of Abraham Lincoln seated between the columns of his memorial at the far end of the pool.

"Your interpreter friend in Sofia was right. The Bulgarians are indeed setting up an invasion of Yugoslavian Macedonia and the Russians are behind it. The assassination attempt on the Bulgarian president was, as she said, an elaborate bit of stage management to give them a pretext for action. That was just the first step. As I told you last night, the Bulgarian authorities have already arrested a Yugoslav and, since then, there've been a couple of explosions at government offices outside the capital. This morning's edition of *Rabotnichesko Delo* is again putting the blame on the Yugoslavs, and is calling for the repossession of Macedonia to create an effective 'cordon sanitaire.' The army meanwhile has been fully mobilized, and is massing on the Yugoslavian border, poised for invasion. It cert—"

"But this ..." Medcalf tried to interrupt, only to be silenced by an imperious finger.

"It certainly won't be a walk-over for the Bulgarians— initially they'll be strictly on their own and it could take them two or three days to wear the Yugoslavs down. But once they're firmly established in Macedonia, the Russians will offer fraternal support to help mop up any remaining resistance from the other five Yugoslavian states. The joint armies will then move rapidly north to Belgrade and establish there a pro-Soviet puppet government, just as they did in Afghanistan. Within a fortnight—three weeks at most— the whole of Yugoslavia will be under Soviet control."

Medcalf tried again. "But this is almost word for word what I told you last night. If this is what you've learned at the State Department, it only confirms what Anelia warned would happen if NATO didn't act quickly to nip it in the bud. We must alert Brussels immediately."

Cunningham was looking uncomfortable. His voice took on an even more portentous timbre.

"The trouble is, as I say, that you've only heard part of the story—and, so it would seem, has your interpreter friend in Sofia. If she and her high-ranking husband had worked in the Bulgarian Foreign Ministry and not in the DS she might have had a better ..."

A brightly colored mallard had landed on the water just a few feet in front of them, hopeful of a crust or crumb. For nearly a minute it had chugged around at Cunningham's

feet like a wind-up toy, punctuating his sober sentences with
an occasional squawk. Annoyed by this threat to his *gravitas*,
he had attempted to shoo the duck away, but it was now acting
even more outrageously, jabbing its head and flapping its
wings less like a duck than like a pigeon auditioning for the
part of a duck. Finally, Cunningham's patience snapped.

"For Christ's sake, Medcalf, can't you do something
about that bloody bird!"

"Just stop waving your hands—it thinks you've got food
for it. But look, what do you mean, I've only heard half the
story?"

With an exasperated *tut*, Cunningham turned his back
on the offending creature but, obliged now to break his
inspirational gaze on Lincoln, he seemed no longer able to
maintain the rhetorical flow. Or perhaps, as Medcalf was
soon to suspect, it was because for the first time he had to
look a fellow flesh-and-blood human in the eye.

"It would seem, Medcalf, that this is part of a wider
plan—an unofficial agreement, if you like—that has been
the subject of discussion between the super powers for some
time." He swallowed hard. "Now, I don't expect you to
understand this straight off. It's exceedingly complex and I
must admit it took me some—"

"Which super powers?"

"Er, America and the Soviet Union."

"Just America and the Soviet Union?"

"Y-yes, although, as the United States' chief ally, naturally Britain has been kept informed, even though we are
not formally a party to it. Anyway—where was I?—yes,
under this agreement the Soviet Union is to be allowed to
consolidate its already de facto control over Yugoslavia, in
return for withdrawing its support from Castro in Cuba and
the various left-wing liberation groups and governments in
Central America—Nicaragua, Guatemala, El Salvador, and
the rest." Aware of Medcalf's look of stupefaction, he continued quickly, "Now, I repeat, this is not an easy concept to

grasp all at once and I do ask you not to jump to any hasty con—"

"You're joking, of course," Medcalf broke in. "This is all part of the same silly game you've been playing since you arrived at the hotel. It's some sort of psychological test, right?"

For several seconds the two men stared at each other. Slowly, Medcalf realized that this was neither a game nor a psychological test.

"You're seriously telling me . . ." He spoke deliberately, every syllable taut with incredulity. "You're seriously telling me that, between them, the Russians and the Americans have done a deal, a super-power carve-up, under which the Soviets will get out of the Caribbean and Central America if in return the Americans will let them have Yugoslavia? In other words, this whole Bulgarian invasion plan is an orchestrated sham being carried out with our full knowledge and compliance! We just sit back and let them walk in. Or am I dreaming?"

"In essence, that is it—although it's not the way I'd choose to put it," Cunningham confirmed. "I can understand your surprise, but frankly your response is the emotional one I feared it would be. The fact is that Yugoslavia is already a socialist country—already dependent upon the Soviet Union economically on account of the Russians being both its biggest trading partners and its main suppliers of oil. In addition to which, since Tito's death, it's become increasingly fragmented and a thoroughly destabilizing influence on East-West relations. But, above all—and this is not just an American viewpoint—one cannot ignore the tremendous advantage to the West of having the Soviets out of the Caribbean and Central America. You may call it what you like—a trade-off, a carve-up, a sell-out—but geographically and politically it makes sense. Personally, I'd describe it, rather, as a . . . a mutually advantageous rationalization of our respective spheres of influence."

"And once the Soviets have got Yugoslavia, what about the other side of the deal—Cuba, Nicaragua, and the rest?"

"I don't know for sure, but I imagine it will be some sort of rerun of the Bay of Pigs—only this time properly coordinated, professionally equipped, and ultimately successful. Frankly, the Russians aren't going to shed many tears over Castro. He's always been too much of a maverick for their taste and he's been muddying the water in places like Africa. Of course they'll bang the table at the UN and protest loudly about imperialist aggression but that'll be purely for public consumption."

"And with Cuba returned to the fold, Nicaragua and the rest will quickly follow suit. Is that the thinking?"

"Within a matter of months, I'd imagine. Without the practical and psychological support of either the Russians or the Cubans, it could even be weeks."

Neither spoke. Even the duck had given up and paddled off. Medcalf still found it hard to believe the evidence of his own ears. And yet the more he thought about it, the more he could see how the arrangement could appeal to both sides. As much as he despised Cunningham's awful euphemisms, it really would be "a mutually advantageous rationalization of respective spheres of influence." Certainly the West had paid a high price. Allowing the Russians into Yugoslavia would give them their first direct access to the Mediterranean. In a time of conflict Greece and Turkey could find themselves quickly isolated from the rest of NATO, while Italy, whose entire Adriatic flank would now be facing three hundred miles of potentially hostile coastline, would be perilously exposed. And yet NATO, of which the United States was both the senior partner and principal bankroller, had presumably been persuaded that this was not too high a price to pay for the removal of that festering thorn in the side of Western Democracy, Cuba—particularly if at the same time it enabled the Americans to clean the Commies out of their own Central American backyard. Overall, it probably did make sense and, seen in the historical perspective, it was no more than the sort of "accommodation" that super powers had attempted to negotiate with one another down the ages. There was just one query in Medcalf's mind:

"What's NATO's role in all this, then?"

"NATO doesn't have a role in this," snapped Cunningham. "I've already told you, you're no longer working for them."

"But if they know about it, they—"

"They don't know about it."

Medcalf reeled. Still recovering from the first blow, he was quite unprepared for this second.

"You mean NATO is deliberately to be kept in ignorance of all this? I don't believe it. Cunningham, this is preposterous!"

The reverberations rippled across the pool. Cunningham swung around to see if anybody else had heard, but the nearest people were over a hundred yards way by the Viet Nam memorial. Even so, he dropped his voice to an urgent whisper:

"For crying out loud, Medcalf, you of all people should know what NATO is like. The place leaks like a bloody sieve!" He paused and, adopting a more conciliatory tone, continued, "Look, it's not that we—ourselves and the Americans, that is—it's not that we *want* to keep this to ourselves. It's the Soviets who are insisting on it being kept under wraps, and you've got to see their point of view. What would the rest of the world say if they were to be seen blatantly trading territory with the West? It would make a mockery of everything Marx said about the world revolutionary struggle ... it would put them in an intolerably embarrassing position. You're the political analyst; you must see that."

Medcalf did—and much else. The global rationalization plan had suddenly taken on a very different aspect. The reason NATO couldn't be trusted, he now suspected, had less to do with Brussels' ability to keep its collective mouth shut than with the awkward questions which the other NATO members might ask. The advantages for America were obvious, but it was hard to see how Western Europe was going to benefit. More to the point, if Yugoslavia could be traded under the table for Cuba and Nicaragua today, who was to say that Austria wouldn't be traded for Angola tomorrow, or Greece for Kampuchea the day after? Where would the line be drawn? How many times could Yalta be revisited?

Just as worrying, though, was Britain's role in the whole affair—assuming it really had one. Now that Medcalf thought about it, Cunningham had been suspiciously vague on details.

"So we've been made privy to all this because we're the Americans' oldest and most trusted allies. That it?" he asked.

"Precisely," replied Cunningham, "and that's nothing to be ashamed of either."

"When?"

"When what?"

"When were we told—when were we let in on The Big Secret?"

Cunningham looked away, his attention suddenly absorbed again by Lincoln.

"I can't tell you exactly—but for some time, I imagine."

The choice of verb was significant. Medcalf moved round to face him.

"You imagine, do you? Well, let me tell you what *I* imagine, Cunningham. I imagine that the first H.M.'s government knew about any of this was shortly after you got in touch with the State Department last night and told them what I'd just told you over dinner. The moment you revealed that we knew not only about the intended invasion of Macedonia but also about the Russians' part in it, your friends at Foggy Bottom would have realized the cat was out of the bag. Don't you see? They'd have had no option then but to tell us the truth. The only way to stop us squawking to

Brussels and blowing the whole thing wide open was to make all three of us co-conspirators—you, me, and H.M.G.! If I hadn't turned up here last night with this can of worms, it would've been Grenada all over again—"Gee, shucks, you guys, we're real sorry about not telling you in advance, but, hey, don't you worry, 'cause you're still our biggest buddy, right?' "

He broke off. He recalled Anelia's taunts about Britain's subservience to the United States and how quick he had been to deny them. Yet she had been closer to the truth than either of them had suspected. Seen in the present light, Britain was as near to becoming the fifty-first state of the U.S. as Bulgaria was to becoming the sixteenth republic of the U.S.S.R. But at least in Bulgaria there were those like Anelia who were willing to risk their lives to alert others, whereas Cunningham would happily have sold his sister into prostitution and his grandmother into slavery so long as he could still flit between Langley and Foggy Bottom.

"Just tell me this, Cunningham . . . ," he said, sufficiently emboldened by anger to grab him by the elbow. "When the Mediterranean has become the new 'Red Sea,' when Yugoslavia, Austria, Greece, Turkey, and Italy have all tumbled and NATO is in ruins, what do you think is going to happen to that faithful li'l ol' American ally off the north coast of Europe? Do you really believe that one fine day the carrier *Nimitz* will appear off Land's End and tow the entire British Isles across the Atlantic to the safe, freedom-loving waters of the U.S. of A.—to be moored off Coney Island as some sort of living theme park?"

Cunningham shook himself free of Medcalf's grasp. For the first time, his eyes flamed with something like passion.

"As a matter of historical record, Medcalf, the scenario you've just outlined—Europe overrun and Britain standing alone—was precisely the situation in 1941. But I keep forgetting that such things are before your time. The answer to your question, however, is that the Americans would no doubt do what they've done in the past whenever we've needed their help—they would give it! And for that reason alone—for the occasions they've bailed us out before and yes, for the fact that you and I wouldn't be indulging in this argument now if they hadn't—we owe them our loyalty!"

An ill-tempered silence fell between the two men. When Cunningham spoke again, Medcalf could barely hear him.

"I saved your life this morning, Medcalf. Frankly, I'm beginning to wonder why."

"What do you mean?"

"I mean that there was a discussion this morning at the State Department as to what would be the best containment policy to adopt. At one point in that discussion there was a majority view that the only way to ensure that your interpreter friend's message didn't get back to Brussels was to dispose of the messenger quickly and cleanly here in situ before he had the chance to pass it on to anybody else, whether deliberately or by accident. It was me, Medcalf—*me*, who pointed out that, if you didn't report back to Brussels in person, Van Kleef might send somebody else out, and that rather than dispose of you, we should send you back to Brussels with a false message. It was me who then had to assure them of your compliance with such an arrangement, of your—to use that outmoded word—loyalty. Had I not thought I was in a position to give that assurance, Medcalf, you would by now have been a dead man—an unidentified corpse in possession of a patently bogus passport and obviously up to no good."

Cunningham was too subtle to point out that the same fate might still await him, but the possibility had the desired effect on Medcalf. The man before him was suddenly no longer a jokey caricature of the British diplomat abroad. There was every reason to believe what he had just said: that he really did have power of life and death over him and, in at least one instance, had already exercised it. Not even in the DS Headquarters in Sofia had Medcalf felt such proximity to the powers of his own extermination.

He turned away and stared back along the Mall toward the Capitol a mile away, its white dome blocked out by the intervening obelisk. Although his brain protested at the overload of information, one thing was clear—that realistically he had no choice but to go along with Cunningham; at least to give the appearance of cooperation. Whatever decision he subsequently took, it could never be implemented by a dead man.

"Perhaps you're right," he said, aware how unconvincing the words sounded even to his own ears.

From Cunningham's expression it was evident that they had fared no better in *his* ears. The about-turn had been suspiciously sudden.

"You'll go along with the plan then? You'll cooperate in sending a false message back to Van Kleef?"

"But I thought the idea was that I should take it back personally."

"That was just one possibility. On reflection, I think it better if you stay here and we send back a coded message via the embassy. We'll need you to check it, though, and there's a chance that Van Kleef will come back with some questions for you."

Each avoided the other's gaze. They both knew what "on reflection" meant. After his emotional outburst, Medcalf was no longer to be trusted out of sight. He was still on the death list—just temporarily transferred to the PENDING section.

"Anyway, we don't have a lot of time," Cunningham said, placing a guiding hand against his back. "I'd better go and consult the head of the East European desk at Foggy Bottom about the contents of this message. I'll see you back to the hotel first and be in touch later in the day so you can look it over and fill in any details. Meantime, I think it's better if you stay in your room. Believe me, Medcalf—with the knowledge you possess you could be at considerable risk."

◆ 25 ◆

"THERE AREN'T enough brandies in the world for you to repay me for what I've done for you in the last twenty-four hours," said Lieberman, seeing DC walk up to his table in the second-floor canteen.

DC laid down his tray.

"Tell me the worst, if it's not going to ruin my digestion."

"You've been so busy you won't believe it—any more, I suspect, than Murphy believed it."

"You mean he's been trying to get me."

"Let's put it this way: I'm surprised your Bellboy hasn't branded a large rectangle on your butt with the heat it must've been generating."

"You think I should call him?"

"I figure it'd be a nice idea. I'm sure he's been worried about you."

Fifteen minutes later Murphy's voice was on the line:

"I'm just saddened, DC, that I should have to tell a man of your seniority that I don't expect one of my heads of section to go AWOL. I'm doubly saddened because I thought you and I had a new understanding."

DC made no reply. Murphy's typically proprietorial attitude to *his* staff made him boil but experience suggested it was best to let the man talk himself out—which was always easier on the phone than in the flesh. To Lieberman's amusement, DC held the handpiece at an angle to his ear as though to avoid steam from a high-pressure hose. Finally, Murphy asked when he was coming back to the Cape.

"Just as soon as I've been to the Airlantic Maintenance Center at Kennedy."

"And what in Christ's name do you plan to do there—if I may ask?"

"I need to run a few checks, go over the records—all within the area of Human Performance, Doug."

"Sounds to me more like a job for Operations," retorted Murphy.

DC said nothing. He was on dangerous ground.

"Okay," said Murphy to his surprise, then added, "I'll send Collins down to meet you there."

DC gagged. The prospect of Collins spying on his every move and reporting back to base was about as welcome as having a one-armed kleptomaniac in a munitions factory. But if that was the price he had to pay for a closer look at Airlantic's Maintenance Center, there was no alternative.

"Fine," he heard himself say. "I'll look forward to seeing him there."

Besides, Murphy was right: It was really a job for Operations, not Human Performance.

♦ **26** ♦

FIVE MINUTES back inside the hotel were enough to confirm Medcalf's worst fears. He was a prisoner.

Beneath his window a plainclothes agent was holding an animated conversation with the lapel of his overcoat; the bedside telephone functioned only for the purposes of calling Room Service; the television and radio had stopped working altogether; and—although he had yet to put it to the test—he had no doubt that the wide-shouldered gentlemen sitting outside at either end of the corridor were there to ensure that he followed instructions and stayed in his room. It was even conceivable that the room itself had been wired for sound.

All, of course, for his own protection. As Cunningham had said, he was at considerable risk.

It was too late now for regrets, but he cursed himself for having so openly displayed his emotions before Cunningham. Cursed himself, too, for not having thought more quickly on his feet and made a dash for it before he had allowed Cunningham to escort him back to the hotel. They would no doubt have tracked him down eventually but at least he would have had a good chance of making a phone call to Brussels before they did. Now the only certainty was that they would dispose of him as soon as he was of no further use—which might be only hours away.

Waves of panic broke over him, accompanied by alternating bouts of sweating and shivering. Feeling sick, he rushed to the bathroom and started retching over the basin. For a while he felt calmer, but again the shivering gave way to sweating as the next wave gathered momentum out on the horizon of his imagination. He looked up and, seeing his face in the mirror, scarcely recognized it. The expression was wild and haunted. Perhaps it wasn't he after all; perhaps all this was happening to somebody else whose body, by a quirk of time and space, he had temporarily inhabited—and would soon vacate . . . He stopped himself. Such thoughts were the delusions of a dying man.

Eventually, a natural stoicism asserted itself. He became almost philosophical, recalling some lines from an Egyptian tomb which, in their rejection of any conventional religious consolation, had always appealed to him: "The end of life is sad. It means the loss of what you once had. It means knowing nothing of the dawn of a morning which does not come. It means sleeping when the sun is in the East." He repeated the words aloud like a mantra. Then he remembered that Hemingway had said much the same thing, but with characteristic bluntness: "We are to make what we can of life by a pragmatic ethic spun bravely out of man himself in full and steady cognizance that the end is darkness."

Again he felt despair take hold of him, the fear rising in his throat, oozing through his pores—a fear of the dark.

He forced himself to think positively. All hope wasn't lost. If, by some self-administered psychological trick, he could convince himself that the global carve-up was justified, it might not be too late to convince even Cunningham of his enthusiasm for it. He might not be sent back to Brussels, but there was still a chance he might live.

After all, when Cunningham had first told him about it, he *had* thought it was right. At least that it made sense; in politics, it was too much to expect anything ever to be as simple as right or wrong.

But that had been when he thought NATO had been consulted and had agreed to the arrangement. Before his loyalty had been split. And, as Cunningham had indicated, this whole business was a question more of loyalty than logic.

But loyalty to whom? That was the real question.

For Cunningham it was simple—"My country, right or wrong!" and, by extension, "My country's ally, right or wrong!" But Cunningham hadn't spent fifteen years of his life working for NATO. He could never appreciate that NATO was as deserving of loyalty as any sovereign state; that it, too, had been brought into existence by an act of political will and was as much concerned with the defense and liberty of the citizens of its member nations as those individual nations themselves were. Since both Britain and America were members of NATO, it was therefore a patent contradiction to imply, as Cunningham had, that in remaining loyal to NATO he was being disloyal to Britain and America. It was not *he* who had changed sides, but they. It was not *he* who was threatening to betray his country and its ally, but they who together were betraying the whole Western Alliance.

The truth was that there was no truth. It was the Law of Shifting Absolutes: The more one argued, the less likely one was to reach a conclusion. The only truth in such circumstances was emotional truth—the "gut feeling" that went beyond logic and loyalty.

His thoughts turned again to Anelia—and a realization which, his mind having been so fully occupied over the last hour, now crept into his consciousness with the lethal stealth of a serpent . . .

He had betrayed her.

Unwittingly, it was true, but no less effectively for that. The night before, when still in ignorance of the whole truth, he had told Cunningham everything he knew—not just the salient facts, but *everything*; Cunningham would then have relayed it to his colleagues in the State Department and, since the Americans were now in cahoots with the Russians, they would have lost no time in revealing to the Russians the identity of the Bulgarian traitor who was threatening to jeopardize the whole agreement.

He was suddenly horrified by the chain of events he had set off. He stood transfixed in the middle of the bathroom, staring at himself in the mirror, like a man who has dropped a cigarette in a cornfield and watches helplessly as the flames run off in all directions.

What would they do to her?

There was only one possible answer. The more painful question was what would they do to her before that. It didn't bear contemplation. He let out a long moan of anguish, hammering his fists on the washbasin. What had he done? The prospect of her exposure, torture, and death was awful enough, but that he of all people—he who had so admired her courage and coolness—should have been the instrument of her betrayal!

A wild resolve was cast within him. She would die and he would die; for both of them the end would be darkness—a shared darkness if such a thing were possible—but one way or another her message would get out. He owed it to her as he had never owed anything to anyone in his life.

He splashed water over his face and, standing now in the doorway, surveyed the bedroom. There *had* to be a way out—if not for himself, at least for the information with which she had entrusted him.

He called Room Service and ordered a glass of milk and a chicken salad sandwich. There was the possibility, he reasoned, that the waiter might be suborned. Failing that, he might be able to overpower him and walk out in his uniform before the thugs at the end of the corridor realized what was happening.

Within seconds of the door opening, he knew the idea was a nonstarter.

Not only was the waiter built like an ex-marine, but a telltale earpiece suggested he probably *was* an ex-marine, for here without a shadow of doubt was another agent.

The irony wasn't lost on Medcalf: The condemned man had unwittingly bidden his jailers bring him his last meal. Looking through the half-open door, he could see one of the corridor heavies hovering outside. Clearly, he was no ordinary prisoner, but the recipient of the full five-star maximum security treatment. It was grimly flattering.

As the "waiter" laid the tray on the coffee table, voices seeped in from the corridor—loud and Italian. Doors slammed. The delegation of visiting parliamentarians had returned from their appointment across the street. It was lunchtime.

Alone again, Medcalf lay on the bed, despairing now of success. The doors still slamming up and down the corridor symbolized all too aptly the death of hope.

The sound of a bedside radio percolated through from the next room. The words were loud enough to be heard but, irritatingly, not loud enough to be understood. He tried to clear the distraction from his mind, but without success. Then he stopped trying . . . and wondered.

If only he could get the message out to one of the Italians, who could then carry it back to Rome and pass it on to Brussels. Certainly any Italian deputy or senator would immediately appreciate the importance of Anelia's information and its implications for the future of both NATO and Italy itself. Just as important, such a man would have the authority necessary to convince Van Kleef that he was telling the truth. With most of the corridor apparently occupied by the Italians, it had to be the best hope. Perhaps now the *only* hope.

He leaped from the bed and walked over to the wall through which the radio could still be heard. Two-thirds of it was covered by a large built-in wardrobe and dressing table. The one-third that wasn't showed no signs of there ever having been an interconnecting door, which was what he was hoping to find.

Undismayed, he inspected the wardrobe unit and found that it had been screwed to the wall with the clear intention that it should stay that way. It was impossible to budge it even a fraction of an inch and casting around, he could find nothing in the room that could be improvised as a screwdriver.

He looked inside the wardrobe cupboard, but its back turned out to be similarly well fixed. He pulled out the drawers but again the back was paneled and screwed in place.

He stood up, frustrated.

Above the drawers was a large mirror that formed part of the dressing table. It was set into the unit but held in place merely by sliding clips which, with a little pressure, it was possible to ease back. As the mirror fell forward, he caught it and laid it on the bed.

Behind, there was wall all right—but still no sign of any door, past or present. There was no point in looking further.

That left only the room on the other side, the bathroom side. But, recalling that the entire bathroom was tiled from floor to ceiling, he was prepared to dismiss the idea without even a cursory look. Besides, he had no reason to believe the room was even occupied.

Yet at this stage even a long shot had to be considered.

As he had feared, the hard white surface gleamed back at him from every wall—except for the area above the wash-basin occupied by a long rectangular mirror that had been permanently fixed in place behind a stainless steel frame.

On hands and knees, he examined every inch of the tilework in the hope of finding perhaps a panel that might give access to the plumbing. There was none. It was hopeless. He pulled the light switch to put out the light and was at that moment—and for the first time—aware of where the light was coming from.

Not from the ceiling but from *above* it.

Looking up, he saw that it filtered through large plastic diffuser panels which, held together by intersecting aluminum strips, constituted what was in effect a false ceiling.

His hopes buoyed, he dragged a chair in from the bedroom and, standing on it, found that the plastic panels merely rested on the aluminum supports—presumably so as to ease their removal when the fluorescent tubes had to be changed.

He removed the panel closest to the common wall by first pushing it up and then pulling it, diagonally edgewise, down through the hole. Then, with his feet on the wash-basin, he steadied himself against the adjacent shower rail so that his head and shoulders were now above the level of the false ceiling.

The first impression was disappointing. By the cold light of the tubes he could see that the common wall continued above the level of the false ceiling. Yet it was no longer masonry or brick, as he assumed the wall behind the tiles to be. He tapped it.

It was wood—a sheet of flimsy plywood.

Its function seemed to be not so much structural as—what? Certainly not decorative, unless the hotel believed that every guest was in the habit of sticking his head through the bathroom ceiling.

A moment's thought suggested the answer.

In order to simplify the plumbing arrangements, the architects of the hotel—or more likely its most recent renovators—had followed the standard practice and arranged the bathrooms back-to-back along each side of the corridor, so that each bedroom suite was laid out as a mirror image of its immediate neighbor. The purpose of the plywood partition was clear: It was to stop the light from the bathroom of one room from filtering into the bathroom of the next room.

Standing now on tiptoe, he clawed at it and, getting a purchase along one side, pulled.

It sprang back with such a whiplash that he was thrown off balance and to save himself had to throw out a flattened palm onto one of the other diffuser panels. For a second—long enough for him to regain his balance—the plastic held, but then burst beneath his weight into a hundred brittle fragments that showered down onto the tiled floor.

His heart flipped. The sound as it ricocheted off the tile surfaces echoed in his skull a thousand times louder. And longer.

Surely someone would come running and he would be discovered. He had a sudden vision of himself—a political fugitive caught in the barbed wire along some strip of no-man's-land, waiting helplessly for the coup-de-grâce from a single pistol shot or burst of automatic fire.

He clenched his teeth till the roots ached. But, whether because the bathroom door was closed or because the guest in the next room was playing his radio so loudly, the noise went unnoticed.

He breathed again. At least it proved one thing: The room had not been wired for sound. And there, looking back through the hole where the partition had been, he could now see the strip lights and diffuser panels of the bathroom next door.

Three minutes later he dropped down on the other side—covered in dust and cobwebs but otherwise unscathed.

The bathroom, illuminated only by the striplights from his side of the wall, was littered with evidence of occupation—but no immediate evidence that it was Italian occupation. The razor on the shelf beneath the mirror could have been bought anywhere, while the bottle of aftershave next to it was French. His hands shaking, he seized on a half-opened shaving kit by the basin and gently tipped its contents onto one of the neatly folded hand towels.

An aerosol can fell out and, as it rolled, revealed just three glorious words—*Spuma da barba*. Shaving lather. He could have kissed it.

But the next step, he belatedly realized, was going to require a fair amount of tact and diplomacy—to which, until now, he had given not a moment's thought.

He put his ear to the closed door and listened. The only sound was the rattling of clothes hangers on a wardrobe rail. Somebody was either packing or unpacking.

He stood up straight, dusted down his shirt and trousers, inspected himself in the mirror, and considered the protocol of the situation. Should he wait till he was discovered, walk straight in, or knock? Whatever he did, he was going to be a source of considerable surprise, but a display of courtesy, however bizarre in the circumstances, might at least make it less offensive.

He knocked.

◆ **27** ◆

ALAN C. FAIRNINGTON had come into the aircraft industry by accident—the fatal one that had buried his elder brother's light aircraft six feet deep in a potato field outside Boise, Idaho.

Had it not been for that, Fairnington would have remained what his father had always intended—public affairs director of an Airlantic subsidiary making plastic moldings, with a token seat at the bottom end of the Airlantic board.

It would have suited him fine, enabling him to devote his time to his passion for music while leaving the macho pursuit of "propelling steam chickens through the sky" to those with a more natural affinity for the job. If he now took any pleasure at all in finding himself, at thirty-eight, head of the sixth largest airline in the United States, it was the perverse one of being probably the only senior airline executive in the world not to have a model of a Boeing seven-something-seven on the corner of his desk or a Pratt & Whitney paperweight next to his blotter.

Instead, the most prominent features of Fairnington's office were an inscribed photograph of Vladimir Horowitz, presented after an Airlantic-sponsored concert, and a set of quadraphonic speakers playing continuous tape recitals of

Bach, Haydn, and Mozart which, by an unobtrusive sliding control let into the desktop, could be turned down to standard elevator volume when a call had to be instigated or answered.

Such concessions were seldom made, however, in the case of face-to-face meetings, and senior staffers had come to accept the expression of distant rapture that would steal over their chief executive's features in the middle of any discussion about profits-per-passenger-mile. Indeed, since it was a mark of special favor to be invited to share such moments, it was not unknown for more ambitious employees to sneak a look at the empty cassette cases on their way through the secretary's office in the belief that the correct identification of a Köchel number might be worth a couple of notches on the promotion scale.

It was an indication of Fairnington's change of temperament—normally so equable and detached—that his office was now silent for the first time in the history of his chairmanship. As DC was shown in, it was immediately evident to him that the man had had no more than a couple of hours' sleep since the accident. Even the perennial tan had gone.

"Ironic, isn't it?" Fairnington said with a weak smile. "I mean, that we should meet again in these circumstances. The last time you were sitting in that chair . . . you remember?"

DC could hardly forget. It had been the day of his departure from the company. Old Man Fairnington—a husk of his former self; broken by the death of his elder son—had sat like a judge in chambers reading out the terms of DC's termination of contract: the company doctor's bogus medical report in return for an agreement by DC that he would never again apply for a pilot's license. Alan, already being groomed by his father to take over the chairmanship, had stood in a corner of the room, a mere witness to the event. DC could recall only that Alan had shaken him by the hand and wished him luck on his way out.

"Look," said DC, "if you'd rather someone else conducted the inquiries, I mean if you feel uncomf—"

Fairnington cut him off.

"No, no. On the contrary, I'd prefer it that someone who knew the company from inside handled this. All I'd say is that, well, our guys are getting kinda jumpy about the way things seem to be going up at Chatham. From what our representatives on the investigation are telling us, it's looking like your guys have made up their minds . . . I mean, this fuel mismanagement theory. Now don't get the wrong idea. We're as anxious as anyone to get to the bottom of this but, well—and I don't have to tell *you* this—it's hard for a dead crew to speak in their own defense."

"If it's any comfort," DC responded, "the fuel mismanagement theory is not one I personally support, but I'm probably in a minority of one. That's why I'm here."

"So what d'you want to see?"

"It's more who than what. I've been through all the SP-3 maintenance records up at Chatham—at least the ones that make sense to me—but I need to talk to the men who did the work."

"You think it could be a maintenance failure?"

DC detected the tone of concern in Fairnington's voice, and knew the reason. An error by ground crew could be even more damaging for an airline than pilot error, since it implied that the fault might lie more with the system than with an individual. Pilots were daily being required to make split-second decisions affecting the safety of their passengers and the public could understand how mistakes could happen, even if they preferred not to think about them. But an error by a lazy, slapdash, or incompetent mechanic who was paid to do no more than perform routine tasks by number—that suggested a failure of screening or training. In short, it suggested something endemic, something rotten in the state of the airline.

*   *   *

Twenty minutes later, DC was down in the Airlantic maintenance hangar. Although a former pilot for the airline, he had seldom had occasion to visit the place and sat now in the supervisor's office, a glass box forty feet above ground level, from where it was possible to see most of what was going on.

Below, a persistent whistler was going through his repertoire out of sight beneath the wing of an aging 727, strains of a Sousa march echoing through the cavernous length of the one-hundred-foot-high, two-hundred-yard-long hangar. The man's colleagues, DC noted, seemed peculiarly resistant to the work tempo being set for them.

"The duty roster for the week before the flight," said the supervisor, handing him a single sheet of paper and adding crisply, "as you asked." He held his head at a slight backward tilt, a model of respectful resentment. Whoever was responsible for Flight 639 falling out of the sky, it wasn't one of *his* boys.

"Right," said DC. He drew breath. "As I understand it, the aircraft would have been in here for about twenty-four hours before the flight to Rome, and that was after coming in from Paris at seven the previous evening. What would your men have done to her during that time?"

"Just rectified any of the A.D.D.s in the Tech. Log that could be completed within the time."

"And according to the records which your company rep in Chatham has shown us, the only acceptable deferred defects noted in the log were a faulty Number Two generator and a weeping junction on hydraulic system 'C'—both of which were rectified and tested. Correct?"

"Correct."

"So, apart from that and the usual ramp check, cleaning and valeting, nothing else would have been done to that aircraft while it was in here."

"Right. It'd had its 'A' check a week earlier and was still well within acceptable flight hours."

"What about the magnetic plugs—the master chip detectors?"

"What about them?"

"When would they have been last changed or checked?"

The supervisor consulted his records.

"The plugs on all three engines were changed during that 'A' check I just told you about—a week before."

"And the occasions when the plugs would've been changed or checked after that but not gone down in the records?"

The supervisor leaned even farther back.

"Look, buddy, I've seen too many episodes of *Kojak* to be impressed by that sort of trick. I've told you, everything here goes down in the book, even if it's only a goddamn fly swatted in the cockpit. You know and I know—and if you don't I'm telling you—the only reason any of those plugs would've been pulled after that 'A' check was if one or more of those engines was having problems. You've seen the Tech. Log—and there ain't nothing there about no plugs. Now, c'mon, we both know the rules."

DC tapped his pen impatiently on the desk. Fairnington had warned him that the men were jumpy, but it was time to be blunt.

"I know the rules. What I don't know is how closely you and your colleagues here stick to them."

"Then let me tell you," retorted the supervisor, suddenly jutting forward. "Scru-pu-lous-ly. That's S-C-R—"

"So the possibility of somebody changing or even just checking those plugs without entering it in the book can be ruled out."

"You've got it."

DC stood up and walked over to the window. He stared down on the 727 below. She was evidently in for a refit; all the seats were out, lined up alongside in theatre-neat rows, and most of the access panels were open or off. About a dozen men were working on her—on, under, in. Mostly on their own.

Rows of clipboards were attached to an angled steel frame close to the fuselage and every now and again one of the mechanics would wander over either to pick one up or to replace one.

To the layman it might have looked like a well-run operation, but it was immediately clear to DC that, however the man behind him designated himself, no one was actually supervising the work on the ground.

Instead, it was all done by the old, time-honored system of work cards: A mechanic would be assigned to a particular job by the supervisor; would either be handed the card or would collect the appropriate card and clipboard from the frame; pick up the relevant parts in their plastic bags from stores; fit them; double check; and sign each step of the job in a small box by the side of the task description on the work card. In some cases, a colleague might be required to do the double-checking and countersign; in exceptional cases it might require the supervisor himself or even an inspector.

It was a good enough system if operated conscientiously, but it was also notorious for the abuse it invited.

DC didn't have to think very far back to cases where mechanics—usually on night shifts—had split the more routine work cards up according to their personal preferences, irrespective of how the supervisor had allocated them, and not only done each other's work, but even signed each other's initials. There was nothing more disruptive to an all-night poker session than having players drop out one after another.

Could it be, he now wondered, that a change in who did what on the night in question had resulted in a mix-up over aircraft and the plugs being changed on the SP-3 by mistake? It certainly wasn't beyond the realm of possibility—although getting the supervisor ever to admit such a thing would be another matter.

"Just out of interest," DC said without turning, "were there any other aircraft in the hangar at the same time as the

SP-3—another which maybe was scheduled to have its magnetic plugs checked or changed?"

"None," said the supervisor flatly, "and don't think I don't know what you're getting at. In fact, forget it."

DC swung round, all set to crease the lapels of the man's immaculately pressed white coat.

He stopped.

Scott Collins was standing in the doorway, fresh in from Chatham on Murphy's orders and wearing an expression like he had lost his way in a theatre and emerged on the wrong side of the footlights. He watched, dumbstruck, as DC picked up the telephone on the supervisor's desk.

"This is Matthew Di Coiano, National Transportation Safety Board, right? Will you put me through to your director of line maintenance? I seem to be having a small communications problem with one of his staff."

The supervisor capitulated.

"There's no need for that. You . . . you guys just don't understand how tense it's been around here these last couple of days. You just breeze in from Washington flashing your I.D.s around the place and treat us like we were . . . like we were a bunch of common criminals or something. You forget there's a human dimension to this."

DC came to within a foot of the supervisor's face. He could count every pore of his greasy skin.

"Save your talk about the human dimension for the relatives of those who died," he said under his breath. "In the meantime, I want the records for every other aircraft that passed through these hangars during the twenty-four hours that that SP-3 was in here. Like *now*. And, while you're about it, you can alert all those who were on shift during that time that I'll be wanting to interview them individually. If any are off-shift at home, call them in."

As the supervisor pushed past Collins, DC sat down.

"Yeah, okay, it was over the top—but he asked for it."

"Can I ask what it was about?" said Collins.

DC explained about the work cards and the possibility of a mix-up, adding, "There's just one problem: After all that, I'm not sure I'll know how to read the damned records when he comes back with them—and, sure as hell, he's not going to help me!"

"Maybe I can help you there," volunteered Collins. "It was part of our air force training to know our aircraft inside out—maintenance procedures included—so that in an emergency we could supervise a ground crew if they were unfamiliar with the type or model. The civilian procedures can't be so different. It should be a simple matter of checking the signatures against the cards and the cards against the sheets."

For the first time, DC saw "Shepherd's Boy Collins" in a new light.

"You've just gotten yourself a job, mister."

For the next three hours the two of them sat at separate desks in the supervisor's office, Collins working through a pile of work cards higher than his head and DC interviewing the mechanics, while the supervisor prowled the hangar below like a spurned bridegroom soliciting sympathy from the wedding guests.

It was a frustrating business: same questions, same answers—"No, sir, never touched any magnetic plugs . . ." "No, sir, never seen anyone else touch them neither"—and another name crossed off the list.

It was further complicated by the fact that the incidence of job swapping on the night shift was so great that a polygraph needle would have been better employed as a windshield wiper.

After the fourth interview, DC got up to stretch his legs. He asked Collins how he was doing.

"Nothing yet, although it would sure help if I knew why I was looking for references to magnetic plugs."

DC hesitated. If Collins was on the snooping mission for Murphy he suspected, it would be folly to tell him in detail of the 1983 Miami incident. On the other hand, since he seemed to know more about the nuts and bolts of aircraft than he himself, it made sense to exploit the man's superior knowledge. He compromised with a half-truth:

"It's just one of a number of theories. If that SP-3 was losing oil and not fuel, then, no matter what the service records may indicate, it could have been because a maintenance man tampered with the magnetic plugs."

"You mean under the impression it was another aircraft?"

"Maybe. The way the night shift seems to operate here, anything's possible."

"Sure, but even if somebody *did* tamper with the plugs, that doesn't . . . I mean you've still got to explain how and why the oil would have escaped. Those engines are so designed that, even if you removed the plugs altogether, you'd get only a very small leak because of the check valve. That's the idea of the check valve—to stop oil pouring out when the plugs are changed. We had cases in the Air Force where the plugs rattled loose in flight and dropped into the engine casing but the oil loss was minimal."

DC stared hard out of the window lest his expression betray him as he said:

"You're forgetting the seals on the plugs—the O-rings. If for some reason those plugs were put in without the seals, that would open the check valve and the oil would pour out around the plug . . . well, wouldn't it? I'm just speculating; you're the one who knows about these things."

"I guess so, but it's kind of hard to imagine a qualified airframe and power plant mechanic not realizing that the seals were off—and making the same mistake on all three engines."

A silhouetted figure appeared at the frosted glass door; it was the next mechanic for interview. DC returned to his desk with the comforting knowledge that, however hard Collins found it to imagine such a possibility, there was at least one indisputable precedent.

Eight interviews later, that comfort had worn literally paper thin. Collins's pile of work cards had been transferred, card by card, from table to floor with not a single reference to magnetic plugs discovered. DC looked at his watch to find it was already half past seven. There was little activity below, the refit of the 727 being apparently a job for the dayshift only. A new supervisor had clocked on and was now chatting to his shift in one of the rest areas.

"I guess it's time we had something to eat," grunted DC, swinging his jacket matador-style over his shoulders.

Collins followed him down the iron stairway.

"D'you mind if we go through the engine shop on the way?" he said. "I'm none too familiar with civilian power plants and, well, I'd sure like to see one of these SP-3 engines stripped."

A pair of swing doors made of soft transparent plastic gave access to the engine shop—plastic so they could be nudged open by the forklift trucks that trundled around the maintenance depot.

The huge engines—seven feet in diameter, three and a half tons apiece and capable of developing a thrust six times that—were stripped of their casings and lined up in bays, some hanging in chains from steel cradles, others nestling on wheeled dollies. DC led the way along a line.

"There's one, same type," he said, indicating one of those on a dolly.

Collins walked around it, stopping at certain points to inspect it on flexed knees. Finally he singled out a gleaming steel pipe about an inch in diameter. His finger was pointing to a knurled knob set in its own housing and let into the pipe.

"And this, I guess, is your number-one suspect—the master chip detector plug. Think anybody would object if I took a closer look?"

Without waiting for an answer, he gave the plug a quick push and twist, and pulled it free of its housing. A couple of drops of oil fell to the immaculately clean floor but that was all.

DC felt he should protest. Mechanics were rightly furious when anybody, no matter how senior, started tampering with their work without asking. The truth, however, was that he himself was eager to take a closer look. He watched, therefore, as Collins first wiped the plug clean with a sheet of absorbent paper and then slowly revolved it between his fingers beneath a powerful lamp on the adjacent workbench.

"That's kinda interesting," mused Collins, pointing to part of the knurled cap. "See there, where the pattern has been filed away—there's a number been engraved."

DC took a closer look. He was right; there was a clear "62."

"It'd sure be interesting," Collins remarked, "to know if they're all numbered that way—and why."

But DC was ahead of him.

"Forget the food," he said. "We're going to the lab."

♦ **28** ♦

THE SENATOR laid his last pair of trousers in the suitcase and, arms in perfect unison, closed the wardrobe doors with an aplomb that a Versailles footman would have envied.

In everything he did, even in the privacy of a hotel bedroom, Senator Claudio Bracciolini acted as though under the scrutiny of an all-seeing observer. As he often remarked, there was no better training for the way one conducted oneself in public than the way one behaved in private. And in seventy years—more than half of them in politics—he had never once been faulted on his public performance.

He sighed and passed an immaculately manicured hand over his wavy gray hair. This time tomorrow, he calculated, he would be back in Rome. And glad of it. At his age, these trips were sheer purgatory. He seemed to have done more "glad-handing" in the last week than in his entire political career. It was worse than campaigning for the American presidency!

He looked at the signed photograph propped against the dressing table mirror and smiled. Like kids going home from a party, they had each been given one on the way out. It had all been very unsubtle—the sort of thing that in Italy one associated more with the world of pop stars and advertising promotions. Still, his wife would be pleased. No doubt she would have it framed in silver like the rest and put in the drawing room along with all the other popes and presidents. Since the restoration of Richard Nixon to the corner table, it might even go next to him—but that was the sort of weighty political decision only she could take.

He glanced at his watch. There were thirty-five minutes to go before they were all due downstairs. Then it would be off on another grueling schedule—mercifully the last. From the hotel they would be bused up to Capitol Hill for a farewell lunch and speeches; then to Washington National Airport to take the shuttle to New York where they were to be guests of honor at a reception organized by the Italian-American Club at the Pierre—before at last being driven to JFK for the flight home. Another six, seven—eight!—hours to go.

Just thinking about it left him exhausted.

He looked around the bedroom, checked the drawers of the dressing table, and made a mental note that he still had to buy a present for his youngest grandson, Claudio II—his favorite grandson, although of course he kept that to himself. He smiled. It had been a touching and felicitous gesture by his daughter-in-law to suggest that the boy should be named after his grandfather and—as though Nature had taken the cue—the six-year-old really did seem, of all his grandchildren, to be the most like him. No, he must not forget to get him something—if necessary, at the airport.

There was a knock at the door. Or was it next door?

He checked to be sure and found the corridor empty except for the secret service men at either end. They had appeared only that morning and, for the life of him, he couldn't understand why he and his colleagues should suddenly be more vulnerable on the last day of their stay than on any of the previous days—unless there had been a death threat, in which case they should have been told.

Again a knock, and coming this time—he could have sworn it—from the bathroom!

He told himself it wasn't possible but, turning the handle, came face to face with a man in his mid-forties with disheveled curly hair.

In his bathroom.

"I owe you an apology," the man said. The accent was unmistakably English and something about his demeanor told the senator that this was not one of the hotel maintenance men checking out the plumbing.

He blinked, but a lifetime in Italian politics had accustomed the senator to almost every situation it was possible to imagine. Compared with catching one's prime minister *in flagrante* with a secretary, this rated quite low on the seismic scale of social shockers.

"Bracciolini," he said, extending a hand and slightly inclining his head, "Senator Claudio Bracciolini."

"Oh, Medcalf—Adrian Medcalf," responded the Englishman, adding uncertainly, "*piacere* . . . pleased to meet you . . . Look, you must think I am mad, or worse, and I promise you I don't make a habit of breaking into other people's bathrooms . . . Sorry, I'm assuming you speak English."

"It is all right. My English is very adequate for the understanding but perhaps not so good for the speaking. But, please, sit yourself."

He indicated the upright chair by the writing table and, taking a couple of miniature Scotches from the hospitality fridge, poured them into glasses. He handed one to his visitor and was pleased to see that, of the two of them, the Englishman was now registering the greater surprise.

"You wish ice?" he asked.

Medcalf shook his head and took the whisky. His hands were shaking so violently that he had to steady the glass on the corner of the writing table.

"There is something that I must tell you," he quavered, "something that is very important for your country but something that will also put your life at risk just to know it. And we don't have a lot of time."

For nearly twenty minutes the senator sat and listened. Although years of practice had taught him to disguise his emotions beneath a veneer of suave skepticism, he was truly alarmed by what the Englishman had to say.

In his own mind he had little doubt that it was true in most respects—the man was who he said he was; had been where he said he had been; and had been told what he said he had been told. Certainly Bulgaria had been in and out of the news for weeks and the latest reports of Bulgarian troops massing on the Yugoslavian border were now leading most bulletins. The Englishman's story therefore had the ring of truth about it—but, more persuasively, his fear for his own life explained the extraordinary lengths he had gone to in order to reach him, as well as the sudden appearance of the secret service men at every corner. Besides, the senator reasoned, a common thief would hardly have bothered to knock!

Yet, was it really possible that the United States would betray her NATO allies—even for a prize as valuable as Cuba?

He questioned the Englishman closely, but, as he did so, he was persuaded as much by his own recollections as by the answers he got.

He remembered how, late one evening more than a decade earlier, he had been summoned by his friend, the U.S. ambassador in Rome, to a private meeting in the American Embassy on the Via Veneto.

It was 1976 and Italy was in the campaign for its most important elections since World War II. For the first time, there was the possibility of the so-called historic compromise becoming a fact—of the PCI, the Italian Communist Party, entering the government as a coalition partner with the Christian Democrats.

The ambassador had told him of the apoplectic reaction of the State Department back home to the possibility of Communists assuming ministerial power in the government of a NATO member and had asked him, as an eminent Christian Democrat and friend of America, how it was possible that he and his countrymen were not similarly scandalized by the prospect of "this red serpent in the bosom of the Western Alliance."

In response, the senator had tried to explain the difference between Euro-Communism and East European Communism and to reassure His Excellency that the Communist Party was no more likely to hand NATO secrets over to the Russians than was his own party.

But he had left knowing he had failed and, for the first time, aware of a gulf of comprehension as wide as the Atlantic itself.

He had often wondered since what would have happened if the Communists *had* gotten into the government at that election—how Secretary of State Kissinger would have implemented his public declaration to "deal with that outcome." Certainly, at the time, the ambassador had left no doubt in his mind that if the other NATO members didn't vote Italy out of the Alliance the Americans would pack their bags in Brussels and take the next flight home.

In truth, NATO had always been a fragile alliance and, a decade later, was no less so.

Although now for different reasons.

On this trip more than any previous trip the senator had detected a disturbing element in the American consciousness— an assertiveness that was not just post-Vietnam, post-Watergate, or post-Iran—but post all of these things put together. He seemed to have spent most of the past week on the receiving end of sentences that began, "What's great about America is . . ." and led inevitably into, "What's wrong with Europe is . . ."

The "Fortress America" mentality, they called it, and if the mentality was now becoming a dangerous reality, it was no great wonder. Even if he could not condone it, he could understand it.

For more than twenty years, America had been kicked around the globe while defending Freedom and Democracy on behalf of peoples who wanted it but weren't prepared to fight for it, pay for it, or even speak up for it. One moment the Europeans were begging for American missiles to protect themselves; the next they were on the streets protesting about the way those same missiles had been "forced" upon them.

If Moscow had now offered Washington the chance to clean out the Caribbean moat, nobody should be surprised that the Americans had been tempted to accept the offer and pull up the drawbridge on the rest of the world. What the Englishman was saying, far from being wild and fanciful, was all too plausible in the prevailing political climate.

"And what are you wishing me to do about this?" he asked when Medcalf had finished speaking.

"You mean I've persuaded you that I'm not a madman?" said Medcalf, as astonished as he was relieved.

The senator smiled. "I would say that in my life in politics I have heard stories which have sounded much more mad but which afterwards have been revealed to be true."

Medcalf leaned forward, hands together. He felt calmer now, although whether on account of the Scotch or the senator's receptive ear he couldn't say.

"There are just two things I would like you to do," he began. "First, tell some of those in your group whom you trust—just two or three will be enough—what I have told you. But please impress upon them that, while they are on American soil, they must not tell anyone else and, above all, must not discuss it over the telephone . . . Second, as soon as you are safely back in Rome, inform either this man Herman Van Kleef, my superior in Brussels, or, if it seems quicker and easier to go through diplomatic channels, contact your NATO ambassador in Brussels so that he can pass it on personally to Van Kleef. It's vital that Van Kleef understand that any message that comes from the British Embassy here in Washington or via MI6 in London is *not* to be believed. But, I must repeat, do nothing until you are back in Rome. I really do fear that your hosts here would go to any lengths to stop this information from getting out."

The senator looked puzzled.

"But explain to me why you wish that I tell my colleagues. Is it not better that I alone keep the secret until we will return to Rome?"

Medcalf hesitated, but decided the senator could take the truth.

"On balance, I think not. It's always possible that they will find out that I have been able to talk to you." He glanced back to the bathroom and the gaping hole in the ceiling. "It is therefore a good insurance policy that you tell two or three of the others."

"You mean in case I am killed."

"I'm afraid that is exactly what I mean."

"You do not think they might be tempted to kill all of us—the whole group? If they think you have talked to me, will they not also think that I have already talked with my colleagues?" He smiled. "We Italians have a bad reputation in this, you know!"

"That's what I'm hoping they'll think," replied Medcalf, "because then it will work both ways. It will be a good insurance policy for the message—and for you. There would be no point in killing you if they thought you might have already talked to the others; your murder would only attract attention and would do nothing to contain the leak of information. As for killing *all* of you, I cannot deny that it's a possibility, but I think it's a remote one. I doubt whether even the American secret service, with all their expertise and technological resources, would be capable of arranging—and guaranteeing—a dozen fatal accidents in the time available. But I repeat, these are only insurance policies; I'm assuming that nobody will ever know I've talked to you." He glanced again nervously at the open bathroom door. "What time is your flight?"

"Eight o'clock this evening, I think, but let me check." The senator removed a typed schedule from his wallet and read, "JFK . . . Flight AL 639 . . . Departure: 20:00 EST."

"At least you'll be flying Alitalia. That's good."

The senator frowned and pulled an airline ticket out of another flap in his wallet.

"No, no, Airlantic. Alitalia's prefix is AZ. Personally I would prefer Alitalia, but our congressional hosts are paying and I think they must be seen to support their own national airlines."

There was an abrupt change in his voice, a sudden concern.

"But you, what will you now do?"

Medcalf gave a smile of resignation.

"Tunnel back into my own room and wait."

"For death?"

"Not necessarily. There's a chance that if I sound convincing enough I might avoid it."

"But is there no possibility that you can escape?"

"I think not. You must have seen the way the place is guarded."

For several seconds the senator was lost in thought. He had taken a liking to the strange Englishman and he was a good judge of character. This Medcalf reminded him of his own elder son, Bruno. They would be about the same age and shared the same contradictory quality of self-sufficiency and vulnerability. He stood up and, hand theatrically to his chin, paced the floor.

"I think there is a way," he said at last, looking at his watch. "My colleagues and I, we are agreed to meet downstairs in the lobby in ten minutes. So why do we not do this: Why do I not telephone three, perhaps four, of them on this floor and tell them to come here to my room—tell them there is"—he threw out a rhetorical hand—"something I am wishing to discuss, a quick drink, perhaps a little celebration before we will leave Washington? We will then put a coat on you, an arm around you, and we will all leave the room together, talking and laughing. We will be in the elevator before the secret service men will notice a thing, because their eyes will always be on your room!" He reached for the bedside telephone. "It is worth a try, as you say."

Medcalf put his hand over the phone.

"It may be worth a try but it's not worth the risk. There are secret service men at both ends of the corridor, which means a face-to-face confrontation at some stage would be unavoidable. There'll probably also be one in the lobby—masquerading as the bellhop, I wouldn't be surprised—and, since I know for a fact that there's one patrolling outside beneath our windows, it's certain that there'll be another keeping an eye on the front entrance."

"But you cannot possibly go back to your room and . . . and wait for them to come and get you. You are yet a young man!"

"I appreciate your concern, Senator. But ask yourself, What would happen if I *did* get out of here? I'll tell you. My absence would be discovered within a couple of hours at most; they'd quickly work out my escape route; and then not just me but all of you, too, would be in danger—as well as the message. I cannot take that risk. I have made it my responsibility to see that this message gets back to Brussels, to those who sent me to Bulgaria in the first place. With your help, it now stands an excellent chance of making it while there's still time for NATO to make a correct, forceful, and, above all, *informed* response to the Bulgarian invasion. My own safety is and must remain of secondary consideration only. When I know you're safely out of the country at eight o'clock tonight, perhaps then I'll try to make an escape. But not before. The person who gave me this message entrusted it to me as I now entrust it to you. She knew the risks she was taking and she knew that, if things went wrong, there'd be no possibility of her escaping—and I fear that I've already betrayed her without at the time realizing it." He paused and looked down. "I cannot now betray her a second time by putting my personal safety above the security of her message." He looked up again into the older man's eyes. "I think you understand."

The senator nodded slowly and sighed.

"I understand. You are a brave man, Medcalf, and I congratulate you. And yes, of course you are right. I will not try to persuade you more. Instead, I will try to be worthy of your example, in the same way that you have proved yourself worthy of the example of your friend in Bulgaria." He glanced at his opened suitcase on the bed. "*Allora*, it is time for me to finish my packing and for you to return to your room."

They stood facing each other—two men of different nationalities, different generations but now, in the space of half an hour, united in a common purpose. They grasped each other's hands and held. There were tears in the older man's eyes.

"I have a small—how you say?—'holiday home' between Florence and Siena. It is very primitive but for me very beautiful, with its own vines and its own olive trees. I wish that you now make a promise to me—a sacred oath!—that you will come and visit with me soon in my small, primitive holiday home. In the spring perhaps. So, now I say, *Ci vediamo!* It means that we will see each other again."

"*Ci vediamo*," repeated Medcalf.

"You have promised."

"I have promised. In the spring."

◆ 29 ◆

THE LAB ASSISTANT was taken by surprise.

"Look, you guys, I'm really not sure I should be talking to you like this. I mean, I'm just one of the Indians around here. Why don't you come back tomorrow morning? The director will be in at eight."

DC acted as though he hadn't heard a word. He slung his jacket over the back of a chair and rested his weight on the windowsill. In his experience Indians of any sort were usually ten times more useful than their chiefs, whose main preoccupation was always to protect the reputation of the company, department, or unit against the possible fallout from a major crash investigation. It was just a matter of overcoming some initial resistance and in this—he grudgingly acknowledged—it usually helped to be part of a twosome.

"Look, just for the benefit of my colleague here who doesn't know about these things," he said, indicating Collins, "just explain, will you, the normal lab procedure for checking the magnetic plugs. And don't worry about the director; I'll clear it all with him in the morning."

The lab assistant wasn't convinced but seemed finally to accept the fact that he was up against an immovable object. He shrugged.

"Well, hell, there's no mystery about it. The plugs are pulled from the engines at prescribed intervals by the mechanics across in the maintenance hangar; a small plastic cap is slipped over the magnetic probe; and each plug is put in a plastic bag and sent along here for analysis of whatever may have stuck to it during the last however many hours of flight. From that—from the size, quantity, and composition of the metal particles—we can tell which engine parts are wearing and which, if any, are likely to give trouble. Most times, it's just routine."

"And the mechanic who removes the plugs from the engines," said DC, as though more concerned with adjusting the fold of his jacket over the chair back, "he'll replace them immediately with a fresh set."

"Right—and same way, as soon as we've finished our analysis here, we'll clean 'em and send 'em back to the maintenance hangar to be used again. It's a continuous cycle."

"You mean the stores—you send them back to the stores."

"No, they're all kept in a cabinet in the supervisor's office in the maintenance hangar. Stores is for new parts; the plugs are recycled parts."

"Got it. Now, the numbering, how does that work?"

The assistant passed a hand nervously through his frizzy red hair.

"Well, again it's no big deal. Each plug has its own number engraved on it. When he removes the plug from the aircraft, the mechanic records the plug number on the tag of the plastic bag it's going into—right alongside the aircraft type and number, and the engine number. That way we in the lab know exactly which engine of which aircraft the plug has come off. Most airlines don't bother to number their plugs but we find it's a useful precaution in case a plug gets separated from its bag when its particles are being checked."

DC nodded at a computer terminal in the corner of the lab.

"And that—where does that come into it?"

"That's the last stage. When we've completed the particle analysis, we log the results on the computer. It keeps a running history of every engine and compares each new entry against all previous entries. That way, if we have an engine that's regularly shedding a lot of debris or debris of a particular kind, it'll alert us to the danger if we haven't already spotted it ourselves."

DC looked at Collins. They both had the sense that there was something important in what the man was saying; it was just a matter of extricating the bit that was relevant. The assistant caught the interaction and, fearing he had said too much, was now worried. He reached for a phone on the desk.

"Look, I'm sorry, guys, but you're getting me into questions which really the director should be answering, not me. Sorry, but I'm going to give him a call at home. Like I say, I'm just one of the Indians around here."

DC saw the chance of any further interrogation slipping away and was about to come down heavy, despite the risk he knew it carried of silencing the man altogether, when to his amazement Collins crossed in front of him and put a consoling arm around the assistant's shoulders.

"Sure, you're absolutely right," he said. "You go ahead. In fact while you're doing that, I'll just phone my wife to tell her I'm going to be home late. Okay if I use the other phone?"

"Sure thing," said the assistant, relieved. "Just press 'Nine' for an outside line."

DC was speechless. His instinctive reaction was to drag Collins outside, slam him up against the wall, and demand what the fuck he thought he was playing at. The last thing they wanted was a paranoid bureaucrat insisting that the lab be put under lock and key and everything submitted to him in writing.

Yet Collins's action was such an outrageous breach of professional protocol that he could only conclude he had some game plan in mind which overrode the deference a junior team member normally paid to a senior.

If he was wrong, he could always slam him up against the wall later.

He watched the two of them pick up separate receivers and simultaneously tap in the numbers, then saw Collins lift his left buttock onto the corner of the desk—and, casual as you like, topple half a cup of cold coffee across a dozen pages of typescript.

"Sh–it," Collins hissed, drawing the assistant's attention to the fingers of milky brown liquid now flexing over the edge.

The assistant was around the desk in a second, frantically pushing other papers out of the way before they, too, were tainted.

"You give me that," said Collins, relieving him of his phone. "Christ, I'm sorry. I'm just such a clumsy bastard sometimes."

It was a performance worthy of a professional magician, and one which DC, standing at a distance, had the advantage of watching from the wings.

As the assistant wiped away the spilled coffee with sheets of absorbent paper, Collins coolly switched the phones and carried on an imaginary conversation with his wife on the line which the assistant had punched through to his chief—while holding the other receiver at arm's length, the regular purr of its dial tone clearly audible. By the time the assistant took hold again of what he thought was his receiver, Collins had already wished his nonexistent children sweet dreams via his nonexistent wife and replaced the receiver on its cradle.

"Your chief seems to be less conscientious than you are," DC remarked.

The assistant examined the still purring receiver as though the answer to his perplexity lay somewhere within.

"I don't understand it," he declared. "Dr. Warner never leaves his phone unattended; if he's not there personally, he always leaves a recorded message saying where he can be reached. It's one of the golden rules of the lab."

"Well, you've done your duty," came in Collins, reaching out for the receiver. "We'll testify that you tried to call but there was no answer. Now, you were telling us about the numbers on the plugs . . ."

"That's right," DC joined in. "Are we correct in thinking from what you were saying that the computer will tell you, at any one time, which plugs are on which aircraft—that in other words you could tell us the numbers of the plugs on that crashed SP-3?"

With an effort the assistant shook himself back into the original conversation. After a moment's readjustment he answered:

"No . . . not by using the computer. It records only the numbers of those plugs that have come through here for inspection. It has no idea where they're going once they've left."

DC felt suddenly very weary. After all their efforts they seemed, like the damned plugs, to be caught up in an eternal cycle.

"So you've no way of knowing which plugs were on that SP-3 . . ." he said, his voice trailing off.

"Oh, sure," bounced back the assistant, "but not by using the computer and I thought that's what you were asking about."

DC could have screamed.

"Well, if not by the computer, *how*, for Christ's sake?"

"By a simple process of elimination. It would take time, but we know how many plugs we've got in total and if we were to list the numbers of the plugs on all the aircraft in the fleet, together with the numbers of those plugs here in the lab and in the supervisor's cabinet, we could easily work out which three were missing. Logically, they'd have to be the ones on the crashed SP-3."

When one thought about it, it was obvious. DC rubbed his face.

"So how long would you need—*will* you need?"

The assistant laughed.

"Oh, no ... This really *is* a decision for the director. Even higher, I'd guess. You're talking now about ordering a special ramp check on every aircraft at its next stop, wherever in the world that may be. By the time that's done and the information's been telephoned or telexed back here ... hell, twelve hours, if you're lucky. More like twenty-four."

"And if the chairman himself were to order it as a matter of urgency—with the same sort of priority that would be given an airworthiness directive, for example?"

"Then I guess we'd be talking about nearer twelve."

It was DC's turn to pick up the phone.

Ten minutes later on their way to find some food at last, Collins asked, "You really think knowing those plug numbers is going to shed some light on this business?"

DC stopped. After the guy's performance in the lab it was hard to regard him any longer as a fifth-columnist. There had also, he had to admit, been some pleasure in working in a ·partnership—even if only as The Great Gaspardi's sidekick.

"If you want to know the truth," he volunteered, "I'm not sure *what* I think at the moment." He wondered again whether to tell Collins about the Miami incident and the missing O-rings, but held back, adding only, "Just go along with me, even if I seem to be developing a fixation about those plugs. I can only explain it as a gut reaction."

To himself he had to admit that it wasn't much more. The facts were against him: There had been nothing in the records or the interviews to indicate that the plugs had been changed before the flight and he hadn't forgotten Collins's own reference to the check valves which would have ensured that, even if the plugs had fallen out, been taken out, or just never been there in the first place, there still wouldn't have been any significant loss of oil. And one last nagging thought—if the plugs had been in place but for some reason without their O-rings, one would still have to explain why it had taken the oil so much longer to leak out of the SP-3's engines than it had taken to leak out of those on the TriStar in the Miami incident.

Logic alone seemed to be on his side—the logic which said that, if the basin was empty, the answer most likely lay with the plug.

"Anyway, since when have you been a member of the Magic Circle?" he asked as they continued along the corridor.

"Oh, that," responded Collins with a self-deprecating grin. "All part of my air force training. One of the things you're taught as a fighter pilot is to react quickly to situations and make use of whatever's on hand. I knew my wife was out tonight, but the cup of coffee . . . well, I guess I was just lucky there."

♦ 30 ♦

IT WAS mid-afternoon by the time Cunningham made his reappearance in Medcalf's hotel room. More like his old buoyant self, he slapped a folded afternoon edition of the *Washington Post* against his open palm.

"Well, they've done it," he declared. "They've gone in." He held up the headline for Medcalf to read. "And what's encouraging is that all the commentators seem to be stressing the historical perspective. Whole paragraphs of editorial on how the invasion has to be seen in the context of the Macedonian issue—together with a lot of emphasis on the fact that it should be seen as a local dispute over a garden fence and not as an invasion by the Warsaw Pact. In fact I couldn't have written it better myself!"

Watching him, Medcalf wondered if Cunningham had been drinking or if this tasteless display of euphoria had a more sinister intent behind it. He had no doubts that his own performance earlier in the day—his lackluster death-bed conversion by the Reflecting Pool—was still fresh in Cunningham's mind, in all its unconvincing detail. This, he suspected, was Cunningham's way of determining the sincerity of that conversion. Attempting therefore to match the upbeat tone, he asked brightly:

"So what about NATO?"

Cunningham beamed. "So far, so good. Utter confusion. It seems the original idea was that the ambassadors should be recalled from Brussels to their respective capitals for consultation. Now it's been decided to convene the full sixteen-nation council in permanent emergency session—the whole bloody shooting match! A bit late in the day, mind you, but what can you expect from an organization that at the last count had four hundred and thirty-five standing committees?" He thought a second. "No doubt, though, your friend Van Kleef will be getting twitchy about your whereabouts"—and, drawing a single sheet of typed paper from his jacket pocket, added, "which is why we must get this off as soon as possible."

Medcalf took it and read. It was the bogus message which Cunningham intended to cable to Van Kleef, the "report" of his debriefing. It was more subtle than he had given Cunningham credit for—a clever mix of truth, half-truth, outright lie, and even humor:

ATTN. H.V.K., CENMON [I.L.]

BULGARIAN MESSENGER BOY RE-ROUTED VIA WASHINGTON. BAGGAGE CONTENTS AS FOLLOWS. ASSASSINATION ATTEMPT BOMBINGS ARREST OF YUGO ENTIRELY BULGARIAN RESPONSIBILITY. CONCEIVED AS PRETEXT FOR

INVASION OF MACEDONIA. STRICTLY NATIONALISTIC AIMS. SOVIETS NOT INVOLVED BUT FEAR GLOBAL MISCALCULATION BY SOFIA. POSSIBLE WARSAW PACT INTERVENTION. SOVIETS ANXIOUS NATO UNDERSTAND. EVEN POSSIBLE SOVIET TROOPS OVER YUGO BORDER BUT SOLELY FOR PURPOSES OF CONTAINMENT. HERE'S LOOKING AT YOU.

Medcalf pretended to be still reading while actually thinking about the likely impact of the cable back in Brussels.

It was a masterly piece of disinformation, right down to the oblique reference to Bogart in the payoff. It was dangerously good.

The question was whether Van Kleef was likely to be convinced by it. Could this cable alone really persuade him that the Bulgarians, who had always shown themselves to be such models of obedience and compliance, had decided, in effect, to thumb their noses at their Soviet masters?

The answer, Medcalf suspected, was that it would depend ultimately upon how much faith Van Kleef had in Bogart as a source. If all her previous material had been high-grade, then yes, it was conceivable that he might on this occasion suspend his natural skepticism.

And even if Van Kleef wasn't taken in, the cable would assuredly do what it was intended to do: confuse an already confused situation. At least until the true picture arrived via Senator Bracciolini. But, whereas this message would be received by Van Kleef within minutes of its being sent, Bracciolini's "correction" might, by Medcalf's reckoning, take another twelve to fifteen hours to arrive. By which time it could be too late.

Even though it might take the Bulgarians two to three days to wear down the Yugoslavs, the psychological battle would already have been lost if, in the face of Bulgarian advances and Yugoslavian calls for help, NATO were seen to be dithering during the hours immediately following the invasion. Already assured of American compliance, the Russians would conclude they had nothing to fear from the rest of NATO, and with impunity would follow the Bulgarians' tank tracks over the border. Within a fortnight, Yugoslavia would be a Soviet satellite.

"Well, what do you think of it?" Cunningham asked.

"Brilliant—quite brilliant," Medcalf responded without a word of a lie, while behind the fatuous, congratulatory smile he ransacked his memory for a scrap of information which, suitably twisted, could be injected into the message to alert Van Kleef to the fact that it was a fake.

But there was nothing. Not a single sentence. He had been too damned conscientious during the debriefing.

"You don't think it's a bit on the bald side?" he said at last.

"That's the style of these things," replied Cunningham. "If your man wants to know more he'll come back for it. The first thing you learn in this business, Medcalf, is never to volunteer more than is necessary . . . I take it then," he added brusquely, "that you have no suggestions to make."

Medcalf could feel his usefulness diminishing by the syllabic second.

"Not really . . . only that, knowing Van Kleef, I'm sure he'll want more specifics." At this stage anything that might suggest his continuing indispensability could only be to his advantage.

"Well, we'll know soon enough," said Cunningham, already heading for the door. He stopped on the threshold. "By the way, you'll find the television's working again."

The door slammed; there was a brief exchange of words outside, followed by footfalls down the corridor.

Medcalf stared at the television and wondered how he should interpret this unexpected resumption of normal service—as a symbol of Trust Renewed or a token concession for the condemned man? A last taste of earthly delights.

As his finger touched the button, he was dimly reminded of a tag he had learned at school. Something about not trusting Greeks who bring gifts.

◆ 31 ◆

DC rapped on the laboratory door. It was locked—an unsubtle reminder, he assumed, that on his visit of the previous evening he had breached protocol by interrogating the assistant without asking his superior.

The impression was confirmed when, unlocking the door, the director barely acknowledged his own identity. The unfortunate assistant was nowhere to be seen.

DC introduced himself and Collins, adding:

"You have some information for us, I believe, Dr. Warner—about magnetic plugs? The chairman figured you'd have the results by now."

He waited for Warner to deliver a lecture on professional behavior and "correct channels," but Warner said only, "I think this is what you want," and handed him a length of computer printout.

It was—a list of the plugs, identified by number, on every Airlantic aircraft throughout the world that was fitted with that type, together with lists of those plugs in the maintenance supervisor's cabinet and those passing through the labs for inspection. At the bottom of the printout in a separate section were the numbers of three plugs described as "unaccounted"—52, 87, 35.

Passing the printout to Collins, DC looked back to Warner. His initial impression, he now realized, had been wrong. What he had interpreted as a frosty formality was in fact unease.

Something was bugging the man.

"So we can assume that the three at the bottom were the plugs fitted to the SP-3 during its last scheduled plug change," said DC by way of breaking the awkward silence.

Warner's reply set him back on his heels.

"No, I'm afraid you can't, Mr. Di Coiano."

"You mean there are others missing as well?"

"No, there are no others missing, but you asked a specific question and I've given you a specific answer. You asked whether the unaccounted plugs on that sheet were the ones fitted to the aircraft during its last scheduled plug change and I have to tell you that, on the evidence available, they were not. If you were to ask me simply whether they were the ones fitted to the aircraft when it took off on its last flight, I would say they were. Do you understand now?"

DC looked at Collins and was comforted to see that he too was mystified by Warner's delphic utterances.

"I don't follow," DC said simply. "We were told it was a straightforward matter of elimination."

Warner walked over to the computer terminal and, removing his spectacles, sat down. He sighed.

"You'd better take a look at this," he said, summoning up a screenful of luminous green figures. "I believe my assistant explained to you last night how our plug inspection system works—how we update the records each time a plug passes through the labs. You will also appreciate, as aviation experts, that these plugs are specific not to the type of aircraft but to the type of engine, so you can expect to find them not just on SP-3s, but on other wide-bodied jets, too. In the same way, because they are returned to a pool, they don't necessarily stay in sets from one aircraft to the next. You understand?"

DC confirmed.

"Right," said Warner. "Then let us see which aircraft those three missing plugs were on immediately before being fitted to that crashed SP-3 . . ." He pointed to three different spots on the screen with the arm of his spectacles. "And here we have them—their last recorded entries." He indicated the first spot. "One of them was on a 747 and, as you can see, was inspected here and entered accordingly on the fourth of this month—ten days before the accident, three days before the crashed aircraft's last known plug change, right?"

DC nodded; there was nothing wrong there. The recycling of the plug through the supervisor's cabinet had simply been fairly rapid.

"However," continued Warner, "the other two were by chance together on the same aircraft, another 747, and they"—he tapped twice on the screen—"passed through here on the twelfth—just two days before the crash and therefore"—he paused and turned—"five days *after* the SP-3's scheduled plug change. And the records show they'd been on that 747 for the previous three weeks." He put his spectacles back on. "What this means, gentlemen—and forgive me if I insult your intelligence—is that at least two of these plugs which are now at the bottom of the Atlantic could not possibly have been the ones which were fitted to the aircraft during its last scheduled plug change, for the obvious reason that they were on another aircraft at the time, quite possibly on the other side of the world."

All three men stared dumbly at one another, and then back at the screen.

"So they must have been fitted to the SP-3 within two days of the crash . . . ," murmured DC to himself. Addressing Warner again, he asked, "You're quite sure there couldn't have been a mistake made here—a wrong entry, something like that?"

But Warner was adamant.

"One hundred percent sure. As a backup check, we always keep the bag tags for six months. In this case, we've cross-checked the plug numbers on the computer against the bag tags and they tally. The dates are correct." He gave a little snort of exasperation. "Frankly, I don't pretend to understand any of it."

DC didn't understand either, but he had no doubt that it was highly relevant to the investigation.

"Have you a room where my colleague and I can be alone for a while to think this thing through?" he asked.

Warner pointed to one of the doors leading off the lab.

"You're welcome to use my office. I'll be working in here today anyway. I'll ask my secretary to transfer my calls."

"Fine—and one other thing: We'll need a box of old-fashioned matches. Real wooden ones, not book matches."

♦ **32** ♦

ON THE UPPER FLOOR of the NATO headquarters in Brussels the secretary-general sat alone in his office. It was eight o'clock in the evening. There were only two sources of illumination in the room—a brass reading lamp on the desk and, built into the bookcase twenty feet away, a television monitor that was relaying via a closed-circuit camera the proceedings in the main hall. It had been one of the secretary-general's first innovations on taking office and, since the relay was exclusive to his office, was jokingly referred to as his "spy in the sky."

In fact it served a number of indisputably practical purposes—not the least of which was that it enabled him, as now, to concentrate on matters that demanded his immediate personal attention while still keeping an eye on what was happening down on "the shop floor."

The emergency session of the North Atlantic Council had been in continuous session for three hours as, one after another, each of the sixteen national representatives around the horseshoe table voiced his government's views on what NATO's response to Bulgaria's invasion of Yugoslavia should be.

Since there was no easy answer, the debate had predictably concentrated on the legalistic niceties of how far, if at all, an attack on a non-NATO, nonaligned country could be said to constitute a threat to NATO itself.

The majority view now emerging was that it all depended on how far that attack went. Implied but never stated was the opinion that the NATO countries could live with a redrawing of the Bulgarian-Yugoslavian border so long as the new line went no further into Yugoslavia than Macedonia—although it was alarmingly apparent that some of the speakers had not the slightest notion of where Macedonia was, let alone where it stopped and the rest of Yugoslavia began.

The secretary-general jotted down the word "maps" on the corner of his blotter to remind himself that it might help if each member were supplied with his own. When he looked up again, the British representative was quoting with approval the words of a German representative—no less an authority than Chancellor Bismarck, speaking a hundred years earlier at the time of another "Bulgarian Crisis":

"Bulgaria, that little country between the Danube and the Balkans, is far from being an object of adequate importance for which to plunge Europe into a war whose issue no man can foresee. At the end of the conflict we should scarcely know why we had fought!"

The secretary-general turned the sound off. The trouble with most British politicians, he mused, was that their exaggerated sense of history stunted their imagination; the conviction that human events were capable of only a limited number of permutations blinded them to dangers and opportunities alike.

His eyes dropped again to his desk and the two pieces of paper that lay, side by side, in the pool of yellow light. One was the cable from Malcolm Cunningham in Washington, deciphered and forwarded by Van Kleef's department; the other, an equally confidential message delivered by hand half an hour earlier in which the Yugoslavian ambassador in Brussels voiced his country's fears of a full-scale invasion by Warsaw Pact forces and appealed to NATO for "every possible assistance."

The secretary-general leaned across the desk and, picking up the telephone, asked to be put through to the gallery of the Council Chamber from where he knew Van Kleef would be watching the debate.

"Herman," he said, "we must talk."

Five minutes later Van Kleef was sitting in the leather chair before the secretary-general's desk.

"So what do you make of it?" asked the secretary-general, nodding in the direction of the television monitor.

"You wish me to be honest?"

"Have I ever wished you to be anything else?"

"Well, in that case . . . My experience in this place has taught me that persons who as individuals have difficulty making decisions always decide as a group that nothing can be done."

The secretary-general smiled for the first time in twelve hours and held up the cable from Washington.

"And this?"

Van Kleef sucked on his teeth.

"That is more difficult. It pleads more questions than it answers, and the one I ask myself most is not why the Bulgarians want to repossess Macedonia, but why they want to repossess it *now*. I do not understand what has happened that has made them ready to risk the anger of the Soviets in achieving their aims. It is as though they are inviting the Soviets to invade them. What I want to know—but this cable does not tell me it—is what has happened inside Bulgaria that has suddenly made Macedonia this big, important issue. It is always hard to tell but I do not think that there are any great internal problems with the economy or with the position of the government. There seems to be no reason, therefore, why they might need to create a diversion— if that is what it is."

"Then let me ask you another question," said the secretary-general. "How reliable a source is Bogart?"

Van Kleef had anticipated it and was fully briefed.

"Well, she has not been wrong yet. This is the seventh time she has passed us information during two and a half years and it has always been of the highest quality. I would say her reputation is very good."

"Good enough for us to trust the Soviets to cross into Yugoslavia? Good enough for us to believe that their only interest is in persuading the Bulgarians to return to their barracks?"

"I cannot say that. As I have said, I do not have enough answers, although . . ." He stopped.

"Well, what?"

"Only this: that if Bogart is right and the Bulgarians really have lost their senses, then the Soviets not only have good reason to fear a global miscalculation but are also in the best position—politically, militarily, and geographically— to exert control over them. In fact, they are probably the only ones who can. The Yugoslavs do not have the strength, and if *we* intervene we risk a nuclear confrontation."

The secretary-general adjusted the shade on the desk lamp to reduce the glare.

"I don't know, Herman. But I am sure of this: The longer we do nothing, the less able we'll be to do *anything* if we have to. The trouble is, as you say, we don't have enough information." He picked up the Washington cable again. "We cannot gamble the security of the Western world on a dozen lines of typescript."

"What do you want me to do?" asked Van Kleef.

"Send a cable to Washington. Tell them to put Medcalf on the next plane back here so we can talk to him ourselves."

♦ 33 ♦

"THE HEADLINES at three o'clock . . . and, first, the Bulgarian invasion of Yugoslavian Macedonia earlier today. A spokesman for the State Department here in Washington has just said that they are monitoring the situation closely and are keeping the White House informed of developments . . . In Moscow, meanwhile, the official news agency Tass has said the Soviet Union regards the conflict among her East European neighbors with the greatest concern. An official of the Soviet Foreign Ministry is quoted as describing the situation in Macedonia as a serious threat to regional stability and one which cannot be allowed to continue indefi—"

The newscaster's voice was interrupted by a knocking at the door. Medcalf turned the television off but didn't move. If it was Cunningham, he could let himself in.

When the knocking was repeated, however, he got off the bed and, puzzled, crossed the room.

It was Cunningham all right—but, as was to become clear within minutes, a different Cunningham. The man seemed capable of more changes of character than a repertory actor.

Yes, he said, there had been a response from Brussels to the cable, and yes, there had been a request for clarification.

But there was something strangely solicitous about the questions that followed—casual but probing, and not the straight matter-of-fact sort that Medcalf had expected to be asked in response to a request from Brussels for clarification. Once again, Medcalf had the feeling that he was being tested, and Cunningham's repeated references to his, Medcalf's, "potentially conflicting loyalties" seemed to confirm it.

For all his subtlety, though, Cunningham was no Arenkov and, compared with the grilling he had been given in Sofia, the cross-examination was no more taxing than filling in a consumer questionnaire.

"So in any further dealings with your former NATO masters," Cunningham concluded, "you'd happily stand by the cable?"

For the first time Medcalf guessed the reason for this latest change in the man's behavior—but dared not believe it.

"Happily, no," he responded. "I personally dislike lying because I'm no good at it, but if it really is in the British national interest, as you say, then yes, I'd stand by it." He cleared his throat and added, "Naturally, though, I'd expect you to acknowledge in any report to your superiors the extent of my cooperation in this whole business."

Cunningham said nothing. Medcalf's refusal to accept the word "happily," coupled with his admission that he made a bad liar, was either unwitting proof of his honesty or a clever psychological bluff.

The question was whether Medcalf was really devious enough to perpetrate such a bluff. The evidence of his own dealings with him suggested to Cunningham that he wasn't and, insofar as he had apparently been chosen by his NATO masters for an ability to get himself arrested within forty-eight hours of arrival in Sofia, it seemed to be also the opinion of those who had known him longer and better.

But it was Medcalf's oblique request to be "mentioned favorably in dispatches" that clinched the matter in Cunningham's mind.

Here was a man who, to use the English expression, seemed to know which side his bread was buttered on—a man who, whatever his other intellectual shortcomings, had the sense to realize that where there was a choice of loyalties, self-interest should be the determining factor.

"Then you'd better pack your bags," he said, handing Medcalf the cable received half an hour earlier from Van Kleef in Brussels.

Medcalf read the words with a relief and joy he found almost impossible to disguise. His facial muscles ached with the effort. He wanted to smile, to laugh, to shout! The caged bird was to be let out. The condemned man, his feet already on the trap, the rope chafing at his neck, was being told that there'd been a ghastly mistake and that, instead of an execution, there was to be a party to celebrate his freedom.

He could only guess at what had happened back at NATO headquarters, but never in his wildest imaginings had he dared to believe that Van Kleef would demand his return in person at this late stage. He had assumed that events were moving too fast for him to be of any further use in Brussels. Had he thought otherwise, he would never have demolished half the bathroom to get Anelia's message out of the hotel.

All that mattered now, though, was that he would soon

be free. He had never felt more truly alive than at this moment. When he saw the Dutchman, he would embrace him and plant a great kiss on each of his ridiculously rosy cheeks. And Senator Bracciolini, too. They would drink the good red wine beneath the spreading vines of his "small, primitive holiday home"—and sooner perhaps than either of them had dared to hope.

"When do I have to leave?" he asked, feigning indifference.

Cunningham checked his watch. "As soon as you're ready. We'll get you to the airport and put you on whichever's the first and fastest flight. While you're packing, I'll use the bathroom."

Medcalf watched in riveted horror as Cunningham walked toward the bathroom door.

The arms, legs, head and torso seemed to move in a succession of still frames, cranked down to an unnatural slowness—as though a divine agent would intervene at the critical moment to freeze the action and keep the hand forever from the doorknob; stop the "ever-moving spheres of heaven, that time may cease and midnight never come."

Like Faustus, he wanted to cry out, to protest. It just wasn't possible that he'd been brought so close to freedom only to be denied it at the last moment by—in the name of all that was absurd and arbitrary—a full bladder! It just wasn't . . . fair.

But the words wouldn't come. There were no words. For what could he say to stop Cunningham that wouldn't itself arouse suspicion? Yet it was impossible that the man wouldn't see the missing ceiling panel and even more impossible that, having seen it, he wouldn't draw the obvious conclusion.

In an instant the decision was made. There'd be only one chance.

He opened the door to the corridor and matter-of-factly addressed the heavy standing outside:

"Mr. Cunningham says you're to call a car to take us to the airport."

As he had hoped, the man wasn't prepared to take the order at face value.

"He's in the bathroom if you want to check with him," he added.

He waited for the man to take a couple of steps into the bedroom—and made his move through the open door. Hurling himself toward the stairs at the end of the corridor, he willed every muscle and ligament in his body to keep pace with his mind, which was already in the lobby, past the concierge, through the front doors, and out of the hotel.

It was, as he had always known, a futile gesture. Before he had gone a dozen paces down the corridor he was cut off by the second heavy. Freedom had been illusory.

Suddenly all resistance seemed not just futile, but undignified. He stopped struggling and allowed himself to be led back into the bedroom by an almost token armlock.

Cunningham stood expressionless by the bed, the telephone to his ear.

"It's too late, you know," Medcalf said, no longer caring about curbing his contempt. "Whatever you may do to me, the word is already out. They know. All of them! The senators, the deputies—they will all know by now."

Cunningham ignored the remarks and continued talking over the phone. It was clear from the curtness of his responses that he was receiving orders. Only once did he look again at Medcalf—and then briefly while repeating his words:

"That's right—all of them. They all know."

Turning away, he added, "I've checked. Their plane doesn't leave JFK till eight this evening . . . Right, and I'll see to things this end."

He laid down the receiver and indicated to the first

heavy to go with him into the bathroom, leaving Medcalf still in the grip of the second.

A minute later he emerged alone, closing the door behind him to cut off the sound of rushing water.

"Take him in," he said, and picked up the phone again.

◆ **34** ◆

DC AND COLLINS sat opposite each other in Lab Director Warner's office, hunched forward in low chairs at a circular coffee table.

DC placed the box of matches on the table and was about to speak when Collins put his finger to his lips, stood up, and crossed to Warner's desk. He checked the intercom, flicking the toggles up and down, and, apparently satisfied, came back.

"Something else you learned in the air force?" DC asked.

"No," replied Collins with a boyish grin. "My father taught me that one. He was an inspector for the Revenue; specialized in corporate fraud. He figured you should always be suspicious if anybody offered you his office for a private talk; it's a standard trick to leave the intercom on, so every word's relayed next door."

Again, despite himself, DC was impressed. It seemed to confirm the decision he had already made a minute earlier in the lab.

"You'd better have a look at this," he said, dropping the report of the Miami incident on the table. "You may think I'm obsessed with magnetic plugs, but the first half dozen pages'll explain."

Collins looked surprised; it was the first gesture of confidence DC had shown in him. He opened the report and read.

For the next ten minutes his eyes didn't leave the page. He seemed to devour whole chunks of text at a glance, his head craned forward at an increasingly sharp angle. It was DC who finally stopped him by laying a hand on the open page.

"The rest you can read later; you've seen the important part."

Collins threw himself back in his chair.

"But that's . . . just incredible! And you think this was a repeat performance?"

DC tipped the matches onto the table and started dividing them up into separate stacks. He spoke in erratic bursts, as though pursuing a line of thought as it suggested itself:

"Not exactly. More like a variation on the same theme. For a start, we have no evidence of any plug change immediately before the flight—so there was no opportunity for a mechanic to forget to put on new O-rings."

"But that's assuming the records are accurate. What if one of them had a brainstorm and changed the plugs without being told?"

DC thought a moment but shook his head.

"You then have to ask what he would've done with the set of plugs he took out. If he'd bagged and tagged them, they'd have come up here to the lab and been recorded on the computer. They're not."

"And if he'd just stuffed them down the garbage chute?"

"Then we'd have not three missing plugs but *six*—three at the bottom of the Atlantic and three down the chute. Whichever way you look at it, it still doesn't add up . . . Besides, the time factor doesn't accord with a straightforward case of missing O-rings."

"Why not?"

DC scooped up the report and opened it.

"On the Miami flight, the first signs of trouble came nineteen minutes after takeoff. Within forty minutes they'd lost every engine. But this flight, the aircraft was already forty-eight minutes out when it started losing engines—just when it was beyond the Continental Shelf and out over the really deep water. It's almost as if . . ." He stopped himself, mindful of deep waters of another kind.

"So where do these come into it?" asked Collins, nodding at the matches.

"It's just an idea, but let's try thinking of this thing as an intellectual exercise. You know the sort of thing—one of those intelligence tests from your Air Force days where you had to carry an imaginary fox and chicken across an imaginary river without the fox at any stage being left alone with the chicken."

He held up a single match.

"Each match represents a magnetic plug, okay? And all the matches here represent all the plugs that Airlantic has in circulation on its wide-bodied fleet." He indicated the three roughly equal piles, pointing to each in turn. "The matches in this pile are those flying around on the various aircraft at any one time; the ones in this pile are those in the laboratory for inspection; and here, the third pile, we have the cleaned and recycled plugs sitting in the supervisor's cabinet downstairs waiting to be reused. Clear?"

Collins's eyes narrowed. "Clear," he confirmed. DC was gratified to find that he had guessed correctly; it was precisely the sort of exercise that appealed to Collins's mentality.

He picked up a red felt-tip pen and colored the ends of three of the matches in the first pile.

"And these," he said, placing them back in the same pile, "are the three plugs that are missing. At the moment, as we have them here, they're still in the air, split between the two 747s." He leaned back against the low chair. "Now, the trick is to devise a means whereby those plugs can find their way onto the doomed SP-3—taking into account the facts:

one, that its last recorded plug change was a full week before the crash, when at least two of the plugs and most likely all three were on another aircraft ... *two*, that no other plugs from that SP-3 have come through the lab ... and *three*, that no other plugs are missing."

It would take two hours to arrive at the solution—two hours during which they would sit like chessplayers, moving the matches from one pile to another and back again; two hours during which every possible permutation would be tried and evaluated; two hours during which a slow realization would steal upon them like nausea.

The truth dawned with the dusk—and with none of the exhilaration that DC had anticipated; no clasping of hands, no slapping of backs.

Just one word that formed on their lips simultaneously but which both men refrained from pronouncing.

Finally, DC stood up and walked over to the large picture window, his hands thrust into his pockets, shoulders sagging. Outside, the winking light of an incoming jet stitched a trail of orange dots across the darkening sky.

"It has to be, hasn't it?" he said quietly, without turning.

"I guess so," responded Collins. "I can see no other explanation. Who was responsible and how they did it, Christ knows—but, no doubt about it, it was sabotage."

The word was out.

✦ 35 ✦

THE CALL for Robert Fischer to re-
pay his debt to society had come at five o'clock in the
afternoon. It had been taken by his wife—a small, nervous
woman who, at the time of Fischer's arrest two years earlier,
had suffered a breakdown from which she had never fully
recovered.

"Tom, for you!" she shrilled, still finding it unnatural to
apply this alien name to the man who for twenty-three years
she had known as "Bob."

It was one of the smaller prices she had been required to
pay for what her husband referred to as his "rehabilitation"—
along with the severance of all former ties, family and
friends alike, and their removal, literally by night, from
the West Coast town where they had both grown up to
New York.

She would never forget the occasion, a few weeks after
the move, when Bob had caught her writing a surreptitious
letter to her mother. He had raged for a week. Didn't she
understand the risk she was taking? Did she really want
some hoodlum to gun him down in a bar or on a street
corner because her mother had left the letter around the
house for it to be seen by a snooping neighbor?

He had shouted at her. She knew the deal he had made
with the authorities! And she knew the rules: one phone call a
month to her mother and no other contact or correspondence!

Sure it was tough, he sympathized, but it would have
been tougher still for her to manage on her own with him in

prison for twenty years, along with the rest of them. Sure he understood that her mother was her only family but—the words that had seared her soul—it wasn't *his* fault that they couldn't have children.

"It's a man," she said, handing him the phone as he wiped the car grease from his hands. "Don't ask me who . . . said you'd know."

She saw the flash of panic, the sudden stiffening of his frame. He took the phone and turned away, excluding her.

"Thomas Wilson," he announced with a shade too much conviction.

There was a light, teasing laugh on the other end.

"You can relax, Bob, it's Phil. Remember Phil?"

"I remember." The cadence was one less of recognition than of resignation.

"Good, good. Got a little job for you, Bob. Something that's blown up real quick. So, how's about if we meet up in half an hour's time?"

Bob scribbled down the address on the back of an old shopping list, his palm leaving a greasy smear on the paper.

"You know Queens Boulevard, right?" said the voice. "Well, you take the last turning on the right off it before Woodhaven, an' it's a hundred yards down on the left. See you there in thirty minutes. And Bob—no later, right?"

Within the appointed half hour, Bob was pulling up outside the run-down automobile repair shop in Queens. He drove in beneath a large, rusting sign for Firestone tires and stopped.

Phil opened the door for him with mock courtesy. Neither Phil's appearance nor his manner had changed in the intervening two years.

"Well, this surely is a delightful surprise after all this time, Robert," he cooed.

"I thought I'd done my bit by helping you put the others away," Bob responded.

"Then you thought wrong, my friend. All you did by that was to save your own miserable hide. You seem to forget the little matter of your new identity—the new passport, the new Social Security number? These things have to be paid for, Robert—as I told you at the time."

Bob followed him into a back room. As they entered, the door was pushed shut by a figure in a neat three-piece suit, taking obvious care to avoid contact with the grease and grime all around.

"Er, Bob, this is ... John," Phil said by way of introduction.

John made no move to shake hands; just a quick peck of the head.

"Now, John here," continued Phil cosily, "thinks you may be just the guy to help him out. He's got a small but rather urgent problem down the road at Kennedy and I've told him how you know all about airports and these things. I guess it's fair to say you could find your way around one without much trouble, yeah?"

"Depends what you mean."

"What I mean, Robert, is that any guy who can help set up a two-million-dollar bullion heist while working as an airline freight handler should have no diffi—"

"That was in Los Angeles and I've told you I had no part in the setting up."

". . . should have no difficulty finding his way around an Airlantic maintenance hangar six miles down the road."

He waited for a response.

"I can't say without knowing what it involves," Bob said at last.

"Just two trips in and out—a little petty pilfering on the first and some routine maintenance work on the second," said Phil.

He steered Bob toward a workbench on which was laid out a map of JFK airport, together with diagrams and photographs of a jet engine.

"I assume your airport experience was sufficient to enable you to tell the difference between a DC-10 and an SP-3," he said, pointing to the diagrams. Without waiting for confirmation, he continued, "This is the turbofan engine fitted to Airlantic's fleet of SP-3s, but all you need to know about it is this little part here . . ."

Given a choice, Bob would rather have gone in on foot. It was his experience that people less often remembered faces than cars—but Phil had insisted that he drive and had fitted out his aging Oldsmobile with new license plates and a JFK staff windshield roundel. Not many people, Phil said, walked to work at JFK.

And Phil was right about one thing: In the below-freezing temperatures, it would have taken a Soviet tank to coax the security guard out of his heated box to check the casually flashed identity card—also thoughtfully provided by Phil with the help of Bob's police mug shot from two years earlier. Not that Bob needed any reminding of the link between past and present.

Phil was right about something else, too: Compared with the passenger side, security screening on the Airlantic staff side was nonexistent. Bob took the bag Phil had given him containing the clipboard and dirty white boilersuit and walked straight from the staff parking lot into the Airlantic complex, following signs for Technical Block K.

Nobody challenged him. Nobody seemed even to notice him.

Checking his watch, he was comforted to see he still had fifteen minutes in hand. He found a lavatory and changed into the boilersuit, clipped the identity card to his breast pocket and, clipboard in hand, set off for the maintenance hangar.

The shift change took him by surprise. According to his watch, there were still three minutes to go when a pack of men started advancing down the corridor, laughing and joking, and he realized that he had less time than he had counted on to get the layout of the hangar.

He needn't have worried. The two SP-3 bays were immediately obvious from their unique configuration. Technical Block K had originally been built with shorter aircraft in mind and, from what Bob could see, was still primarily used for Airlantic's medium-haul 727s and DC-9s.

To accommodate the longer SP-3s, a pair of boxlike extensions for the tail section had been let into the rear wall of the maintenance hangar, with the advantage that, having fixed stairways and pivoting platforms, they enabled the entire tail section, including the Number Two engine, to be worked on without ladders or scaffolding.

There was only the one SP-3 in the hangar, dwarfing the other aircraft like a dinosaur in a farmyard. All the other wide-bodied jets were evidently serviced in the adjoining, larger hangars.

He walked across the floor and, feeling suddenly exposed, reconnoitered the scene from the shelter of a DC-9 trailing edge.

John had described the supervisor's office as "like an aquarium hanging from the wall" and, yes, there was no mistaking it—strategically placed about forty feet off the ground against the rear wall at the halfway point.

Two men were standing in it, apparently talking, just as John had said. This was the changeover of shift, and the supervisor of the day shift was handing over to his counterpart on the night shift, notifying him of progress made and problems encountered.

Bob ducked back under the wing and, for the sake of

appearances, scribbled some numbers on his clipboard. Not that anybody seemed to be taking the slightest notice.

Next time he peeked out, he was comforted to see one of the supervisors, now without his white coat, descending the steel stairway. He watched him leave the hangar and then, shedding the protection of the wing, he walked casually across the floor to the area directly beneath the supervisor's office.

And waited.

The new shift—about twenty-five men in all—were milling around the metal frame that normally carried the clipboards and work cards. They, too, were waiting, waiting for orders.

Finally, he heard the *tip-tap, tip-tap* of the supervisor's feet above him and watched as the white-coated figure crossed to the group, a bundle of fresh work cards under one arm.

This, he had been warned, would be the tricky bit. He had to curb any natural instinct to bolt straight up the stairway in case it looked as though he had been waiting for the supervisor to leave. Yet the longer he held back, the less time he would have to find what he was after.

About half the pack of mechanics had drifted off to various parts of the hangar when he decided to go.

The supervisor's back was to the stairway, but there were still half a dozen mechanics on the periphery of the group who Bob knew would be able to see him if they looked up.

It was a risk he had to take.

It felt like the longest climb of his life as, with every step on the clanking metal stairway, he waited for the cry, "Hey, buddy, the super's down here!" His legs dragged like lead, his breath came in gasps; and, by the time he reached the top, the steel of the door handle cool against his sweaty palm was as welcome as water to a drought victim.

He opened the door and, now inside the aquarium, imagined every pair of eyes below focused on him. Two years of being on the run from his own past, of never knowing who would be at the door or even round the corner, had shredded his nerves and, whatever Phil's judgment, he felt in his heart—even more so in his bowels—that he was the least suited person for this sort of caper.

Phil had talked about "the cabinet" but, as he now scanned the office, he saw nothing that remotely resembled a cabinet. He was almost relieved; if there was no cabinet, there was no job—and nothing more he could be expected to do except turn tail and leave.

Then he saw it, half-hidden beneath a carelessly tossed white coat.

After a moment's hesitation, he crossed the floor, knees tingling, and pulled on the handle.

Nothing gave.

He pulled again, his trembling grip giving the handle an inadvertent twist. This time the door flew back, tipping the tall steel structure fractionally forward.

The blue plastic box was on the second shelf at the front.

He checked the contents against his mental picture of the photograph Phil had shown him, then scooped up three of the magnetic plugs and half a dozen O-ring seals, stuffed them into his pocket, and pushed the cabinet door shut.

As he turned, he glanced out of the window. The group below had dispersed. There was no sign of the supervisor, and if he wasn't down below, he had to be . . .

A criminal's instinct told him to meet any unavoidable challenge head-on. Quickly retracing his steps across the office, he closed the door behind him and started back down the stairway.

The supervisor was coming up.

"Looking for Dave," Bob said. "You seen him anywhere?" In any group of more than twenty men there was always a Dave.

"If y'mean Baker," said the supervisor on his way past, "you'll find him on the DC-9."

* * *

"You did well," said Phil, showing the plugs and O-rings to John twenty minutes later. "The next trip'll be even easier. Now why don't you just go and sit in your car and relax awhile."

Bob obeyed, well aware that Phil's desire for his departure had little to do with any concern for his welfare.

He raked the car seat back and stretched out. His blood seemed to be moving around his body in spurts and squirts, but the smell of his own sweat was strangely comforting in an animal way.

He lowered the car window an inch and took deep, controlled breaths. There was a high-pitched mechanical whining coming from the back room and, now that he thought about it, he recalled seeing a small, vertically mounted drill on the end of the bench where Phil had laid out the map, diagrams, and photographs. He counted the number of operations—one . . . two . . . three.

Fifteen minutes later he was summoned back into the workshop.

He sniffed.

There was a different smell about the place. No longer the smell of grease and grime—but, familiar though it was, he couldn't place it. His eye, meanwhile, was caught by a number of shiny metal curls below the drill on the bench, and he persuaded himself it had to be the smell of the oil used to cool the drilling bit.

Phil was holding the plugs, now with their rubber ring seals in place. Even he, Bob noticed, was looking a touch more ragged than previously.

"Right, let's go through the details of the second run," said Phil, pointing again to the diagrams and the photographs.

Bob didn't like what he heard and said so; Phil had said the second run would be easier, whereas it was obvious that the risks would be ten times greater.

"On the contrary," countered Phil. "Since you've already been seen around the place, they're going to take even less notice of you than they did before."

"What? When I'm dismantling a fucking aircraft!"

Phil's genial mask slipped.

"You're dismantling fucking nothing," he retorted. "I've told you, each plug will take a maximum of forty-five seconds if you follow instructions. It's—it's as easy as changing a light bulb."

Protest was pointless. Bob tried a polite inquiry.

"D'you have any objection to telling me what this is all about then?" With a dash of irony he added, "I mean, psychologically speaking, it might help me with my motivation."

Phil looked to John. John sucked his lower lip for several seconds and then said:

"You're no fool, and that's for sure, Bob—and, well, I figure you'll have guessed by now that this is all at a pretty high level—national security, that sort of thing." He slowly brought the tips of his fingers together in a gesture that reminded Bob of a presidential aide briefing the press corps. "Now, ah, obviously, as you'll understand, there's a limit to, ah, how far I can let you in on the details—even I don't have a total overview—but"—he glanced at Phil—"I think we can safely let you in on at least a part of it."

He took one of the plugs from his colleague and pointed the end toward Bob, inviting him to take a closer look.

"What we've done is this: We've drilled through the core of each plug and placed a microfilm in the cavity—one microfilm per plug—and then, as you can see, we've filled in the hole at each end so nobody'll notice. The point is that these things have to be checked and changed every so often as a matter of routine and, if I tell you that there'll be somebody at the next stop who'll be real anxious to carry out a quick change of this particular component—well, I'm sure you get the idea."

Bob recalled the countless spy thrillers that formed the staple of his reading diet.

"You mean an airport mechanic who's actually an undercover agent for us and who's—"

"Now just hold it there!" John cut in. "I never said that. And you just forget everything I've told you, you hear me?"

Bob heard all right and, despite his sarcastic remarks about knowledge improving motivation, he found he really did feel better about the whole business. Seen in a certain light, he was putting his criminal talents at the service of the State; it was almost an honor to be selected for such a job—or, as it had now become in his own mind, "mission." No doubt about it—the SP-3 was headed on its next flight for someplace behind the Iron Curtain. As for the microfilm, that would almost certainly contain secret instructions for the network of U.S. agents working undercover in Eastern Europe.

There was one other question that occurred to him but John had anticipated it:

"Obviously, ah, it would've been easier if we could've brought Airlantic in on the operation, but in this instance the security is at, ah, such a high level that the risk of widening the involvement was felt to be just too great." He took the two remaining plugs from Phil and handed them to Bob. "But, as I say, you know none of this."

Half an hour later, Bob was back in the Airlantic hangar, the belief that he was on the side of the angels giving him the winged confidence he had lacked on the first run.

From what he could see, there were only a couple of mechanics working on the SP-3. One of them was visible only by his legs, the rest of him in the belly of the aircraft, while a colleague held a two-foot light bar at arm's length for him to see by.

Clutching his clipboard, Bob strode purposefully over to the port engine.

As Phil had shown on the diagram, the oil filler access door was unmistakable—low down on the side of the engine pod and bearing bold black lettering to indicate the make and grade of oil to be used. He released the four flick catches and let it drop down.

Inside, it looked exactly like Phil's photographs. A jumble of different gauge pipes filled the frame, but conspicuous in the bottom left-hand corner was the large oil filler cap and there, right by it, the master chip detector housing and plug.

Following Phil's instructions to the letter, he removed one of the plugs from the pocket of his boiler suit, palmed it, and, placing his hand inside the cowling, laid it temporarily on top of the oil filler cap.

Then, moving his hand to the left, he gripped the head of the plug already in the engine and removed it, taking special care, as Phil had warned, not to let it slip from his hand into the casing.

Finally, he fitted the drilled plug in its place, checked that it was properly seated, and slipped the original plug unobtrusively back into his pocket—so that to anyone watching, the most likely impression would have been that he was merely checking the filler cap.

Considering the trouble Bob habitually had fitting light bulbs, it had been a breeze.

A rerun of the operation on the starboard engine also went without a glitch.

Only the tail engine remained.

Phil had said this would involve the least risk of all because the tail was out of sight in its own custom-made cubicle. Also, since the cubicle was fitted with walkways and platforms, one could gain access to the tail engine without the aid of a cherry-picker, even though it was thirty feet off the ground.

Phil had been right about everything else so far and Bob actually found himself whistling as he crossed to the steps that led up to the walkway. He felt good—a professional doing a professional job. On the way, he passed a mechanic at a bench, squirting aerosol lubricant into what looked like part of one of the SP-3's electrical generators. Bob was intrigued to see that it was exactly the same stuff he had been using on his car when Phil had phoned him earlier at home.

"Great stuff, that," he remarked with a grin. "Y'could fuck a mouse with it!"

The mechanic gave a short, hiccup laugh.

"I'll take your word for that, buddy."

A minute later, Bob was up on the lower walkway of the tail cubicle, the top of his head almost level with the tail and the access panel for the Number Two engine right there before his eyes.

The only difference with the procedure this time was that he had to balance the replacement plug on a ledge inside the cowling instead of on the oil filler cap.

Apart from that, no problem. Phil had been right again.

He snapped the panel clips into place and, confident of being safely out of sight, removed all three oily plugs from his pocket, rolled off their seals, and carefully cleaned them with a large sheet of absorbent paper. Phil had said it was important that not a trace of oil was left on them—"as pristine as the papal pecker!"

There was only one thing more to do, and that involved a return to the supervisor's office.

He knew it would be more difficult than on the first occasion, because this time he would have to wait for an opportunity to present itself before he could act.

He positioned himself again beneath the trailing edge of the DC-9 and for the next half hour watched as the white-

coated figure moved around the aquarium-like office—
sometimes standing, sometimes sitting at the desk when only
a bobbing, balding head could be seen.

Bob waited, craving a cigarette like he had never craved
one before and snatching increasingly anxious glances at his
watch.

The supervisor gave every sign of spending the night in
the place, whereas Phil had assured him that he would have
to come down at some point, if only to stretch his legs or
take a leak.

Bob could feel his confidence draining away like water
through sand; the high that he had been on earlier had
already peaked and he was now entering a dangerous phase
of withdrawal. Nervously, he started fingering the plugs in
his pocket and questioning the point of this last phase of the
operation. Phil and John had said it was vitally important,
but they'd said everything was vitally important. Since the
microfilm was now safely inside the aircraft, it didn't seem
worth the risk—and a man had to use his own judgment on
such occasions. So why not just drop the old plugs down a
ventilation shaft and lie when he got back to the workshop?
Who was ever to know?

He had almost made up his mind when he noticed movement in the aquarium.

The supervisor was now standing at the window, a walkie-
talkie to his lips and, judging by the direction he was facing,
talking to the mechanic who had been working on the SP-3
generator fifty or more yards away. Bob could no longer see
the mechanic but it was clear that there was a problem of
some sort. Sure enough, a few seconds later, the supervisor
was out of the aquarium and climbing down to the hangar
floor to make a personal inspection.

He took a deep breath; it was going to be a straight-in-
straight-out operation. And not without risk, for, if the
supervisor could see the mechanic's bench from his office,
the line-of-sight had to work both ways.

He moved across the floor, up the stairway, and within seconds was inside again. Recalling that he had been able to see only the supervisor's head when the man had been seated at his desk, he scuttled across to the cabinet on all fours like a chimpanzee, reached up, pulled the door open, and, taking all three plugs in one hand, tossed them grenade-style into the blue plastic box from which he had earlier taken the other ones.

Twenty minutes later Robert Fischer was back on the Van Wyck Expressway, the airport an arc-lit mirage receding in his rearview mirror. His debt to society repaid with interest.

It would be later that same evening, slumped before the television with a six-pack of Budweiser, that the truth—the enormity of what he had done—would hit him.

In disbelief he would listen to the flash report of the missing Airlantic SP-3 off the coast of Nova Scotia—and at last identify what it was he had smelled in the back room of the auto repair shop.

Wax.

He had no idea of the running temperature of a jet engine, nor of the precise melting properties of wax—but only an idiot could have been ignorant of the likely effect of the one on the other.

PART FOUR

♦

♦

♦

♦

♦

♦

♦ 36 ♦

DC spent most of the two-hour flight back to Chatham wondering how Collins could have missed it. They had split at Airlantic headquarters because DC had wanted to check the security on the staff entrances to the maintenance hangars, but the arrangement had been quite explicit: that they would rendezvous at La Guardia at 6:30.

Back in the Chatham motel he was to encounter more mystery.

From the moment he entered the investigation conference room he was aware of a tension in the air for which, unmistakably, he was in some way responsible. He found himself shunned by men who three days earlier he had thought of as colleagues but who now seemed to regard his presence as an offense to the eye or, worse, the nose.

Unable to see Murphy anywhere, he asked the only person in the room who was prepared to meet his gaze, the girl at the typewriter.

"Mr. Murphy went to his room half an hour ago," she responded with an embarrassment that suggested she had broken a vow of silence.

On his way there, DC prepared himself for what he assumed would be another verbal shoot-out, having now no doubt that some part of his unofficial sleuthing had found its way back to Chatham. Certainly, if Murphy had tried to contact him at Airlantic, he would have quickly discovered that the "few checks" he had been running there had far more to do with Power Plants and Operations than with Human Performance—in short, that he had been trampling over everybody's turf except his own. With hindsight, he should have briefed Fairnington about the possibility of Murphy calling, but it would have been unfair to have involved a man in Fairnington's position in his deception. Unprofessional, even.

It would also have been a help to have had Collins alongside him now to back up his theories about the cause of the crash—instead of being obliged to fly solo into the thunderhead of Murphy's wrath.

He rapped on the hollow door. A door two down opened and shut again as quickly. He rapped again and this time heard Murphy's voice.

"Yeah, come in."

Murphy was standing on the threshold of the bathroom, a towel around his sagging belly, water at his feet. He looked genuinely surprised to see him.

"I thought the chairman had spoken to you," he said. "Didn't he contact you at Airlantic?"

"About what?" DC asked.

Before replying, Murphy crossed the room to pluck his spectacles from the end of the bed, as though in the absence of clothes they might confer some dignity on him.

"You're off the investigation," he said bluntly.

It took DC several seconds to respond. He had expected to be chewed out, not benched.

"The hell I am! When you hear what—"

"Save it for the chairman, DC," Murphy cut in with determined calm. "From now on, he's the one you'll be doing your pleading to."

Whatever had happened in his absence, it was more serious than he had at first imagined. Why should he have to do any pleading to anyone? He took a step toward Murphy.

"I'll report to the chairman when I get the order—from him. In the meantime, you owe me an explanation—and I'm staying here until I get it." He pulled out a chair and sat down, arms folded.

There was a pained smile on Murphy's face.

"I owe *you* an explanation—oh, that's rich, that's rich!"

In the gurgle of ironic laughter DC recognized the slow whip-curl of Murphy's tongue. He was ready for the lash that followed—

"And how about the explanations that you owe *me*? How about the explanations that you owe all of us working on this investigation?"

—but not for the snap in the tail:

"How about your trip to Derby, England?"

He flinched. So that was it.

"It was on board business," he said defiantly.

"*Unauthorized* board business," retorted Murphy, "except insofar as you thought the board's name could help you ransack Rolls-Royce's technical library."

It added up. He remembered now that George Schofield had given his name to get a photocopy of the report of the Miami incident. He had thought at the time that it might start telexes flying but had forgotten about it amid all that had happened since.

Yet how he had got the information was now irrelevant; the important thing was that he *had* got it. Even Murphy had to see that.

"Do you know what turned up in that 'ransacking'?" he asked.

Murphy didn't and, having wound himself up for the big performance, he wasn't going to be sidetracked now.

"DC, I neither know nor care. It's not the result that concerns me; it's the principle. No investigation can tolerate mavericks. An investigation is a team effort or it's nothing; there's no place for the glory boys. It has to be said, DC: Temperamentally you're just not cut out for investigation work. I don't deny you have the perseverance but you lack the patience; you want to be ahead of the pack at every turn and that's just not fair on the other guys. Well, you can't say I haven't warned you before about operating outside the loop. It's no—"

"Okay, Doug, okay." DC raised his hands in surrender. "I did wrong and I admit it. I was shooting from the lip just now and I'm sorry. You're right—it's me that owes you the explanation, and if you'll just listen a moment, I'll—"

In retrospect, the word "listen" had been ill-chosen.

"It's no longer a matter of *me* listening," Murphy sputtered. "Any listening that's going to be done from now on will be strictly between you and the chairman. You're no longer a part of this investigation, DC—and that's final."

The combined effects of the shower and the heightened emotion had misted Murphy's spectacles. He removed them and, wiping the lenses on a corner of the bedsheet, continued:

"I have nothing more to say to you, and there's nothing more I want to hear from you. It was my understanding after talking with the chairman that he was getting in touch with the two of you at Airlantic and was going to call you both back to Washington from there. If you insist on having the order from him personally, I suggest you take the next flight back and go and see him. Frankly, by the time you get there, I'd be surprised if you're still even an employee of the board in any meaningful sense." He paused to adjust the towel around his ill-defined midriff. "The chairman's thinking when I last spoke to him was that you should be suspended immediately from all board work pending either your resignation or your dismissal. I've submitted a report on your conduct to the board and I guess you're entitled to do the same—although personally I wouldn't bother."

DC stared at him in silence. Neither of them had emerged from the confrontation with any credit, but there had been some satisfaction in seeing Murphy obliged to play his big scene without the benefit of wardrobe. He stood up to leave.

"You look absurd," he said and slammed the door behind him.

*   *   *

His own room was as he had left
it—except for a note that had been pushed under the door.
The writing was unfamiliar but not the initial:

Meet me at Coast Guard beach at ten tonight—T.

All thought of the investigation and the fact that he was
now out of a job was on the instant banished from DC's
mind. It was not that he had forgotten about Terry but
rather that, since his failed attempt to contact her from
England, he had not dared to hope for fear of further
disappointment.

He looked again at the note and then at his watch. It
was already half past nine. He picked up the telephone and
ordered a taxi through the front desk.

While he waited and paced, a thought occurred to him:
since he had been away from the motel for the previous two
nights, how could he be sure that the assignation was for
this evening and not for one of the previous evenings?

He couldn't. The only comfort lay in the belief that the
maid who checked the room would have been unlikely to
have left the note on the floor. But that was assuming . . .

His fretting was interrupted by the squeal of the phone.
The taxi was waiting.

Outside in the motel parking lot
there was at least one indicator that he had got the right
night: Terry's dark blue Pontiac was nowhere to be seen.
That and the fact that her room key had been in the slot
buoyed his hopes throughout the fifteen-minute journey north
up Route 6.

At the Visitors Center there was still no sign of her car
but, recalling the wording of the note, he hadn't really
expected any and instructed the taxi driver to follow the
twisting road down to the beach. The driver let out a long
sigh that could be taken only as a general condemnation of
all crazy, out-of-season off-Capers.

They rounded the last bend and there, behind the old white clapboard Coast Guard house, was what DC most wanted to see in all the world at this moment: a low silhouette which, caught in the headlights, revealed itself as a dark blue Pontiac.

There was nobody in it, but the license plate confirmed it was Terry's.

He paid off the taxi and watched the tail lights weave back between the pines to the main highway.

In his hurried departure from the motel he had failed to bring a flashlight with him, but any fear he might otherwise have entertained at being abandoned on a wild, winter coastline in the dark was soon dispelled by the thought of Terry waiting down on the beach. She would be certain to have a flashlight. She thought of these things.

Guided only by the cloud-filtered glow of a weak half moon, he scuffed his way down to the shore and, breasting the wind, headed up the beach.

He was aware of his heart pounding, and not only from exertion. All the old feelings that in the last couple of days he had tried so hard to suppress welled back up to the surface. Whatever impression she liked to give the world, she was in reality as romantic as he was. Why else go to such lengths to arrange such a rendezvous when she could so much more easily have arranged to meet him in the motel bar? But no, the beach had a sentimental significance for them. It was her way of indicating that the misunderstanding in New Jersey had been forgotten—that they should start again where they had left off.

The sea was calmer than on the previous occasion. The waves, dimly phosphorescent with plankton, lapped the shoreline with a regular, lazy slap. After a time, he found his eyes were able to distinguish shades of black in the darkness and quickened his pace, wondering how far along she could have got.

There was a sound behind him. He stopped.

His first thought was that she was playing a game, and he smiled to himself in the darkness before realizing that it was only a trickle of shale from high up on the cliff face—just part of the never-ending erosion of the coastline. He stumbled on, wondering whether he should now call out. But even in the dark, he reasoned, it was impossible that they should miss each other.

Then he saw it—the beam of a flashlight dancing in the distance.

He ran now. The smell of the sea was again the smell of her damp hair; the sound of the foam the sound of her teasing laugh when she had asked whether their trip to New Jersey would be strictly business.

He remembered her story about the mooncussers—how they, too, used lights to lure their innocent victims onto the coast, to wreck and then plunder them. It was an appropriate metaphor, except that on this occasion there had never been a more willing candidate for emotional shipwreck. He plunged forward and, the flashlight now less than twenty yards away, called out:

"Hey, mooncusser, where've you been all my life?"

The beam did a jig in response but there was no answer. He laughed.

"C'mon now, quit the games! I haven't come all this way for—"

Arms were around him—iron pincers that snapped about his ribcage from behind. The flashlight was advancing.

For several seconds he was paralyzed by shock. Then, struggling for breath, he was aware of his whole body being lifted off the ground and gave an instinctive backward kick. There was a sharp "Aar!" as his heel dug into his assailant's shin. The grip around his chest eased a fraction but the flashlight was now full in his face—so close that the horseshoe coil of the bulb branded its image on his retina, filling every corner of the sky with its ghosts.

He waited for the blow to fall—from which direction he could only guess. Still the flashlight was in his face, still he waited, but still it didn't come. Even stranger, the only sounds from his attackers were the grunts and groans of their exertion. He was being mugged by mutes.

Again he felt himself being lifted but this time the flashlight was on the sand. Whoever had been holding it was now grabbing him around the ankles, while the other assailant still had him around the chest. He lashed out with feet and head in the hope of catching something, but still, inexplicably, there was no attempt to immobilize him by the most obvious means—a blow to the groin or solar plexus.

Yet it was a hopeless struggle.

Finally overpowered, he was aware of being borne horizontally like a rolled-up carpet toward the sea—and at last he understood.

His brain reacted in the way it had been trained to react in the cockpit in the face of an emergency, distancing itself from the immediate action in order to analyze the available information. To calculate the odds.

On the minus side, he was outnumbered at least two to one by men whose undoubted intention was to drown him. On the plus side, his assailants seemed bound by whatever contract they were under not to leave any mark on the body. His death had to look accidental. The key to his survival therefore lay in exploiting that advantage—and the only other thing on his side: the dark.

The icy water took his breath away a second time. But again his pilot's mind stood outside the situation, viewing it rationally and objectively, consigning the shock of the assault to a separate and sealed mental compartment.

Whatever their numerical superiority, it would be no easy matter for two men to drown a third of comparable strength without ropes or recourse to disabling violence. While one of them would be fully occupied holding the feet together, the other would have to keep the head below water—and to do that he would have to slide his grip up above the victim's elbow joint. The only alternative would be for the two of them to wade with him into the waves right up to their own necks—and risk being tipped off balance by the powerful undertow.

His only hope of escape, therefore, lay in persuading his attackers that they could do their work in waist-deep water.

He stopped fighting. Went limp.

It seemed to work. He felt the grip move up his arm and, taking a last gasp before his head went under, found he now had sufficient movement in the lower arms to crook his left forearm up behind his back.

He waited for the the next big wave and then, with full and sudden force coupled with all the finer fighting instincts of a New York street kid, drove his fist up into the soft, yielding flesh of his assailant's groin.

Instantly, the iron grip sprang open. His torso free, he backed into a hairpin, grabbed one of the ankles of the other attacker, and jerked it off the seabed, plunging them both into the surf.

For the first time he had the advantage. Kicking out in the dark, he felt his foot connect with something that elicited a satisfying snap and groan. Behind him he could hear the retching of his first victim.

For a moment all was still. Even the waves paused to draw breath.

He reckoned he had five seconds—certainly no more—in which to plan his next move. Already, as he struggled to clear his head, the groaning at his feet was giving way to swearing. The next move had to be the right move or it would be his last.

The only thing to catch his eye was the flashlight, still glowing where it had been left on the beach. The instant he saw it, he knew what he had to do. Just as it was the flashlight that had lured him into the trap, so the flashlight

was now the only thing that could deprive him of his sol
remaining advantage—the cover of darkness.

He started to run toward it but was scythed off at th
knees by a crippling spasm in his right ankle. Whateve
damage he had inflicted on the second attacker had been a
a cost. On all fours, therefore, he scrambled toward th
beach, scooped up the flashlight, and flung it far out to sea
Like a dying star, it looped through the air, blinked, an
was no more.

From the surf came the sound of voices.

The logical move—the expected move—would be to shi
up the sandy cliff face or set off at full speed back along th
beach. But with his sprained ankle, he knew that climbin
and sprinting were both out of the question. Instead, h
limped in the opposite direction and, arcing around, rolle
back into the freezing surf.

As the in-shore wind rebounded off the cliffs, it carrie
toward him snatches of conversation—of a sort that left n
doubt about the fate that would await him if caught
second time. For what seemed an eternity the two me
roamed up and down the beach in search of their prey, a
one point coming so close that he had to push himself bac
into deeper water.

For the first time he started to worry about the possibl
effects of the cold. He knew that if he had been out of hi
depth, he'd most likely have been dead by now—a victim o
cramp followed by respiratory collapse. The danger wher
he was, buffeted by the surf, was not drowning but a
equally lethal loss of body temperature.

Already his limbs were numb and his breathing wa
perilously shallow. It was becoming an effort to maintai
his grip on the shifting shingle. He could feel his brai
shrinking to the size of a walnut; could actually visualize it
wrinkled and rattling within his skull, as mind and bod
slipped away into a voluntary, terminal hibernation.

With alarm, the part of his mind still functioning registered that his body had stopped shivering. The systems were closing down. The end could not be far off. Another minute and he would be pulled out to sea by the undertow, to float for a few seconds before spinning like a dead fish in slow spirals, head down, to the bottom.

Then there were no more voices. He wondered if his hearing was failing him like the rest of his body but, no, the surf and the sea were still audible. They had gone.

He dragged himself back up the beach like a wounded seal and for five minutes and more lay in a fetal ball, his knees beneath his chin. With tingling stealth, he felt sensation return to his limbs and was even relieved to feel the ache in his ankle again.

He now regretted having so hastily disposed of the flashlight but after several minutes found what he was looking for—a length of driftwood that could be improvised as a crutch.

It took him half an hour to hobble in his sodden clothing the couple of hundred yards back to the Coast Guard house but at least the effort generated warmth, and the warmth in turn invigorated the muscles.

His mind took longer to recover but, the immediate danger over, he started to question the reasons behind his present plight and, more specifically, what part Terry could have played in the setup. The last thing he wanted to believe was that she had consciously lured him to what should have been his death; yet how else could he explain the note and the presence of her car behind the Coast Guard house?

Unless . . .

Painful though it was, the possibility had to be faced that, like him, she could have been followed all the way down to their planned rendezvous on the beach. And murdered while waiting for him.

A ghastly image filled his mind: of her body even at that

moment lying in the freezing surf just a few yards from where he himself had taken refuge. It was so overwhelming that he stopped and considered returning to the spot, even though he was now in sight of the Coast Guard house. A second time he regretted his reckless disposal of the flashlight. Why, instead of throwing it away, had he not just turned the damned thing off?

But there would be one fair pointer to the truth—the car. If her car was still parked behind the Coast Guard house, he told himself, the probability was that she, too, had been attacked.

And if it wasn't?

Then he would have to acknowledge that she had been part of a conspiracy to lure him to his death, and, since there had been no sign of any other vehicles, might even have provided the transport by which his attackers had reached the beach.

As he pulled himself up the last few yards to the Coast Guard house, he didn't know which would cause him more pain—to mourn her death or curse her life.

He rounded the side of the building and, surveying the parking lot by the fitful moonlight, felt the sudden blast of wind plant the kiss of Judas on his cheek. It was empty.

Oblivious to cold and pain alike, DC stomped the half mile back from the beach to the main highway, fueled by an anger that burned deep within him.

He was in luck. A truck driver had stopped at the Visitors Center pull-off to relieve himself. He looked at the sodden bundle of humanity before him and, not the least deflected from the business in hand, listened to DC's request for help. Sure thing, he smiled, it'd be no trouble to give him a ride back to his motel.

* * *

A quarter of an hour later, DC was standing again in the motel parking lot. There was no sign of Terry's Pontiac.

It was after midnight. In the lobby, the only service still operating was an automatic dispenser for the *Boston Herald*. The front desk was deserted.

Seizing the opportunity, he removed both his own key and Terry's from their slots and hurried to his room before his extraordinary appearance raised any unwanted questions.

Never had a hot shower felt better. His flesh rippled beneath the jets as they injected life and color back into his wax-white body. He dried himself off and filled a glass with hot water from the tap, mixing it with a whisky miniature from the refrigerator. The whisky masked the foul taste of the water and by the second glass and second whisky he could expand his lungs without the feeling that his ribs had been welded together.

Gently he probed his ankle, which was assuming pumpkin proportions. Nothing seemed broken, and with the aid of a knotted sock he improvised a support bandage, tested it, and found it worked tolerably well.

Dressed again in dry clothes, he locked the door behind him and limped down the corridor to Terry's room, key in hand.

It gave every appearance of still being occupied—dresses in the wardrobe, toiletries above the washbasin, suitcase on the rack. For a moment he was puzzled. Was this seeming normality a further indication of her complicity in his near demise, or not?

A few seconds' thought convinced him it was. If his attackers had been successful in making his death appear like accidental drowning, the local cops would have soon checked back at the motel and questioned those who were known to have had contact with him—Terry included. For her to have checked out the night he drowned would have aroused precisely the suspicion she was no doubt anxious to avoid.

That she wasn't there now was easy enough to explain: She and her accomplices would have assumed that he would report the attack to the police and were even at this moment no doubt deliberating how best to kick over the traces of their bungling. In all probability she would turn up in the morning with some elaborate alibi to explain her movements.

But not before he had carried out his own investigation. In fact, the last thing he wanted was the police involved. The satisfaction of tracking her down and confronting her with her guilt was going to be his—and his alone.

He searched the entire room but found nothing of interest. Not a single incriminating scrap of paper. But, as he rummaged, explanations for her behavior throughout their brief relationship began for the first time to suggest themselves.

Slowly, one pivotal truth emerged: that she had been working all along for whoever was responsible for sabotaging the SP-3. That alone made sense of everything else. Although it pained him to have to admit it, Murphy had been right about one thing—she was no innocent guest who just happened to have booked into the motel at the same time as a high-powered N.T.S.B. team working on one of the biggest air crashes in years.

But Murphy had been wrong in suggesting that she was a top-notch journalist working undercover. She was there to snoop all right, but more particularly to monitor the progress of the investigation and, if necessary, alert her masters, whoever they were, if it ever looked as though the investigators were about to hit on the real reasons for the crash. Using all her feminine guile, she had attached herself to the first member of the team who'd made a pass at her and had then subtly milked him for information.

Subtly? No, he was flattering himself.

Looking back, he could see she had made a monkey of him, tickling his male vanity with cosy dinners *"à deux"* and romantic clinches on windswept beaches. And all the time secretly laughing at him.

Little wonder then that her mood had changed so suddenly in New Jersey. After the interview with Aldridge's widow, it would have been alarmingly clear to her that here was one investigator who was not going to be satisfied until he had unearthed the truth. It was her good fortune that she had attached herself to him, and her duty to inform her masters as quickly as possible that he represented the greatest threat to their well-planned cover-up.

At last he understood the reasons for her abrupt change of plans that night—the lies about the girlfriend in Manhattan and her precipitate departure for La Guardia. He also realized that he need not have worried about how long her note had been waiting for him in his motel room. She and her accomplices would have been dangling the same bait every night until his return.

The only thing he hadn't checked during his search of the room was the plastic folder on the writing desk. It was identical to the folder in his own room and, he assumed, in every other room in the motel.

Flipping it open, he found the usual collection of creased stationery, flattering postcards, and promotional material for local restaurants—while, tucked into one of its transparent pockets, was a copy of *Cape Cod Life* in case the awful anonymity of the motel caused the visitor to forget where he was.

He closed it. Then paused and reopened it.

There had been something wrong about the cover of the magazine.

It showed Hyannis Port, which was fine—but in summer. The only explanation was that it had to be a back number. He checked. It was. According to the date, six and a half years back! But only when he saw the words

"QUILTS"—a reference to one of the articles inside—did he make the connection.

He slid the magazine out of its transparent pocket and flicked through to the article which he had formerly seen only in photocopy—in the motel bar the evening they had first met.

"DO YOU HAVE A QUILT COMPLEX?" asked the familiar headline. Beneath it, the byline: "Karen Davies."

He read the name again. Stared at it. Mouthed it. Even spoke it out loud.

He could swear that the name on the photocopy had been "Terry Morrow." In fact, he knew it had been, because he remembered her pointing it out as proof of her harmless credentials. And it was inconceivable that the magazine would have run two such articles, with identical headlines and identical layouts, but by different authors.

There could be only one explanation: She had used the article to give credibility to her phoney identity. She had taken a real article by a real writer—Karen Davies—and photocopied her own name or, more likely, her professional pseudonym, over the byline. And by choosing an article published six and a half years previously, she could be reasonably sure that nobody was going to blow her cover by stumbling on the original. Unless that somebody searched her room. That had been her only mistake—not destroying it.

He sat down on the bed. All the proof he needed was in his hands. The last vestige of hope that she might after all have been an innocent victim of extraordinary circumstances melted before his eyes.

He felt suddenly vulnerable. Before knowing the true extent of Terry's complicity and the sophisticated nature of the surveillance exercise she was involved in, he had thought he would be reasonably safe from

ny further attempt on his life, if only because his assailants
would assume that he had alerted the police.

Now he wondered. If, as appeared to be the case, he had
been singled out as a target from the start because of his
investigative zeal, it followed that he would remain a target
at least until he was able to share what he knew about the
sabotage of the SP-3's plugs with an authoritative third
party.

In retrospect, his action in returning to the motel seemed
suddenly foolhardy. Now to compound that recklessness by
returning to his room and staying the rest of the night alone
there would be like checking into a funeral parlor.

It was imperative to change rooms, so that anybody
inspecting his present room would assume he had panicked, packed, and run. Even if they were more suspicious,
they would hardly go knocking on all the other doors in the
motel to be sure. Yet he also had to be ready and waiting for
Terry's return to the motel, whenever that was going to be.

The solution was obvious: He would move into her room.

It took just fifteen minutes. Only
one thing then remained to be done—to return both keys to
the front desk, so that Terry would not only not suspect any
interference with her room but, seeing his key there, too,
would assume he had never returned to the motel or had
already left.

Leaving the door on the latch, he walked back along the
corridor to the lobby and slid the keys into their respective
slots. As he did so, his eye fell on the file of guest registration
slips, tucked away on a shelf beneath the desk. He pulled it out
and ran through it until he came to the card for Room 128.

It was as he had expected. The name "Morrow, Ms.
Teresa" was there, but the only address was "c/o *Cape Cod
Life*, Osterville, Massachusetts."

If for nothing else, she deserved credit for consistency.

*   *   *

The vigil had been in vain. By seven o'clock when the dawn seeped over the window sill, DC had to acknowledge that the chances of Terry returning to the motel were diminishing by the minute.

The only hope lay in the thought he had had earlier—that, after spending the night concocting an alibi, she might return sometime during the morning just for the sake of appearances and to collect her belongings. But there was a limit to how long he could wait, for just as pressing now was the need to return to Washington to see the chairman.

At eight-fifteen he phoned N.T.S.B. headquarters and got through to Shepherd's secretary. The chairman wouldn't be able to see him before late afternoon—5:00 P.M. at the earliest. He had an exceptionally full schedule, including one meeting that had to be kept open-ended. DC sighed. Five P.M. it would have to be then.

He called the air taxi company to arrange a flight. They had no aircraft in Chatham at the moment but were expecting one in from New York late morning. It was scheduled to return to New York by nightfall, but a detour via Washington could be arranged. How would a 1:30 P.M. takeoff suit him? "Just fine," he said, and ordered a cab for 1:00 P.M., taking the precaution of talking to the firm direct instead of asking the front desk to do it for him.

He settled back on the bed with four hours to kill—four hours during which he dared not even leave the room in case Terry returned. Not that he wanted to anyway. As a persona indisputably non grata, he had no desire to bump into Murphy, Kaplan, Seeward, or any other member of the team at the moment. He would save it all for the chairman.

It was with a sense of relief that he took to the air again just after one-thirty. Neither Terry nor anyone else had appeared during the morning, and he had left the room as he had found it. Almost.

He had taken two things with him. First, the copy of *Cape Cod Life*, with which to confront Terry at some later date. And second, a cashmere scarf which he had recognized as the one she had been wearing the day they had gone up to Provincetown. Finding that it still smelled of the sea and perfume, he had folded it flat and tucked it inside his waistband. Why, he couldn't explain—except perhaps in terms of emotional masochism. Like a hair shirt to a penitent, it satisfied a psychological need too complex to be rationalized.

The pilot was the chatty type. As the twin-engined Cessna wheeled over Nauset Beach to head south, he pointed to the horizon where layers of dense cloud merged with the Atlantic swell.

"Kinda scuzzy, huh?" he shouted above the threshing of the engines, "Cloud base must be down to about seven-fifty. Did they tell you about the deer that swim over to Nantucket? Imagine that! It must be all of twelve-fifteen miles." He half-turned. "You're a pilot yourself, right?"

Sitting diagonally behind him in the cabin, DC grunted. "A few years back."

Martha's Vineyard was coming up on the starboard side. Without warning, they dropped to within a couple of hundred feet of a panhandle spit of land.

"Chappaquiddick!" the pilot yelled, again pointing. "See the bridge? That's where it all happened. Yes, sir, that's where brother Teddy sank the Kennedys' last hope of getting another man into the White House! Leastways, that's what I figure . . . D'you still get to put enough hours in to keep your license topped up?"

DC responded that he preferred to read rather than fight a decibel duel with the engines. No offense intended.

The pilot looked around, obliging him to pull from his

jacket pocket the only reading material close at hand—the copy of *Cape Cod Life*.

Half an hour later he had read every article except the one on quilt-making.

"How's the readin' goin'?" yelled the pilot, looking again for a conversational opening.

"Just fine," responded DC and reluctantly turned to the quilts article, persuading himself that one of the greater regrets of his life had been his ignorance of the finer points of needlework.

The strangest sensation stole over him as he read, and with every snappy sentence, every sassy aside, the conviction grew.

He *knew* the writer; would have sworn it on a stack of Bibles. The style was as immediately identifiable as if . . . as if she had been sitting and chatting next to him.

Or opposite, across a steaming bowl of quahog clam chowder.

He told himself it wasn't possible. Anyway, it didn't make sense. She had wanted to make out she was something and somebody she was not and so, with the help of a photocopier, had poached the identity of—he flicked back to the beginning of the article—this Karen Davies woman. Her choice of article had been purely opportunistic, almost arbitrary, the only requirement being that it be both innocuous and out of date.

Or had he got the whole thing back to front? Had she in fact been Karen Davies the writer all along but, wishing on this occasion to keep her true identity secret, had chosen a pseudonym which then required her to modify the byline on her *own* article?

The more he thought about it, the more it came to seem the obvious explanation. And if so, he had a good idea how he could track her down.

*   *   *

An hour later he stood hunched in a telephone booth in a Washington shopping mall, the copy of *Cape Cod Life* propped at eye level before him, open at the page which listed the magazine's personnel.

His eye tracked down the column, past circulation manager, distribution coordinator, and newsstand distributor, until it reached the telephone number for the editorial office in Osterville, MA. He punched it out and, as he waited, stared through the glass at a sign opposite advertising gourmet popcorn. It was good to be back among the big-city sophisticates. What he wouldn't give right now for a Cordon Bleu hot dog!

"*Cape Cod Life*. Can I help you?"

He asked to be put through to the editor. The speaker apologized—the editor was out of town right now but she was sure there'd be somebody in the office who'd be able to help.

There was—a young woman with a mallow-soft Massachusetts accent who described herself as the magazine's production assistant.

DC introduced himself as a New York literary agent. He reeled off an imaginary name, sticking an "Associates" on the end to add a little classy authenticity. One of his clients, he said, had seen this article in a back number of the magazine and had been particularly impressed. The writer's name—he paused as though checking—yes, Karen Davies. Did they by any chance have a contact address or phone number for Ms. Davies so he could talk to her on his client's behalf? There could be a pretty lucrative commission in it for her.

He read out the details of the article. The production assistant gave a low whistle when she heard the date of the issue—"That's really going back some!"—and asked him to hang on while she checked.

As he waited, he could hear the whoosh and clunk of filing cabinet drawers. Not one but half a dozen. Ms. Davies, it seemed, was either a most irregular contributor to the magazine or had simply not worked for them for a very long while—perhaps even six and a half years.

"I think we could have a problem here," said the production assistant at last. "We've no Karen Davies listed in our contributors' index, and I've checked back through our payment records for the issue in which that article was published. The only address—if you can call it that—is a Washington post office box number."

"Washington?" It was as though he had brushed against a high-voltage cable.

"That's right, sir."

He took it down.

"And that's all—no telephone number?"

"I'm sorry, no."

"What about your editor? Wouldn't he have some way of contacting her?"

"Could be, sir, but he isn't expected back in his office for at least half an hour. I can ask him then if you want. If you give me your number I'll call you back."

"There's no way of you or me getting in touch with him before then?"

"No, sir. If I knew where he was I'd have suggested that."

There was a hint of resentment in her voice. To push harder would be counterproductive.

"Okay," he replied. "Look, I appreciate your help, but, instead of you calling me, I'll call you—about an hour from now. You did say that the P.O. box was in Washington, right?"

"Right, sir. Washington, D.C."

He put down the receiver and pulled out the C & P directory for the Washington metropolitan area. Now that he thought about it, one of the many things that Terry had avoided in their talks together had been any discussion about where she lived. He'd asked, but the question had been deflected with a vague "Depends where I'm working and what on," leaving the clear impression that further inquiry would be unwelcome.

He thumbed through the Ds until he came to Davies. There were plenty but no Karens. The only K. Davieses were Karls, Keiths, Kurts, Kenneths—and a single Katherine. He called Information but they had nothing either. In fact, the more he thought about it, the more it seemed likely that she would be unlisted—and that was assuming that, all these years later, she was still in Washington.

He felt a kind of despair setting in. She could be on the other side of the street or on the other side of the world, and—but for a chance encounter—he might die without ever knowing which. As he flipped the directory closed, his eye was caught by an entry that had been ringed in red ballpoint by a previous occupant.

It read: the Mental Health Crisis Resolution Service (Suicide).

◆ 37 ◆

THE CHAIRMAN was in no mood for polite preliminaries.

"I'm not sure what you hope to achieve by this meeting, Di Coiano," he said, glancing at his watch. "I've already talked to Collins, and Doug Murphy tells me he's already talked to you. It seems to me we both know all we need to know."

DC ignored the low-slung armchair that Shepherd had indicated and instead brought in close to the desk one of the upright chairs which, physically at least, would put him on an equal level. The news that Collins had already been interrogated was as he had feared. Certainly Collins would have been able to explain the technicalities of what they had discovered in the Airlantic labs—better even than DC himself—but, in attempting to argue a case before Shepherd, he would have lacked the experience to handle the sort of verbal intimidation of which Shepherd was a master practitioner.

"Collins told you our thoughts about sabotage then," he said tentatively.

"Told me them, yes, although whether it adds up to sabotage is another matter."

"You mean you think we've got it wrong?"

"Let's say that with hindsight I'm not sure it was a good idea to team the two of you up. Quite apart from your own buccaneering attitude toward the feelings of your colleagues, it looks to me like you got carried away and read more into matters than a strictly professional approach would have warranted. But that'll be for somebody else to decide. All the relevant material has already been impounded."

The more DC heard, the less he liked it. As usual, Shepherd was trying to wind him up, but this time he was determined not to repeat the mistake he had made with Murphy, when the argument had degenerated into a shouting match almost before it had begun. Shepherd was a far more formidable adversary—able to grasp the significance and nuances of a complex situation before anybody else, and then exploit it to his own advantage. As DC now saw his task, it was to focus that ability on the situation that he and Collins had discovered in the Airlantic labs and then, by taking him through the facts carefully and calmly, lead Shepherd to the same inescapable conclusion they had arrived at. The key word was "calm."

"Look," he began, resting his forearms on the desktop, "I accept that I am now off this case and okay, I may have been guilty of a degree of professional misconduct in the way I've gone about things in the last few days. Putting that to one side, though, I am convinced that there is no way that plug change on that aircraft could have happened accidentally. If I had a reputation still to stake on it, I'd stake it. Collins and I went through every other possibility, and every time we arrived back at the same place. Those plugs were tampered with. No question."

"Well, let's just take one thing at a time, shall we?" said Shepherd with an ominous lift of the eyebrow. "Are you saying that those plugs were changed or that they were tampered with? There's an important difference, and, if I've heard you correctly, I'd sure like to know *how* they were tampered with."

It was the one question to which DC had no answer—which no doubt was why Shepherd had seized upon it.

"I don't know," he said—with what he hoped was disarming candor. "It could have been done in any one of a dozen different ways. I get the clearest impression, though, that whatever was done to those plugs was intended to ensure that the engines lost their oil at a point in the flight when the aircraft could be assumed to be beyond the Continental Shelf—and suddenly; the crew seem to have had next to no warning from their instruments. As I read it, the intention was to bury that flight in the deepest water possible, together with its black boxes and any other potentially incriminating evidence. And since the engines were the heaviest items on the aircraft—the ones that would therefore sink to the greatest depth—they were the ideal candidates for sabotage."

"So you still can't tell me *how* they were sabotaged."

There was an incipient sneer in Shepherd's voice. Don't let the man get to you, DC told himself. Just hang in there and he'll come around.

"No, not exactly, but—"

Shepherd turned away, spinning his executive chair to face the picture window overlooking the Mall. Dusk was giving way to dark. One by one, the arcs were picking out the capital's landmarks, while around them the lights of a thousand commuter cars wove their rush-hour spaghetti.

"And what about this 'Miami incident' report that you dug up in Derby, England?" Shepherd asked at last. "Collins seemed to think it was important."

DC saw the trap.

"It's important only insofar as it establishes a precedent," he said, picking his words carefully.

"You mean you think the Miami incident was also sabotage?"

"No, that was accidental, beyond doubt. When I say precedent, I mean it would have indicated to any potential saboteur where the SP-3 was at its most vulnerable—its Achilles' heel, if you like."

Shepherd continued to gaze contemplatively out of the window.

"So how do you know this wasn't also a case of carelessness? How can you be so sure that this time it wasn't a pair of *Airlantic* mechanics who forgot to fit a couple of two-bit washers?" He swung around to face DC again. "And don't give me any garbage about there being no 'record' of a plug change. I had all that from Collins. There's no record of a lot of things in this industry, but they still happen—and most often on night shifts. Ask any investigator in this building."

It was as DC had feared. Collins had been subjected to one of Shepherd's classic demolition jobs—and by the sound of it had caved in. Personally, though, he still felt on firmer ground.

"The records themselves are only the bottom line in this," he answered. "More relevant are the lab procedures which Airlantic follows in compiling those records. If you take the procedures and the records together, you arrive at only one conclusion—that at some point within two days of the flight, perhaps even two hours, somebody changed those plugs without authorization and *then*—this is the important point—cleaned up the ones he had removed and returned them to the supervisor's cabinet. In other words, he tried to cover his tracks. He knew that Airlantic numbered its plugs and realized it would be possible for an investigator at a later date to add up the total and check that there were no more than three missing. Six missing plugs would have raised suspicions. What he overlooked—or simply didn't know—was the precise way the plug numbers were logged on the lab computer. That was his undoing. Those computer records prove not only that the plugs must have been changed on the aircraft within two days of the crash, but also that whoever did it had the presence of mind to put the ones he had removed back into circulation without going through the labs where the change would have been noted. Technically, mathematically, and logically, a deliberate act of sabotage is the only possible explanation."

Shepherd remained unimpressed.

"It's one opinion. Other people may have others."

DC felt crushed. The whole burden of what he had just been saying was that it was *not* a matter of opinion, but a verifiable certainty! Yet it was apparent that Shepherd had made not the slightest attempt even to grasp it, let alone argue it. In spite of all that he had vowed, DC couldn't stop himself.

"Well, how for Christ's sake do *you* explain it?" he burst out. "Did those plugs just walk off that aircraft and jump into the supervisor's cabinet of their own accord—or what? I'm asking. If what I've just said is only a matter of opinion, you give me your opinion!"

It was not the way to address one's esteemed chairman but it was too late to take it back. From now on, he realized, the more passionately he argued his case, the more clearly he would demonstrate in Shepherd's eyes how temperamentally unsuited he was to make *any* rational judgment.

Yet he couldn't understand it. Why was the man apparently so determined not to see the truth, when in this case it was as much an intellectual effort not to see it as it was to see it? It was as if . . . as if he didn't *want* to see it.

"So you're saying," said Shepherd, looking again at his watch, "that whatever happened, you don't know how it happened, only that it did happen."

DC had no answer. He thought of going over the whole history of the last week, from the burned oil stain on the tail plane to the attempt to drown him—but, with the man in his present frame of mind, he knew what the response would be: Why, in each case, had he not notified the appropriate authorities—Investigator-in-Charge Murphy and the police, respectively?

Something inside him crumbled. He felt bewildered and bruised. Once again, he seemed to have fought the wrong fight, or, rather, fought the right fight but the wrong way. He sat, punch-drunk, while Shepherd lifted the phone to call his driver to take him home. He tried one last throw.

"Shepherd, please—if you're not prepared to listen to me, will you just take a look at those computer records with Airlantic's lab director, Dr. Warner. He'll explain it better than I can."

The chairman pulled his briefcase up onto the desk and scooped papers into it.

"You seem to have a lot of faith in computers, Di Coiano. I just hope that at the end of all this you'll still think it was worth blowing your career for."

"And that was it. He got up and walked out!"

Lieberman was sympathetic but not surprised.

"DC, I figure there are a couple of things you should know," he said, placing a cup of black coffee on the table. "You haven't been around this place for the last thirty-six ours and, well, things've been happening here that have otten some of us thinking—and it looks like they're connected with whatever you found up at Airlantic."

He paused, checked the corridor outside the audio lab nd, closing the door, returned to the listening room.

"The chairman had a lunchtime meeting today," he said a a confidential whisper, sitting down opposite DC at the ble.

"So?"

"With the President's adviser on national security."

"Anderson?"

"Right, and it was at Anderson's instigation. I was going) say 'request,' but according to the rumors that have been ying around the chairman's office there was no request bout it."

"What are you saying, Ben?"

"I'm saying that the President's adviser on national secu- ty doesn't summon the chairman of the Safety Board at the eight of a major air crash investigation for a cosy tête-a- ête about their golf swings."

"You think the chairman's being leaned on?"

"That's the way it looks. Collins had a session with him esterday evening as soon as he returned from Airlantic and ame out looking twenty years older. Now, I don't have to ·ll you that Scott Collins has always been the golden boy in ne eyes of our esteemed chairman—but I swear to you, I've ever seen anybody who'd more obviously been put through ne wringer. He was that shocked, he wouldn't even talk bout it. Then, first thing this morning, the summons to the Vhite House was on Shepherd's desk."

DC sipped his coffee, tapping the plastic spoon on the abletop. He didn't doubt that Terry's surveillance activity, he attempt to murder him, and the sabotage of Flight 639 vere all links in the same chain, but to suggest that that hain then clanked all the way up the steps of the White Iouse—that was one hell of a speculative leap. Even if it did help explain Shepherd's peculiar reluctance to come te terms with the evidence of the plugs.

"I don't know, Ben," he said with a shake of the head "Certainly what Collins and I found up at Airlantic is dyna mite, but Jesus ... Okay, we both know that this place i subject to political pressures, but pressures from within th aviation industry or from our friends upstairs in the FAA— the rewriting of a crash report, a change of emphasis to giv more weight to one probable cause than another, that sor of thing. But what you're suggesting is that the Board ha agreed to be muzzled in a case involving sabotage and th death of more than two hundred and fifty innocent civilians."

Lieberman's voice was barely audible.

"DC, the chairman is a presidential appointee."

"Sure, but he's also answerable to Congress."

"President first, Congress second. And I tell you, in a matter of national security it would never get to second base. Now do you understand what I am saying? As a friend, I'm worried for you."

DC hesitated, and then told Lieberman about his experi ences on the beach the previous evening, as well as Terry' part in it. As though the testimony required proof, he raised his leg to reveal the swollen ankle. The blood drained from Lieberman's face.

"So what the hell are you doing *here*?" he hissed. "DC do yourself a favor—just get as far away from this place a possible. Go on vacation—anything. Anywhere, but away from here. I tell you, I've never yet enjoyed a Christian funeral and yours I'd enjoy less than most."

"Yeah, okay, I hear you," DC said, hand raised.

Lieberman's fear was infectious but it wasn't going te solve anything. He considered calling his attorney but tha smacked of panic. Anyway, he'd probably have left hi office by now. He looked up at the clock—and banged the table with such force that the coffee jumped in the cup.

"Sh-it!"

His mind dominated by so many other matters, he had clean forgotten to call back *Cape Cod Life*. It was a quarter past six—and he had promised to call them back at a quarter *to* six. He lunged for the phone.

"What are you doing?" asked Lieberman.

"Don't worry. It's all connected."

Lieberman placed his hand over the telephone.

"DC, don't be crazy! If it's connected with the investigation, make it from somewhere else. It's too risky here."

DC wrenched the hand away and, holding the machine out of Lieberman's reach, started tapping in the area code for Osterville.

"Ben, I don't have the time to go and find another phone. I should've called half an hour ago. As it is, I'll be lucky to catch them." He tapped in the remaining numbers and waited, bouncing his fist on the table to the rhythmic purr of the dial tone. Aware of Lieberman's continuing gesticulations, he added, "Ben, if nobody in this building is willing or wanting to listen to me, I have to get to the bottom of this thing myself—and there's only one route I know."

He was in luck—but only just. Another thirty seconds, the production assistant told him, and she would have locked up the office and gone home.

"So what news have you got for me on Ms. Davies?" he asked, glancing at Lieberman, who was now delivering a prayer—maybe an imprecation—to the ceiling.

"Well . . . ," she started. He recognized the tone. It was the sort of "Well" that was intended to prepare the hearer for disappointment. ". . . I don't know whether this is going to be a whole lot of help to you, but the editor has checked back through his correspondence file and he's come across the letter in which Ms. Davies first offered us her services."

"With an address or still the box number?"

"No, there's an address all right. Trouble is, it could be six years or more out of date."

"But it's Washington?"

"Uh-huh. I'll give it to you if you really think it might still be any good."

He scribbled it down, blessed her, promised to take out a life subscription, and put the receiver down. It was the first piece of good luck in twenty-four hours.

Lieberman wasn't disposed to share in the celebration.

"You're crazy—and crazier still if you now do what I think you're going to do."

DC looked again at the slip of paper, then stuffed it into his back pocket. On his way out of the door, he gripped Lieberman by the shoulder.

"Ben, I promise you, it's okay. It may be dark out there, but I know the way."

A quarter of a mile away, in a nondescript government building on the other side of the Mall, a man in rolled-up shirtsleeves had also scribbled down the address. He removed his headphones, stubbed out his cigarette, and picked up an internal telephone.

"Mike? I've got something for you."

It was archetypal Georgetown, right down to the brass carriage lamp by the front door—the sort of pastel-painted, louver-shuttered Washington townhouse which, just to rent, would cost between a thousand and fifteen hundred dollars a month; and to buy, well over a quarter of a million. Whatever Terry was, writer or professional snooper, she was doing well out of it.

The curtains were drawn but a single light glinted through the open-weave fabric. Once DC thought he saw it cast a shadow, but he wasn't sure. A thin trail of smoke rose from the chimney.

He stood on a patch of grass beneath a high brick wall on the upper reaches of P Street, watching the house from the other side of the old tram tracks. An unspecifiable form of moisture was dropping from the sky—not rain, not sleet, not snow; more like chips of ice. Anybody with any sense was inside.

The sole passerby in the hour and twenty minutes he had been watching had been a woman with an ill-disciplined retriever which she addressed with increasing exasperation as "Bugsy." DC guessed the family name had to be Malone and, by the effort the woman required to drag the animal past, that he was standing on Bugsy's pooping patch.

The mercury was plummeting. He could feel the grass beneath his feet crisping with the cold and he knew that, if nothing happened soon, he would have to take the initiative.

Although it was the one thing he had been waiting for, the opening door caught him by surprise.

The silhouetted figure hugged itself against the sudden cold and, struggling to retain balance on the icy brick sidewalk, teetered downhill away from where he was standing. It was unmistakably a woman and, despite his previous experience with the flashlight on the beach, he felt sure that this time it was Terry.

Cars were parked on both sides of the road but she passed them all. Had she been getting a cab, he reasoned, she would surely in this weather have called for one to collect her from the door.

Then he remembered that there was a small general store across the next intersection. It was within walking distance and in the direction she was heading. He looked back to the house. The light inside had been left on. It all seemed to add up.

To the extent that he had formulated any plan, he now

started to put it into action. Stalking his prey on foot had always been out of the question, and not just because of his ankle. Any encounter with Terry, he had vowed, was going to be face-to-face, in a place that was both private and secure. And if that involved a little amateur breaking and entry—even violence—he had only to remind himself of how close he had come to death just twenty-four hours earlier to firm his resolve.

He crossed the street.

Although the house was to all appearances the standard two-story frame structure, a quick peek over the white picket fence alongside revealed that below street level there was in fact another floor which gave on to a small paved patio about eight feet down. In the normal way, the patio could be reached only by the basement back door, but even for a cripple with a sprained ankle it required no great feat of athleticism to get a leg over the fence and, holding on to a spindly sapling, shimmy down like a fireman.

He paused at the bottom. Until now, it had never occurred to him that Terry might live with somebody or even be married. He had no doubt that there had been offers by the truckload, but she had struck him as just, well, too independent for any sort of permanent relationship. And, like her address, it was another area of her private life that she had skillfully avoided talking about.

Cautiously, he pressed his ear to one of the panes of the single basement window. There was no sound. He cupped his hands against the glass and peered in.

A straight staircase, the lower part of its banister and balusters exposed, led up to the softly lit ground floor, but there was no suggestion of habitation—no movement, no shadows.

He couldn't afford to wait. If he was right about the shopping expedition, it was a walk of no more than ten minutes each way. Perhaps fifteen on the icy sidewalks.

Testing the door and window, he found both locked. But

the window was made up of small six-inch panes and, so far as he could see, without the benefit of any antitheft catch. He chose the middle top pane of the bottom frame and gave it a jabbing punch with his gloved fist.

The pieces tumbled inside, their fall only partially deadened by a thick pile carpet. If anybody was inside, they would now be alerted to his presence. He listened but, hearing only the sound of his own breathing, reached through, flicked the locking lever, and raised the lower frame enough to let himself in. He paused again for several seconds, then moved on—and up.

He emerged into the ground-floor living room, his head still at the level of the polished pine floorboards. Straight ahead, a log fire hissed in response to the moisture dropping down the chimney.

A few more steps brought him into the room. Along the far wall was a deep buttoned chesterfield and, before it, a cane coffee table strewn with magazines. In the corner by the window a large, straggling pot plant was drooping beneath the weight of its own leaves.

Another flight of stairs, identical to the one he had just climbed, led to the upper floor and the bedrooms. He stood on the bottom step and listened. Still nothing—the only sound the hissing of the fire and the comforting creaks of the old wooden frame house.

He felt an animal desire to warm himself by the fire, to rub life back into his frozen limbs, but since it was barely fifteen feet from the front door and there was no porch, he would then have no warning of her return. Instead, he removed his coat, pushed his scarf and gloves down one arm, and settled himself on the stairs leading up to the bedrooms. Hidden by the barred shadows of the balustrade, he would be able to observe her for a vital few seconds before she realized he was there.

*   *   *

As he waited, the homey atmosphere of the place, the sweet smell of the sizzling applewood in the grate combining with the waxy warmth of the pine floorboards, seeped into his senses, seductive and soporific. He had to keep reminding himself why he had come; had to stoke up his anger and outrage.

And yet it was just such an atmosphere, he realized with an ache, that he had been missing over the last week of his barren hotel and motel existence. Longer than that even— for the truth was that he had been missing it ever since the breakup of his marriage two years earlier.

Again, he had to remind himself that he had come not to lick his wounds but to bring the fight to the enemy, to exact answers and, if necessary, retribution.

There was the rasp of a Yale key in the lock, followed by the rattle of the external screen as the front door was opened and slammed shut.

Out of sight around the corner, he pushed himself deeper into the shadows—and listened.

The only sound was of something being put down on a table in the kitchen off to the left of the front door. There was a rustle of paper, followed by the pneumatic wheeze of a refrigerator door. Then the gurgle and splash of pouring liquid.

"And I'll bet you could do with a little something too, huh?"

He froze. It was Terry's voice. No doubt about it. But who was with her—a lover, a kid? It was that sort of voice. His hand on his coat, he glanced over his shoulder, ready to make a dash up to the bedrooms.

"How about a small saucer of milk on this f-f-f-freezing night?"

He heard—or perhaps just imagined—an appreciative purr in response. He closed his eyes and drew a long even breath, as the sound of more pouring liquid was followed by the regular, contented slap of a feline tongue.

A minute later, footsteps came into the living room to within a few feet of him. Glass in hand, Terry snapped on the television built into the shelving beneath the stairs and fell back onto the sofa, kicking off her shoes. In a single fluid movement, she raised both feet and tucked them, protectively, beneath her legs.

Still unseen, he stared at her from behind the balustrade and felt again what he had felt the first time he had seen her in the mirror in the ghastly bar of the Pilgrims Motel—the sense of privilege of watching a beautiful, elegant creature without its knowing; a creature that, observed or not, was as incapable of an awkward gesture as the planets were of breaking orbit or water of running uphill.

She rapped out a succession of taps on the remote control, switching in turn from a quiz show to an old movie to a studio discussion on abortion, then sighed, and hit the Off button.

For several seconds she stared, lost in thought, at the dying screen, then sighed again and sipped her drink.

✦ 38 ✦

THERE WAS no start, not even a sudden intake of breath, as she caught sight of the figure hunched behind the balustrade. Nor, knowing her, had DC expected any. Of the two of them, he thought he was probably the more nervous.

"So are you going to tell me how you tracked me down or do I have to guess?" Her voice was as controlled as if she were addressing a tiresome child.

"You left your calling card—your real calling card—in your room at the motel. Remember the quilts article?"

She looked down at her drink and gave the ice cubes a prod with the swizzle stick. Her display of insolent coolness, whether real or feigned, suddenly infuriated him. He stepped from the shadows and seized her by the wrist, sending the contents of the glass over the back of the sofa.

"Terry, I didn't come here to play intellectual fucking games! What I want to hear is your explanation for what happened last night."

He grabbed her other wrist and, resting his full weight now on her curled-up legs, effectively immobilized her. He half-expected her to shout or scream, then realized that would never be her style. Instead, she stared back at him with a look of outraged innocence.

"Last night? I was *here* last night. I've been here since the night I left you in New Jersey."

"You mean the night you supposedly spent with your girlfriend in Manhattan—the night you went via La Guardia airport. Remember? Or would you like some time to consider which story might fit your purpose better?"

He could smell her perfume now—strong, and, for all her outward composure, sharply accentuated by fear. Like a shark sensing blood, he forced her hard back against the sofa, squeezing her wrists with such force that the splayed fingers quivered like tuning forks. He could feel the blood pumping furiously through her veins and for the first time understood how intermingled were the passions of sex and violence, how a man could commit rape out of hatred. He wanted to violate her, to tear her apart with his own body—to enter, ransack, and defile her most intimate recesses in a welter of blood and sperm.

She, too, seemed to understand something of the uncontrollable brutality now asserting itself and, for the first time, her composure cracked.

"DC, stop! . . . Just listen to me, just for a moment . . . let me explain!"

There was real alarm in her eyes. Her whole body shook. It was so unlike any state he had ever seen her in before that he instantly released his grip and stepped back. Despite his right to retribution, he felt suddenly ashamed and frightened by his capacity for violence.

"It'd . . . it'd just better be good. That's all, that's all," he repeated, breathlessly. He sat down on the sofa next to her, still within arm's reach in case she had a mind to make a break for it. "I tell you, my patience is limited."

"I p-promise you, DC," she stammered, "the night I left you in New Jersey I came back here, straight back here. I've barely been out since. Only, like tonight, to go to the store. You must believe me!"

"Like you expect me to believe you had nothing to do with the attempt to kill me last night down on the Coast Guard beach?"

The terror in her eyes gave way to surprise. Or a clever counterfeit of it.

"*Kill* you?"

"Yes, kill me!" He could feel his muscles tensing again. "The message in my room; your car in the parking lot behind the old Coast Guard house; the romantic rendezvous with the illusive mooncusser—and your prick-teasing complicity in the whole fucking business!"

She shook her head, the loose curls falling across her face.

"DC, I swear I don't know what you're talking about. The car, if you mean the Pontiac, was rented. I left it up on the Cape at the motel—together with all my belongings in my room. I've told you, I've been here ever since I left you in New Jersey. You *must* believe me!"

He tugged his billfold from a back pocket and held the still uncreased note within inches of her eyes.

"You're telling me that's not your writing?"

She stared at it.

"That? Never! You can check for yourself." She reached forward, but he caught her wrist.

There was a half-finished letter on the coffee table, the pen still resting diagonally across it. Keeping hold of her, he picked it up and examined it at arm's length. It was true; the writing was quite different, although the address at the top was hers. Still he wasn't persuaded.

"How do I know you don't share this place with a girlfriend and that this isn't her letter?"

"Look underneath. You'll find the letter from my mother that I'm replying to."

He glanced down. The opened letter started, "My dearest Kerry . . ."

"My family has never called me 'Karen'—but always 'Kerry,'" she explained. "That's why I chose 'Terry' as a pseudonym. It was close enough for me not to be fazed when anybody called me it."

Again he released his hold on her. He had been wrong about the note. And if he had been wrong about that . . .

She sensed his confusion.

"DC, I swear I had no idea that anybody was going to try to kill you. I thought . . ."

He looked up sharply.

"You thought what?"

"I thought—I was told—that the idea was merely to keep an eye on you so that, if necessary, you could be taken off the investigation. There was never any indication that you'd come to any harm. I'm telling you the truth. I swear it."

For a sickening second he wondered if he had made a total fool of himself, had gotten *everything* wrong. But no. The fact remained—and she had just confirmed it—that she had been sent to spy on him, or at least on whichever dumb bastard was first to show himself susceptible to her pretty face and shapely legs. He heaved a sigh.

"Let's go back to the beginning. What is your job—your *real* job?"

She seemed to relax. Some of her former composure restored, she answered.

"I'm both a writer and an occasional government agent— paid snooper, if that's what you want to call it. They're both my 'real' jobs. The one is the perfect cover for the other. Being a writer enables me to be in unlikely places and ask probing questions without arousing suspicion. At least normally—when I don't leave copies of my original work around for other snoopers to find."

"And you were sent to Chatham to spy on the investigation."

"Yes—to keep an eye on its progress and report back any developments. I latched on to you and got an early break."

"The tail up at Provincetown."

"Right. After you pointed out the significance of the oil stain on it—remember how carefully you explained it all when you were examining it on the truck?—I phoned my superiors before meeting you back at the car and they took care of it on its way back to Chatham. Your hunch about the cops was right."

"And then?"

"Then it all became more complicated. I guess I started to like you. As simple and corny as that. I tried not to. It's like being a nurse, this job—you mustn't get emotionally attached to the patients. I always thought I could handle my own emotions, but when we went to New Jersey for the interview with Aldridge's widow, well, that was a kind of turning point, I guess."

"In what way?"

"I thought I had you all figured out. Poor Italian boy made good. Typical macho male, liked to impress, to shoot a line. Easy to string along."

"And?"

"Then I realized you were more sensitive than you let on. I don't mean just more vulnerable—that type's always vulnerable if you know where to look. I mean more willing to admit your vulnerability and lay yourself open. And there was something else I learned about you in New Jersey. I realized that you were not just a nice guy but genuinely—I don't know what the word is—honorable, I guess. I couldn't believe that anybody who'd lost his job like you'd lost it would then turn around and fight for the reputation of the man who'd screwed him. It would've been so much easier for you to have done nothing. I still thought you were a fool, but an honorable fool."

"And that was why you left so abruptly?"

"That was why. Doing this job is like being an actress but having to improvise a whole play, and with an element of real risk if your performance doesn't convince. Normally I get a real buzz out of that, but for the first time I felt bad about myself, and that was hard. I could justify what I was doing on the rational level, but emotionally I knew it was affecting my performance. So I came straight back here and got them to take me off the case. I told them I'd caught a virus and been confined to bed."

"And the interview with Aldridge's widow—what did you tell them about that?"

She didn't miss a beat.

"The truth, of course. If I hadn't, they would've suspected my reasons for wanting to be taken off. I told them the interview had confirmed your belief that this wasn't a case of crew error and that you were more determined than ever to keep digging—with or without the help of your colleagues. I imagine that as a result they would've monitored your movements even more closely. From what you say happened to you last night, they did more than monitor."

*   *   *

DC's head teemed with conflicting
otions. The only comfort was that the truth was margin-
more palatable than he had thought. She had good
son to feel bad about herself, but he believed her when
said she hadn't known about the plan to kill him. He
perately wanted to believe more, but—as any air crash
estigator knew—desperately wanting to believe something
somebody was always dangerous.

He looked at her again and wondered how far she was
playing a role—indeed, whether her psychological makeup
s such that she was capable of ever playing anything else.

"Do you know why that aircraft fell out of the sky?" he
ed, fearing her answer.

"Not exactly, but I can guess. I assume it was sabotage. I
't see any other reason why I should've been told to
ort back on how the investigation was going."

"You mean you knew that and yet still agreed to do the
?"

"Yes."

Something inside DC gave way. The thread of faith he
d been clinging to snapped. How could she, who had just
agratulated him on being honorable, have knowingly got-
involved in such a cover-up?

"Listen, DC," she added with a sudden assertiveness, "I
n't want you to get the wrong idea about me. I am not
at you think I am or what you want me to be. I'm not a
ty Hearst figure. You're not looking at a little innocent
o's gotten caught up in the big bad world and now needs
be rescued and returned to the bosom of her family. I'm
t of that big bad world—of my own free will and with
baby-brown eyes wide open. This wasn't a one-time
apade. Do you think my bosses would have accepted at
e value my reasons for taking myself off the job if they
ln't had good reason to trust me? This is my job, DC—
t as investigating air crashes is yours. You and I have set
rselves different priorities, which along the way involve

different concepts of morality. Yet in our different w
we're both government employees, both public serva
The reason I came back here was not that I thought
snooping was wrong or immoral, but because I knew t
my emotional involvement with you would interfere w
my ability to do a good job. Far from being sentimenta
was actually being ruthlessly professional. If you want me
be really honest, the only thing I regret is not having
turned to the motel that night to clear my room."

She paused and, correctly anticipating his next questi
went on:

"How can I live with myself? Do I sleep easily at nig
You want to know?"

"If you want to tell me."

"First things first. Now you know that I wasn't invol
in trying to kill you and now that I know—at least thin
know—that you're not going to try to kill *me*, why don
get us both a drink? I figure we could do with one."

DC nodded and watched her go out to the kitchen. I
stockinged feet on the bare boards aroused in him stra
feelings of domestic sexuality—a fleeting vision of a life t
he now knew could never be but which, until a min
earlier, a small part of his subconscious had still hop
possible.

She returned with two glasses—one, a rye and dry.

"You see, I remembered. That was what I spilled o
you when I left the bar in New Jersey. The refill is on
house."

He forced a smile.

"You were going to tell me how you sleep at nigh
Despite himself, the sexual innuendo had crept into his voi

She curled up on the sofa as before, her stockinged t
now nudging against his thigh, insidiously cosy.

"You mean how I justify the official murder of t
hundred and fifty-four innocent people and my part in p
verting the course of the investigation into it?"

"That, too, if you want to be specific."

"It's very simple. Two words: Freedom costs. If our mocratic system is to survive, there are occasions when me uncomfortable decisions have to be taken and, once ken, implemented."

"And what about the freedom of the individual to get on plane and not be blown out of the sky by his own vernment? What do they teach you on the training course out *that*?"

His sarcasm failed to ruffle her.

"I see no inconsistency," she continued coolly. "Is it so democratic a notion that in exceptional circumstances the inority should be sacrificed for the sake and survival of the ajority?"

Instead of responding, he looked away. Every time he ipped away a layer, he seemed to find a different person neath—and this was the least attractive yet.

"Look," she said, for the first time reacting emotionally his disapproval, "you asked me to explain myself—how I stified my existence. I'm not trying to convert you. You're e sort who'll always do what is 'right,' and I envy you that ility to see everything in terms of good and evil. All I ask u to realize is that the reason decent, fair-minded, freedom-ving liberals like yourself can walk with your heads held high along the paths of righteousness is that there are ople like me who are prepared to go down on their knees d get their hands dirty to keep those paths clean! So if casionally, like now, you step into something nasty and u choose to look down, perhaps you should do so more in preciation than revulsion."

"And what then?" he retorted. "Ignore it, just step over Cross to the other side?"

"That's up to you. The mere fact of something's being cret doesn't give you the right to expose it. There are good crets and bad secrets. But if you insist on stopping for closer look, you should help clear it out of the way or,

if you don't want to soil your pretty hands—then, y
walk on."

He shook his head.

"Just tell me this, do you know why that jet w
sabotaged?"

"Of course not—and if I asked I wouldn't be told. I ha
no right to know."

"And that doesn't bother you, for Christ's sake?"

"Why should it? Do you think the man who works in
government missile factory is 'bothered' by not knowi
who they're going to be used against? This is not a busine
for bleeding hearts, DC. You have to take the overvie
There are times when 'in defense of freedom' has to
justification enough."

She leaned forward and quite unexpectedly took h
hand. It was an ironic but significant reversal of roles aft
his earlier attempts to shackle her.

"DC," she said, softly now, "I've told you all I know
ask for nothing in return except your understanding. I'm n
asking you to believe what I believe; only to see that I
believe it. Do you see that?"

"I do, but . . ."

She sealed his lips with a finger.

" 'I do' is enough. Don't make things more complicat
than they need be."

His hands moved up her forearm to pull the finger awa
Instead, he found himself lightly kissing it—and was awa
again of the comforting warmth of his surroundings, t
crackle of logs in the grate, her presence beside him.

"You can stay here, you know that," she whispere
strands of her hair now catching against his unshaven chee

He could feel himself being bound hand and foot
scented, silken bonds—emasculated by his own masculinit
as his lips traveled down the slope of her neck into the so
swell of her cleavage.

*   *   *

The bedroom was warm and dark.
They lay side by side on the crumpled sheets, she on her
k, he face down. His arm rested across her, the hand
ping her breast. He rolled over onto his back, his body
ped but his thoughts churning.

"You realize the truth'll come out eventually. They may
e to wait a few months for the weather to improve but at
e stage that wreckage'll be raised. There's no problem
n the technology; it's only a question of money."

"Exactly," she sighed sleepily.

"Meaning?"

She shifted her position to face him, even though there
s no light to see by. "Well, where do you think the
ney's going to come from?"

"Federal funds, I guess . . ." He saw what she meant.
ou think they'd refuse? No, it'd be too obvious. I don't
eve that."

"Depends how it's done. What if they were simply to
ue that the salvage money—ten million, a hundred million?
vould be better spent on funding FAA research into fire-
stant fuel or cabin interiors or something? It'd look
ressively public-spirited in view of the number of passen-
s who die every year as a result of fire. By comparison,
number who drown in ditchings is infinitesimal."

DC had to admit that such an argument stood a good
nce of being accepted. If so, the real reason for the crash
uld never be known. Collins would already have been
midated into silence by Chairman Shepherd, while he
l no doubt that Airlantic's computer tapes would by now
e been suitably modified—wiped, even.

Which left only the plugs themselves—the smoking guns
the case—and each one of them was safely embedded in
ee and a half tons of turbofan jet engine three miles
vn on the floor of the Atlantic. Safer from scrutiny than
hey had been cast in concrete; too deep even to be
feted by the tides.

Tides.

As he drifted in and out of consciousness, he had uncomfortable sensation of the icy water of the Atla lapping his feet; of two hundred and fifty-four bodies b borne in toward him on the floodtide, bobbing and bloa And he, ignoring them, walking along the beach arm in with Terry, seduced both physically and mentally, hav persuaded himself that this was one of those occasions w innocent people had to be sacrificed to the cause of f dom; that it was in everybody's best interests if he just l walking.

The figure of Gerald Aldridge rose before him out of surf, neck craned forward, immaculate as ever in unife but, absurdly, without shoes or socks and with his trou rolled up. And smiling, for God's sake! No, no, not smil Smirking. Aldridge was staring at the two of them, arm arm, taunting him for trading his conscience for a one-n stand. "At least, Di Coiano," he was saying, "at leas might have been more acceptable, more forgivable in eyes of the Almighty, if you had traded it for someth more permanent."

DC put out his hand and, finding Terry's head, pus her hair back gently over her ear.

"You awake?"

"Hmm."

"Can I ask you something—something important?"

"Like what?"

"Like would you ever consider giving up all this if were asked to?"

"Who's asking?"

His lips took some time to phrase the answer.

"*I'm* asking."

She gave a teasing laugh.

"And offering?"

"Whatever you want ... a permanent relationship marriage?"

Her hand reached out to touch his face in the dark. She
lled his head toward her and kissed his cheek.

"DC, you're an incurable romantic. It must be the Italian
ood. But thanks for the offer."

He lay again in silence. The "but" had been his answer.
e hadn't even taken him seriously.

By dawn, he had made up his mind.
He would go back to New York, back to Alan Fairnington
Airlantic. In the face of official indifference or outright
enace, it was the only course of action. The computer
pes might have been modified but there was still an expert
tness in the form of Lab Director Warner. Warner had
t only seen the figures on the screen, but it was he who
d first pointed out the discrepancy. With his testimony,
e Airlantic chairman's backing, and the report of the
iami incident, it might yet be possible to put together a
ima facie case which, even if it wouldn't convince a court,
uld interest the press. Thereafter, the public pressure to
ise the wreckage from the seabed, at whatever cost, would
come irresistible.

But the journey to New York would require care and
cumspection. Taking the shuttle was out: It was doubtful
hether he would even get through the airport doors, let
one pass the barrier. Renting a car would be equally
zardous, since he would be required to produce a driver's
ense and credit card.

That left only one form of transport that could ensure
onymity and get him there in reasonable time—three and
half hours, if he remembered right.

She was turned away from him,
ll asleep, the covers thrown back. He raised himself on his
bow and for more than a minute observed the regular rise

and fall of her breathing, tracing with his eye the line of h
profile against the pillow, the angle between neck and sho
der, traveling the rippling length of her spine to where t
sheet bisected her buttocks. Meticulously he stored it all
his memory. He wanted to kiss her—more in blessing tha
desire—but feared that it might wake her.

He gathered up his clothes and, remembering that t
bedroom door grated on its hinges, eased himself around
and tiptoed downstairs.

From the kitchen he made two calls—one to Amtra
information desk, who told him *The Virginian* was due
leave Union Station from track L-25 in three-quarters of
hour; the other to Diamond Cabs to order a taxi to pi
him up at the front door in ten minutes. No later.

He placed the receiver carefully back on its cradle a
listened. Upstairs, all was quiet.

He washed his face under the kitchen tap—there was
time to shave—and used the lavatory in the basement. The
quickly and quietly, he dressed and checked his briefcase.
an afterthought, he pulled out the cashmere scarf he ha
taken from Terry's motel room, gave it the kiss he ha
forgone ten minutes earlier, and placed it on the coffee tab
where she would be sure to see it. It would speak mo
eloquently than any hastily scribbled farewell.

The freshly gilded eagles abov
Union Station sparkled in the morning light as, twenty mi
utes later, he paid off the cab and, with a glance at h
watch, headed for the ticket office.

Inside, he paid in dollar bills and, by a circuitous rou
dictated by renovation work, eventually arrived at t
waiting area for passengers traveling to Penn Station, Ne
York City.

Again he checked his watch. It was barely five minut
before the scheduled departure time but the Amtrak barri

guard was exercising his petty prerogative and holding everybody back.

He felt an almost panicky desire to get away. Whereas the Cape had been menacing, Washington was corrupting—a place where a man's soul was in more danger than his body. As though in sympathy, his ankle started to throb.

A woman with a baby slung in a pouch asked him if the train stopped at Wilmington. Not knowing, he referred her to a man in a blue parka standing beside him. The man brushed her off with a curt "Don't know, lady" and looked away. The woman shrugged. He was tempted to remonstrate with the man, but he didn't. The last thing he wanted right now was to draw attention to himself.

PRING-NG-NG-NG-NG-NG!

She opened her eyes and, propping herself up, shouted through the partially open door.

"DC? You down there?"

" 'T'sonly the mailman!" she heard him reply.

She sank back on the pillow, looked at the bedside clock, and puckered her brow. The mailman hadn't come at this hour in months.

The front door slammed, then a car door. A second later she heard the car start up and pull away.

She was out of the bed and across the room, tearing at the window catch just in time to see a Diamond cab disappear around the corner.

A thousand thoughts pierced her semi-consciousness, as she threw open the bedroom door and screamed down the stairs.

There was no response. She snatched the telephone from the beside table and, from memory, punched out the number of Diamond Cabs.

Busy.

She pulled on a pair of slacks and a shirt and, still struggling into her shoes, tried the number again.

"Diamond Cabs. Can I help you?"

Her words tumbling over each other, she gave her address and added:

"One of your drivers has just picked up a fare from here ... I must know where he's heading ..." She thought quickly. "He's left something behind; I have to get it to him."

With practiced calm, the woman on the other end said she would have to ask her colleagues, as she had only just come on duty.

Ten seconds later, she was back on the line. Yes, a gentleman had ordered a cab for that address. It was taking him to Union Station. If he had left something behind, they'd gladly pass on a message to him over the driver's radio.

"No, no, that won't be necessary—but thank you," she blurted. "I'll catch up with him at the station." A belated thought occurred to her. "This gentleman, did he say which train he was taking?"

Another pause, another discussion. Finally:

"My colleague's not certain but she thinks he mentioned *The Virginian*—seemed he was in a real hurry to catch it."

She abandoned the car directly in front of the station, discarding it with no more thought than if it were a candy wrapper.

The first Amtrak official she saw directed her to track L-25. He started to add that she would have to be quick if she wanted to catch *The Virginian* but never finished the sentence.

Running through corridors of builders' plywood, she had the impression of moving without covering distance. Physical objects conspired against her—unmanned baggage carts moved across her path, the heels of her shoes forced themselves into grooves and gratings, while signs managed of their own accord to be deliberately ambiguous. In her frustration she started to weep, so that her already unsteady vision became still more blurred.

Rounding the final corner, she saw the knot of people at the barrier that led down to the track. Her brain tried to separate the crowd into its component parts but her eyes refused to focus through the tears.

She screamed.

"DC! DC!"

Faces turned. Then one part of the crowd detached itself from the rest.

She ran forward, anxiety and relief flowing through her now in equal measure.

"DC, don't go! If you do, they'll kill—"

The word and the deed fused in a single sound—an absurdly theatrical *"CRACK!"* echoed by the duller impact of a Samsonite briefcase hitting the ground. She rushed forward but, as he fell, a second bullet ripped into the neck and snapped his head back in a silent howl.

The only other figure to move was wearing a blue parka. Fleet as a shadow, it swept past and back down the plywood corridor.

He was in the surf again on the Coast Guard beach. Face up. Above him, hands were struggling to keep his head above water but it was impossibly heavy. He could already taste the salt in his mouth as the waves seeped in at the corners and then closed over him.

Staring up through the flecked surf, he could see she was saying something. He struggled to comprehend but his ears, too, were now stopped by the water. With a sudden desperation, he grasped for the shingle and the reassurance of the shore beneath him.

It wasn't there. He willed his arms to move, to claw his way back to the surface, but his mind had lost the power of command over his body. The systems were closing down. Floating and sinking, he was being pulled out to sea by the undertow. Now spinning, head down, in slow spirals.

Epilogue

Time past and time future,
What might have been and what has been
Point to one end, which is always present.

—T.S. ELIOT, "Burnt Norton"

THE TWO MEN stand side by side on the terrace, glasses in hand, surveying the valley of vines and olives that fall away below. The air is warm and laced with the fragrance of wild myrtle. The Italian, the older of the two, turns to face the house and points to the crumbling stonework.

"I warned to you that it is primitive, eh?" he says. "But at least you are seeing it at the best time of the year. Of all the seasons, the spring is the most beautiful here. The handsome prince, the Sun, he kisses his sleeping beauty, the Earth, and she stretches her limbs, opens her eyes, and awakes. Adonis is slain by the boar and is sent to the underworld, but the gods take pity and allow him to return to his beloved Aphrodite for just six months of every year. Myths, legends, even fairy tales—they are all about the same thing. About renewal and regeneration. About hope!"

"It was kind of you to invite us," says his guest.

"Kind? But how can I *not* invite you? When you tell to me that you will be staying in Florence with your family only twenty kilometers away, of course you must be invited! I am sorry you can stay only for lunch."

He glances behind him. The Dutchman's daughters are playing on the other side of the house; from the kitchen comes the sound of cooking.

"Also . . . ," the Italian continues more quietly, "also, I think it is right that you and I are here today and I am glad of it for that reason. You know, I obliged your Medcalf to

349

promise to me that we will meet here, but I think we both knew that it will not be possible for him." He looks down into his glass, then into the distance at a wave of dark cypresses coursing down the hillside. "So, let us together think of him for a little moment. Let us drink to his memory, for he was a brave man and we all owe him much."

They raise their glasses, drink, and lapse into silence.

"Did NATO not ever investigate his death?" the Italian asks suddenly.

The Dutchman pauses before answering. "All things considered, it was thought best that the official verdict be accepted. In America it seems many people die in their baths of natural causes. A hundred and fifty a year on average." He catches the Italian's eye and says no more.

The Italian nods. "It all seems a very long time ago since I was talking with you and the secretary-general that night in Brussels. So many things have happened in a very few months. Good things, too, I think. The Yugoslavs have lost Macedonia, it is true, but they are fortunate still to have the other five-sixes of their country. And look at NATO—how much stronger she is now, how much more confident. You know, I think perhaps those people are right who say that a little adultery can make wonders for a marriage! Sometimes we need a shock to make us understand what is truly important." His tone changes. "But two hundred and fifty people die to make us realize it, that is a heavy price! For me, the loss of my colleagues was very great, you can imagine, but I think more great for their families. Sometimes I am wondering if it is not better if they know what really happened and why." He notes the twitch of the Dutchman's head, the sudden scrutiny in the eyes, and lays a hand on his arm. "Do not preoccupy yourself, my friend. You can trust me never to say nothing. Like the death of your Medcalf, we must always accept the official verdict. Yes? So it will always remain an accident and a mystery."

The Dutchman's daughters emerge onto the terrace bear-
plates and cutlery which they proceed noisily to arrange
the lunch table. The two men move farther down the
ey.

"About that night," says the Dutchman. "You asked me
ut Medcalf. I wish to ask you a question also."

"But I think you know everything."

"What happened, yes. I know that, instead of taking the
ht you were booked on—the Airlantic one to Rome—
took another one direct to Brussels. What I have never
derstood is why you changed. It was as if you had, well, a
monition of the crash."

The Italian shakes his head. "Ah, sadly no. You think I
allow my colleagues to get on that aircraft if I know it is
ng to crash? No, it was only what the English call com-
n sense. Your Medcalf was brave and he showed great
iative, but I think he was not very practical. If his mes-
e was so important—and naturally I could see how im-
rtant it was—then it was obviously very foolish for me to
first to Rome and then to Brussels, or to waste perhaps
more time to try to use the diplomatic channels. No, no,
soon as I am thinking about it, I know immediately that
nust fly directly to Brussels. And because the NATO
lding is only a couple of kilometers from the airport,
at could be more straightforward?"

He pauses. There is the suggestion of a smile on his lips.

"But of one thing perhaps, yes, I am a little proud."

"What is that?"

"That I also had the sense not to cancel my ticket on the
me flight—so my name, it remained on the passenger list.
ink that is what your Medcalf would have called a good
urance policy. No?"

Postscript

THE "MIAMI INCIDENT" of May 5, ▮3, was actually the subject of an exhaustive investigation ▮ the N.T.S.B., and if the members of my own fictional ▮-team had been half as competent as they should have ▮n, they would have known about it immediately—and ▮rtened the book by about two-thirds. In fact, my account ▮ the incident is based entirely on N.T.S.B. report no. ▮R-84/04, even though for purely dramatic purposes I ▮y seem to have deposited the sole extant copy of it in ▮ls-Royce's technical library at Derby, U.K.

▮ I should also add—just in case any aspiring saboteur ▮nks this book could be a handy blueprint—that, follow-▮ the Miami incident and the widespread alarm it caused, ▮ world's airlines changed their maintenance procedures in ▮umber of crucial respects.

▮ Finally, to anybody who is as fascinated as I am by the ▮ject of air crash investigation I would commend one ▮k of nonfiction above all others—*Impact Erebus* (Hodder ▮ Stoughton, 1983) by Captain Gordon Vette, the account ▮ the inquiry into the crash of the Air New Zealand DC-10 ▮ the Antarctic in 1979. The debt I owe to it will be ▮vious to anyone who reads it.

353